Previous Praise for Lacie Waldon and *The Layover*

"[A] breezy enemies-to-lovers romp with just enough heart to keep it grounded . . . The couple's sparkling chemistry and flirtatious fighting make this sing. Readers craving an armchair getaway need look no further." —*Publishers Weekly*

"[A] tale of learning to let go of the past to be open to whatever's ahead." —*Library Journal*

"[A] tropical, fun, and flirty summer read ideal for a beach day." —*USA Today*

"Once I started *The Layover*, I couldn't put it down! Lacie Waldon has written a super fun, witty, and romantic enemies-to-lovers rom-com that had me flying through the pages. And as a bonus, I loved the peek behind the curtain into the lives of flight attendants. This is a lovely escape full of sun, swoons, and sexual tension."

—Kerry Winfrey, author of *Waiting for Tom Hanks*

"A highly recommended read for fans of enemies-to-lovers and anyone who feels the pull of wanderlust."

—Sarah Hogle, author of *You Deserve Each Other*

"A stand-out debut! Witty banter, sizzling chemistry, and perfect pacing had me flying through *The Layover*. A must read for rom-com fans!" —Samantha Young, author of *Fight or Flight*

"*The Layover* is an ideal escape—from the intriguing insider's view of air travel to the picturesque setting on the shores of Belize, I was swept away on Ava's journey as she spars with Jack, wrestles her feelings, and learns to trust her own heart. A fun and irresistible romance that soars."

—Libby Hubscher, author of *Meet Me in Paradise*

"A sexy, dazzling debut, *The Layover* is a jet fuel-powered rom-com that had me dreaming of sun-soaked beaches and a view from 35,000 feet. Plus the delicious, slow-burning romance, sizzling banter, and crackling chemistry? *Swoon*. If you're an enemies-to-lovers fan—or have even a speck of wanderlust in your heart—*The Layover* is the romantic escape for you!"

—Angie Hockman, author of *Shipped*

"A breath of fresh air! Lacie Waldon's exceptional debut combines sharp, clever writing with crackling sexual tension for pure enemies-to-lovers gold. *The Layover* is the ultimate summer beach read and a new favorite. Waldon is one to watch."

—Devon Daniels, author of *Meet You in the Middle*

"*The Layover* is the perfect escape—a hilarious, compulsive, swoony rom-com from an exciting new voice in contemporary romance. Lacie Waldon's witty banter and laugh-out-loud fresh take on enemies to lovers stuck together on a twenty-four hour layover in Belize are sure to satisfy readers and keep them smiling to the very last page. I absolutely loved it."

—Robin Reul, author of *My Kind of Crazy*
and *Where the Road Leads Us*

ALSO BY LACIE WALDON

The Layover

From the Jump

Lacie Waldon

G. P. PUTNAM'S SONS
New York

PUTNAM
— EST. 1838 —

G. P. PUTNAM'S SONS
Publishers Since 1838
An imprint of Penguin Random House LLC
penguinrandomhouse.com

Library of Congress Cataloging-in-Publication Data

Names: Waldon, Lacie, author.
Title: From the jump / Lacie Waldon.
Description: New York: G. P. Putnam's Sons, [2022]
Identifiers: LCCN 2022011390 (print) | LCCN 2022011391 (ebook) |
ISBN 9780593328279 (trade paperback) | ISBN 9780593328286 (ebook)
Subjects: LCGFT: Novels.
Classification: LCC PS3623.A35688 F76 2022 (print) |
LCC PS3623.A35688 (ebook) | DDC 813/.6—dc23
LC record available at https://lccn.loc.gov/2022011390
LC ebook record available at https://lccn.loc.gov/2022011391

Printed in the United States of America
1 3 5 7 9 10 8 6 4 2

Book design by Ashley Tucker

For Isaac, who's always there when I jump.
Parkour.

From the Jump

*M*y hair felt like it was melting beneath the beaming LA sun, and I pressed my hands against my thighs, preventing them from rubbing at my face in search of leaking blond dye. The university courtyard had no shade, and the line for student IDs was crowded enough to break the breeze. A trickle of sweat broke free of my hairline, prompting an irrational mental image of bottle-blond rivulets trickling down my forehead. I couldn't believe I'd placed my trust in something called Hair Cair. The egregious spelling had seemed an especially bad omen the day before I started my freshman year of college, but the sale price had simply been too good to pass up. Surely my new roommate would tell me if I looked like my pores were leaking lemonade.

Wouldn't she? She seemed like the type who would. Phoebe seemed like the type who would say anything that came to her mind, without considering how it might be interpreted. Not that she was rude. She just had confidence—the kind of self-assurance that was rare in anyone, much less a teenager. She was warm and charismatic and paralyzingly intimidating.

I was, in contrast, attempting to play it cool. Phoebe seemed to think our random room pairing destined us to be friends, and I was desperate to prove her right. Blaire Barton, author of *How to Impress*, which I'd checked out from the library the moment I received my acceptance letter, claimed shared interests led to deeper connection, so I searched Phoebe's words for context and parroted it back to her.

"Oh, totally. Me, too. I *love* Monkey Balls," I said, hoping I was expressing interest in a movie or a band and not some kind of sexual deviancy.

The stocky guy in line in front of me turned around, smirking before opening his mouth to deliver some crass remark. I shot him my iciest stare, and he froze for a moment before quickly shifting his gaze toward a couple of guys pelting candy at each other in the grass nearby.

"Right?" Phoebe beamed with pleasure at this shared sentiment, causing me to silently praise Blaire Barton for coming through once again. "They're so talented. But what about Andre? He's . . ."

Phoebe trailed off, her eyes drifting closed and her chin tilting up. Her dark skin glittered at the edges of her Afro, the same perspiration that was threatening to make me look like a microwaved Peep only making her more striking. My mind scrambled for the words to end her sentence: *The lead singer? The guitarist? The drummer?* It wasn't a pop quiz. Phoebe couldn't be looking for me to offer facts she already knew. The correct answer had to be an adjective.

"Pretty grimy in person, actually," a voice behind us said. "Andre is, I mean. Long hair in pictures and long hair in person are two very different things."

I turned around, simultaneously grateful for the answer and annoyed that someone had interrupted the conversation. My chest tightened when I saw the pretty girl with the almond eyes and glossy black hair who'd spoken. A tiny *S* dangled from her necklace, comprised entirely of diamonds. Her words refiltered through my mind, morphing from a knowing observance to a brag.

Simone Zhang. I hadn't yet met her, but I'd noticed her on move-in day, bossing around what appeared to be actual hired help. So, it was unsurprising to discover she'd seen a famous person up close. She was clearly wealthy. All the effort I'd put into my outfit wouldn't trick her. She was almost certainly rich enough to know my cotton sundress had been worn just a little too thin, and the sandals I snagged at the Goodwill—the best one, where the trophy wives up in the Hills discarded outfits that couldn't be worn more than once and bags with a single scratch—might be Loeffler Randall, but they were from three seasons ago.

"Grimy can be sexy," Phoebe said, turning toward Simone like she'd already been a part of our conversation.

My heart raced, but I kept my face blank, lifting my chin slightly to project confidence. Most people were easy to fool, but truly rich girls could always spot the things other kids missed. They were police dogs, trained to sniff out weakness. And if they found it, they would make sure you never lived it down. I pressed my thumbnail into my thigh, reminding myself that things were different now. I was just a normal college student, living in a dorm like everyone else. There was nothing for her to find out.

"Maybe it *can* be," the girl said, "but not when it's paired with perverted."

"No." Phoebe breathed out the word, looking both horrified and intrigued. "What did he do?"

"Well, let's just say that I thought drummers were sexy, too.

It's why I begged my father to get Monkey Balls to play for my seventeenth birthday party. I just wanted to meet him. It's not like I really thought anything would happen between me and a grown man." Her eyes narrowed. "But apparently, he doesn't have a problem with going after young girls."

Phoebe gasped. "Did you hook up with him?"

"No." Simone's mouth twisted at the thought. Her cheeks flushed with anger. "He tried to kiss my sister. My *little* sister."

The way she said it made me understand jealousy didn't play a part in her disgust. She was simply a big sister, protective of someone she loved. My chin lowered as I softened toward her. I'd never had a sister, but I'd always wanted one. I'd imagined we'd look out for each other, freeing my mom up to look out for herself.

"You stopped him?" I asked, without intending to.

She barked out a laugh, flashing perfect white teeth. "Are you kidding? My sister's a terror. She kicked him in his monkey balls and went right back to watching *Gossip Girl*. But I did grab him by the hair and drag him to the door when I heard. I'm not kidding when I say I had to wash my hands five times afterward. The man is *dirty*."

I ignored the faint chant in my head. *Livvie smells like rotten meat. That's because she lives in the street!* That was a million years ago. And it was ridiculous even then. I might've stayed in a car that just happened to be parked *on* a street, but I certainly didn't live there. If I'd vacationed in Paris for twenty-three days, I guarantee nobody would've allowed me to claim I'd *lived* in France.

"Well, that's it, then," Phoebe said, exhaling with disappointment. "Monkey Balls is dead to me."

I nodded my agreement, distracted by the two guys to my

left. The two boys had been messing around next to us long enough that I'd picked up their names. The one called "Dice" was average height and unremarkably dressed, with straight dark hair to his shoulders and scruff that covered half his face. The other—Mac—was the most gorgeous guy I'd ever seen. He was almost pretty, his features delicate and his eyelashes visible from ten feet away. It was only his height and broad shoulders that balanced it out, making him proper Ken doll material.

I couldn't tear my eyes away from him, despite the fact that I knew better than to be interested in anyone that good-looking. I'd already learned overly attractive men, like rich girls, were dangerous. It wasn't his looks that had me captivated, though. It was how much fun he was having. They'd stopped pelting jelly beans at each other, and now Dice was tossing them up in the air while Mac attempted to catch them in his mouth. It was the most idiotic thing I'd ever seen. That was a game for popcorn, not a candy-coated bullet guaranteed to break teeth.

I wanted to play.

I wouldn't, of course. But I wanted to.

Mac caught a red one in his mouth and spit it toward Dice, who batted it away. I laughed at the face Dice made when he wiped his red-streaked palm on his jeans. To my shock, he glanced over, winking at me before lobbing two yellows into the air. Mac trotted dutifully underneath them, opening his mouth toward the sky. But as they plummeted toward his face, he seemed to have doubts, swinging one oafish hand up and catching them in the air before they hit his face.

"Yum," Simone murmured.

I glanced over to find that her gaze had followed mine to the boys.

"I want a jelly bean," she called out, her voice taking on a

breathy quality. She tilted her chin up, opening her mouth sug-
gestively.

I cringed, looking to Dice without meaning to. His mouth
curved the slightest bit, like he was vaguely amused but wasn't
taking the bait. Mac, on the other hand, had no such reserva-
tions. He flung one of the yellows across the ten-foot gap between us. My eyes widened as the jelly bean descended, visions
of future plurals hissing through the inevitable chip in one of
Simone's perfect white teeth. *Should I do something?*

A sharp *snap* of two fingers ricocheted through the air, and
Simone's gaze dropped instinctively toward the sound. The
jelly bean pinged against her forehead so hard it traveled out
and forward at least three feet before falling to the ground. Her
hand went to the spot of impact, already turning a purplish
red, her eyes widening in confusion. They turned glassy with
unshed tears, likely from embarrassment as much as pain.

"Sorry," Dice said, taking long strides across the grass and
stopping in front of her. Up close, he smelled like an intoxicating mix of something smoky and spiced.

"You distracted me!" Simone looked down at his hand like
it was evidence of a crime.

"I had to." He reached for her forehead, brushing a thumb
over the mark. Strangely, I felt the gesture deep in my belly.
"We couldn't let anything happen to that gorgeous smile of
yours, could we?"

She looked into his eyes uncertainly and seemed to notice
at the same time as me that they were a dark, mesmerizing
blue. Beneath them was a sharp-cut jaw and the sexiest mouth
I'd ever seen. It was disconcerting. Why was he masquerading
as an unremarkable college boy when he was packing all of *this*
beneath the hair and the chin scruff? If he hadn't had such a

detached air about him, it would've felt dangerous, like seeing a hidden dagger suddenly unsheathed.

"I'm Simone," she exhaled.

He nodded and, seemingly reassured that she'd survived her candy-coated injury, took a step away from her.

"And you are?" she prompted.

"Lucas Deiss," he said, waving toward his friend. "And that's Logan MacKenzie, but you can call him Mac."

"I can't believe you thought you were going to throw a jelly bean that far into someone's mouth," Phoebe said, shaking her head at Mac. "Don't you know how dangerous that is?"

"Is it?" Mac asked with a hint of southern twang. He looked genuinely curious, and he wasn't the only one. We'd gotten the attention of the people around us, which wasn't surprising; the line was moving at a pace that made snails look speedy. LA was one of the most image-obsessed cities in the world, after all. Students were probably setting up their own portable light rings before each photo.

"Yes!" Phoebe's hands went to her hips. "If it had gone in her mouth, it definitely would've choked her."

"Huh." Mac seemed to think about this for a moment. "But it's so small. Her throat tube has to be bigger than that."

Phoebe squinted.

Mac lifted his shoulders.

"Higher education is going to be good for you," she pronounced.

Mac ran a hand through his shaggy blond hair, smiling sheepishly at Phoebe. "I know. I do dumb things sometimes. My mom says my enthusiasm carries me away."

"You probably don't want to start your college career talking about your mom," Phoebe said.

"Right." Mac nodded agreeably. His happy-go-lucky vibe was disarming.

Maybe it was because of that, or maybe Phoebe was simply too nice to continue giving him a hard time, but she smiled and added, "I get carried away sometimes, too."

A wide smile split across his face. "You do?"

Phoebe held out a slender arm, pointing at the scar that sliced through her dark skin from wrist to elbow. Mac ran a finger along it, and I could've sworn I felt the air spark between them. Beside me, Deiss had moved away from Simone, but she was still peering at him from beneath lowered lashes. I wondered if I was witnessing the moment I lost my first two prospective college friends to their future boyfriends.

"I got this jumping off the roof with the wings I'd constructed from cardboard and pillow feathers," Phoebe told him. "I really believed they'd make me fly. Broke it in three places."

"That's not stupid," Mac said. "You have to be really smart to make your own wings."

"Maybe," she said. "But it was definitely stupid when I revised the wing design and broke my leg jumping off the roof a second time."

Mac guffawed, and Phoebe grinned ruefully before slipping into laughter with him.

"We should do something," Simone announced.

I looked to her, but she was singularly focused on Deiss. He glanced toward me and took another step back.

"All of us," she added quickly. "I have the key to the rooftop pool at the Aqua. We could go swimming?"

"Let's do it," Mac said. He lifted Phoebe's arm by the wrist and slapped his hand against hers in a high five.

"I'll catch you back at the room later," Deiss said to Mac, his eyes sliding past us. "I've got to get something to eat."

"My family has a tab at the pool." To her credit, Simone managed to keep the desperation out of her voice. But I could see it in the way she stared at the side of Deiss's head, like she was trying to tunnel inside his brain and change his response. "And I guarantee the Aqua's burgers are better than anything you can get on campus."

Deiss shrugged, but his eyes brightened. "I do like a good burger. You up for it?"

I blinked at the realization that his question seemed to be directed toward me. Was he picking up on the pairing off that seemed to be happening? Was he hoping I'd be his buffer?

Did it matter? He clearly wanted me to go, and who was I to pass up the first college hangout I'd been invited to? At my nod, the line was abandoned and we were on our way to procure swimwear, like we were one big group. Apparently, that's all it took to make friends in college: free food and the key to a pool.

I followed along, thrilled to be a part of something, not yet realizing how important we'd all become to each other. I had no idea that Phoebe and Mac would end up dating for the next six years. That Deiss, despite having what was rumored to be a very active sex life, would somehow always make his way back to us, almost every single day, without fail. That Simone's fear of missing out would lead her to abandon her legacy status in Kappa Delta (or that she'd end up dragging us to all sorts of Greek events after her mother declared this resistance an unforgivable betrayal to the family name).

I was simply grateful to have found friends.

It took a year or two before I realized what I'd actually found was a family.

CHAPTER 1

*J*t's the third Thursday of the month. If I were asked to pick my favorite holiday, Christmas or Halloween wouldn't even stand a chance. I'd choose a third Thursday every time. The first third Thursday of the year. The last. The third Thursday in April. They're all winners. Third Thursdays are the day all five of us commit to venturing out of our neighborhoods and making our ways to each other. It's my grounding post, the evening that saves me from feeling like my entire life is a role in a play with a rigid and repetitive script.

A Third Thursday is not a day to get caught up in the stresses of everyday life. Yet caught up is exactly what I seem to be. Actually, panicking is a more accurate description. I've had to pinch my wrist three times to stop myself from picking anxiously at the manicure I got during my lunch break. *Take on a mountain of debt or give up my home.* I twist the glass of chardonnay on the sticky high table I've scored, weighing the equally distressing options in my mind.

The busy bar buzzes around me, muddying my thoughts.

Or maybe that's the wine. I gave myself an hour and a half to get a handful of miles across town because that's how you have to budget your time if you're brave enough to attempt an exit from Santa Monica at the end of a workday. Shockingly, though, the roads chose today to be somewhat functional, and I arrived early enough to not only procure a table and drink but also make my way through most of a glass. It's enough of a miracle that I pull out and reread the mostly memorized letter in case the date has miraculously been pushed back as well.

Sadly, it's all still there in black and white. The building that contains my rent-controlled apartment has been sold, and I have until the end of tomorrow to declare my intention to buy the place I've been living in for the last seven years or let it go. Which is why I've made sure to always have at least six months' worth of rent in my savings, just as *Seeking Security: A Woman's Guide to Securing Her Own Future* told me to. It's going to be fine. I've prepared for this.

Except, of course, I have no idea what I've prepared myself to do. Am I supposed to buy my apartment and bury myself under a mountain of debt when I was just starting to see glimmers of light from beneath the boulder of student loans? Or am I supposed to start over somewhere else? Both options cause my chest to tighten, my heart hammering. I always imagined I'd have a partner by the time I attempted homeownership. There was supposed to be room for a child, or maybe even two.

But I don't have a partner and, for now at least, I only need space for myself. I've made my apartment my home, and I swore to myself that I'd never be forced out of my home again. And maybe walking away won't leave me homeless in the way I've experienced before, but I'll know I can't trust myself any more than I could trust my mother. So who's left to make sure everything doesn't crash and burn once again?

"You look lonely," says a guy who leans an elbow on my table, pressing into one of the many glasses left behind by its previous occupants. He has artfully mussed hair and a rakish grin that says he knows exactly how attractive he is.

"Alone and lonely aren't necessarily the same thing, though, are they?" I keep my voice light because the internet's Husband Huntress insists it's important to never pass up an opportunity to practice the art of flirtation. This guy is barking up the wrong tree, though. Even if I weren't currently pondering the breakdown of my entire existence, I wouldn't go for someone this flashy. My mom used to date someone who wore a pinkie ring very similar to this one; he left her for a woman with bigger breasts and longer purse strings.

"You're right," the guy says. "I'll rephrase that. You look beautiful."

"Thank you."

His grin widens. "Can I get you another drink?"

"She'll take a chardonnay," says a familiar voice behind me. "And a lager for me, as long as you're making the trip."

"Hello, Deiss." I turn around with a warm smile. In all the Thursdays we've met, this might be the first time he's ever shown up early. It's a rare treat, having him all to myself.

"Hello, Liv." He flashes a smile, bright white against the darkness of his full beard. "I see you're collecting your usual stable of admirers."

"Apparently, I looked lonely," I say.

"I amended it to beautiful," the guy reminds me.

"Oh, yes," I say to Deiss. "I forgot that we decided to rewind."

"Are you going to fast-forward to the part where you break his heart," Deiss asks, "or should I grab our drinks and give you two a moment to talk?"

"Thank you for the offer," I say, glancing over at the guy, "and for the compliment, but I'm going to have to pass on the drink."

"No problem," the guy says, backing away. "I was just trying to be friendly."

"That's what I love about LA," Deiss says, turning his attention to the mess on the table. "Everyone's so friendly. They'll give you the shirt right off their back."

"As long as it's guaranteed to end up on the floor at the foot of your bed?"

"Exactly."

We grin at each other, and my skin flushes warm.

"Slow day at the shop?" I ask, referring to Studio Sounds, the record store Deiss owns.

"No more than usual. I saw your text, though, and figured I'd head over so you wouldn't be stuck here alone." He reaches for a dirty glass as he glances back at the slick guy, who has rejoined his friends. "Should've known there was little chance of that."

I search my brain for a clever response but am distracted by the sight of him transferring the mess from our table to one next to us that has just opened up. Usually, he's lounging against something, surveying everyone else's efforts like we're all putting on a show for his personal entertainment. Still, as strange as it is to see him *tidying*, he manages to do it in a way that looks like no effort at all. It's like he's yawning, his arms stretching out lazily, just happening to accomplish something in the movement.

"How *is* the shop?" I ask instead. Business has been slow because, shockingly, in the time of streaming music, records aren't exactly a hot commodity. But last year, Deiss rearranged it to be able to host after-hours concerts with local bands.

"Poorly managed." Deiss grins and leans against the now emptied table. He makes it look so comfortable that I want to slide off my chair and copy him. "I keep getting distracted by the new guitar stock, Booker is worthless, and Mia scares all the customers off. I *am* looking into getting a liquor license, though."

"For the basement shows?"

He nods. "The door money is good, but a lot of the profit comes from liquor sales."

"How do you know if you haven't gotten the license yet?"

"I've been charging people for shots and pouring it into their mouths from the bottle."

"Deiss!" I force a frown, even though I can't help secretly being a little delighted by his insubordination. I've always been jealous of the way he seems so unencumbered by the rules.

He offers a shrug in response. "No cups, no proof, right?"

I tsk my disapproval, but thanks to the arrival of our friends, I don't feel obligated to verbalize it. They come in together, conspicuous despite the crowd. It's probably Mac who draws the most attention. Men of his height and good looks tend to be noticeable, especially if you've seen his latest underwear ad. But it's Phoebe, dark and willowy with an Afro that makes her look several inches taller than she is, who my eyes go to.

As always, she's wearing mismatched pieces she's likely uncovered at a thrift shop. They shouldn't work to make an outfit, but of course they somehow manage to. She looks effortlessly cool, like she belongs on one of the pages of the magazine she writes for, the complete opposite of me and my carefully chosen neutrals and fresh blowout. I want to take a picture of the textures and patterns, the shocks of color, so I can study it and figure out how it all works together. It's the kind of understanding that's invaluable for my work in graphic design.

Next to her, Simone is a study in subtle elegance. Hers is a look that does not require dissection. It can be summed up in brand names and dollar signs. I know this because I'm like the version of her on a budget. It's not something I'm jealous of, simply a fact. Even her flawless skin and gorgeous bone structure scream *money*.

"The Ice Queen and King Cagey are having fun without us!" Phoebe points an accusing finger at us, even as she beelines toward Deiss to tackle him with a hug.

Mac hurries behind her, wrapping his arms around me so that my face presses into his chest. Weirdly, he smells like cotton candy. He's probably spent the afternoon in bed with some model who wears body spray designed for teenage girls.

"You feel good," Phoebe says, patting at Deiss's chest with one explorative hand while the other stays draped around his neck. "Have you been working out?"

"Have you?" Mac asks Deiss, seemingly delighted at his ex-girlfriend groping his best friend. "We should try picking a fight later to see if you hulk out."

I look for some sign that he's joking, but naturally, there isn't one. Mac's greatest quality is also his worst: he's impulsive and enthusiastic about everything. It's what makes him one of the few people brave enough (or just oblivious enough) to bear-hug me, a woman most people barely risk approaching with a handshake. But it's also what makes him think of picking a fight with someone for an entertaining experiment. He's not violent by any stretch of the word. He just hasn't thought through the fact that fights involve both causing and receiving pain.

"Someone has to move all the boxes at the shop." Deiss rubs his hand over his head from front to back so dark hair spills into his face. He's trying to disappear, but it's a useless effort. "Booker certainly isn't going to do it."

"That bag is gorgeous, Simone," I say, attempting to help him out by deflecting attention. It's an easy pivot. I've greeted Simone with compliments ever since freshman year when I learned it was the way of the sorority girls. Although, upon further inspection, I discover that her bag is, in fact, gorgeous.

"Isn't it?" Simone leans in and kisses the air beside my cheek, leaving a cloud of Côte d'Azur in her wake as she pulls back. "I'm loving your new highlights. Honeyed blond is totally your color."

"Thanks." I expect her to recommend for the hundredth time that I try her salon (where Groupons are never *ever* accepted), but her gaze has already shifted from me to Deiss. Her eyes narrow as if they can x-ray-vision their way under his black leather jacket to the muscles Phoebe claimed to have discovered beneath. She has that look on her face that I recognize from freshman year—the look that says she wants to stuff him in a syringe and shoot him into her veins.

Eleven years.

I know Simone hasn't been pining for him for all this time. That look of hers has appeared a lot less frequently over the years, especially since Deiss's beard thickened enough to cover half his face. But I also know if Deiss ever went up for sale, she'd whip her black Amex out so fast, anyone it its path would be sliced to ribbons. She pushes around Mac to sit next to Deiss as Phoebe slides onto the stool across from me.

"So, updates." Phoebe looks at me excitedly. "I need them."

I blink, my stomach lurching beneath her attention. She probably thinks the idea of buying my apartment is exciting, but *how does she know?* I haven't been able to talk about it to anyone because there's no way to explain my fears without re-vealing my past. Did I call her in my sleep? Have we finally gotten so close that she just feels these kinds of things, like a twin whose foot aches when her sister kicks a soccer ball wrong?

"On Operation: Kale," she prompts. "They loved it, didn't they! I knew they would."

My stomach lurches again before sinking like a stone. Op-eration: Kale. I can't believe I wasted an hour of Phoebe's time brainstorming ways to make my latest superfood assignment from Infinity Designs into something original. It was demoral-izing enough when they sprinkled so many suggestions on it that it ended up as watered down as every other project I'd turned in this year. Now Phoebe'll be just as disappointed as I was.

"Yes," I lie, forcing the wide smile I've practiced in the mir-ror. "They did love it, mainly because of your suggestions. Thanks so much for your help."

"Anytime." Phoebe claps her hands together. "I'm so glad it was a success."

"Operation: Kale is over?" Mac asks, as if he's heard any-thing about it before ten seconds ago. "Does that mean you can get the time off work to go to Africa after all?"

It's a stupid question—if I intended to go on a trip to a dif-ferent continent with them *tomorrow*, I clearly would've in-formed them long before today—but everyone's reaction hurts. Phoebe, in her infinite understanding of my money fears, looks sorry for me. Deiss glances around for a server, as if, after seven years of my excuses for missing their annual trip, he can't be bothered to hear another one. Simone looks confused, like she's actually begun to believe I'm incapable of leaving the state of California.

"Sadly, no," I say coolly. "Also unfortunate: we still don't have drinks. Anyone want to come with me to grab the first round?"

"I guess I should," Deiss says, "since you'd have had a refill by now if I hadn't shown up."

We collect everyone's orders, and Deiss leads us toward the bar. With the dark clothing, the beard, and the hair in his eyes, people can barely see him, but it doesn't seem to matter. It never has. Girls have always wanted to be with him, and guys have always wanted to be his friend. Deiss, naturally, isn't overly interested in either.

It's a fact that's never seemed quite fair to me. What's cool on him—his aloofness and self-contained personality—is perceived as cold on me. But I suppose you can't compare the two of us. Not when Deiss makes no effort at anything, and I feel like I never stop trying to get every little thing right.

"Do you think they're going to talk about South Africa all night?" I ask once he's ordered the drinks.

Deiss shrugs and leans against the bar, surveying the room. "It's a pretty big trip for us. Everyone's excited."

"And it's tomorrow," I agree, his response making me feel petty. It's not their fault I'm never able to make it. "You should probably all be home packing."

"Probably."

"I'm surprised you guys didn't just cancel tonight. You're going to see each other tomorrow anyway." Fishing for affirmation is beneath me, but I want to hear the words. *Third Thursdays are sacred. We'd never pass up the opportunity to see you.*

"Are you sad you're missing it?" Deiss says instead. He turns toward me, catching me by surprise with his undivided attention.

"It's fine," I lie quickly. "It's ten days. It's not like I would've seen you guys in that time anyway."

"That's not what I meant."

I falter under his gaze. His eyes are piercing, and it feels like they can see right through me. I feel myself weaken, even as I remind myself that nobody likes a woman who whines.

"I hate that I'm missing it," I hear myself admitting. "I've never been anywhere, and I hate that you're all having adventures and making memories without me. I worry, by the time I have the money to go to all the best places, you guys will have already been there and won't want to go back. And I'm scared you'll get used to being without me and stop inviting me at all."

The confession leaves me breathless, and I can't believe it's come out of my mouth. I've invested so much into sculpting myself into someone impressive. How could I expose the writhing mess of uncertainty and fear that lies beneath?

Even more surprising is the fact that Deiss simply leans back and lets his gaze drift over the crowd. "That's what I thought," he says, seemingly to himself.

"*That's what you thought?*" Something sharp and hot shoots through me. It's equal parts incredulity, rage, and hurt. Never once, in all the time I've known Deiss, have I shown anything other than absolute confidence. Now I admit to being worried and scared, and his only reaction is to congratulate himself? "You're not going to tell me I've been making the wrong decision choosing work over these trips? Or that I won't get left behind?"

"They're just trips," he says blandly. "You'll go when you want to. And as long as we all stay friends, I'm sure you will, too."

"That's comforting." My words come out spiked like icicles. "Thanks so much for the advice."

"Was I supposed to give advice?" He shifts to his side and

drags his eyes back to me. "You seem to be doing fine on your own."

"I do?" It's embarrassing, needing this approval, but I can't help myself.

"Sure." He shrugs. "If you like that treadmill."

"What treadmill?" I'm certain Deiss isn't talking about my stationary runs three times a week. The Husband Huntress says there's nothing more annoying than a fit woman who brags about her workouts.

"You don't ever feel like you're on a treadmill?" He waves his hand lazily, like it's something we've talked about, even though it's definitely not. "Staring at the same wall as you keep clocking your progress, even though you know you're just going to keep running and running?"

"And what if I have felt like that?" *I have. I* definitely *have.*

"I don't know." He shrugs, distracted by something happening behind me. "Personally, I'd probably want to find out what was on the other side of that wall."

CHAPTER 2

I t's Friday afternoon, and my colleagues are hustling to wrap things up so they can leave straight from our weekly summary meeting. I take one last glance over my cubicle. It's perfectly in order, exactly how I want to come back to it on Monday. There's nothing worse than returning from the weekend to find last week's chaos already seeping into an unblemished new week. The picture of the five of us at the fair is crooked, and I straighten it, pressing my thumb against the tack that holds it up. We look so young. But not as young as my mom and I look in the picture next to it.

As much as I love these snapshots, I can't help wondering if I shouldn't have some more recent memories worth decorating my workspace with. What have I been doing for the last seven years? Is Deiss right that I've been staring at a wall? If I have, it's a cubicle wall made of felt, which I'm sure is even sadder than whatever wall he was envisioning.

I feel a flare of annoyance at his audacity to judge me, but it fades as quickly as it arrives. Like Deiss puts any thought at all into anything other than music. Unlike me, he's almost certainly already forgotten about it.

"I'm telling you, Olivia." Elena waits for me to slide my suit jacket on. "You have to go to a psychic. If I hadn't tried it, I'd never have discovered that my future husband will be wearing a red t-shirt when I meet him. Do you have any idea how much that narrows my search? It'll save me countless bad dates."

"So, you're only going to accept dates from red-shirted men?" Despite the effort to keep my voice neutral, my skepticism cracks through. I've been off my game today, my brain sluggish from churning over Deiss's words and the enormous decision due by the end of the day. *The loss of my home or crippling debt.* I should know by now what I'm going to do.

She takes a step back in surprise, which is actually helpful as we have a meeting to get to, not that Elena seems to care. In her striped stockings and fuzzy sweater, she looks like she's on her way to pick up one of her bad dates at a carnival instead. For all I know, she might be. She's seemingly oblivious to the bustle of work going on around us. Her desk is still littered with task lists that need to be addressed, and I can see from here that she has approximately thirty-seven open tabs on her computer.

"Well, no," she says. "But the pressure will be lifted if I show up and he's *not* wearing a red shirt, because I'll know nothing will come of it. That's what makes a date bad. The pressure."

Is it? I think back to my last date, unable to recall any pressure. I simply followed the Husband Huntress's dating guidelines and maintained a sense of mysteriousness. (She's proven herself right again and again—men seem delighted to project their desires onto a blank slate.) Even without any *pressure*, though, the date was inarguably bad.

The thing the Husband Huntress neglects to mention is

how unsatisfying it is, sitting there politely, playing the part of the perfect listener while a man named Roger fills all the space with cycling talk. *Leading out and half-wheeling. Lycra, slippery roads, and gel packs.* I'd successfully feigned interest in all of it while fiddling with the loose press-on nail on my pinkie. I kept imagining a game of table football where I tugged it off and flicked it with my middle finger, his steaming soup bowl the goalpost.

"That makes sense," I say, hoping my skepticism didn't hurt her feelings. Elena has real friends whose responsibility it is to ground her in reality, a whole circle of people she seems to constantly be doing fun things with outside of work. Things she never invites me to. I just happen to be her cubicle neighbor.

She expands on her point as we head down the hall, while I punctuate her thoughts with murmurs of agreement until I spot Marian Hammersmith outside the conference room we're meeting in. She's talking to a couple of higher-ups, her chin tilted up like it does when she's putting someone in their place. I lift mine as well. Running my tongue over my freshly bleached teeth, I try to think of anything I could use to start a conversation with her. To my surprise, the effort proves unnecessary.

"Good morning, Olivia," she says, turning my way just before I walk through the conference room door.

My knees threaten to drop into a curtsy. Marian Hammersmith is so elegant, so perfectly put together that being acknowledged by her feels like being greeted by the queen. She's wearing a beige suit today, with a crisp white shirt underneath and a gold necklace to give the whole look a touch of glamour. If she's had a face-lift, the surgeon has done excellent work. There's constant speculation in the office as to her age. Guesses land as low as forty, all the way up to mid-sixties. I have too much respect for her to weigh in with a vote, but I'd love to hear the verified answer. It's not that I want her to retire. It's just that I can't have her job until she leaves it.

"Good morning, Marian." To my dismay, my voice has gone up an octave like a nervous schoolgirl's, even after seven years of working together.

"Nice work on that kale project you turned in last week," she says.

"Thank you." I feel the corners of my mouth tug toward a frown and have to force them back up. Obviously, Marian's approval is one of my main goals in this job, but this particular praise stings. I would hope that she, of all people, would recognize the paint-by-numbers outcome my ideas had been reduced to. Did she even consider my original pitch? I want to believe she liked it, that perhaps it was the people above her who decided to keep things at status quo, but it's difficult to believe when she's complimenting me for staying between the lines.

Sometimes I wish I'd never come up with the concept for celeriac. If I'd gotten management's attention with something style-related, maybe I'd be their go-to girl for boutique branding instead of foods that need to be triple-washed. Maybe they wouldn't see cassava and immediately think of me.

"We should have a lunch meeting next week." Marian's eyes drift off me, following someone into the conference room, but the loss of her attention doesn't prevent me from perking back up at her words. "There are a few things I'd like to discuss with you."

"I'd love that," I say coolly, despite my desire to jump in the air, contort my legs into one of those shapes cheerleaders make, and yell hooray.

She focuses back in on me. "Great suit, by the way. The cut of the jacket is flawless."

"I was just going to say the same about yours." *Dress for the job you want*, they say, *not the one you have.* I wonder if Marian realizes I've modeled myself off her. She must at least suspect my ambition. What lowly in-house designer doesn't dream of one day rising to creative director?

She smiles graciously and nods me into the conference room. I scurry forward in submission, instantly bumping into Elena.

"Oh, did you not see me there, either?" Elena mutters, but I can tell by her tone she's more amused than offended. "Marian certainly didn't."

I tilt my head and study Elena as she and I make our way toward two empty seats back along the wall. With her hair pulled into a messy bun on top of her head, Elena looks more like Marian's disgruntled teenage daughter than her peer. I'm not sure why she's always so surprised to be treated as such. I've offered her some of my books on how to live life more successfully, but she never seems to get around to it. If I'm being completely honest, I'm always a little relieved when she returns them unread. I want to help Elena, but I'd hate to see her free spirit shackled.

"She saw you," I say. "She just knew your psychic hadn't predicted her speaking to you yet."

"Eddie Radner." Elena points left across the room and turns right, not noticing as her purse bangs into the knee of the man next to her. In her defense, the room is chaotic. Everyone has taken advantage of the free coffee and cookies and is wandering around with fistfuls of caffeine and sugar, talking over each other in an effort to catch up on any gossip they've missed over the week and compare plans for the weekend. This is how all our Friday afternoon debrief meetings go, which is the reason we all keep arriving a little earlier each week. It's a liquorless happy hour, the roundup behind the release gates that will soon open to freedom.

"Thanks," I say, sliding into the seat she motions at. It's behind a man who's both tall and wide enough to hide me from Eddie's view. "This is perfect."

"Can I ask you a question?" For once, Elena's volume is at a two instead of the ten it's usually dialed to.

I nod, despite the fact that her uncharacteristic discretion makes me nervous.

"Eddie seems to really like you," she says. "And I do hear you when you're regurgitating the tenets of *Success in the Workplace*, but I also listen when you quote the Husband Huntress. And *she* says you shouldn't count someone out before you get to know them."

"That's not a question." I know where Elena is going, though. Her argument is that I shouldn't keep rejecting Eddie's advances without getting to know him, despite the fact that there are at least three other women in the office who can claim to know him quite intimately. What Elena doesn't understand is that I'm well acquainted with men like Eddie Radner. They swept in and out of my house throughout the entirely of my childhood, drawn to my mother's beauty and eagerness to please. What I learned from them is that compliments and charm are the well-documented signs of a bad bet.

"Why won't you go out with him?"

I do a quick sweep to ensure no one is listening to us. "I'm not interested in him."

"But you were interested in Boring Roger?"

"I was willing to give Roger a chance."

Elena squints with confusion. "Then why not give the same to Eddie? If you thought it might not work out either way, wouldn't you rather hit the sheets with someone who knows what he's doing in them than someone who likely irons them?"

I shudder. "You do remember that I didn't sleep with Roger, right?"

"But you would've," she says, "if things had gone well. So, my point stands."

"Roger checks all of the boxes," I say. "He's the kind of man who would make a perfect life partner."

She laughs, but it fades as she realizes I'm being serious.

"Hmm," she murmurs. There's something in her expression I don't like. It looks a lot like pity. It's the kind of look that should be directed toward someone like my mother, not me.

"Is there something wrong with that?" I can hear the defensiveness in my voice and am aware it's a very unappealing quality. "He's nice," I say more softly.

Her nose wrinkles. "But does he excite you?"

"Excitement doesn't factor into the equation," I explain. "Attraction fades. You're supposed to choose your dates according to your long-term relationship goals."

"But sometimes you go wild and have a fling just for the fun of it, right?" Elena grins knowingly. "I mean, you can't live your entire life doing what you're *supposed to do*."

I blink, unsure how she's managed to make good strategic decisions sound so silly.

"Oh my gosh, Olivia!" Her eyes widen and she leans forward, fascinated. "You do, don't you? No wonder you're so perfect!"

I flinch beneath what feels like an accusation rather than affirmation. If it's actually working, and this is what perfect looks and feels like, I'm suddenly terrified I've bought into a lie.

"I don't know how you manage it," Elena says. "I never do what I'm supposed to do. I tell myself I'm going to diet or date the right men or read the right books, and the next thing I know there's an ex-felon with dreamy eyes on the couch next to me with a pizza in front of us and Netflix has paused to ask if we're still watching. Does that really never happen to you?"

"I don't even remember what pizza tastes like." It feels silly to admit it, but I don't know what else to say. A simple *No, none of that has ever happened to me* might sound judgmental. Anyway, the truth is the night Elena has just described sounds amazing. Obviously, I would prefer a guy without a record, but I like the sound of his eyes. And why shouldn't I get a night on the couch?

Be fit, they say. So, every day I spend an hour of my evening under the strict instruction of my personal trainer. My legs might be perfectly toned, but my stomach is in a perpetual state of growling unrest. *Be healthy. Be financially responsible. Dress for success. Be your best self. Look your best. Find a partner. Settle down. And don't forget to go out and have fun!*

But none of these goals quite go together.

For as long as I can remember, I've been doing everything I'm supposed to do. And look where it's gotten me. I'm stretched thin, literally.

I'm supposed to be an independent woman. Everything I believe in is pressuring me to buy my condo. I took this stable, boring, increasingly life-sucking job with its good salary for this very reason. But everything else I've been told to do—the gym memberships, the skin creams, the organic almond milks and coconut waters, the overall *maintenance* required to play this role of the advancing career woman—eats up all the money the job brings in.

And even if I'd saved more, or if my job does provide me the credibility necessary to procure a loan, what next? I'm supposed to be able to buy my own place, but I'm also expected to believe I can achieve the plan on my inspiration board. And if I do? Well, in that case, I should have a family coming my way any minute. And I can't raise kids in a one-bedroom apartment with a stove full of books and a stand-up shower. They'll feel like they're being waterboarded.

"No pizza?" Elena gapes at me with an awe that's embarrassingly misplaced. "I want to be you when I grow up."

"You are grown up," I say. "And we have the same job. Only I'm here late every night while you're out living your life. If someone's winning, it's you."

Elena looks as shocked as I feel at the admission. Maybe my confession to Deiss last night has left a crack in a door I never meant to open. Thankfully, no one around us seems to have heard me.

"You don't have to stay late just because they ask you to," Elena says. "None of the rest of us do. I thought you were just kissing up for a promotion."

"Sure." She doesn't know I often have nowhere else to go. Or that I keep naively hoping the extra work might finally result in a creative project the higher-ups will approve as is. "Isn't that what I'm supposed to do? That doesn't mean I'm not sick of it."

"But you could just stop. All you have to do is say no." Elena's eyes light up, and she leans in to whisper, "It feels so good saying no to them."

Before I can formulate any kind of response, Mr. Dailey calls the meeting to order. Like a switch has been flipped, the party-like atmosphere fades. Seats groan as people settle in. Smiles sink into frowns. It's the flaw of the Friday afternoon meeting. We've all just been given a glimpse of the relief of the weekend, but now we're about to be reminded of the fresh hell awaiting us next week. It will niggle at the back of our minds on Saturday, but by Sunday night, it will be wailing like a siren, obliterating any effort to hold onto the remaining joy of the weekend.

"I'm sure you've all received the memo about bathroom etiquette," Mr. Dailey says sternly.

I turn toward him and sit up straight to present the image of an enthusiastic, attentive employee who cares greatly about her coworkers' bowel movements. My mind, however, sinks into the simplicity of Elena's suggestion. *No.* For only two tiny letters, the word is strangely compelling. Intoxicating even. *No.* It sounds so firm. So decisive. I whisper it silently, and my tongue clicks off the roof of my mouth in a satisfying way, even as my chest tightens.

That word is the antithesis of everything I learned growing up. My mother taught me to not end up how she did, abandoned, alone, scraping to get by. If I would only do as I was told, by her and everyone else, I'd become someone better. One of the bright, beautiful people we watched on TV instead of the tired, worn-down scraps we always felt like. If I did everything right, I'd be financially solvent, have a home, and be loved. If that were true, though, why am I not? Technically, I haven't reached any of those benchmarks yet.

The truth is, I'm not even happy.

Should I be happy that I've somehow become the go-to designer for foods so gross that they need to be rebranded so people will put them in their mouths? Should I be happy that my shoes feel like mousetraps have snapped shut on my toes? Should I be happy that Roger was willing to take me on a bike ride so long that we'd have to smear packs of chemical gel onto our tongues just to survive it?

No. I whisper it silently again, rolling it around in my mouth, savoring the feel of it.

Maybe it's still there twenty minutes later when Mr. Dailey addresses me in front of the group. Maybe it has settled itself on my tongue like a runner crouched at the starting line, taut with the desire to be released. Or maybe it's been building since Deiss pulled away the curtain to reveal a wall. Whatever the reason, when Mr. Dailey announces that my next project is not only another food project but *bone broth*, the most disgusting one I've received yet, I'm as surprised as anyone that I don't just nod politely as I'm expected to do.

"No," I say instead.

The word comes out simply, coolly, decisively. There are a few gasps around the room, but the biggest show of surprise comes from Mr. Dailey himself. He looks positively stunned, and who could blame him? I've always been his yes-girl. In fact, if our office had a yearbook, I'd probably be in there as *Most likely to give away her firstborn if formally requested by management.*

I brace myself for my impending regret—regret for behaving rashly, for embarrassing myself in front of my coworkers, for disappointing my boss, for endangering my career—but it doesn't hit. All I feel is a thrill of excitement working its way up through my chest, powering me like a surge of electricity. This might possibly be the most alive I've ever felt.

"But—" Mr. Dailey begins to speak, almost certainly intending to explain that the bone broth project wasn't an offer as much as an assignment, but he's cut off by the wave of my hand.

I engage my beauty queen smile. "No."

And it turns out Elena was right. It *does* feel good.

THEN

J had refused to get out of the car. In fact, I'd gotten behind the wheel and moved the car farther away, just to physically mark my objection to the night's event. Graffiti was an eyesore. It was also illegal. And I didn't care how many times Simone declared it decorative or Mac claimed it would be good practice for my graphic design classes; I had no intention of participating.

I'd been sitting in the driver's seat in the dark for about twenty minutes when the cop came flying into the gravel parking lot like a stunt driver on crack. He did that thing where you hit the brakes and the car keeps moving, spinning around so his headlights spotlighted the crumbling wall my friends were marking up. It would've been badass if it weren't such overkill. Actually, it *was* kind of badass, especially the way it caused my friends to whip around, gaping at the headlights like startled deer. If I hadn't been so terrified, I might've laughed.

Oddly, my first instinct was to look at the drawings that the moonlight had been too dim to illuminate from this distance. I made a mental note to ask Phoebe to jot down those flowers for me when we got back to the dorm; they would be the perfect addition to a digital sketch I'd been working on for my Editorial Layout class. And I swooned a little at the sight of Mac's *Mac & Phoebe* and the halfway-completed *4* that was presumably meant to have become *4ever*.

My second instinct was to check on my friends. Unsurprisingly, Deiss was stepping back to lean nonchalantly against the wall, even as the hand that held the spray paint can slowly lowered from the word *Deftones* down to his side. Mac and Phoebe had covered their mouths like they were trying not to laugh. Simone had fluffed her hair and was unsubtly adjusting her cleavage. Belatedly, I ducked down, praying the officer would assume the car was empty.

I was convinced he was going to arrest them, maybe even take them directly to prison, so I kept my grip tight on the steering wheel, determined to provide a getaway car if he tried. It proved unnecessary, though. Less than twenty minutes later, he was gone and they were back in the car, laughing and comparing tickets.

"My dad is going to kill me," Phoebe said, looking at me with wide eyes even as she giggled.

"My dad is going to lawyer me up and demand I contest it," Simone said.

I wondered what Deiss's dad would have to say, but I didn't bother asking. He'd never even confessed aloud to being born to human parents, leaving us to wonder if he might've been created in some lab with excellent speakers and a varied playlist. After two years of friendship, we'd yet to be able to get him to share anything of his past. Once, Simone pushed too hard to figure out what state he was from, and he'd walked out of the room, strolling back in three days later like nothing had happened. We stopped asking him questions after that.

I pulled Phoebe's ticket out of her hand, my mouth falling open as I read the print.

"Four hundred dollars?" My gaze shot between their hands, taking in the tickets. "You each have to pay a four hundred dollar fine?"

"At least we didn't get arrested," Mac said.

I shook my head as I started at the car. "Sixteen hundred dollars. Just so you could doodle on a wall. What a waste."

"Was it?" Deiss was in the passenger seat beside me, and he slid on his seat belt.

"Yeah." I think of how much of the semester's bills that could've paid for it. "What else would you call it?"

"I don't know." He shot me a grin I could only half see in the moonlight. "It felt more like an adventure to me."

CHAPTER 3

*T*hat's not what I meant!" Elena scurries down the street after me. "I just wanted you to say no to staying late like one time."

"I know." I glance up at the sun, which has begun its slow descent. It's still bright with the joy that spring brings, and I realize it must have been a beautiful day. The air is crisp with the promise of a new season. Away from this strip of cement, there are entire parks full of blooming flowers and burbling birds. It's been way too long since I've walked through one.

"Can you please just stop and talk to me for a minute?" The frantic edge to Elena's voice causes me to slow and turn toward her. Someone bumps my arm as they hurry past. We're gumming up the works. The sidewalk is no place for existential crises. And really, I don't need it to be. Mine has already happened.

"Elena." My tone softens as I take in the tension etched across her face. "I'm fine. Everything is fine."

"So, you didn't just quit your job?" I can see the relief shining from her eyes. Somehow, she's taken on the responsibility for the last hour. The irony isn't lost on me, given the fact that this might be the one time in my whole life I've actually done something because I wanted to.

"I had six weeks of vacation built up," I say, tweaking the truth about my meeting with Mr. Dailey into something more palatable for Elena's digestion. Vacation sounds better than the unpaid leave he's gifted me to deal with, as he so delicately termed it, my "personal issues." "We've agreed that I'll use that time to get my priorities straight."

It's a miracle he didn't just fire me, but it doesn't matter either way. I'm done with Infinity Designs. If I want to work on the kind of projects I want to work, I'll clearly have to find them on my own. I, Olivia Bakersfield, am officially going freelance.

"Six weeks of vacation? That's perfect!" Elena bounces on her heels. "He's always liked you. You'll take a little break, and then you'll come back. Everything will be right back to normal."

I don't bother to correct her.

"You don't need to worry about me," I say when it becomes clear she's not going away. "I'm fine."

"Are you sure?" Her face scrunches up with doubt. "Maybe we should get a drink or something and hash all of this out."

I blink, surprised by the offer. Surely Elena already has plans for a Friday night. From what I've deduced, her social life is usually overflowing. More than once, I've heard her groan aloud at the realization of having double-booked. But, I realize, she hasn't really invited me to get a drink. She's only suggesting it might be something we *should* do.

"But that's silly," she says, squirming at my silence. "I'm sure you have other friends you'd rather be with."

"My friends all left for South Africa this afternoon." Realizing how ridiculous my timing has been distracts me enough to allow the words to slip out. If I'd only quit a few weeks earlier, maybe I'd be with them. But that's not right, is it? I would've been too concerned about money. "They've gone on vacation without me."

"*Of course* you have friends who vacation in South Africa," Elena says, a strange smile slipping across her face. "I always pictured them sipping low-calorie cocktails at polo matches, but frolicking abroad sounds about right, too."

"What?" I search her face, but the mental image of Deiss in a leisure suit distracts me, causing me to laugh aloud.

"Is comparing them to me so funny?" she asks, hurt tinging the edges of her words. "Not everyone sees me as the ridiculous person they got stuck next to at work, you know. A lot of people actually like me."

"What are you talking about, Elena?" I cringe at the implication of her words. There's no way I could've made her feel like that. "Everyone likes you. *I* like you."

"Sure." She smiles wryly. "That must be why you're always offering me books on how to behave differently."

"But . . ." I stutter, taken aback. "Those were books I read *myself.* I offered them because I thought they might be helpful, not because I wanted you to be different."

"Did it ever occur to you that I didn't need help?" She throws her hands out in front of her. "That I was *sharing* my mistakes as a way to connect with you? Typically, people—at least the ones who are interested in being friends—respond by offering a sympathetic ear. Or even better, they share something in return. They don't just offer professional help before returning to their keyboard."

For the second time, I'm left blinking speechlessly at the woman in front of me. I have no idea what I'm supposed to say. An apology feels most appropriate, but something tells me Elena would only be insulted by more polite words. Unlike me, she's a person driven by feelings, and apparently, without realizing, I've hurt hers repeatedly.

"I'm sorry," I blurt out, despite all indications something better is required. "I didn't realize . . ."

What? This is like a Sunday crossword puzzle in the *New York Times*. I didn't realize *what?* That she needed more sympathy? That can't be right. It will sound like I think she's needy. That I wasn't sharing? That's too obvious a lie. Elena and I have worked with each other for years. If I hadn't made the active decision to keep to myself, some personal details would've naturally slipped out by now.

"You know what?" she says before I can solve the riddle. "Just forget about it. I don't know why we're talking about this. It's obviously not the time. You've had a crazy day at work, and the last thing you need to be thinking about is me and my silly insecurities. Go. Have a fun night and leave all of this behind you."

"Elena," I say as she backs away.

"We're fine." She offers a reassuring smile and waves me forward. "I'll see you in a few weeks."

"No." Apparently the word has still been hovering on my tongue, eager to be repeated. "Please don't go."

Elena stops, looking at me questioningly, but I have no other words lined up for release. The momentum I had in the meeting has dissipated, but I summon it back. *Forget what I'm supposed to say or do. What do I want?*

"I didn't know how to respond to your sharing," I say, closing the gap between us, "because sharing isn't something I normally do. With anyone. People can't take advantage of your weaknesses if you don't expose them. But it's recently been brought to my attention that I don't have to always do what I'm supposed to. And I think I want to . . ." I can't bring myself to say *share*. It sounds too cheesy. And I'm not even sure it's true. I'd like to stop holding everything in, but I don't actually want to stand here on the sidewalk spilling my guts like a drunken teen outside a football game.

"You want to what?" Elena prompts.

"Do more things I'm not supposed to do." As far as declarations go, it's not exactly specific, but it sends a thrill through me nonetheless.

"Yeah?" Elena grins mischievously, her eyes sparkling. "Like what?"

"I don't know." I shift uncomfortably on my heels. "Just . . . things."

"Come on, Olivia. Name one thing off the top of your head that you're not supposed to do."

I aim for the top of my head, but the omnipresent growl of my stomach weighs down the expedition. "Eat. My trainer has banned all sugar, dairy, processed foods, and anything fried from my diet."

"And you want?"

"All of the above." My mouth waters at the thought. Donuts. Pizza. Cookies. Potato chips. So many things have been off-limits for so long.

Elena laughs, clapping with excitement. "Please tell me you also want company. Everyone knows calories don't count when you're eating them for a friend. It'll be like breakup ice cream but without the tears."

I flush that she'd refer to me as a friend after all the ways I've unknowingly offended her. "You still want to hang out with me?"

"Are you kidding? I've never wanted to hang out with you more." She grabs my hand and starts pulling me down the street. "Where should we start?"

As I totter after her on stilettos, a terrible thought occurs to me. My suits are so perfectly tailored that even an extra glass of water can make them feel tight around the waist. It's an outfit for eating lettuce or nibbling on a carb-less nutrition bar, not decadence.

"I have to change," I say. "Can we go to my condo first?"

"Are you inviting me into your home?" Elena's mouth drops open in exaggerated shock. "Olivia Bakersfield, you *are* opening up."

I roll my eyes to cover my uncertainty. But after four years of working together, I finally manage to get out, "You shouldn't call me Olivia. My friends call me Liv."

"*Ice cream and* liquor? Are you sure?" I push open the door to my apartment, placing the keys in the delicate rose-gold leaf on the floating shelf.

"Baileys was specifically created to go in milkshakes," Elena says. She follows me in. Like mine, her arms are laden with the bags of alcohol and junk food we've picked up at the bodega down the street.

"Cat Stevens is not going to be pleased. He hates it when I use the blender."

I cross to the kitchen, drop my bags on the island, and pull the blender out anyway. One of the bags topples over, sending Doritos and Oreos and candy bars sliding across the white countertop.

"Who's Cat Stevens?" Elena pulls the ice cream out of her bag and slides it toward me.

"My cat."

"You don't have a cat," she says with unwarranted certainty. She doesn't even look around for one as she says it. "I'd have seen pictures."

"Clearly, you wouldn't have." I find a grapefruit spoon for the ice cream because I don't have a proper scoop.

"There would be cat hair on your clothes."

"You think I'm the kind of person who would choose a cat that sheds?" I'm a little offended by the thought of it. "He's probably hiding under the bed from us. Feel free to try to lure him out."

While she goes in search of Cat's doubtless disapproval, I carve off chunks of ice cream, dump them into the blender, and tilt the Baileys up until half the contents have glugged out. It smells delicious, like it really is some magical ingredient specifically created to improve something as already delightful as ice cream.

"This is nice," Elena says as I pour them into my sixteen-ounce smoothie glasses. She seems to have stalled in the living room and is standing in one place, slowly spinning to take in my apartment from different angles.

"Very elegant," she adds politely.

I cross the room and hand her one of the milkshakes before studying the decor with her. It surprises me that I've been more excited about the food than to show off my home. I faithfully followed the principles of *Chez Chic* after the Husband

Huntress explained that your living space is a potential partner's best insight into who you are behind closed doors. The
place turned out well, despite all *Chez Chic*'s warnings about
color being tacky making me too nervous to buy anything that
wasn't museum white. I do, however, worry what, exactly, this
place says to potential partners. *If we have children, I'll have to
keep them in cages to prevent stains* was not my intended message,
but it does seem to be the one I've landed upon.

My nose wrinkles as I see it all through Elena's eyes. The
expensive couch that's as comfortable as a church pew. The tasteful art that makes me feel nothing. This isn't a home; it's a
Friendsta post. And if that really is the case, maybe I can walk
away without breaking any promises to myself.

I could rent someplace cheaper. Create a strict budget. Maybe
even sell some things to add to my financial cushion, giving myself time to find work as a freelance graphic designer. It's not
what *Seeking Security* would advise—a responsible person should
invest in property instead of spending on rent—but it's not crazy.
I could do it responsibly. I'd just have to think of it as an investment in my dreams. *My* dreams—for once—not the dreams I'd
been instructed to have.

"Thanks," I say. "But it's not mine anymore. I'm moving out."

I'm doing a drunken version of yoga when Elena has the
idea. The Baileys is long gone, along with the first bottle of
wine. I've got a straw in my wineglass, though, and I've found
that I can bend my head toward it no matter what shape the
rest of my body is stretched into. Cat Stevens is watching me

from under the entertainment center, clearly unimpressed by my efforts. Or maybe it's just the loud music he's taken umbrage at.

"You should go to Africa tomorrow and meet up with your friends now that you're on vacation," Elena yells as she dances on the coffee table. "Do you know where they're staying?"

"I could check the emails." I do downward dog and sip the wine through the straw. "They planned most of it on our running group chain."

"I'll check flights while you pack." She intentionally falls backward from the table to the couch, wincing as she hits the cushions.

I laugh and reach for the remote to turn down the music. "Did you forget how hard it was?"

"I don't know how you sit on this." She wriggles around as if there might be a more comfortable spot. "Go on. Start packing. And don't worry about Cat Stevens. I can pop in and feed him while you're gone."

I shake my head. "I can't go to Africa tomorrow." *Can I?* "What if customs thinks my passport is fake because it's never been used before? And what about shots? Don't you need shots or something to leave the country?"

"My cousin works at a clinic. If you need shots, I'm sure he can fit you in tomorrow morning to give them to you. We'll just book you on an afternoon flight."

It's a crazy idea. Obviously, if I was worried about the cost of it before I lost my income, I definitely can't afford to go now. But I've gone about five hours doing the things I'm not supposed to and it seems to be working out pretty damn well.

"Call him," I say with a drunken shrug.

Elena narrows down the flights and calls out questions to

me as she fills in the necessary information. When it's time to submit, however, she hesitates.

"It's nonrefundable," she says, her hands pulling back from the laptop.

Without a word, I plop down next to her and hit the purchase button.

CHAPTER 4

$\mathcal{B}$y the time I arrive in Durban, South Africa, it's been almost forty hours since I've last showered. I've consumed eighteen coffees, watched six bad movies and two good ones, and read until my eyes began to cross, and my skin has sucked in my foundation in what I can only assume was a desperate attempt to rehydrate itself. Still, I feel better than I did the morning after my slumber party with Elena. The next time I decide to abstain from alcohol, it won't be because of calories. It will be because of hangovers and inadvisable purchases of cheap flights that involve four layovers before reaching your final destination.

I stop in a restroom before leaving the airport and use the last of my bottled water to brush my teeth. When she got my email, Phoebe offered to make the three-hour drive from St. Lulia to pick me up, and it doesn't seem fair to reward her generosity by releasing the nuclear bomb that has been living inside my mouth. Despite my stop for hygiene, I beat most of my fellow passengers outside. It seems the majority of them decided to check their luggage and are now being held captive audience to the empty conveyer belt making its slow, creaky loop.

Rather than feeling superior for restricting myself to a carry-on, I'm freaked out imagining what they've packed that I've failed to bring. I've never been out of the country. Maybe they know about things I didn't realize I needed. Or maybe they just weren't rip-roaring drunk when they were pulling clothes out of their closets and throwing them gleefully into a bag. By the time I got back from my appointment with Elena's cousin, I barely had time to find a spot for the malaria tablets he'd given me, much less double-check what had been done the night before.

There's a cover over the area outside the door I exit, but its shade can't diminish the brilliance of the day. The air smells different. It's earthier than in LA, rich and full of possibility. The sun feels closer, and I fumble in my purse for my sunglasses. Once they're on, I lift my arms above my head and stretch my entire body, trying to restore it to the shape it was before I decided to live in tinfoil cans for two days. My effort is interrupted by a honk from the little brown hatchback that coasts to a stop in front of me.

"Want a ride, gorgeous?" Deiss leans over from the driver's seat to speak through the open window on the passenger's side.

I freeze with my hands in the air, too stunned by his unexpected appearance to react appropriately. It's not just the fact that he's showed up instead of Phoebe but that he's shaved off all of his hair. Not only from his head but the beard, too. All that's left is a dark stubble on his cheeks and a black buzz on his head that I can't help imagining feels softer than it looks.

The overall effect is . . . shocking. Overwhelming, actually. Without the hair, there's nothing to distract from his piercing blue eyes and sharp cheekbones. It's his mouth that's the real unearthed treasure, though. I stare at it, unable to think.

"Deiss?" My voice comes out breathy.

"At your service." His lip curls as if in response to the spotlight of my thoughts. He pulls back into his seat and I hear the pop of the ancient car's trunk.

His disappearance breaks the trance, and I jerk my arms back to my side. They pop back up as if they've been spring-loaded, smoothing at my hair and face and clothes like any of it can be fixed. While it's reassuring that I've brushed my teeth, the image I caught in the mirror while doing so was much less comforting. I happen to know for a fact that, beneath these sunglasses, the green of my eyes is so dramatically surrounded by ribbons of red Deiss is likely to break into Christmas carols if he sees them. My hair is limp, hanging down my back like a batch of sunflowers that have been forced to survive in the shade. I really hope I don't smell, but there's no way of knowing for sure.

Deiss climbs out of the car, and I mirror his movement to the trunk. "I wasn't expecting you."

"Disappointed?" He doesn't seem offended by the idea. He doesn't even seem particularly curious as to my answer. He merely reaches for my roller bag and tucks it gently into the trunk.

"Of course not." No wonder he's kept his face and mouth under wraps. He was probably doing it as a public service because he knew their beauty was too much for the world to handle. The emergence of them has thrown me completely off my game. "I just feel bad. I know it was a long drive."

The minute the words come out, I realize they're true. I feel terrible, actually. It was one thing when Phoebe offered to drive me; I knew she'd enjoy three hours of gossip about the ridiculous things Mac has done since they left LA. But Deiss? I can't believe my arrival has cost him a full day of his vacation.

"It *was* a long drive. But I figured I should be the one to do it." He places the bag inside and closes the trunk, pulling the mirrored aviators from where they dangle off the top button of his linen shirt and sliding them over his eyes. "I know you like me best."

My body relaxes at his words, and I smile as he turns to head toward the driver's door. My guilt is a wasted effort. He's Deiss. If he hadn't wanted to drive all this way to pick me up, he wouldn't have.

"Actually," I say, sliding into the passenger seat, "I made a list. Phoebe, obviously, ranked first. You almost came in second, but then I remembered Simone. And Mac."

The rattly old car smells faintly of gas, and the seat is made of a faux leather that's peeling in parts. A piece of it digs into my linen pants, threatening to snag the material. Since I've never been out of the country before, I've also never been in a car made for driving on the opposite side of the road. It's disconcerting, like everything is normal but also slightly off-kilter.

"Just wait. Phoebe will be plummeting to the bottom of that list soon enough." Deiss pulls the car out, and my hair tickles my neck as the air from the open windows slips through it. "You've never been on one of these things, so you don't know, but that woman is a nightmare to travel with. Always talking about the schedule. It's like vacationing at basic training."

"Uh-huh," I say, remembering the time Phoebe missed dinner because she'd decided to hitchhike to Tucson. It turned out she'd been "craving a cheese crisp," although I'd had to come up with a better excuse for her professor to explain the classes she'd missed. If she couldn't even be bothered to figure out the schedule for a bus back then, I'm certain she's not enforcing one of her own on others. "I'm going to tell her you're lying about her."

"Please don't." Deiss's eyebrows lift over the mirrored frames as he merges onto the highway and picks up speed. There's enough fear in his voice that I laugh, wondering what Phoebe did to finally break Lucas Deiss. My guess goes to the time she held a box of his records over the edge of a balcony, threatening to let go if he wouldn't admit Taylor Swift is the greatest songwriter of our generation.

"I don't know." I pause, pretending to think it over. "I suppose I owe you my silence, considering you drove all this way."

He grins knowingly, like this is proof he's my favorite after all. My hair whips around my face, and I wonder if this car is too old to have air-conditioning or if Deiss can feel the richness of the air, too, and wants to soak it all in. Two days ago, I would've been worried about tangles in my blowout. Now, I can't seem to care enough to even rope it back in a bun. It's ruined anyway, and I like the feel of whirling through this foreign land.

I'm not sure what I expected from this place, but it wasn't the long stretch of highway surrounded by a surprising amount of green we're barreling through. It's beautiful, but the sky is the real showstopper. It stretches endlessly above us, cotton candy blue and vast in a way I never get to see in Los Angeles. It makes me feel like I'm flying.

"Seriously, though," I say, "why did you come to pick me up? I thought Phoebe was going to."

"They wanted to go snorkeling."

"And you don't snorkel?"

"Not with sharks."

"They went snorkeling with sharks?"

Deiss's head tilts. "Not *with* sharks, exactly. But there were reports of sharks at the beach this morning. And they went snorkeling *at* the beach. So . . ."

"So, they went snorkeling in a shark's playground."

Deiss makes a sound with his tongue that signifies his agreement.

My eyes widen. It occurs to me for the first time that this is not an entry-level trip into the world of vacations. I've been so focused on catching up to my friends that I never stopped to consider where I was going to end up. I have spent the entirety of my adult life doing everything in my power to curate my existence. Not once have I considered inserting sharks into the picture.

"Do you think they're okay?"

"Phoebe and Simone should be fine, but Mac's probably worth worrying about. Since his brain is made of the same material as jellyfish, the sharks are definitely going after him first."

I nod. "So, you could've hidden behind him."

"Maybe," he says. "But the last girl I dated tried to set my pants on fire while I was wearing them. Ever since then, I've had a real phobia of biters."

I search him for signs of a teasing smile, but Deiss's eyes don't leave the road. It's impossible to tell if he's kidding or serious. I can't imagine Lucas Deiss arguing with anyone, much less a woman. It requires an energy I've never seen him exhibit.

In my search for signs that he's kidding, my eyes get stuck on his mouth again. I suppose I should feel lucky that he's kept it hidden for all these years. It's so distracting. Certainly, my grades would have suffered if my professors had been in competition with this.

"What about you?" His question causes my eyes to jerk back toward the windshield. Thankfully, he doesn't seem to notice. "Any phobias?"

"Do I have any *phobias*?" I turn back toward him, too surprised to worry about his mouth trap. "What's happening right now? Are you actually trying to make small talk?"

He gives a rare, genuine laugh that I feel through my whole body.

"I kind of was," he admits. "Is it that obvious I don't have much practice with it?"

"I've known you for eleven years, Deiss. It doesn't have to be obvious. I'm fully aware you're not one for idle conversation."

"But in the last eleven years, I haven't been trapped in a car with someone for three hours."

"How flattering to hear that you feel trapped with me."

He glances over with a grin, and I catch a glimpse of my face in his glasses. I look absurd, like I'm not just amused but could actually be on the verge of giggling. It's disconcerting, like looking into a mirror and finding my neighbor's face instead of mine. It's the lack of sleep that has knocked my mask crooked.

Since the moment I said no at work, something strange has been happening inside me. There's this little ember of rebellion smoldering in my belly. It's why I watched movies and read novels on the plane instead of listening to my informative podcasts. It's the reason I opted for the regular in-flight meal over the vegetarian one. And I think it might be why five flights over the course of two days actually felt fun instead of the nightmare it could've been.

"It's not like I'm planning to tuck and roll out mid-highway," he says. "I'm just saying it did occur to me that it might be weird if we sat in silence all afternoon."

"Well." I pause thoughtfully. "You've spent a lot of time with women. What do you talk to them about?"

"Surprisingly little, actually."

I groan, but without the disgust I'd feel for anyone else. I don't see Deiss enough to have any personal evidence of what his dating life is like, but I gather it's similar to how it was back at school, active but fleeting. Phoebe lives within walking distance of him, and she claims she's yet to be introduced to anyone special.

"Do you care about anything other than music?" I ask.

"Again, I have to admit, surprisingly little."

I laugh. "I suppose if we had anything in common, we would've discovered it by now."

"Most likely," he agrees. "Do you want to tell me all about your life?"

"What about it?"

"I don't know. Past, present, and desires for the future?"

I shudder. "Definitely not. And I know you're not going to tell me about your past, but do you want to update me on your present or future?"

"The very idea has me rethinking the tuck-and-roll plan."

"Noted." I peer up at the endless sky. "It always creeps me out when people refer to themselves in the third person," I say finally. "Could that be considered a phobia?"

"Ugh." He cringes. "Definitely phobia-worthy. That's the worst."

"This woman in my office does it. I think she's trying to develop her own catchphrase, too. She keeps saying, 'Melanie has *feelings* about that.'"

"Have you considered trying to get her fired?"

"I did steal the boss's wallet once and put it in her desk."

He visibly perks up. "Really?"

"No, Deiss," I say dryly.

"I'm disappointed." He shakes his head and does something with his mouth that's probably supposed to emphasize his point but only manages to highlight the fullness of his lips. "You've disappointed me."

"Now you know how I felt when you pulled up instead of Phoebe."

"Fair enough."

"But if it makes you feel better, my friend Elena printed out a fake memo officially banning feelings and left it on Melanie's desk." My chest warms at the thought that I can legitimately call Elena a friend now.

"It does, Liv. It makes me feel much better."

"And that wraps up phobias," I say decisively. "Moving on to favorites. Shall we begin with movies?"

"*Fight Club*," he says without hesitation.

"I haven't seen it. But it sounds charming."

"You haven't seen it?" He looks over at me in disbelief.

"If I had," I say, "we'd have something in common."

"Deiss is very glad you gave into the small talk plan," he says with an evil grin.

I suppress a smile and feign gagging instead.

CHAPTER 5

o my great surprise, the small talk takes us through not only the three-hour drive but also through a leisurely early dinner stop at a town on the water. We sit beneath a brightly colored umbrella, comparing favorites as we share a spicy bean relish called chakalaka and a rich minced-meat dish called bobotie. The flavors are unlike anything I've ever had, and I savor each bite before washing it down with a local beer that's made from corn. When I've eaten all I can, I lean back in the woven chair, my stomach swelling with fullness as the sea-soaked air caresses my skin.

Before I'm ready to leave, Deiss is up and moving toward the car. I scurry after him reluctantly, but it's not until we're closing in on St. Lulia that his urgency begins to make sense.

"Keep your eyes open for hippos on the road," Deiss says, causing me to stiffen in the passenger's seat.

"Pardon me?" I blink at his profile, highlighted by the orange glow of the setting sun.

"It's possible it was recommended that we return straight

here from the airport. Apparently, there are no lights on the road, and hippos tend to wander in the path of oncoming cars. They're hard to spot once it gets dark."

I study the road that has gotten progressively narrower since we exited the highway. "And you thought it was a good idea to stop for dinner?"

"I was enjoying having you all to myself." He looks over, and the orange from the sky reflects off his lenses. "It seemed like a good way to make it last longer."

I blink beneath my sunglasses, but before I can read too much into this startling confession, he turns back toward the wheel.

"Besides," he says lazily, "everyone should have corn beer at least once in their lives. You said you liked it."

"I also like hippos," I say, scurrying past the momentary shift between us. "But I'd rather not see one of them mowed down by your car."

"If it makes you feel better, there's no way this heap of junk is capable of mowing down a hippo. It's way more likely to crush in on itself and burst into flames."

"Thank you," I say dryly. "That *does* make me feel better."

He tugs his glasses off and tosses them on the dashboard. My fingers twitch with the desire to pick them up and cradle them gently in my lap. I don't want them to get scratched. I scan the area for hippos. Beside me, Deiss's hand remains casually slung over the wheel, but as the sun drops beneath the horizon, I feel the speed of the car drop with it. I look over and catch his eyes, narrowed with concentration.

"You're nervous," I say.

"Do you want to be the American who comes to South Africa and provokes a war with the hippos?" Without looking over to see the shake of my head, he says, "Neither do I."

The vegetation around us changes just before the road turns to dirt. It's tropical, but not like the well-spaced palm trees on the beaches back home. It's more like a jungle, wild and interwoven. The air is ripe with the collision of earth and sea. It feels thicker, like it's filling my lungs with something alive.

Deiss eases the car over a pothole. "We'll pass our cabanas to get to your guesthouse, but it's a small town, so they can't be far apart. Would you rather stop and see everyone first or get checked in?"

I'd kill for a quick shower, but obviously it's more appropriate to stop and say hello first.

No.

The word pops into my head, unexpected and insistent. *I don't want to do things because I'm supposed to.* These are my friends, my family even, and I am on vacation. There's no reason to temper my desires here. Especially not with them.

"I'd prefer to get checked in first." The words come out so confidently, I can't even hear the question in them myself. But I find myself waiting for Deiss's permission anyway.

Unsurprisingly, it doesn't come. He merely nods and leans a little closer toward the windshield before turning sharply. And then there's a glow of light that gets brighter as we move into the town. Still no road lights, but a strip of restaurants and lodges lights the street through their windows. Up ahead, shadowed people shuffle down the strip with the lazy saunter of vacationers. We pass a restaurant lined with tables. Its door is propped open, lively music spilling out. A string of Christmas lights is haphazardly draped along the front wall, more likely decor than leftover holiday cheer. In the distance, I hear the roar of the sea.

Then, almost as quickly as it appeared, it's gone again and we're back in the jungle as if the stretch of civilization was merely a mirage. Ten minutes later, Deiss pulls the car to a stop in front of my soon-to-be home. Neither of us speaks as we collect my luggage and approach the front door. The jungle around us rustles with the sounds of living creatures, but the building itself shows no signs of life.

"Are you sure this place hasn't been condemned?" Deiss eyes the sagging wooden building doubtfully. Unlike the other places we've passed, there's no welcoming light over their door. The only sign we've arrived at the right place is the piece of cardboard propped against the wall with the words *Holiday Guesthouse* written in block letters across it.

My stomach drops. "Since Friday when I made the reservation?"

His look of doubt remains.

"No," I admit. "I'm not at all sure."

He sets my bag on the gravel porch and raps loudly on the door.

My breath catches in my throat as I wait for it to open. I can't believe this is the place Elena chose to book for my first trip out of the country. I'd be furious with her; however, since I opted to get drunk on alcoholic creamer instead of dealing with logistics, I probably shouldn't place blame.

Deiss lifts his hand to knock again, but the door opens before he makes contact. A small, wiry woman peers out, seeming to look past us. Slowly, her bright eyes focus, taking us in. She has a distracted air, making it impossible to determine if she's pleased or annoyed to see us. I suspect she's neither, and that she'd be perfectly content to see us in a room or back on the road, as long as the chosen option removes us from her doorstep.

"Hi," I say, wishing I'd thought to at least learn the local greeting. Shifting my tote bag to the other shoulder, I proceed in English because, sadly, that's the only language I know. "I'm Olivia Bakersfield. I've booked a room for tonight."

"Here?" She glances behind her as if she's checking some invisible registry in the air. "Oh, right. My brother mentioned trying that out. I suppose he's giving you his room."

"His room?"

"I hope you didn't pay him much for it." She wags a finger at me. "I guarantee not one cent of it will go toward keeping this house running. Do you know he showed up two years ago and still insists he's my *guest*?"

I position my face into an appropriate expression of disapproval but am spared the effort formulating a reply when Deiss speaks up.

"The thing is," he says, "Olivia's only here to confirm that her reservation was canceled. She wouldn't want any confusion that might result in her having to pay for the mistaken booking."

"I see. Well, there's nothing to worry about there." The woman waves her hand in a way that seems to brush both any potential confusion and us away in one swoop. "My brother takes payment in cash. Unless she already gave it to him? If so, that was your mistake, girlie. Getting money out of him is like trying to pry your hand out of a crocodile's mouth."

Deiss looks at me, and I shake my head. I'm incapable of saying more. Obviously, there's not even the tiniest part of me that wants to stay in some strange man's bedroom. On the other hand, I'm nearing fifty hours without any real sleep. Without the distraction of small talk, exhaustion has reared its ugly head, rendering me wobbly.

"We're good then," Deiss says firmly. "Sorry to take up your time."

Before he's even done speaking, the woman is nodding and offering a kind smile as she slams the door in our faces.

I stand there stunned for a moment, my eyes tracing the worn wooden rectangle in front of me. The touch of Deiss's hand on the small of my back jolts me out of my reverie. It's warm and firm, and completely unexpected.

"Let's go," he says, already guiding me back to the car. "There are two beds in my room. You'll stay there."

I shrink at the suggestion. There's no way I'm allowing Deiss to see me without makeup on, in the harsh light of morning with unbrushed teeth and hair. I wouldn't even let Phoebe see that. I don't care how out of character I've been behaving. There's a reason I haven't had a roommate since college, and why I prefer not to spend the night with the men I date. Nobody can hold their head up high in front of someone who has seen it resting in a pool of drool on their own pillow.

"I can't stay with you," I say once we're back in the car with the engine running.

"Sure you can," he says confidently.

"I'll ask Phoebe if I can stay with her." The compromise offers no relief. Even if I didn't mind Phoebe seeing my drool, I don't want to be a burden on her. That kind of weakness ruins things, changing a relationship forever.

"Perfect," Deiss says. "Just out of curiosity, do you think Mac will try to talk you into sleeping in his bed, or are you assuming the idea of two beautiful women on the bed next to him will be enough to make him opt for legroom?"

My stomach sinks. "Phoebe and Mac are staying together?"

"Yep."

"You could have just said that."

"I could've." Deiss looks unfazed by the glare I shoot him.

He pulls the car back onto the road, leaving the "guesthouse" behind.

"I can't stay in your room, Deiss."

"Then stay in Simone's." He offers the suggestion as if we weren't both witness to the Sister Standoff of 2016, in which Simone and her little sister stopped speaking for nine whole months because Ashley showed up for a weekend visit. "She breathed like a crank caller," Simone would grumble every time one of us would try to remind her how much she loves her only sibling. "She never breathes like that in public. It's like she saved it all up and then came into my beautiful apartment and exhaled every germ she'd accumulated over the past month." Her face would scrunch up with disgust. "And did I mention that she brought coffee inside? My living room smelled like an Alcoholics Anonymous meeting for days after she finally left."

"I will," I say, convincing myself as much as him. "It's one night. I'll just wait until breakfast to drink any coffee."

"And," he prompts.

"And I'll keep my breathing to a minimum."

"And . . ."

It takes a minute to figure out what he's referring to. Once I do, I shake my head.

"She doesn't still do that," I say. "She's an adult now."

"An adult who needs Disney music playing at full volume in order to sleep." He smiles. "I could hear it from my balcony last night."

I exhale loudly, my eyes fluttering closed. I am so unbelievably tired.

"Just stay with me," Deiss says. "What's the issue? It's not like I'm going to cop a feel. You'd spear me with icicles if I tried."

"I would not."

He lifts an eyebrow.

"I'd use ice rays," I say. "They beam out from my eyes."

"See?" He grins. "You know I'm a self-preservationist. There's absolutely nothing for you to worry about."

Except waking up and accidentally torching you with my dragon's breath.

"It's settled then," Deiss says, choosing to take my silence as affirmation. "You'll stay with me, at least for tonight. Then tomorrow, when you haven't just traveled from one continent to another and I haven't spent six hours behind the wheel of a car, we'll look into alternative options."

"Right." I don't even think about what I'm agreeing to. I'm too distracted by the reminder that Deiss has wasted an entire day of his vacation on me. *Of course* he wants to get this settled so he doesn't have to feel obligated to spend even more of his time finding a new place for me to stay. "Thank you," I add, flushing with embarrassment. I can't believe I've allowed myself to become such a burden. A needy woman is a weak woman. I know this, yet I've shown up on a trip where no one was expecting me and have forced them to take care of me.

It's mortifying.

"No problem," Deiss says, turning into the Elephant Lodge. Unlike the last place, this one has a real sign that's lit by a spotlight shining up from the ground. It's a perfect logo, the kind of thing I'd be proud to have created. It straddles a line between classic and rugged, exactly what you'd want to see when you're playing adventurer but secretly hoping for all the comforts of home.

We park and, rather than walking toward the lobby door, Deiss leads me around the side of the building on a dimly lit, slatted-wood pathway. Palm trees rustle in the wind as we walk past, and a song that's heavy on the bongos plays in the distance. Deiss pulls my bag behind him, and the wheels make little clacking sounds over the boards. The path branches off on either side every few yards, but we keep going until I begin to wonder if the joke is on me, and I've accidentally agreed to camp in the jungle.

"That way," Deiss says, tilting his chin toward the last path on the right.

It leads to a small wooden hut. Deiss slides around me to unlock the door, and his shoulder brushes against mine, warm and hard. The contact sparks something inside my chest, a jolt of adrenaline reminding me that I'm not a person who shares small spaces. Even as a child, it was only me and a mother who was usually gone, working one of her two jobs. Most of the time, I had the house to myself. First thing tomorrow morning, I'll find somewhere else more appropriate to stay.

"What do you think?" Deiss asks, flipping on the light. Inside, it's less primitive than the outside led me to believe. White tiles line the floor, and a ceiling fan whirs above. There's a hand-painted elephant above the bed, bookmarked on either side by woven basket lids. "Nice, right?"

My eyes drop back to the bed. "Um, Lucas?"

"Yes, darling?"

"You said there were two beds."

His lip curls. "Did I?"

I sputter in response. *No.* No way. Not happening. Fortunately, I've been practicing for this. The word *no* now lives on the tip of my tongue.

"Kidding, Olivia," he says before I can get it out. He pulls the beige quilted cover off and presses into the middle of the bed, revealing a deep line beneath the sheets. "It's two singles pushed together. Why don't you hop in the shower, and I'll hunt down our friends and two new sets of bedsheets. Mac will help me drag them apart when we get back."

I blink at him, still prepared to say no. But no to what, I can't decide. I'm so tired that I can't even imagine insisting on going with him to find our friends. Plus, it's definitely in everyone's best interest if I bathe.

"Fine," I say, pursing my lips. "Thank you."

The moment the door closes behind him, I rip my clothes off and jump in the shower. At first, I flinch at every sound, peeking outside the curtain to make sure Deiss hasn't returned. Within a few minutes, though, I'm too caught up in the feel of the water against my skin to care. It comes out in a trickle, and it smells different from back home. Unlike in LA, it's not permeated with chlorine, and it has a salty tinge that seems wrong. The soap is different, too. No matter how vigorously I rub it between my palms, it won't foam up. I end up using the shampoo on my body, spreading the suds until every part of me is slick and fragrant.

Afterward, I pull a pair of shorts and a t-shirt out of my bag. I need to go through it and figure out what I drunkenly packed, but first I should at least put on mascara and some blush. I'll have to do something with my hair as well, before everyone arrives. I find a brush, but the act of lifting it to my head feels overwhelming. Heavily, I sink onto the bed. It'll be easier this way, with just my arms active while my legs rest. As if my body is engaging in a revolt, my back slumps against the headboard and my legs stretch across the bed. The world blurs. My eyelids flutter once, twice, and then they close.

CHAPTER 6

*O*h, Deiss." Phoebe's voice breaks through my sleep, ruining a very lovely dream in which I've been swimming with a new hybrid animal, spawned from a questionable mating of a koala bear and a turtle. "You wouldn't!"

I squint against the light that's streaming through the window and discover that my cheek is pressed against a t-shirt that's covering a well-muscled back. Apparently, it's the koala side of my swimming partner I've decided I relate most with, because I'm currently mimicking one, one of my arms wrapped around Deiss's waist and my leg slung over both of his. It's so wildly out of character for me that, rather than unhand him and scuttle backward like a normal person, I freeze in place.

"And good morning to you, Phoebe." Deiss's voice is gruff with sleep, but his body isn't stiff with it. Smoothly, he turns toward me, wrapping warm fingers around my wrist and lifting my hand from the impressive ladder of abs they're spanning.

My cheeks flush with embarrassment as he places my hand gently on my own stomach before pulling himself into a sitting position. His legs slide out from under mine, separating our bodies completely. The whole extraction is performed with the practiced hand of a dispassionate surgeon.

"You know Liv doesn't like messes," Phoebe says. "If you pull a dice on her, she's going to end up running away from all of us. And who will keep us in line then? We'll all be out of control."

I rub the sleep out of my eyes, but it doesn't go away. I've heard of jet lag, but I never dreamed it would feel so tangible. It's like a thick wool blanket weighing down not only my body but my head, too. Even my fingers feel heavy and useless.

Phoebe, on the other hand, looks wide awake. She's wearing a navy-and-white-striped top and a pair of white shorts with boat shoes. It would look annoyingly preppy if it weren't for her glorious Afro and slew of accessories. As it is, it looks quirky and stylish. I'd like to re-create her image in illustrated form and attach it to a logo for a yachting company.

"We're supposed to play dice?" I ask, trying to catch up.

"No," Phoebe says. "He's going to pull a *Deiss*. You know how he is. He can't help himself."

"This sounds like it's going to be offensive." Deiss's mouth curls with amusement.

I force my eyes away. *We're in bed together.* I have no makeup on, and my hair probably looks ridiculous. Worse, Deiss has had to peel me off of him like I'm some stray cat that snuck in during the night. This is more embarrassing than him seeing me yesterday, unshowered and covered in plane filth. It's more embarrassing even than the time we stayed up partying all night at Phoebe's and I awoke on her floor to find a green Jolly Rancher stuck to my cheek. No wonder Deiss was so sure he wouldn't be tempted to cop a feel. I pull the sheet up to my neck and subtly begin to scoot toward the opposite side of the bed.

"No offense intended," Phoebe said, coming toward us. "It's not like you mean to be infuriating. If you were capable of giving women more, I'm sure you would."

"Oh, that's nice," Deiss says. "As long as it's my incompetence that's the problem and not anything hurtful."

"Exactly." Phoebe settles on the bed beside me and leans over, smothering me in a hug. "You're here! Please know that I don't blame you at all for giving in to Deiss now that he's all shaven and sex-panther-y. It's one hundred percent his fault for unleashing himself on womankind."

Her hair smells like coconuts, and I breathe it in, savoring her closeness. I've long suspected there's something about me that gives off a warning signal. A kind of *Do Not Touch* sign that people seem scared to disobey. Like Mac, though, Phoebe doesn't adhere to it. She never has. She's always treated me as if I belong to her in some small way. I like it. It's nice to be claimed by someone.

"I missed you," I say, squeezing her back.

"Interesting," Deiss says. "I'm sure you'll be thrilled to hear that the Ice Queen had no emotional response to seeing me. I let her stay in my bed and didn't even get a hug for my generosity."

I look up at the reminder. "You were supposed to separate them."

"And you weren't supposed to pass out on them before I had the chance."

"Wait," Phoebe says. "Are you saying you didn't sleep together?"

"No need to sound so relieved," Deiss says. "I've never had any negative reviews before."

"He's probably never stayed around long enough to receive feedback," I say to Phoebe.

"You should go," Deiss says to Phoebe. "She was much more pleasant before you arrived."

"I was so tired yesterday my brain was barely functioning," I say, despite the fact that today is not much better. I've traded exhaustion for haze. "That wasn't so much pleasantness as stupidity."

"Actually," Deiss says, "I was referring to the cuddling this morning."

I roll my eyes, hoping Phoebe's groan distracts from the redness I can feel creeping into my cheeks. While my eyes can be counted on to hide any emotion, my skin isn't always as accommodating.

"*You* should go," Phoebe says to Deiss. "We need coffee."

"There's some on the table."

"The instant packets? Those didn't pass for coffee at the hotel in Spain, and they still don't here. We need the real stuff, Deiss, and you've been nominated to find it for us."

Deiss sighs and leans forward. "Fine."

His white t-shirt is so threadbare, it's almost see-through. My eyes catch on the muscles that pop out beneath it as he pushes himself up. I force myself to turn to Phoebe, but she's busy watching the show.

"You sleep in shorts?" she asks, scanning the length of him.

I breathe a sigh of relief at the confirmation of real clothes on his bottom half. If it had turned out I'd cuddled a boxer-clad Deiss—or, worse, a Deiss in briefs—I'm not sure I ever could've looked him in the eyes again.

"When I'm sharing the bed with Liv, I do," he says. "What time do we board the boat?"

I look over in surprise, but Deiss is looking down at the floor, shuffling into a pair of low-profile white trainers. "Boat?"

"We've got the wildlife cruise today. I already called, and they confirmed there's space for you." Phoebe glances over at Deiss. "It leaves at ten. So, you'd better get on that coffee."

"Aye, aye, Cap," he says dryly, grabbing his phone. As he strolls out the door, he glances at me and says, "Told you she was bossy on vacation."

I don't defend her because I'm already reaching for my phone to check the time. It's 8:37, and I'm guessing the boat doesn't depart from the lobby. We'll have to get to a dock, which means I probably have less than an hour before we leave. It's not enough time. Waterproof mascara always takes longer to apply, and I'll need to do a Google search on boat hairstyles that are flattering but will prevent me from ending up with a mouthful of honey-blond highlights. Thank goodness I took care of shaving last night.

"Can you do me a huge favor?" I get out of bed and head toward my suitcase. "I need to find somewhere else to stay tonight, but I also have to get ready. Would you mind searching some options?"

"But I have so much to tell you. And this might be our only time alone all day. Plus, we have a patio!" Phoebe darts to the door on the other side of the cabana and flings it open, gesturing outside like the assistant on a game show.

Her smile is so wide that I feel my mouth mirroring hers. Unfortunately, I don't have the luxury of sitting around and catching up. I have new accommodations to find. More importantly, I don't go out into the world without my armor on. As much as I love Phoebe, she should know me well enough to understand this. When we were at school and half the girls on campus were wandering around in pajama pants and sweatshirts, I was swapping out purses to better accessorize my outfits. As my mother always told me, if you look like a mess, people will assume they can mess with you.

"It's fine," I say. "I can figure out a place to stay after I get ready. Why don't you go on the patio and I'll be out as soon as I'm done."

"No." Phoebe's shoulders slump, but to her credit, she manages to hold onto her smile. "That's okay. I want to help. I'll sit on the bed so I can talk to you while you're in the bathroom."

Her tone carries no judgment, but her words provoke a mental image that makes me cringe. There's nothing wrong with choosing to get ready for the day if that's what I want to do. But is it? Do I really want to spend my morning staring into a mirror when I could be on a patio with my best friend?

No.

The realization makes my breathing speed up. I know it shouldn't, but the thought of being around people all day with a bare face and a poorly thought-out outfit feels like the equivalent of going into public with my breasts out and a fig leaf between my legs. It's not vanity. It's protection. But should I really have to protect myself against the people I love most in the world?

Again, the answer is *no*.

I look down at the t-shirt I dragged out of my bag last night and am shocked to discover words on it. On principle alone, I don't wear novelty tees. The idea that I'd own one is ridiculous. I can't imagine where Elena and I found it.

The thought of her name solves the mystery. The shirt was given to me the year she was my Secret Santa at work. I can't believe I've forgotten. She laughed so hard she snorted when I opened it and read the words *If you can read this, you're standing too close*. She tried to make me put it on, but I refused. It smelled like the plastic it had been shipped in. If I'm going to say no to prioritizing appearance over experience, I suppose her gift is the most apt uniform for my rebellion.

"Actually," I say, "I'd like to see the patio. Just let me brush my teeth, and I'll be right out."

Phoebe squeals and runs for the door, and I head into the bathroom to face the music. As feared, my hair looks like a place birds might build their home. And without contouring, my cheekbones have all but disappeared. I must have slept hard, though, because the dark smudges that were under my eyes yesterday seem to have been erased along with my bone structure. I brush my teeth, run a brush through my hair, and take a deep breath before joining Phoebe outside.

It's easy to see why she was so excited about the patio. It's on the edge of a sharp incline, layering the exotic tropical trees and bushes so they stretch from ground to sky without feeling claustrophobic. The fronds sway in the breeze like they're dancing to music. Phoebe is lying on one of the loungers, but I settle in a patch of sunlight at the small table in the other corner. The air smells green and wet.

"I can't believe you made it," Phoebe says. "How did you get the time off?"

"It turns out, in-house designers aren't as essential as I convinced myself we are. We actually get vacation days, too."

Phoebe laughs. "Who'd have thought?"

"Well, I've gone seven years without taking advantage of them, so clearly not me." I know I could—and maybe even should—tell her the truth, but I'm not ready to talk about it yet. I need to figure out a game plan first, not for telling her but for successfully going freelance. Without a concrete strategy and breakdown of the numbers, I'll look foolish.

"I should've come on one of these trips before," I admit. "Although, apparently, I wouldn't have been rooming with you. Is that not weird, you and your ex sharing a hut?"

"No." Phoebe waves a dismissive hand, but there's something in her eyes I don't like. "It's fine."

"Is it?" I choose my words carefully, not wanting to give her any reason to feel defensive. The problem is, while everyone else might think Phoebe and Mac's six-year relationship miraculously wrapped up with no hurt feelings, I was the one she ended up crying to about it. She probably didn't intend to—it took a large part of a bottle of tequila to loosen her tongue—but she did. And while she started out the night insisting it was mature of Mac to admit to wanting to see other people (translation: sleep with all the models who were suddenly his co-workers), she ended it declaring she never wanted to see his stupidly gorgeous face again.

My heart still breaks remembering her confession. But that was also one of the most terrifying nights of my life. If Phoebe couldn't be friends with Mac, it would spell the end of our little group. And if I could've gone back in time and strangled the talent scout who spotted Mac wolfing down tacos at the Pink Cantina, sending him down the path toward gorgeous, scantily clad women, I would've happily procured a rope and gone hunting.

"You were together for a long time," I say. "I could see how it might feel complicated."

"It's the fact that we were together for so long that keeps it from getting complicated," Phoebe says with a breeziness that doesn't quite ring true. "Mac and I always share a room on vacation. It splits the cost in half."

"I guess that makes sense," I say diplomatically.

She squeezes her eyes shut. "What *could* complicate it is the fact that I accidentally walked in on him getting out of the shower yesterday."

"Oh, Phoebes." My stomach sinks. "I don't suppose you closed your eyes and backed out of the room?"

"Eventually. But he's so . . ."

"Chiseled?" It's probably not the right thing to focus on, but facts are facts. Mac's underwear ad made me want to lick the glossy page, and I've seen him eat an entire hot dog in one bite and then burp like a mating call for whales.

"Exactly." She smiles gratefully. "He's so very chiseled. It's confusing, you know?"

I nod sympathetically, even though I don't find it confusing at all. Mac won the lottery when he got Phoebe, and true to form, he was too stupid to hold onto her. I don't care how much fun he is to be around. Phoebe deserves better.

"Did anything happen?" I ask.

"No. And it can't." She squints at me. "Can it?"

No.

This time, I hold the word in, even though it takes considerable restraint. "Do you think you're capable of being friends with benefits with him?"

"I doubt it," she admits. "There's too much history there."

"Do you want to get back together?" I brace myself.

"Definitely not," she says firmly. "I love Mac to death, but if he broke my heart again, I'd have to kill him. And I can't go to prison. I look great in a jumpsuit, but even I can't make an outfit sparkle if I'm not allowed to add accessories."

I exhale my relief.

"Do you not want us to get back together?" She peers at me curiously.

"It's not my call." I avert my eyes, embarrassed that I've been so obvious in my reaction.

"If you have something to say, Liv, please say it." There's no sarcasm in her tone. If anything, there's a pleading quality that's contrary to her usual confidence. "I need a friend's advice right now."

I hesitate, comparing how I'm supposed to respond with how I want to. Finally, I decide to brave the latter. "You and Mac were good together. And if you think it could be good again, I'd be happy for you. But selfishly, I'm scared of what would happen if the two of you fell out. I don't think the group could survive it again."

I stop myself before admitting how crucial these people are to my life. That they're the closest I've ever felt to being a part of something. It would put way too much pressure on Phoebe.

"I know exactly what you mean," she says, sinking into the lounger. "I was worried about the same thing when we broke up. And then, last night! Liv, you have no idea how much I was panicking when Deiss said you were staying in his room. I was convinced the two of you were going to hook up and, after that, we'd lose you for sure."

I wave off the thought, surprised by the change in focus. "It wasn't like that at all. But why would that make me lost?"

"Oh, you know how it is. Deiss tends to take a kind of love-them-and-leave-them approach to women. And you tend to go cold when you've finished with someone. It's not like I'm worried about either of you getting emotionally involved, but I can't picture a scenario where you don't both end up retreating. And that doesn't really work for a group like ours, does it?"

I nod eagerly. Obviously, she's way off base about Deiss and me, but she's not wrong about the rest of it. "That's exactly what

I'm saying about you and Mac. When you two broke up and you never wanted to see him again, it meant I was never going to see him again. And I could handle that if that's how it had to be, but it wasn't that simple, was it? Because where Mac is, Deiss is. And Simone has a bunch of sorority sisters and a weakness for handsome men, so she's not exactly likely to choose time with us over Mac and Deiss. It's all just a domino chain, waiting to fall."

"It *is*. And me seeing Mac naked again has made the first domino teeter."

"Exactly."

"But we can't let them fall," she says emphatically. "Olivia Bakersfield, we must keep the dominos upright!"

I lean back a little in the face of this sudden zealousness. I'm not quite sure how this benign conversation warrants declarations involving full names.

"Hear me out," Phoebe says, holding up a hand. "Now, I'm not saying we have to be some creepy cult where we all get to tell each other what to do. However, as a group, we're all basically in a relationship, right? Just because it's not one person and not romantic doesn't mean it's not a relationship. And, like any relationship, one person can't only take themselves into consideration when making a decision."

"Okay?" I'm pretty sure, if there's an actual need to specify the difference between your own philosophy and that of a creepy cult's, something has gone off the rails. But it's Phoebe doing the specifying, so I'm not prepared to argue quite yet.

"Do I sound crazy?" she asks. "Because I actually think this is really going to help me."

"Is it?"

"Monkeys!" She shrieks the word.

Truthfully, she *is* starting to sound a little crazy.

"Behind you," Phoebe says, gesturing toward the knobby pieces of wood functioning as a railing to the patio. She jumps to her feet.

I turn slowly and am shocked to discover not one monkey but three. They've got gray backs and fluffy white fronts and are scampering up the trunk and fronds of the tree in front of us. One peers at me with its tiny black face. Without conscious decision, I rise to greet it. It screeches, and I feel a thrill go through me. I've never seen a monkey so close, and certainly not one just hanging out like it has arrived to have coffee with us. Its friend swings from one branch to the next, chattering loudly.

"What I'm trying to say"—Phoebe raises her voice to be heard over the monkey sounds—"is that I can't be weak with Mac. Not just because it's a bad idea for me, and maybe even for him, but because it's bad for everyone."

"It's bad for the group," I say, catching on. It makes sense: Phoebe has always found it easier to look out for everyone around her than just for herself.

"So, for the sake of the group, I solemnly swear that I won't allow anything to happen between Mac and me again. And you . . ." Phoebe holds out her hand like I'm supposed to shake it.

I grab it without thinking, but then I'm stumped. "And I . . ."

"Solemnly swear . . ." she prompts.

It hits me that she wants a promise that I won't hook up with Deiss, which only causes me to laugh awkwardly. I'm happy to do anything that might help her not get hurt in the long run, but I can't say the words she wants to hear. Deiss has zero romantic interest in me. I'd sound delusional.

Phoebe's eyes search my face. "Oh my gosh," she whispers. "Do you like him? Have you *always*?"

"Of course not." My voice has gone prim, and the sound of it makes me cringe. I hate when I talk like this. It makes me seem cold, and people always seem to shrivel in response. I grab Phoebe's hand before she can recoil, and I shake it firmly. "I solemnly swear that I won't ever allow anything to happen between me and Deiss."

"That sounds final," a voice says from behind us.

I whip around to find Deiss standing in the open door, three cups of coffee balanced in his hands. Heat surges up my back, flooding into my face. I have no doubt I've gone a blistering shade of red.

"Interesting." Deiss tilts his head, his gaze perusing the length of me in a way that feels like actual hands on skin. "I didn't realize that hadn't been decided until now."

CHAPTER 7

"Y ou're quiet," Deiss says forty minutes later as we head down the wooden path through the jungle to meet the group for the estuary cruise. "Are you trying to prevent yourself from flirting with me?"

"Funny." I still can't look at him. And not just because he caught Phoebe and me making that ridiculous pact. Despite having taken a clear and deliberate stand against makeup this morning, I still feel naked heading out into the world without it on. Even my own mother hasn't caught me with a bare face since she took me to get a free makeover at the Macy's counter two towns over and delightedly declared, "*Now* you're ready to be seen in public."

My hand reaches for the hem of the printed skirt that swishes against my thighs, but I stop myself before I can smooth it down. In the five minutes I had alone, I was able to unearth a simple, fitted white tee to wear with it in hopes it will make my au naturel face and hair seem like a fashion choice rather than an inability to groom myself. Strappy leather flats finish off the look. It's classic, a style I always revert back to when one of my design projects starts to feel fussy or out of control. Today, however, it's failing to deliver the comfort it usually provides.

"I'm not sure what you heard," I say coolly, "but you've misinterpreted my part in the conversation."

"Did I?" It's ridiculous how blasé he's capable of sounding, like he's whistling carelessly without making a sound. "It seemed pretty clear-cut to me."

My bare toe stubs against a wooden slat that's slightly higher than the others, and I stumble. Deiss's arm flies around my waist. He holds me firmly against his side. It's warm and unyielding, and I stay there for only a moment before pulling myself free.

"Uh-oh," he says. "Do we need to confess that to Phoebe?"

I ignore him and walk faster, rounding the corner toward the lobby. I can feel the flush in my cheeks, and as an unwilling victim of his mouth trap and the participant in a wildly embarrassing pact, it feels more imperative than ever that I don't allow Lucas Deiss to affect me. Luckily, the rest of the group is waiting outside for us, and Mac spots me first. He bounds our way like an excited puppy. Before I can properly brace myself, he's got me in a bear hug and is swinging me around like a tetherball.

"Livitron!" He plops me down and dips his head so our faces line up. "You got freckles! They're so tiny, like your cheeks have been sprinkled with fairy dust."

He smiles like a kid, and I don't have the heart to tell him that people don't just sprout freckles; they're born with them and are quickly trained to smother them under a dewy layer of very expensive foundation.

"They were giving them out on the plane ride over," Deiss says, coming up behind me.

Mac looks intrigued, like he doesn't believe him, but he'd like to.

"They gave me an option," I agree. "Beef and a spray tan or chicken and freckles."

"Both only last for six to eight washes," Deiss says.

"We should start an airline that really does that," Mac says.

"We can call it the Sky Spa," Simone says. Her focus shifts to me. "I heard your room fell through last night. How awful! You could've stayed with me, you know."

I blink in surprise. I can't help wondering whether her sudden generosity is due to my need or the fact that she doesn't like the idea of me staying with Deiss any more than Phoebe did. That's unfair, though. Simone has always been generous in her own way. I can't count the number of times she's claimed a beautiful dress wasn't her color or lamented the way it hung on her figure, insisting I take it off her hands. Miraculously, this always seems to happen right when I'm getting ready for a date or some other social event. Also miraculous: this trend started right after the first time she and I went shopping, when Simone ended the day with her arms full of bags and I hadn't even been able to find a decent pair of earrings that wouldn't max out my card.

"Really?" I hesitate. As much as I don't relish a night of walking on eggshells and attempting to sleep to the blare of Disney music, it's probably best to get some space from Deiss. "Well, Phoebe and I searched everywhere online, but we couldn't find any vacancies for tonight."

"Seriously?" Simone shakes her head. "You finally make it out of the country, and nothing is going right."

"At least I made it," I say. "But I will need someplace to stay tonight."

"Oh." Simone's sympathy quickly transitions into a look of surprise, then unease. "Well, I'm sure you're all set up and comfortable in Deiss's room now. And I doubt I could even find the other bed in my room under all of the clothes. Why scrunch them up into drawers when you can lay them out and let them breathe, right?"

"Right." I grin in spite of the round-about rebuff.

We are who we are. Even Simone's fear of me sharing a bed with Deiss can't overcome her need to have a Simone-specific space. I have no doubt she'd be willing to pay for any one of us to get our own room, but sharing is just a little bit further than she's capable of going. I can relate, if for different reasons.

"I guess we're still roomies," Deiss says.

"Just for one more night," I clarify. Phoebe and I might not have been able to find an available room, but we were able to book a single-person tent for tomorrow's safari.

"That's probably best," Deiss says. "Too much time alone together might tempt you."

"Tempt you to what?" Simone's nose tilts up, like a dog catching the scent of something.

I shoot Deiss a warning look, but he just smiles.

"Apparently," he says casually, "my sexual allure is so staggering, our Ice Queen had to make a vow to Phoebe that she wouldn't succumb to it."

Simone gasps.

"Wrong," I say. "First, it was not a *vow*. It was a pact. Second, it wasn't about you or your sexual allure. It was about you *and* Mac."

"So, you're tempted to sleep with Mac, too?" He looks over

at a very astonished Mac and nods in a congratulatory way. "Nice."

"Wait," Mac says before I can speak. "You're into me?"

"No," I say firmly.

He shakes his head, seeming not to have heard me. "I knew this face was going to get me into trouble. I can't control it, you know. I was just *born* with it."

"Please," Phoebe says. "I've seen pictures of you with braces and enough dots of acne cream across your forehead that it looked like you were being treated for poison ivy."

"Well, that didn't stop Liv from wanting to sleep with me."

"I do not want to sleep with you!" I inhale deeply and lower my voice. "Phoebe and I were simply agreeing that we'd never do anything to mess up the dynamic of the group, which happens to include—"

"Getting naked with us," Mac interrupts.

"It's smart of you," Deiss says, his lip curling smugly, "to recognize your weakness in the face of such temptation."

I can see his childish attempt to provoke me and will not rise to it.

Unfortunately, Phoebe either doesn't see it or is unable to muster the same restraint.

"Please," she says. "We were just kidding around. You couldn't tempt us if you tried."

"You think?" Deiss looks annoyingly amused.

Phoebe's eyes spark with challenge. "Give it a shot."

Deiss's amusement is muted by a flicker of apprehension. "What?"

"You heard me. We're smart, savvy, gorgeous women. It takes more than a sex-panther makeover"—Phoebe flicks to indicate his newly bare face before turning her attention toward

Mac—"or a decent set of abs to attract women like us. If you really think you're so irresistible, let's see you prove it."

"You want us to come on to you?" Mac looks delighted by the idea.

"Yes," Simone says quickly, her eyes darting toward Deiss. "That sounds entertaining. I'm willing to participate. For science."

I snort indelicately, and everyone's head turns toward me.

"Is that our van?" I deflect the attention by gesturing to the dinged-up scrap of metal that's rolled to a stop in front of the lobby door.

"Allow me to get the door for you ladies," Mac says gallantly.

"Well," Phoebe says, "that's Mac's super suave move, so he's clearly in. How 'bout you, Lucas?"

Deiss slides an arm over her shoulders and hits her with the full force of his gorgeous mouth. "Sure, I'll give it a shot."

I groan loudly, but nobody seems to care.

CHAPTER 8

The boat is single-leveled and covered, with benches lining both sides. The middle is empty, presumably so passengers can race from one side to the other when wildlife appears. There's been a lot of both racing and wildlife appearances. There's also been a lot of indiscriminate flirting from the guys. I say *indiscriminate* because the focus of their attention seems to shift with the sway of the boat, although it *has* been strictly limited to me, Phoebe, and Simone. Never mind the group of four women who are also on the tour, appear to be single, and are far more likely to yield results. The attention would be annoying if it weren't so comical.

"You know," Mac says in a deeper voice I've never heard him use before today, "I could probably wrestle that croc."

"*That* croc?" I point at the seven-foot crocodile the group of women are frantically photographing. Its slow, predatory approach on us is terrifying, as are the guide's insistent reminders to keep our hands in the boat.

"Yep." Mac nods confidently. "I'd probably win, too."

"Probably?" I study his perfect face, taking in the chiseled jaw, straight nose, and clear blue eyes, no thoughts or troubles to darken them. I'm looking at a man who has the flirting capabilities of a twelve-year-old because he's never had to develop his game. He was lucky enough to spend years with a woman way too good for him, and since then, he's managed to get by solely on good looks and enthusiasm.

"Definitely," he says smugly.

"Why are you doing this, Mac? Go flirt with Phoebe."

He glances over at her. "Deiss is flirting with Phoebe."

I follow his gaze. Mac is right. Deiss has been flirting with Phoebe since we got in the van. He tossed a little attention Simone's way when we first got on the boat, but when she slid off her see-through button-up and started prancing around in just the pink cami beneath, he quickly backed off.

"You don't really expect anything to happen between the two of us, do you?" I ask Mac.

"Nah. But it's fun trying." He slides his arm around my shoulders and smiles broadly. "I've never been allowed to flirt with you before."

"Let's take a picture," Simone says from behind us.

I turn reluctantly, shifting my sunglasses higher on my nose. At least they cover half my face. Simone's insistence on projecting my makeup-less image to all 112,000 of her followers feels personal, but of course it's not. She needs this proof that her life is something to aspire to. There are thousands of people on Friendsta who put up travel photos taken with cameras much more high-tech than her phone. Her brand is all about lifestyle. And I, more than anyone, can respect the importance of branding. Anyway, Deiss's refusal to appear in any social media has basically made it impossible for any of the rest of us to take such a stand. The last time I tried, Simone lost her temper. Apparently, we were ganging up on her and trying to make her look thirsty.

Mac swings his arms over our shoulders, pulling us into his sides as Simone frames the selfie. On the screen, I look washed out next to Mac's striking features and Simone's artfully applied makeup. My smile is real, though, widening as Mac turns and presses an unexpected kiss against Simone's cheek.

He looks pleased by her resulting giggle.

"You want me, don't you," he says proudly. Before she can answer, he turns to me, waggling his eyebrows. His thumb begins to stroke my arm.

"Mac." I try to keep my voice stern, but I can't help laughing with Simone. It's like being pawed by a puppy.

"I love this game," Simone says brightly, snapping another picture. "I still don't really understand what prompted it, but I'm game."

"It's all about the challenge," I tell her, rolling my eyes. "This madness only started because Deiss overheard Phoebe and me saying we'd never mess up our friendships by getting romantically involved with Mac or Deiss."

"But not really me," Mac says to Simone. "I don't count."

"Of course you count," I say.

"Well, yeah. For *you*." Mac laughs. "Sorry. That was confusing. I meant I don't count for Phoebe."

Simone and I look at each other, then look slowly back to Mac.

"Phoebe was specifically talking about you, Mac," I say.

"But Phoebe and I have slept together a thousand times," he says.

"And then you broke up with her," I say. "Remember? Five years ago? It's why you don't sleep together anymore."

"Right," he says. "But there's nothing to stop us from getting back together."

"It kind of sounds like there is, though, doesn't it?" Simone sets an uncharacteristically gentle hand on Mac's shoulder. "Isn't that pretty much what Liv is saying?"

Mac looks at me with wide eyes.

"This is not a revelation," I say. "You guys have been broken up for ages. All Phoebe said is that she wouldn't do anything to risk your friendship."

"Well, that's good," Mac says, although his face says something different. "She's my best friend."

"And you're hers," I say. "See? That's not the kind of thing either of you would want to ruin."

"Yeah." Mac nods, but his eyes linger on Phoebe and Deiss. "I'm just going to go find out what they're talking about."

Simone and I stare after him together, and then Simone leans in closer.

"Do you have a bad feeling about that?" she asks.

I sigh down at the crocodile that is slowly moving away. "I don't even know what just happened."

"I think you just told him the love of his life had closed the door on him."

"If she was the love of his life, he wouldn't have broken up with her," I say.

"No," Simone says firmly. "If she wasn't the love of his life, he would've cheated on her instead of breaking up with her."

I roll my eyes. "Am I supposed to be impressed by his restraint?"

"Yeah, actually. They'd been together since they were kids, and they both needed to see what else was out there. You know Mac. He's all impulse. That might be the only time in his life that he thought a situation through and did the right thing."

I open my mouth to argue but am cut off by someone yelling about hippos. The guide points to the other side of the boat, and like everyone else, I find myself running to the other side. It's a whole pod of them. I've never seen a hippo before. I've never even thought of them as real. They've always been cartoons in my mind, but there's nothing cartoonish about them. They look old, even the baby at the edge of the water. Their skin is like thick, weathered leather. They're massive, bigger than I imagined, and the thoughts of Phoebe and Mac fade against their enormity.

I take a couple of pictures, but it seems silly. I'll never forget these animals. I'll never forget any of this. It's hard to imagine that I've gone from my cubicle to here in a matter of days. Not one of my books told me what it would be like to hear the lap of water and feel the sun on my face as I float down an estuary. They didn't describe the awe of seeing things I've only ever seen on TV. But they should have.

I leave the crowd and return to the empty side of the boat, leaning against the railing to search for my own discovery. Wind ruffles my hair, and I pull my sunglasses to the top of my head to keep it back. With the blanket of jet lag still hovering over me, it feels like this could all be a dream. A bird trills above as I search the water for a crocodile. When I don't find one, I scan the banks for another exotic bird. Instead, I spot more monkeys.

"Having fun?" Deiss appears beside me and leans against the railing. His eyes follow mine to the monkeys.

"I'm supposed to be working on a project about bone broth right now," I say. "So, yes. This feels particularly fun in comparison."

"Bone broth? No wonder you jumped on a plane."

I turn to look at him. "Have you come over because of Phoebe's challenge?"

He glances over with a small grin, but then his eyes return

to the monkeys. "You're safe. I think I got it all out of my system with her."

I feel a twinge of disappointment that I don't approve of at all. "Too bad. I was curious what it was like when you actually made an effort."

He laughs. "What is it, exactly, that you think I don't make an effort at?"

"Anything."

"Fair enough."

"See?" I turn to him triumphantly. "You can't even make an effort to defend yourself."

"What's there to defend?" He turns to meet my eyes.

He's taken off the mirrored glasses, and it's strange, being this close to him and having his full attention. The blue of his eyes is so different from the lightness of Mac's. It's dark and swirling with all of the things he never says aloud. I find myself leaning a little closer, wishing I could read something in them.

"Your hair looks different today," he says quietly. He's not looking at my hair, though. He's still looking into my eyes.

"Does it?" I ask, even though the fact that I didn't style it was a pressing concern merely an hour ago. I pat at it without thinking.

"I like it." He reaches up and runs a lock of it through his thumb and forefinger slowly. As his hand gets lower, the back of his thumb trails lightly down the side of my neck. Goose bumps break across my skin, and my skin flushes hotly. "It's pretty. You always look beautiful, though."

"I do?" I ask, too distracted by whatever is happening to realize I've spoken at all.

"I can't keep my eyes off you sometimes." As if to demonstrate his point, his eyes drift over my face like a caress. "You're like this serene, brilliant pool, with all of these things swirling below the surface, just out of view. Sometimes, when I see one of them, it feels like treasure."

His tongue slips out over his bottom lip, pulling it in, and my eyes finally leave his, locking in on his mouth. His thumb traces my collarbone, and my hair moves with it, tickling the skin on my chest. My stomach flips, sharp and hard.

He leans closer still, and his thumb breaks free of the lock of hair and lifts to my chin, tilting it up. His mouth comes closer before moving past mine, the stubble delightfully rough against my cheek. And then his hot breath is tickling my ear.

"That's what it looks like," he whispers, "when I'm making an effort."

His words filter slowly through my mind. Once the meaning of them works its way through my brain, I brace myself for embarrassment. But it doesn't come. I'm disappointed at the realization I'm not the treasure he's described, but more than that, I'm caught up in the wonder of what Deiss has just done. I can't remember a single time of my life that I've so thoroughly forgotten myself. And the *skill* he's exhibited. As someone who spends most days pretending, I'm in awe of his mastery of it.

"Lucas Deiss," I say admiringly. I pull back, but I have to grip his arm to steady myself. "You are good at that."

He smiles a wolfish smile that's an entirely new level of gorgeousness. Simply, confidently, he says, "I know."

CHAPTER 9

Safaris have always brought visions to my mind of trekking through tall grass in a dry African heat with a wide-brimmed hat to protect my face from the sun. A set of binoculars would dangle from my chest, and a herd of giraffes would graze in the distance as a single zebra wandered in front of me. In my head, there were always other people with me, but they were blurry, somewhere to the side, spread out across the land.

In reality, a safari turns out to be an extended visit to a very large natural zoo, with no directions as to where its inhabitants are. We don't walk because there's too much ground to be covered and, outside the confines of our Land Cruiser, lions and leopards and other things would happily make a meal of any one of us. It's endless hours of riding across bumpy terrain, excitedly recounting the elephant that just flapped its ears at me before I eventually settle into my seat and listen to my earbuds as I scan the landscape for my next discovery. It's hundreds of pictures, at first zoomed-in frames of exotic wildlife but eventually of Mac choking on his attempt to eat a Clif bar in a single bite, or of Phoebe and Deiss napping in the back seat. In other words, it's nothing like I've imagined. But it's fantastic.

I shift in my seat, feeling my shirt slide against the sweat on my back. It's almost comical to think earlier this week I was so nervous to show my bare face. Now, three days into camping, all I can do is hope my deodorant is working and nobody has seen me flash my butt while peeing behind a large bush.

"You look tired," Simone says from the seat next to me. She peers at my face. "Did you get any sleep last night?"

"I slept fine," I lie, not wanting to admit how scared I've been sleeping alone in a tent. I don't worry about her because she's used to ordering things around. If a lion showed up, she'd probably demand it lie down beside her to keep her warm. But I can't get over the fact that there are no locks. It's impossible to turn your brain off knowing anyone could tug on a zipper and drag you out into the blackness.

Her eyes squint, unconvinced, and I feel a surge of affection for her. Simone is remarkably perceptive when she chooses to focus on someone other than herself. So much so that I've never minded that she doesn't do it very frequently. I actually admire how self-focused she is. It would be easy to say she's living off her daddy's money and avoiding getting a real job, but she's put more hours into becoming an influencer than most people do in the office. She's constantly networking and reaching out to companies to further her own brand.

She has a passion that makes her lose track of everything else. I remember feeling that way about graphic design, back when I was creating stuff I loved. It's a fact I haven't been able to stop thinking about, despite my efforts to focus on this moment with my friends in this wild land. Something about the ease of this trip makes striking out on my own feel more possible than it ever has. If I can live like this, covered in dust with my hair tangled by the wind, I can certainly get by on my savings until I start making enough to support myself.

"Are you sad that it's almost time to go home?" Simone asks, like she can read my mind. "You missed the first couple of days, so it probably feels like a pretty short trip to you."

"No," I answer, honestly this time. "I needed to do this, and it's been great, but I'm excited to get back. I've got stuff to do."

"Like what?" Phoebe asks from the back seat.

"I'm guessing it will involve lots of personal grooming," Deiss says. His head is on her shoulder, which can't be as comfortable as it looks. My butt is bruised from all the bouncing around, and Phoebe is significantly bonier than the seat cushion.

"Do I sense judgment in your tone?" I ask. "Because that would be pretty rich coming from someone who shaved everything from the neck up because he was too lazy to use shampoo."

"No judgment," he says, directing his mirrored lenses my way. "But I'll have you know I still use shampoo. It was the brush I was too lazy to use. Between searching for it every morning and lifting my arm for all those repetitive strokes, it was like waking up to a full workout."

"How did you ever pull yourself out of bed?" I ask.

"With a lot of effort. And you know how I feel about that." He flashes a cheeky grin, and my cheeks flush at the memory of the last time he *made an effort*.

I can't stop myself from laughing aloud.

"What's happening here?" Simone looks back and forth

between the two of us, her eyes pausing only momentarily on Mac's sleeping form. "Do the two of you have an inside joke?"

"No," I say. "It's common knowledge that Deiss shaved his head. All you have to do is look at him and the evidence is right there."

Rightfully, Simone's brow furrows in confusion.

"She's deflecting," Phoebe says thoughtfully. "I think Simone's called it. There's something weird going on."

"Thank you." Simone looks properly vindicated. "They've been bickering like this for days. Neither of them ever talks this much, especially not to each other."

My brow lifts in surprise at the realization that she's right. I have been talking more than usual. The less I've worried about what I'm supposed to say, the more I've been able to contribute to the conversation. And not just in response to something someone else has said. I've actually shared my own thoughts a few times.

"I think it's the small talk," Deiss offers. "We had to resort to it when I picked Liv up from the airport. Now we can't stop."

I swallow a smile at his explanation.

"Small talk and bickering are two different things," Simone says.

"So," I say, "you see why we've been practicing. Neither of us knows exactly how to do it."

Deiss nods. "You can hardly expect us to iron out the kinks if we don't practice."

"Well, you're certainly not going to learn from each other," Simone says. "You only care about something if you're heard it on a record player, and Liv isn't saying a word unless she's read it in a book first."

The unexpected criticism hits like a sharp jab to the abdomen.

"She doesn't get all of her directives from books," Deiss says. His face stays expressionless, but I know, underneath his glasses, his eyes are sparkling with amusement. "I think the Husband Huntress is a blog."

I stuff down the bark of laughter that comes from deep within me. How *dare* he? I've certainly never mentioned the Husband Huntress in front of a man, not intentionally at least. If Deiss has heard me speak of her, he was eavesdropping.

"Thato," I call out to our guide, "if someone were to unknowingly have raw meat in their tent, what's the likelihood they'd be eaten by a lion?"

Deiss laughs, and Simone's head whips toward him.

Thato smiles cheerfully through the rearview mirror. "Don't worry. I keep the raw meat locked in the cooler. The lions can't smell it in there."

"And yet, somehow, I do feel a little worried," Deiss says, quietly enough that Thato can't hear him.

I flash him a wicked smile. "You always have been smarter than you look."

"I don't like this," Simone mutters. "I don't like it at all."

I accept the after-dinner tea Thato offers, even though I know caffeine this late at night is probably a bad idea. Never have I had so much tea as I've had in South Africa. It appears after every meal and again between them, thick with sugar, wafting wispy tendrils of steam that smell of bitter leaves. I take a sip, ignoring the way the glass teacup burns my fingers.

The sky has almost faded to black, and the only light at camp comes from the fire we're sitting around and the Land Cruiser's headlights, which Thato has pointed at the makeshift kitchen behind us. I shiver in the chilly night air and scoot closer to the fire. Its yellow flames lick at the sky and illuminate everyone's faces.

"I miss tacos," Mac says. He pokes at the fire with a stick he's found, doing nothing to improve the flame.

"We've been gone a week," Phoebe says.

"And how can you even think about more food after that dinner?" Simone asks. "I've never been so full in my life."

"It doesn't matter how long it's been or how full you are," Deiss says. He's leaned back with his hands on the ground, and his face is tilted toward the sky. "You can always miss something. Sometimes, I wake up in the morning and miss last night's whiskey."

Phoebe laughs, and Mac's gaze goes toward her, doing that strange peering thing I've noticed him doing over the last few days. It's like he's searching her for something. Or studying her. I can't imagine what he's looking for. You'd think after all the years they spent together, he'd have her face memorized by now.

"I'm not sure that's the kind of thing you're supposed to say aloud," she says to Deiss. "It could be considered cause for concern."

Deiss just grins, not bothering to drop his gaze from the sky.

"What do you miss now?" Mac asks him.

"Nothing," Deiss says.

Phoebe scoffs. "Sure you do. What about your bed? You must miss that when you're sleeping on the hard ground in that tent."

"Not really. I like the ground." He tilts his head toward her. The buzz of hair across his head and jaw has gotten darker and thicker over the last few days, leaving him shadowed and mysterious. "Why? What do you miss?"

"Lattes," she says without hesitation. "Big travel cups filled with steamed milk and espresso."

"I love the coffee here," Simone says. "It's like a shot to the brain."

"It's tasty," she agrees. "But it lacks the volume I require."

"So," Deiss says, "'quality over quantity' isn't for you?"

"Nope," she says firmly. "It's right up there with 'it's the thought that counts.' I mean, who came up with that nonsense? Clearly, it's the result that matters."

"For the record," Mac says, "she's talking about presents, too. And romantic weekends away."

"There is no reality in which hunting UFOs near Area 51 is considered a romantic weekend away," Phoebe says.

I laugh in spite of myself.

"And I'm not sure you can claim to have booked anything," Deiss says to Mac. "Didn't you just stop at a motel on the side of the road?"

"In Mac's defense," Phoebe says, "it did have an ancient microwave. And the smell of stale smoke permeating the room made me grateful to go to sleep at night."

I take another sip of my tea, and the sweetness of it bursts against my taste buds. It reminds me of Sunday afternoons with my mother. The memory is a strange contrast to the moment—the vastness of the night, the idle chatter and wild, crackling fire, versus the two of us still in our church dresses with a flowered teapot and tiny cups. It's nice, though, to have a little part of her here on this adventure.

Like me before this week, my mom has never been out of the country. She's a small-town beauty queen, through and through. Our tea parties were always the height of sophistication to both of us. Often, we'd attempt British accents while nibbling at our low-fat cookies, freed from their single-serve packets and placed reverentially on the mismatched china she'd found at the Goodwill. I'd steal a sugar cube when she wasn't looking, squirreling it in my cheeks and feeling its slow dissolve. Then its sweetness would hit my bloodstream, and I'd find myself chattering away, giggly and eager to entertain.

Or maybe it wasn't the sugar that fueled those conversations. Maybe it was just that, for a few hours each week, it was just the two of us, best friends. My mom wasn't pulling yet another double at the diner, and no men were allowed. We didn't even talk about them, especially not if they were backing away, or losing interest, or growing colder and curter, or whatever the current strategy was for leaving us behind. I didn't talk about the bad stuff, either. Not the kids who had made fun of my ill-fitting clothes or the sleepover I hadn't been invited to that weekend.

Instead, we reveled in the prettiness of the moment. The colors on the teapot and in our dresses. The tilt of our pinkies as we lifted the teacups to our painted lips. We talked about the things that brought us joy, and for a couple of hours, we felt like the kind of people who lived in a world of tea and sweetness. To this day, I always make it back home at least one Sunday each month so the two of us can have tea together.

"What do you miss, Liv?" Simone asks.

"Cat Stevens," I say without thinking.

"The singer?" Deiss looks over with interest.

"My cat," I say.

"You don't have a cat." Simone's mouth twists like the word itself insults her.

"I do."

"She does," Phoebe agrees. "I've met him. He's not very friendly."

"He's not," I admit. "If I open a window, he jumps up on the sill and spends a significant amount of time debating whether staying with me or leaping to his death is preferable."

"But so far, he's opted to stay with you?" Deiss asks.

"I always end up closing the window before he can decide," I say. "Usually, that decision coincides with him edging close enough that I'm forced to acknowledge I'm coming in second to death."

"I bet he'd like me," Mac says. "Cats always do."

"I'm sure he would," Deiss says. "Olivia, why have you been depriving Cat Stevens the pleasure of meeting Mac? Do you not want your cat to experience one of the greatest pleasures life has to offer?"

"Is he being sarcastic?" Mac asks Phoebe.

"No," Phoebe assures him. "He just wants Liv's cat to be happy."

"I live all the way across town," I say. "Nobody wants to go to my house."

"I want to go to your house," Mac says.

"I'd make the drive," Simone says, "but it's so much easier for you to come to me."

"What I don't understand," Deiss says, drawing out the words, "is how Phoebe and Simone have gotten invites when Mac and I haven't."

"Because we can be trusted on a white couch," Phoebe says.

"I didn't actually invite Simone because I knew it was too far," I say. "And Phoebe invited herself."

I don't mention that she needed somewhere to go because she was devastated that Mac had posted a picture of himself with another woman on social media. Despite the fact that he and Phoebe had already been broken up for a few years, it was the first time Mac had indicated he might be in a real relationship with someone else.

In the end, it turned out to be nothing. But that night was the first time I realized how much Phoebe had been pretending to be okay with how things had ended up between the two of them. I think it was illuminating for her as well. She never said anything to Mac about it, but she did break things off with the guy she'd been seeing. I guess she figured, if she could still feel like that about her ex, she had no business being with someone new.

"Hey," Phoebe says, clearly offended. "I assumed the fact that it's my best friend's home meant no invitation was required."

"I thought I was your best friend," Mac says to her. He leans toward her, doing that strange searching thing again. I'm surprised no one else has mentioned it.

"You are," Phoebe says. "All of you are."

"But *best* means one," he says. "We can't all be best. If we're all best, then that means none of us are."

"Then none of you are." She laughs, but I can hear the exasperation in it. And rightfully so. Nobody expects to be forced to rank their friends, especially as a full-grown adult.

"But . . ." Mac trails off. I once heard him assert, "Baseball is going to be better when it's played by drones," and passionately defend it, but this kind of emotional honesty is out of his range.

"But I've seen you naked," he says. "A lot."

"In the past," she says sharply. "That was a long time ago."

"So, back then," he says, "was I your best friend?"

"Mac." There's a warning in the word that makes me flinch. It's like hearing Mom and Dad on the verge of a fight. In all the time Phoebe and Mac were together, I rarely saw them argue. But since they've split, I haven't heard so much as a minor disagreement between them.

"What?" To my surprise, Mac doesn't back down. "I'm just trying to figure this out. You never said that, just because I stopped being your boyfriend, I wouldn't be your best friend anymore. Is that what you're saying?"

"I'm not saying anything," Phoebe says. "Common sense should take care of that for me."

I feign a yawn, lifting my arms above my head for full effect. "It's getting late. I guess I should probably get some sleep."

"Well, it's not," Mac says, seemingly referring to common sense's failure to communicate with him.

Deiss lets out an ill-timed chuckle, earning a glare from Mac.

"I'd probably better get some sleep, too," he says, the amusement clear in his voice as he gets to his feet.

I feel none of his amusement as Simone and I stand up to go to our tents. A niggling sense of dread threads through me as I leave Phoebe and Mac to hash out their breakup, a conversation five years past due. My dread is only amplified by the rustling in the bushes out beyond camp. Reluctantly, I change into my pajamas before burrowing down into the sleeping bag and closing my eyes.

Sleep, however, proves elusive. The caffeine zips through my veins, sending my thoughts galloping in every direction. Luckily, my terror of the prowling wildlife outside is able to distract me somewhat from my worry for Phoebe and Mac. And when that fails, there's always the new and ever-present fear that I'll fail in my efforts to make money as a freelancer once I get back home.

I toss and turn, burying my face into one side of the pillow and then the other as I work through the worst-case scenarios. At some point, I must wear myself out. I don't realize I've fallen into a light, anxious sleep until I'm jolted out of it by the tremor of the earth beneath me. The hammering of my heart blocks out all conscious thought for a moment. I blink in the darkness, slowly remembering where I am.

The realization brings no comfort as something metal crashes outside. I'm alone, protected only by the flimsy material of a tent. Our campsite seems to be under attack, and my suit of armor was purchased in the sleepwear section of Bloomingdale's and is made entirely of silk.

CHAPTER 10

I lie on my back, clutching the sleeping bag to my chin as my body trembles beneath it. My eyes blink rapidly at the top of my tent, as if my gaze alone can prevent it from crushing in on me. My breaths come in short, quick gasps. I don't know what's out there, but the rumbling of the ground tells me it's big, and never in my life have I felt smaller. My guess is wild hippos. Or bulls. If it's a stampede, nothing could stop them from trampling my tent. The first night, a sturdy wind almost did the walls of my tent in. I felt like one of the little piggies facing down the Big Bad Wolf.

"Liv?" The zipper lowers an inch, and I jerk upright, clutching the sleeping bag to my chest. "It's just me."

"Deiss?" I yank down the zipper and am so grateful to see him that I grab him by the forearm, tugging him inside. It doesn't occur to me until he falls on the ground next to me that this tent is called a single for a reason. I've been sleeping diagonally just so I can stretch my legs all the way out.

"Whoa." Deiss pushes himself up and rearranges himself so

that he's in a sitting position in the tiny amount of space available. "If I'd known you'd be so excited to see me, I would've shown up the first night."

I gape at his dim figure in the darkness, grateful. If I have to die, at least I won't have to do so alone.

"What's out there?" I whisper, barely able to get the words out. I'm not sure I want to hear the answer.

"We have visitors." He leans forward, like he's going to look out the tent flap, but I beat him to it. Only, rather than looking outside, I zip it up with shaking fingers, wishing I had a padlock on hand.

"Is it bulls?" I ask. "It is, isn't it. It's bulls." Visions of horns ripping through my nylon house fill my mind. It will be like an Easter egg hunt for them, with me and my silk pajamas as the little milk chocolate surprise in the center.

"No," he says reassuringly. "It's just elephants. I think Thato must've forgotten to lock up some of the food."

I stare at his shadowed face in disbelief. *Clearly*, elephants are not better. They have much longer, thicker legs. Even if they don't attack the tents, which they could easily do with their tusks, there's nothing to stop them from stepping on us.

"You can see them," Deiss says, misinterpreting my disbelief. "The moon and the stars are pretty bright, so it's lighter outside than it is in here. They were all around that tarp over the kitchen area when I came out. Hopefully, they'll get whatever they smelled and keep moving."

"I don't want to *see* them." I'm still panting. Strangely, this doesn't seem to deliver any more oxygen. I gulp at the air, but the tent is too small. There's no air left in it. "I want to get the hell out of here."

"To where?" Deiss laughs. "We're safer here than running around like a midnight snack."

My eyes widen, and my fingers squeeze at my thighs. The dry, oxygenless air gets caught in my throat. I try to cough it out.

"Hey." Deiss's voice softens, and he leans toward me. His hand strokes my back. "Are you all right?"

No.

I think I'm having a panic attack. At the very least, I am very definitely panicking. I don't want to get stomped on by an elephant. Thanks to the personal trainer I've only recently parted ways with, I haven't been consuming any dairy. My bones probably have the consistency of old chalk.

I shake my head, unwilling to admit to any of this aloud. Not only is Deiss fine, but he left his tent for mine. He went outside, *where the elephants are*, because he knew I'd be scared. There is no way I'm confessing that the basic act of breathing is beyond my current capabilities.

"What can I do?" Deiss asks.

"I'm fine," I say. But what I really want to say is, *Make me forget where I am.*

Deiss might be, I realize, the one person who actually is capable of making me forget where I am. He's already done it once, on the boat. I could ask him to do it again.

"Distract me," I blurt out.

"What?"

"Do what you did on the boat."

He stills, as the meaning of my words sinks in. Something sparks through the air between us, a kind of heat, probably from my own embarrassment.

"You want—" Deiss's voice has gone deep, making him sound like a stranger.

"I just wanted to be distracted." I wave my hand. "Forget it. It was a dumb idea."

"They'll be gone soon," he says gently.

There's another loud clatter outside, and my heart leaps from my chest to my throat. I tense and peer at the flimsy top of the tent, my hand reaching for Deiss's arm. I don't realize I've made contact until his fingers come to rest over mine.

"We're okay," he says, gently trying to pry my hand loose.

I'm squeezing too hard, but I'm not sure I can stop. It's his fault if he ends up with bruises; I'm meant to be alone in here. If Deiss had stayed in his own tent, I would've managed to present as cool and calm by morning. He's peeked under a closed hood, and everyone knows that's how you get burned by the engine.

"We're going to be fertilizer," I say more to myself than to Deiss.

"What?"

"Our bodies will be trampled, so they'll just leave them here." The details unveil themselves as I work through the scenario. "Why would anyone want to load up a bunch of bloody corpses and drive them back to town? It would be like chumming the waters in a sea of sharks."

"Liv," Deiss says, a little louder this time.

"Wild animals would be diving teeth-first into the vehicle." I can hear the shakiness in my voice, but it sounds farther away than it should. I squeeze into Deiss's forearm, finding the bone beneath the muscle. "They definitely wouldn't risk it. They'll leave us here. Maybe they won't even tell anyone that we died. I wouldn't, if my business depended on people feeling safe. It sounds much better if we just disappeared, doesn't it?"

My voice cracks at the thought that my mom will assume I'm yet another person who has abandoned her.

"Nobody's dying," Deiss says. "And nobody's disappearing, either. It's just elephants."

He sounds so earnest that I find myself laughing in response. It's *just* elephants. It's just a herd of animals that weigh
up to fourteen *thousand* pounds each. Of course Deiss isn't
worried. He's so loose that an elephant could step on him and
his organs would probably slide to one side and take a nap until
the pressure let up. My organs, on the other hand, would pop
like tightly stretched rubber bands. My heart and lungs already
feel stretched beyond their limits. They don't even need to be
fully stepped on. A little swing of one of the elephants' trunks
should be enough to shatter them like ice.

"Hey," he says.

My laughter has turned into sharp little gasps. I look into
his face. His eyes are just dark orbs outlined in white. I try to
focus on them, but there's another crash outside the tent. It
sounds nearer this time, and a shriek rips out of my throat.

He leans toward me, and the padding of his thumb presses
lightly against my lips, silently warning me to be quiet. I don't
know if he's worried about me freaking out the elephants or our
friends, but I hear the whine in the back of my throat that says
another scream is on standby, straining to be released. Deiss
seems to hear it, too, because his fingers slip down my jaw and
over the tension before wrapping behind my neck and pulling
me forward.

I feel the heat of his mouth on mine before I realize what
he's doing. Actually, even then I'm not sure what, exactly, he's
doing. Because it's not a kiss. Not really. For a moment, his lips
brush against mine, but then they still, so close I can feel them
like a whisper, but not quite making contact. My heart pounds,
and I start to lean back, but his hand on my neck holds me in
place, despite the lack of tension in his grip.

Our breath mingles, mine fast and his slow. His fingers slip
up into my hair and come back down again, leaving a tingling

trail in their wake. I feel the strange urge to bite at his lower lip with my teeth and tug it into place against my mouth. His forehead leans lightly against mine, and I feel the brush of his nose on the tip of my own. I focus on the pacing of his breath and am shocked to discover mine has slowed to match his. It's overwhelmingly intimate, like he's taken control of my insides and pulled them into a slow dance to some silent melody.

Through a haze, I hear the loud pounding near our tent, but the sound of it disappears when Deiss pushes through the invisible barrier between our mouths and captures my top lip between his. His tongue swirls against mine, sending an aching need through my belly. Before I can appease it, Deiss's mouth is gone.

He says something I'm too distracted to hear, flashing a grin I can see in the dark.

I blink at him. I want a repeat of what just happened. It's the only way I'll be able to determine how it felt eternal and like a blip at the same time. "What *was* that?"

"You were panicking," he says, "and I didn't want to slap you."

"So, you kissed me?"

"In my defense, it wasn't meant to be a kiss. But then the elephants came closer, and . . ."

"You decided to shove your tongue in my mouth to keep me from screaming again." It's an ugly, unfair way to phrase it, like insisting silk is actually burlap. I can't help myself, though. What was funny on the boat feels embarrassing now. By hypnotizing me with his pheromones, or whatever that magic was, he's made me look as malleable and eager as my mother.

"It was a mistake," he says quietly. "But I stopped. As soon as I realized I could distract you with my most embarrassing secret, I did that instead."

"Your secret?"

"What I just told you," he prompts. "About when I was a kid."

I search my mind, but all that's there is the memory of his mouth teasing at mine.

"When you peed your pants in the cafeteria?" I guess.

"I wish." There's rustling in the tent as he stretches his legs out and leans back on his arms. "It would mean my most embarrassing moment lasted for minutes instead of years. And that I'd actually been able to go to a school and eat lunch in a cafeteria like a normal kid."

"Hmm." I'm not going to ask. It's what he wants, and he's already proven he's more than capable of playing me like a piano. Well, he can press that key all he wants, but there's no sound coming out of this mouth. As if I care about some silly little embarrassment that happened to Lucas Deiss years before we even met. An embarrassment that apparently lasted for years. Something so traumatizing that he'd admit to its impact all this time later.

I can't imagine what it could be. Not that I need to. Imagine it, that is. But really. Mac once stole his clothes while he was showering at the campus gym. I saw Deiss walking back to the dorm afterward, dangling a notebook over his nether regions as he chatted casually in the courtyard with Professor Cordero. If his bare butt flashing a game of touch football didn't rank as an embarrassment, whatever did must have been really bad.

I hold my breath, but it's not enough to keep the words inside. "What was it?"

"This is between the two of us," Deiss says in a low voice. "The others don't know."

"Not even Mac?"

"Definitely not Mac." There's an edge of seriousness to his voice.

"But Phoebe knows." It's inconceivable that Lucas Deiss would share something with me that he hasn't already told someone else. I've never been the kind of person people confess their secrets to. I don't have the required warmth. Or maybe it's simply because I'm incapable of sharing in return.

"Nobody knows," he says. "And if anyone finds out, I'll know they heard it from you."

"I wouldn't do that." I'd *never*. Just because people don't trust me with their secrets doesn't mean I don't know how to keep them.

"I know you wouldn't. I just need you to understand how important this is. It would pretty much be the worst thing in the world if everyone found out I used to be a child star." His voice catches on the last words like his body physically objects to the use of them.

"You used to be . . ." I trail off, trying to wrap my brain around what Deiss has just said. All I can picture is a shorter version of him in profile, too cool to bother turning toward the camera.

"The baby in *Family Fun*." His nod draws my eyes back to his. "Well, at first, I was the baby. Then I became the toddler who said cheesy one-liners and took baths in front of a million viewers."

"No." My hand goes over my mouth, but a giggle sneaks around it. I lean forward, searching his face, but it's too dark to find any sign of resemblance. Even in my memory, there's none.

But there wouldn't be, would there? Deiss has always had long hair or a beard. "Are you telling me you were Noah Riley?"

"For eight long seasons. It was *funnn-tastic*," he says dryly, using Noah's famous catch phrase. "Honestly, it wasn't that bad. The thing about pretending everyone is family for that long is that they really become one. At least that's how it felt as a kid. I got to grow up with a brother and sister, even though technically I was an only child. And I had two extra parents who could spoil me rotten because they got to hand me off to my real parents at the end of each day."

My head spins. Lucas Deiss is a former child star. That's why he's always been so tight-lipped about his past. Why would he tell me this? And why, after all this time, would he choose to tell me *now*?

To distract me. This was Deiss's version of throwing himself on his own sword. And it's worked. The elephants seem suddenly tiny in comparison to such massive news.

"But I used to watch that show." I can still hear the theme song in my head, if not every individual word. "I'd remember if I'd seen your name in the credits. Brandon Davis played the part. He was super famous."

"Brendan Davis, with an *e* and an *a*. My parents thought it sounded more 'Hollywood' than regular Brandon." He grins. "They thought they were protecting *their* privacy when they gave me the stage name. It never occurred to them that people would develop such an obsession with a little kid. Luckily, my real name never leaked. When the show ended, I continued with homeschooling. By the time I went to college, I'd grown up enough to be unrecognizable."

"But what about all the time in between?" I shake my head, the math not adding up. "That had to be seven or eight years.

Are you saying your parents just locked you away like some witness to a mafia murder? All so some little girl with pigtails wouldn't go into hysterics when she spotted you?"

Deiss is quiet for a moment, and I cringe, remembering belatedly that this is his life I'm being so flippant about.

"It wasn't just little girls with pigtails they were worried about," he says finally. "There were salary negotiations in the final season. The cast's decision to stick together made the news. Unsurprisingly, a kid raking in that kind of money makes for a pretty big target. None of the threats turned into anything, but it scared my parents enough to cause them to pack up the house and start over somewhere new. Continuing to homeschool me after the show ended was an obvious choice."

"I'm sorry," I say. "That's terrible."

Deiss shrugs. "For my parents, maybe. I didn't mind, though. After a lifetime of being on a studio's schedule, it was nice being at home. And I was so used to being around adults that it didn't even occur to me that I was missing out on having friends my age. My mom is as obsessed with music as I am, and we'd spend hours listening to albums or competing over who could make the best playlist for the day. By the time I realized there was a reason I never left the house, poolside studying and the ability to grade my own tests seemed like a pretty sweet trade-off for a lifetime of anonymity."

"And nobody has ever figured out that you were Noah?"

"Not a soul knows," he says. "Until tonight. So, as I'm sure you realize, you now have leverage over me. What do you say, Liv? Care to even the playing field with a secret of your own?"

I don't *care to*. Obviously, I don't. Except that there's something about this night. His grand gesture. The specialness of my being the person he's finally chosen to open up to. The darkness. And the way we're holed up against the wildness out-side. The breaths we shared, and the long-awaited glimpse into Deiss's past, so different from anything I would've ever imag-ined. The combination of all of it pulls at me, makes me want to lean deeper in. It makes me feel reckless and alive.

"I quit my job." I blurt the words out, not aware until I hear them aloud how paltry a confession it makes. People leave their jobs every day. It's nothing like admitting to having a whole other identity.

"Did you?" To his credit, Deiss manages to infuse enough surprise in the question that it seems like I've said something interesting.

"I did. Well, mostly," I say, embarrassed. "They're not pay-ing me now. And I'm not going back. So, I've quit, even if they don't necessarily realize it yet. And I know it was just a job, but I was supposed to stick with it, you know? The security it of-fered, and the salary, it all fit perfectly into my plan. And now I've walked away from it, and it feels like the first time in my life that I'm completely off book."

"And is that scary? Or exhilarating?" Deiss says the last word in a way that makes it sound infinitely appealing.

"Exhilarating," I repeat without thinking. My brain catches up, so I add, "And scary," because it feels important that I be honest. Anything less would cheapen the moment.

"Is it scarier that you've lost your income or that you're off the perfect plan?"

I freeze in the face of this line of interrogation. It's unsur-prising that Deiss would be so perceptive, but still—admitting to quitting my job only reshapes the image of my life. To admit the rest will reshape the image of my personality.

The darkness gives me the strength to answer him. "It's

scariest that I'm off the plan. All of a sudden, there are these questions in my head. And there used to be obvious answers, because they were fed to me by articles or books or podcasts, all of these instruction manuals for life. But now it's just me, trying to figure out what I want to do, or say, and it's freeing, but it also feels like I'm taking steps that might not be able to be retraced."

It's funny how you sometimes don't realize something until you've said it aloud. I haven't done anything truly outlandish since I said "no" at work, but each little thing has chipped away at the veneer I've spent a lifetime polishing. Even if I somehow end up back at Infinity Designs, management will never again trust me to be their ultimate yes-girl. Elena will always know my perfectly flat stomach gets rounded when filled with alcoholic milkshakes. Enough people have seen my freckled cheeks that they'll know I'm wearing foundation if they don't see them. These things might be small, but they're still irreversible.

"I don't think there's any such thing as who you *are*," Deiss says. "So, I wouldn't worry about getting back to it."

"What do you mean?"

"Well, it's all fluid, isn't it? You walk around in this body, but that changes according to what you eat, or your level of physical activity, or the years that pass. And inside, especially, there's nothing constant. Every moment, you're making a different decision. If you decide to start hitting strangers in the face, you're a person who hits strangers in the face. It doesn't matter if you spent the last ten years of your life behaving like a saint. Nobody you hit in the face is going to thank you for the good you did yesterday. To them, you're just the asshole who clocked them with a right hook."

"Is that meant to be reassuring? The fact that no amount of

correct behavior protects against an isolated moment of bad behavior?"

"Not particularly." He laughs. "I'm just making a point. Tonight, you were scared of elephants. But tomorrow, in the light of day, you won't be. And you'll look at me through those cool green eyes, and I won't be able to imagine that you've ever been afraid of anything in your life."

I smile, liking the person he sees me as: someone trustworthy and without fear.

"Speaking of the elephants," I say, "I don't hear them anymore."

"They left a few minutes ago." He gets to his knees and unzips the flap, peering outside. "Probably to get some sleep, which we should do as well."

I nod despite my disappointment at the sight of him crawling out of the tent. I didn't mean to imply that I had no more need of him now that we weren't under siege. Still, he's probably right. We don't need a repeat of the other night, with one of us passing out on top of the other.

"Thanks," I say as he begins to zip up the tent behind him.

"For what?"

For trusting me with your secret. For saving me from a panic attack. For making it feel okay to leave my job and attempt to strike out on my own.

"For showing up," I say simply.

He winks at me for the first time since freshman year, the day we met on the lawn. "That's what friends are for."

*P*hoebe was never one to pass up a dare. Still, I didn't think she'd do it. I didn't think she *could*. Slate Devers was standing no more than ten feet away from his precious skateboard, an energy drink gripped tightly in his hand like he was scared it might jolt into the air and pour its power into someone else's mouth. Little did he know something much more important to him was about to be yanked away.

I would've felt sorry for him, but he was an asshole. There was no other word for him. I imagined the girls he dated convinced themselves he was *edgy*, but I'd heard him yell at enough of them to realize he was truly awful, that the ripped clothes and ornate tattoos were a deliberate shield to distract people from looking any deeper. My smile widened as Phoebe pulled his skateboard out of the grass and onto the paved path.

"Hey!" The energy drink must have done its job because Slate whipped around with the reflexes of a snake. "That's mine!"

"I know." Phoebe grinned, putting one foot on the board and taking off.

The laughter bubbled up, bursting out of me as he began to run after her. Next to me, Simone's hands had gone over her mouth, trying to hold it in, but Deiss and Mac had given in to loud guffaws. There was something about the way Phoebe rode, her arms waving all around her like she was having a party, while Slate ran desperately after her, shouting for her to stop. I kept expecting her to yell back at him, to explain that it was just a dare and she was bringing it right back, but she didn't. Her left leg just kept pumping against the pavement, pulling her farther away from him and out of sight.

"Ride-ola free-ola!" Phoebe hollered as she zipped away.

"You said you talked to her." Deiss tried to scowl at me, but the corner of his mouth tilted up, betraying him. "I refuse to be a part of a group that has its own secret language. Especially one that just adds *ola* on the end of every word. It's like living with Oompa Loompas."

"I-ola *did*-ola talk-ola to-ola her-ola." I smiled serenely. "In Ola-Speak."

Deiss shook his head but grinned at me in a way that looked almost like admiration.

"Who's next?" Simone asked when she finished cheering Phoebe on.

"The Ice Queen," Mac said.

"Truth or dare?" Deiss asked.

I didn't know why they were looking at me so expectantly. I always picked truth, and they were always disappointed.

"Truth," I said.

Simone groaned.

"Ask her something embarrassing," she ordered the guys. "Something filthy."

Deiss nodded, and my heart sped up.

"What's the worst thing that ever happened to you?" he asked.

"Deiss!" Simone glared at him.

He shrugged innocently. "Maybe the worst thing that ever happened to her was really dirty."

I smiled as gratefully at him as I could, but my mind was already deep-diving. The worst thing that had ever happened to me. It was so obvious I didn't even have to think of it. More accurately, I didn't want to. Yet there it was, flashing through my mind in Technicolor.

Surprisingly, it wasn't the time Mom and I lived in the car. It wasn't even everyone in school finding out and taunting me about it. That was bad, but I knew I couldn't have done anything to prevent it. My mom was the one who'd foolishly trusted her boyfriend when he said was taking care of the rent.

The *worst* thing didn't happen until I was eighteen, just a couple of months before I left for college. My stomach cramped as I remembered opening the box I kept under my bed. I was so shocked to find it empty. For years, I'd kept everyone at school away from my house. But Cara was different. She'd already figured out that my carefully cultivated look was nothing more than a facade. And she liked me anyway.

Still, I was nervous the day I invited her to come over. I couldn't help worrying she'd unearth some secret I'd forgotten I was hiding. The money I'd worked so hard for, bundled into a shoebox and tucked out of sight, hadn't even been on my radar. It never once occurred to me that she would find it, much less steal it.

Obviously, it should have.

I wasn't sure if I was more devastated about the loss or the realization I was destined to follow in my mom's footsteps. I just knew I was devastated.

"Come on," Simone said, squirming restlessly. "It's my turn next. What's the worst thing that ever happened to you?"

I met her gaze, feeling my mask shift softly into place.

"Bangs," I said simply.

"Bangs?" Deiss's obvious disappointment made me feel horribly shallow.

"Bangs," I repeated with a flippant shrug. "They made my face look like the moon."

CHAPTER 11

The sun fills the tent early the next morning, waking me from a restless sleep. The only sign that I didn't dream the events of last night is the way my neatly folded clothes were smooshed when Deiss scooted into them. The tent is so tiny, it's hard to believe we both were able to fit without being on top of each other. The memory of his mouth on mine flashes through my mind, and my cheeks flush with embarrassment.

I wish we were already back home. I'm not ready to see him again. I just want everything to be back the way it was.

Everyone is sitting around the campfire when I climb out of the tent. There's a chill in the air, but I'm guessing the fire is more for the hot water for coffee than to provide heat. I clock Deiss leaning back against his backpack to the right but avoid his eyes, veering left to sit by Phoebe. The sky is cloudy and gray, rendering the green-and-brown landscape a drabber shade than it was yesterday. The bags Thato strung up last night are on the ground now, tattered and torn. I shiver at the sight of them.

"The elephants got them," Phoebe says, sounding more excited than concerned as her eyes follow my gaze. "Thato said they ate most of the food."

"We're eating Phoebe's Clif bars for breakfast," Mac says. "I have dibs on the chocolate chip one, though."

"You already ate two of them," Deiss says, presumably to Mac, although I refuse to look at him to confirm. "If you want a third, you can eat the oatmeal raisin one that nobody wants."

"Maybe Liv likes oatmeal raisin," Mac says.

"She doesn't," Deiss says. "She only eats the peanut butter ones."

Deiss has paid attention to my food preferences? Thankfully, Simone shifts toward me before I can react.

"Were you okay last night?" She's pulled off a tiny bit of Clif bar and is nibbling at it like a squirrel. "I wanted to come to your tent so we could protect each other, but I was scared of getting trampled en route."

Without thinking, I glance at Deiss. Thankfully, he's busy throwing an oatmeal Clif bar at Mac, which Mac promptly bats back at him.

"I was fine," I say. "I slept through most of it."

"So did Mac!" Phoebe shakes her head in disbelief. "I don't know how you guys managed that. It sounded like an earthquake. I almost had a heart attack."

"Same," Simone says. "What about you, Deiss? I suppose you slept right through it, too?"

"Nah," Deiss says. "I was up for the whole thing. It was pretty exciting. Maybe even fun-tastic."

My head jerks toward him, but his face is perfectly blank. In spite of myself, I laugh.

"I haven't heard that in forever," Simone says. "I used to be obsessed with that show."

"Were you?" I shrug, managing to restrain myself from laughing again. "I thought *Boy Meets World* was much better."

"Are you kidding?" Simone looks at me like I've just claimed sardines are better than champagne.

"It's-ola the-ola truth-ola," I say, pulling out the big guns.

As expected, the group breaks into Ola-Speak, everyone laughing and trying to outdo each other's speed. Everyone except for Deiss, of course. He's shaking his head, but I spot the relief in his eyes when he looks at me.

With an enigmatic smile, *I* wink at *him*.

To my relief, the rest of the day goes smoothly. Whatever weirdness might have spilled over from last night was wiped away by the reference to his past. I suppose that's why it's so easy to be grateful for his offer to share a room when my debit card gets declined in the hotel lobby. Or maybe I've simply resigned myself to the fact that Africa is a place where I end up spending my nights with Deiss. It's the same hotel we stayed in when I arrived, so I know the room will have two beds, even if they have been pushed together.

"Should I be worried about the fact that my card was just declined?" I ask the group, despite the fact that the guy behind the desk just assured me that their machine frequently struggles with debit cards.

"You should be worried that you live in the 1800s," Simone says. "Who doesn't bring a credit card when traveling overseas?"

"I've never traveled overseas," I say, squaring my shoulders at her tone. She's managing to sound awfully judgmental for someone whose own credit card is tied to a family bank account. "Nor do I use credit cards. I have *one*, as recommended by *Seeking Security*, and I buy one thing each month on it and pay it off immediately, in a responsible effort to build my credit rating."

"I have like six," Mac says, reaching for his wallet as if he's going to display them for me like a proud dad with pictures of his kids. "But I like to use the blue one best because it's made of metal."

"Quick question," Simone says, holding a finger up in the air. "If your credit is so spectacular, why did that man just reject your payment?"

"You *just* heard him say a lot of debit cards are declined," Phoebe says. "It's a problem with his machine."

"I need a shower," Deiss says decisively. "Liv, let's go."

"Wait," Simone says. "Not together, right? All showering is being done separately, right?"

Because I don't appreciate her, of all people, questioning my spending, I choose not to reassure her. I arch an eyebrow instead, allowing the corner of my mouth to curl in a suggestive smile. It's a move that makes me feel petty, but her territorial attitude toward Deiss is beginning to grate.

His hand presses against the small of my back, sweeping me away. Over his shoulder he calls out, "Downstairs for dinner in an hour."

"I'll need longer than that," I say once we're outside. The moon is full, and the lighting along the wooden-slatted path is a welcome change from the darkness outside the campsites we've been staying at. But the density of the jungle feels strange after several days of vast land and open skies.

"Your beauty routine for the last four days has consisted of wet wipes and sunscreen," he says. "You'll do fine. Plus, I'm starving. Man cannot survive on Clif bars alone."

I nod, too pleased he hasn't noticed my secret applications of mascara and tinted moisturizer to argue for more time. I might have learned that I don't have to wear a face full of makeup, but I've also discovered that old habits die hard. As Simone keeps reminding us, pictures last forever, and a safari calls for lots and lots of camera time.

Our room turns out to be almost identical to the last one we stayed in, only this time the beds have been separated already. I wait for the awkwardness to hit, but it doesn't come. Apparently, trading secrets during an elephant invasion is the trick to achieving comfort with someone. Or maybe it's just that there's no time for things to get weird. Deiss tosses his stuff on the far bed the moment we walk in and insists I take the first shower. When I get out, tugging my shirt and skirt over my damp, sticky skin so as not to risk a falling towel, he's not even there.

He doesn't return until ten minutes before we're supposed to leave. I'm tempted to ask where he's been, but it doesn't feel appropriate. I've never appreciated those kinds of questions directed my way. Still, my gaze follows him covertly as he strolls into the bathroom.

I don't understand his confidence—how he moves through life without feeling like he owes anyone anything. When I walk into a room and don't speak, it's because I don't know what to say and make the choice to opt for silence over a potential mistake. When he does it, I doubt he's thinking about anything in particular beyond the shower he wants to take, or the song lyrics running through his head. To him, a nod of acknowledgment is all that's needed when someone else appears.

"We can't keep teasing Simone," he says, coming out of the bathroom as I'm pulling a brush through my wet hair. Like me, he's opted to put on clothes in the steamy bathroom. His t-shirt has stuck to his skin and is off-center on his shoulders, pulling against his chest. I catch a glimpse of tight abs before he shifts it into place. "She's freaking out."

"You saw her?"

"She came by Mac's room. We were trying to figure out what time we're going to the airport tomorrow."

"Oh." They're probably expecting me to get my own ride. I leave several hours after them, and the back seat of their car isn't made for three to sit comfortably. I'd better figure out what's going on with my card before then. A three-hour taxi can't be cheap.

"Phoebe used Mac's points to get you on the same flight as us," he says casually, as if booking me on a different flight is the most natural thing in the world, "so you can just give him whatever refund you get from the airline."

"He's got to cancel that, Deiss." A last-minute flight will be crazy expensive. The only way I was able to justify the price before was the circuitousness of the route bringing down the cost. "I don't even know if they'll refund me. They'll probably just offer credit."

"So, see if you can transfer the credit into Mac's name." Deiss shrugs and pads over to his shoes. "Or buy him a beer. His agency books all of the flights to his modeling jobs, but the points end up in his name. You know Mac. He's not using them. He probably thinks they're a user rating and he gets bonus points every time a flight attendant wants to sleep with him."

"Um." I hesitate. "Well, thank you."

"Thank Phoebe." He grabs the keys and holds one out. "And Mac, I guess. But mostly Phoebe. She booked you on the flight. All I did was call dibs on driving so I wouldn't get stuck in the back with you and Simone. Speaking of whom . . ."

"We can't tease her anymore," I say obediently, reaching for my key.

He doesn't let go. Instead, his eyes meet mine over the joined line of our arms. They're sharply blue, and the intensity in them makes my stomach flip. His tongue slips over his bottom lip, drawing my attention down to his mouth.

"Listen, Liv," he says hesitantly. "About last night. I really was just trying to calm you down. I had no intention of kissing you."

"I know," I say quickly, feeling a pang of hurt. It's not as if I thought he was actually coming on to me. Surely he doesn't feel like I'm some naive girl who believes he's going to become her knight in shining armor overnight. He's Lucas Deiss, and I'm the Ice Queen. I understand exactly who he is. It's offensive that he doesn't have the same understanding of me. "You were trying to distract me from the elephants."

"Exactly." He still doesn't let go of the key, and for some reason, I don't, either. "So, I think it would be best if we don't mention it to anyone."

"There's nothing to mention."

"It's just that Simone was convinced we were in here showering together, and then Phoebe started talking about that pact again." He shakes his head and lets go of the card. My arm drops to my side. "It's amazing to me that we've all managed to stay tight for eleven years without any rules, and now, suddenly, swearing under oath is required to keep the peace."

"So, Phoebe made you say it, too? That you wouldn't hook up with me?" My breath catches as I wait for his answer. A part of me hopes he didn't say it, because I like that Deiss doesn't adhere to social rules. But another part of me hopes he did, because bending to something like that would be a sign that, like me, he needs this group. He's always felt like the most tenuous of the five of us. Every time he appears at Third Thursdays, I find myself breathing a sigh of relief.

"Yep. Me and Simone both." He grins wryly. "I had to hold up my hand and repeat after her. I told you she becomes a dictator on vacation."

I exhale a laugh of relief. "I hope you feel bad now for teasing me about saying it on the patio."

"If I feel bad," he says seriously, "it's because I seem to have just joined the one cult in the world that bans communal fornication."

I stifle a laugh and roll my eyes instead.

"Let's go to dinner," he says.

I shake my head. "I need to blow-dry my hair."

"Please, Liv." He makes his eyes unfairly soulful. "I need food."

With a sigh, I toss my brush on the dresser and follow him toward the door.

"*I can't believe* Deiss never came back last night." Simone pushes her plate away from her like the sight of the fresh, vibrantly colored fruit she's chosen from the breakfast buffet disgusts her. We're on the restaurant's patio, despite the clouds and smell of rain in the air. Phoebe has insisted we soak in every bit of St. Lulia we have left, which was also the excuse she used for forcing Simone and me out of bed and dragging us down here before I'd fully even woken up.

"I can," I say. The real mystery is who Deiss ended up with. Obviously, it was one of the women on the birthday trip we met at the hotel bar last night, but which one? My vote goes to the sultry brunette with the husky voice. Her name was Zoe, and even I was entranced by her. We talked about graphic design for a while out by the pool before her attention turned to Deiss. After that, she seemed to forget about me completely. It was unfortunate, as she's been doing freelance for some time, and I really wanted to pick her brain. *Apparently*, she'd rather get laid on vacation than talk shop.

"We got ditched," Phoebe says, scowling into her coffee.

"Mac didn't sleep in your room, either?"

"He did." She sighs. "But he walked *Lara the Birthday Girl* to her room first."

I pause in peeling my naartjie and study her. Like Simone, Phoebe has barely eaten any of her food. There's something tight about her that makes me nervous. Usually, she seems to flow like water, but today she's choppy with waves.

"Can I ask you something?" I lift the round citrus fruit in front of my face like a shield.

"Of course."

Despite her permission, I hesitate before saying, "Are you jealous?"

Her eyebrows lift, but then her head tilts. "I don't know," she says, looking perplexed. "Probably a little. I mean, it's so easy for him. It's not like he's looking for a *mental* connection or anything. He just gets to jump on anyone who gives him the go-ahead. And he's got this job that pays tons of money and requires absolutely nothing of him. And he gets to live by himself, while I'm stuck living with a roommate who labels their food and accuses me of taking too long in the shower."

"No—" I try to interrupt, but Phoebe barrels on.

"Like, how does she *know*, Liv?" Phoebe throws out her hands. "She's never even home in the mornings, but she acts like she's got a timer on the showerhead and is counting the chips in her labeled bags. She's *so confident* in her accusations."

She looks at me like she expects an answer, but I shake my head.

"I didn't mean jealous of Mac," I say. "I meant jealous of Lara the Birthday Girl."

"Oh." Phoebe averts her eyes. "Why would I be jealous of her? She had that terrible giggle. It was like the helium being forced out of a balloon, right? It's perfectly natural that I wanted to stick a pin in her."

"Um, Phoebe?" Simone says. "Her laugh was completely normal."

"Was it?" Phoebe shrugs and takes a sip of her coffee. "I thought she sounded like a cartoon chipmunk. But I guess Mac heard what you heard."

"He's been kind of weird on this trip," Simone says.

"Right?" Phoebe looks around furtively, as if the patio isn't completely empty aside from us. "He's been quieter than normal. It's almost like he's thinking about something, which is bizarre, because he's the sweetest guy in the world, but let's face it—Mac isn't exactly one for introspection."

"It's like he's been studying you," I admit reluctantly.

"He has?" Phoebe looks way too intrigued by this nugget of information.

I nod and shove a piece of the naartjie in my mouth. The sweet, tangy flavor explodes against my taste buds. A single raindrop sneaks through the clouds and lands on my arm. Monkeys chatter in the distance.

"And what about the campfire, when he was rambling about best friends?" Simone says. "*Awkward.*"

"If you think that was awkward," Phoebe says, "you should've been in our tent that night."

"Did something happen?" It takes effort to ask the question

in a neutral tone. I'll support Phoebe in anything she wants to do—*of course* I will. But she created the pact for a reason. She was the one who said the two of them getting back together would be a terrible idea. And selfishly, I've never felt that more intensely than I do now, after the escape from my dreary life this trip has provided.

I need to know there are more of these adventures to come. I need to believe I haven't missed all my chances to see the world with the people I love most.

"Not intentionally." Phoebe grimaces. "I woke up to the stomping of the elephants, and his arms were around me. He must've started cuddling me in his sleep, which is innocent enough. But then I got scared, so I scooted closer into him. And his arms tightened around me." She sighs. "He never even woke up, but it was a reminder I wish I hadn't gotten."

"A reminder of what?" Simone asks.

"Of how it felt to be connected to him like that. I've never met someone else who's so completely themselves." Phoebe looks at me pleadingly like she needs me to understand. "He thinks something, he says it. He wants something, he grabs it. It was like Mac was this other half of me, making everything okay. And now that he's gone, I don't know how to enjoy anything the same way."

"Yes, you do," I say confidently. "You've just forgotten because you've been here with him. Remember how you celebrated when you got your first feature piece in the magazine? Mac wasn't even in the state. He was in New York on a job. And remember the time you spent with that British businessman before he went back home? You certainly seemed to enjoy yourself then. For two weeks, the only texts I received from you consisted entirely of eggplant emojis."

"Oh." Phoebe's eyes drift toward the ceiling. "He *was* fun."

"Exactly." I dig my spoon emphatically into the gelatinous seeds of a halved passion fruit. "This might be my first time traveling, but I'm already realizing it has a way of blurring all the boundaries between people. It's like it's too much contact, you know? And you're in this strange place and you totally forget who you even are in real life. But none of that matters because we have a pact. You care too much about the friendship—with him, and between all of us—to break it. Right?"

"Right." Her response is lacking the conviction I'd prefer, but it will do.

"Right," I agree. Resolutely, I spoon some passion fruit into my mouth. The tiny black seeds in the center crunch between my teeth.

Naturally, I'm attempting to pick them out when Deiss shows up. He doesn't seem to notice, though. He just snags a coffee mug so tightly it looks like he wants to tilt it up over his face and lick the insides. He'd probably look haggard if he weren't so tan. As it is, he's half sunshine, half sultry evening. It's tremendously unfair. If I'd spent the night being bounced around a bed, I'd be a tangled mess the next morning. I certainly wouldn't look like I was searching for sustenance to get me through the next round.

He sinks into the empty chair next to me and plucks the ripe fig off my plate. Without a word, he shoves the entire thing into his mouth.

"No," I say sharply, like I'm chastising an errant puppy. "We do not touch Olivia's plate."

Unabashed, he reaches for my half-eaten naartjie. I slap his hand away, and he groans like he's been wronged.

"I need sustenance," he says, reaching in his pocket and pulling out my phone and debit card. He drops them next to my plate, and I remember that I failed in my drunken efforts to type in the twenty-four-hour customer service line's thirty-seven-digit number after I got back from the pool. He must've made his way back this morning and spotted them on my nightstand.

"There's a whole buffet of sustenance inside," I say, picking up the phone. "But thanks for this."

He shrugs off my gratitude. "I didn't know if you'd gotten a chance to call yet."

"You would've known," Phoebe says, grinning dirtily, "if you'd spent the night in your own bed."

I spot a voicemail from the office and listen to it as Phoebe and Simone mine Deiss for details. To my surprise, it's Marian Hammersmith following up on her suggestion that we meet over lunch. I hang up quickly, as if she might come through the phone and physically drag me away from this adventure and back into work. Grabbing the debit card, I dial the help number on the back.

Beside me, Deiss is giving Phoebe and Simone nothing, not even a line about gentlemen never telling. Instead he squints at them like they're speaking Greek and successfully snags the rest of my naartjie. In between pressing prompt after prompt designed to get me to settle for a robot's help, I manage to snatch the last two slices back.

"I just want to know which girl it was," Phoebe says as I finally manage to convey my issue to a real human.

Deiss leans back in the chair and crosses his arms over his chest. The sun beams through the clouds, making his eyes glint in a way that doesn't match the dark smudges of sleeplessness under them. When he finally speaks, it's in a lazy drawl. "How do you know I was with someone? Maybe I wanted to spend my last night in Africa alone, communing with the hippos."

I shake my head as the representative puts me on hold.

"No," I say to Phoebe. "There would've been crocs out there, too. He's got a fear of biters."

Phoebe beams at me and turns to him. "Well? It clearly wasn't that."

Deiss shoots me a look, but his mouth twitches with amusement.

"It's not my fault you wanted to talk about phobias," I say, volleying his look right back at him. "If you didn't want anyone to know, you shouldn't have admitted to it."

His head tilts, and a slow smile stretches across his face. His eyes hold mine, reminding me his fears aren't the only thing he's admitted to. Rather than seeming to fear it as another secret I won't keep, he looks entertained by the knowledge it's something I'll forever have to hold in. His confidence in my restraint is disconcerting. He's right—I couldn't out him even if I wanted to. I've spent too many years trying to overcome my past to destroy someone's effort to do the same. Somehow, Deiss has figured me out in a way that I haven't managed with him.

The representative comes back on the line, and I wave Deiss away as if he's speaking aloud instead of beaming messages at me through his piercing blue eyes. I must not be prepared for real words because the ones I hear through the phone make no sense at all. Blankly, I repeat after him. But rather than coming out like a statement, big fat question marks make my words go high at the end: "You didn't put a block on the card? The account is empty?"

CHAPTER 12

The trip home is a nightmare. It's hours upon hours of being trapped—in a car, on a plane—unable to do anything whatsoever to rectify whatever is happening with my finances. It's not just my checking account that's empty; my savings is, too. Everything has disappeared. I have an appointment at the bank the morning after I get back to figure out how to restore the funds, but until then, I'm flat broke.

In the meantime, all I have to my name is the wrinkled hundred-dollar bill that Mac pressed into my palm "in case you need to buy extra water for the flight." He laughed off my effort to refuse the offer, reminding me that looks like his pay way more than is fair. Even if I had my credit card with me, it would be worthless. The bank has issued a new one with different numbers, which should arrive at my home within the next forty-eight hours. It's part of the security alert they've attached to my name, in case I've been a victim of identity theft.

My friends have a plethora of theories, and I get to hear all of them, whether I want to or not. Simone, of course, thinks it's all a big mistake and that the bank will take care of it. Phoebe suspects a shopkeeper or cashier copied down the numbers when I used my card to pay for something. Mac believes it's a prank. By whom, he hasn't determined. But he feels confident that I'll get home and someone will be there, doubled over in laughter at the scare they've given me. In his version, we'll all end up chortling with them.

When I open the door to my condo, that is not what happens. Although there *is* someone inside waiting for me. It's Elena, sitting on the floor with her legs crossed beneath her. Rather than laughing when she sees me, she begins to cry. Likely because she's managed to lose my couch. Or possibly because she's also misplaced my lamp, TV, dining room table, and everything else I own.

"What the hell?" Phoebe pushes past me and stops inside, her head twisting as she surveys the empty space. "Where's your stuff?"

I stand in the doorway, too overwhelmed to take another step forward. My home is like a swirling black hole, but the Alhambra Cream paint-color version of white rather than black. It's a relief that Phoebe is still standing instead of being sucked into its abyss. Behind me, Deiss clears his throat.

I whip around, eager to find something else to focus my rage on. I *told him* he and Phoebe didn't need to drop me off. And I certainly didn't ask them to come upstairs with me. Now he has the nerve to act impatient because I'd *dare* take a minute to collect my thoughts in the midst of losing *every single thing I've ever owned*? The accusation shrivels on my tongue the moment I see his expression. It's soft, sorrowful even, and his eyes are filled with sympathy.

"Is there any chance you left it this way?" He squints, as if he's genuinely hoping that's the case.

I shake my head and turn on my heel, striding toward Elena in search of answers. I already know what happened, though. The details don't matter. Only the root cause does: I broke the rules. All of them. I quit my job, went off budget, turned my back on my home, and ran away like a child to play with my friends. Did I really believe there wouldn't be consequences?

Elena scrambles up to meet me, wrapping her arms around me like a soggy blanket. I stiffen. If she expects me to be the girl who drank alcoholic milkshakes with her last week, she'll be disappointed. That girl had a blender. And a framed certificate that proved her submissions were the most valued at Infinity Designs in 2019. And all the things she'd spent her hard-earned money on over the years to prove she could provide a home for herself.

But more important than the loss of my things is the absence of a disdainful cat, mewling in response to the loss of his hiding place.

"Where's Cat Stevens?" My voice is sharp enough that Elena freezes for a moment before beginning to sob anew.

"I've lost him," she cries. "*Twice*."

I feel a sharp pang in my chest, but this news is just as inevitable as the rest of it was. I knew better than to get a cat. My mother and I had to get rid of Boots when I was nine because Paul Davenport (my mother's boyfriend for long enough that I'd begun to tentatively and pathetically refer to him as Dad) went into a rage over her litter box. He claimed it reeked, despite the fact that I was diligent about cleaning daily. Despite Boots's banishment and a three-day deep clean on the house, the damage was insurmountable. We'd become tainted by association, as smelly and pervasive as cat poo, and Paul-turned-Dad soon joined the list of men who'd deemed my mom and me lacking.

In truth, I never missed Paul nearly as much as I missed Boots. I visited her sometimes at the pound, before a more faithful family adopted her. Even after she disappeared, I kept going. Playing with the other cats. Nervously petting the dogs. The habit followed me to LA, which is where I found Cat Stevens. He was as haughty as I pretended to be and equally distrustful.

"What do you mean twice?" Phoebe's eyes blaze like she's ready to combust. Stretched up to her full height, she looks less like a willowy reed in the wind and more like a lightning rod. "What happened to all of Liv's stuff?"

"I don't know," Elena wails, jerking her head back and forth between the two of us. "I think I messed up!"

"It's going to be fine," Deiss says, crossing the room to stand by me. "Just tell us exactly what happened."

Elena's eyes widen at the sight of him. In a shaky voice, she says, "I came to feed Cat, but the door must not have latched behind me. It was closed, though. And I was trying to be patient, you know? Give him time to warm up to me? But then I got off the phone, and I looked behind me, and it was open. Like, all the way. And I searched the whole place, but Cat was gone."

"You said twice, though," Deiss says gently. "Did you find him the first time?"

She nods eagerly. "I raced through the streets searching, but there was no trace of him. Finally, I gave up, but when I got back, there was a man here. He'd found Cat and gotten the address from his collar and brought him home."

Phoebe waves her hands in the air with exasperation. "And then what happened?"

I'm completely numb.

"He brought Cat back?" Deiss asks. "That was nice of him."

"Right?" Elena gazes up at him, relief shining in her eyes at the thought of an ally. "I wanted to give him a reward, but I didn't have any cash. So, I offered him a drink. I thought it was the least I could do."

"I would've thought the least you could do would be to close the door," Phoebe mutters, pacing across the living room, right through the space where there would normally be a couch.

"I'm sure he appreciated the offer," Deiss says. "Did he accept the drink?"

"Yes. But I took him to the bar down the street. Obviously, I wasn't going to invite a stranger into Olivia's house." She looks to me as if for approval, but I can barely see her. My vision is too full of white. Alhambra Cream where my paintings used to be. Chantilly Lace on the walls beyond my bedroom door. I guarantee, though, if I were to walk through that door, I wouldn't see the cotton sateen duvet on my bed. Nor would I see the bed.

I take a step toward it, but stop before my suspicion can be confirmed. I'd rather not know. The couch might've been ridiculous, but that bed was like sleeping on a cloud. I won't miss it as much as I'll miss Cat Stevens, but I'll probably never sleep as well again.

"So," Deiss says. "He never came inside?"

"Well." Elena hesitates. "For a minute. Just to get Cat Stevens through the door."

"And did he start robbing Liv right then?" Phoebe asks. "Or did he wait until after you bought him a frosty lager?"

"He couldn't have done it." Elena tears up again, her chin wobbling as she looks to Deiss for reassurance. "He came all the way here just to bring Cat Stevens home. A cat rescuer doesn't rob houses."

"I'm sure you're right," Deiss says. "But just for argument's sake, did you happen to mention that Liv was out of town?"

Elena's tears start to flow in earnest. Miserably, she nods. "I guess I must've mentioned it when I told him I'd be checking in on Cat until Liv got back on Tuesday. I thought, if he lived in the neighborhood, he might want to meet up again."

"And did he?" Deiss's voice quickens with excitement. "Did he want to meet up again?"

"Tell us you got his number," Phoebe demands before Elena has a chance to answer. "Better yet, tell us you went home with him."

"I got his number," Elena says, not meeting our eyes. "But when I called it, it was for a pizza place."

Phoebe shakes her head. "And did you go home with him?"

"No." Elena studies the floor. Her shoulders droop with shame.

"You brought him back here," Deiss says, his voice kindly devoid of accusation, "didn't you?"

"No." Phoebe slaps her hand against her forehead. But her disbelief is pointless. It's obvious by Elena's lack of response that Deiss is right.

"You did," I say in a deadened tone.

"You don't understand," Elena wails. "We had talked for hours. We had so much in common."

I stare at her, and she crumples.

"But when we were talking, I must've mentioned you were moving," she admits through her tears. "Because your neighbor said he saw them taking everything. He even asked where you were. But they said you'd hired them. That they were professional movers. They were even all wearing white shirts. And they had a key!"

Just like that, I know exactly what happened. It hardly takes Sherlock-level deduction on my part, which is convenient, because Mr. Holmes would certainly be smarter than to leave a spare key in plain sight. Like the fool that I am, I kept it in the same rose-gold leaf on the floating shelf next to the door where I drop my regular set of keys.

The spare was for runs; when I needed a single key I could zip into yoga pants. Normally, I only had one, the one I gave Elena, but Mr. Rosenthall had returned my emergency copy when he decided not to buy his apartment. With his back in my possession, I had two. One for Elena and one, conveniently, for Cat Stevens's rescuer to find. The poor man hardly had a choice. A key and the neighbors' expectations that I was moving all my stuff out? I was practically begging to be robbed. I might as well have flung my door open and announced an Oprah-style giveaway.

I pull out my phone and begin dialing.

"Are you calling the police?" Phoebe asks.

"They should arrest me," Elena says, holding out her hands like one of us has handcuffs. "This is all my fault."

"Whoever robbed the place deserves to be arrested," Deiss says. "But you'll need to be here to give them all the details you can remember about him."

"You know the police department's number by heart?" Phoebe leans over my shoulder, peering down at my phone.

"I'm not calling the police," I say, holding up my hand to indicate the need for silence. My heart races with the importance of what I'm about to do. I can't mess it up by sounding unprofessional. Not now, when the stakes are so high.

"Who are you calling?" Phoebe asks, just as my finger is about to make contact with the call button.

"My boss," I snap, waving her away. Panic has caused my voice to go up an octave. It's the only thing that gives me away. Other than that, my mask has snapped firmly back into place. "I need to make sure I can return to my job."

"Why wouldn't you be able to return to your job?" Phoebe's brow furrows in confusion.

Deiss is the only one I've told about my dream of quitting. Instinctively, my eyes go to him. But he's already taken a step forward. His hand settles on mine, squeezing my fingers for a moment before easing the phone out of my hand.

"Let's just take a beat." Despite the casualness of his tone, there's something about Deiss that makes it clear he's not to be argued with. "We'll call the police. Then, we can figure the rest out afterward."

I meet his eyes for a moment, my jaw squaring with resolve. But to my surprise, my hand drops down to my side. Finally, I nod.

CHAPTER 13

I move silently through Deiss's loft, trying to figure out how I've ended up here. I blame the jet lag. It has merged with the shock of everything that's happened, leaving me blunted and dull. Everything feels fast and frantic after the slow days in South Africa. Even the Los Angeles air, dry and thick with exhaust fumes, is working against me, making it difficult to breathe.

The space is stuffy from ten days with closed windows and the air turned off. It's not a bad place to end up, obviously—Phoebe and Simone and I have speculated more than once about how Deiss managed to afford a two-bedroom loft in one of the most expensive cities in the world. (It was a question we knew better than to ask, and one I alone now know the answer to.) It's actually surprisingly clean.

The furniture is mismatched and well-worn but tasteful. Granted, Deiss clearly hasn't read *Chez Chic*. The walls are as far from white as it gets; every area is a different color, although they all go together in a unique way. It's like they're from the same family, but one where some of its members were forgotten before they found themselves at a reunion filled with vaguely similar facial features.

"Did you do that yourself?" I gesture toward the mossy green color in the living area. If I'd seen it on a color wheel, I wouldn't have even considered painting it onto a graphic background, much less on physical walls. I would've assumed it would resemble mold. But in person, it turns out to be soothing, like I've hiked through a forest and found myself in a shaded spot beside a burbling stream.

"I did." Deiss puts down the remote, abandoning his effort to explain how to access streaming on his TV.

"I like it." And I *do*. But the claim doesn't sound authentic when I hear the words hit the air. I cringe at the sound of them because I am so very grateful for his generosity. It's just a bit unsettling.

Matching vibes to colors is something I excel at. I've built an entire career out of it. Deiss is dark gray with something unexpected like a pop of cherry mixed in. Maybe a deep midnight blue with a streak of yellow. Finding out he's opted for earthy hues makes me feel like I've missed something crucial about his personality.

"I like to paint," Deiss says, reading my uncertainty. "Not in an artistic way. Just walls. I like the monotony of it, the way I end up zoning out, caught up in the satisfaction of watching the old color disappear stripe by stripe. I also like how exhausting it is, how tight my back is by the end and how my arms ache, and how I can't wait to collapse after that last stroke and just take in this environment that's entirely new."

"You do it frequently?"

He nods.

"Do you do it when you're stressed?"

Something flickers across his face. I could swear it's reluctance, but it must not be, because he answers my question.

"I guess," he says, leaning against the wall. His arms cross loosely over his chest. "But not always. Sometimes, I'm trying to think through something, and the only way to get to the answer is to distract my brain long enough for the mess to untangle on its own. But sometimes, I guess, I just want a change."

"I didn't know that." I look toward the leather couch, so worn in it's spidered with creases. He probably chose the light brown color so it would go with any wall shade he wanted to paint.

With quick steps, I move to the kitchen, then onward, surveying his home with new understanding. A patternless bedspread. Photos on the wall instead of art. All of it deliberately noncommittal to a color scheme.

I stop in the doorway to what's supposed to be my room, taking in the aggressively red walls (some shade between maroon and the color of video game blood) and the sofa bed. A desk sits in front of a window, a record player on top. The wall beside it is lined with stacks of records. In the corner, there's a bass guitar. I didn't know Deiss played music.

"I love it," I say. This time, the honesty in my words is clear. While my home was a kind of museum, his is like a living extension of himself, shifting according to his moods. What's not to like? "But I can't stay."

"Sure you can," he says simply.

I shake my head. "I need to be close to my office."

"You have an entire month before they expect you back."

"I can't wait that long, Deiss." I sigh, reluctant to explain myself. "My savings are gone."

"They'll be back after the bank does an investigation."

"I need to make money to live on until that happens."

"You're going to. If you needed motivation to hustle as a freelancer, here it is."

"How does a graphic designer make money without a laptop?" It comes out snappier than I've intended. But I've never known Deiss to be such an optimist, and this does not feel like the ideal time for the emergence of the trait. "Mine was stolen. Remember? That's how he got into my bank account."

Deiss scoffs. "You'll have your credit card by tomorrow. And I'm sure they'll restore your account soon."

A $2,000 credit limit. A good laptop will cut that in half, leaving me with a small safety net to get me through however long it might take to resolve all this. I can't even apply for another card if things get rough. Not while there's a security alert on my name.

"But what if they don't? Restore my account, that is. It wasn't the bank's fault. They didn't let some cyber thief sneak into their system. He came in through *my* laptop." I train my eyes slightly past him and square my jaw. "I let this happen, Deiss. I broke the rules, and there were consequences for my actions. All I can do now is try to get back on the right path."

"Hey." He puts his hands on my shoulders, not speaking until I give in and look up at him. "You didn't break any rules. You made a choice to go on vacation, which, by the way, is a very normal thing to do. But if you go back to your job now, you'll be walking a very difficult path to reverse from. Right now, you have the option to try out freelancing, knowing that your boss has provided a safety net if it doesn't work out. But he's not going to provide that twice. If you tell him you've decided to continue working for him, you're going to feel stuck there for a very long time."

I blink at his closeness, trying to think of an argument but coming up short. He's right. I wouldn't dare walk away from my job again, not with the knowledge that the first try ended in such spectacular failure. And if my life felt unsatisfying before, I can only imagine how going back to the same thing will feel now.

"I'll only stay until I get everything figured out," I say firmly.

"Perfect." Deiss gives me a slow, dazzling smile. "That's exactly how long the invitation is good for."

I feel silly following Deiss to Studio Sounds, but I really would like to see his shop. I haven't made it to his part of town since the grand opening. There's been little reason to visit. He's certainly never asked me to come to one of his after-hours shows. In fairness, they're open to the public, but I've taken his lack of personal invitation as proof he doesn't think I'm cool enough to enjoy them.

I use my need for a laptop as my excuse to tag along. A Google search has revealed an electronics store a few blocks past Studio Sounds. Obviously, I can't buy anything tonight, but I can check out some models and figure out what I like the feel of before I search for cheaper comparisons. Hopefully, I can find something nearby so I don't have to wait for delivery. The sooner I can start working, the sooner I can generate some income. But a laptop is key to that plan. I can make do with the clothes and makeup I took to Africa until my account is restored, but I can't do graphic design on flowy skirts with a mascara wand.

Despite the fact that we sat at my condo for over an hour

waiting for the police, then another hour with them once they finally arrived, the sun still hasn't set. It's at that angle where it makes the fronds of the palm trees that line the street glow like they've been lit from within. The air smells like tacos from a Mexican place we pass. There's a general sense of relaxation in Los Feliz that contrasts starkly with Santa Monica. Bikers pedal by. Most of the people who pass us on the sidewalk have on headphones, their hands free instead of occupied by iced coffees and shopping bags. In the entire seven-minute walk, not one passing car honks with rage.

A bell dings over the door as Deiss swings it open and waves me through. It's dim inside, with spotlights over the record bins but ambient blue lights lining the walls. A song I've never heard pulses through the speakers, louder than a normal establishment but not aggressively so. It has the kind of beat that moves its way through your body, making you feel unexpected things. The back wall is lined with guitars for sale. To my surprise, Phoebe is sitting on the counter, talking to a guy with dreadlocks that skim his shoulders. He's on a stool behind a cash register and a mounted iPad.

"What are you doing here?" I ask, passing a couple with their heads bent over a bin to get to her.

"It would be more shocking if a day passed without her here," the guy behind the counter says. Up close, I can see that his arms are covered in tattoos. They almost blend in against his dark skin, giving the impression they're ridged in a way you could feel if you ran a finger over them.

"You come here every day?" I ask her, unable to keep the hurt out of my voice. This whole time, I've assumed we all look forward to seeing each other on Third Thursdays. I knew Phoebe and Mac and Deiss live closer to each other than Simone and me, but I assumed they saw each other occasionally. Once a week, maybe. Certainly not *daily*.

"It's walking distance from my house," she says apologetically. "The last time I went to your place, there was a wreck on the 10, and it took me two hours to get back."

"I take it you're Olivia," the guy says, clearly hoping to curtail the weirdness I've just brought into his den of chill. "Phoebe told me what happened. I'm really sorry to hear it."

"Thank you . . ." I trail off, my mind churning over the realization that my failure to participate in group trips isn't the only way I've distanced myself. My actual physical distance has left me on the outskirts. While I've been living life alone, my friends have continued on living it together. Absentmindedly, I proffer my hand like an accountant meeting her new coworker.

"Booker," he says, an amused smile flashing across his face. His teeth are even and so white I immediately wonder if it's time for me to get mine bleached again. He slides a large hand into mine, despite the fact that I can tell by the curl of his mouth that my awkward formality has been noted. "Booker Zane. Nice to meet you."

I smile, but I'm distracted by the stack of flyers for Saturday night's show. The info is written in Sharpie, and the handwriting is terrible. This underwhelming display of craftsmanship must be his doing. I've heard more than one story about his laissez-faire approach to employment.

"Z," Deiss says, coming around me to go behind the counter.

Booker lets go of my hand to slap Deiss's; then they hug like Deiss has been gone for months rather than ten days.

"How did it go?" Deiss asks when they let go of each other. "Any issues?"

"Please," Booker says. "Your job is easy."

Deiss nods. "What I'm hearing is an offer to do next year's taxes."

"You think I'll still be working here next year?" Another gleaming grin breaks across Booker's face. "That's adorable. Movie stars don't have side jobs."

"But they do usually have roles in movies," Deiss says.

"He has an audition for some action flick on Thursday morning," Phoebe says.

"Nice," Deiss says. "Let's do some stocking and see if we can bulk you up a little before then. The bins are looking as weak as your biceps."

"I couldn't watch the store *and* unload the boxes," Booker says, holding up a flexed arm and prodding at it appraisingly. He looks pleased by his assessment of the bulge. "Someone could've robbed us while I was in the back. Liv knows what I'm talking about."

"Booker!" Phoebe slaps his arm, widening her eyes at me.

"Your foresight is admirable," Deiss says before I can feel forced to respond. "Phoebe, could you please take over Booker's vigilant watch against the criminal element and their desperate desire for the eighteen dollars and fifty cents we most likely have in the cash register?"

"It's the instruments I was worried about," Booker says, still contentedly propped on the stool. "There are a lot of people lusting after that Gibson Les Paul, you know."

"Defend the Les Paul at all cost," Deiss says to Phoebe. "If at any point you feel your life is in danger . . ." He tilts his head and holds up an inspirational finger. "Sacrifice it."

"Aye, aye, Captain." Phoebe offers a sharp salute from her relaxed perch on the counter.

"What about her?" Booker gestures toward me. "Why can't she help you stock?"

"Because she doesn't work here," Deiss says.

"I need to buy a laptop." For some reason, maybe because I'm the one who's just scored a free place to stay from his boss, my excuse comes out apologetically.

"That's right. You're a graphic designer, right? Why don't you just use this one?" Booker gestures toward the counter, presumably where an invisible laptop is sitting.

"Oh." Deiss looks over in surprise. "You should do that, actually. The iPad works to look up stock. Booker never even pulls the laptop out anymore."

"It makes you type everything in." Booker wrinkles his nose and holds up his phone. "It's basically manual labor. This has voice prompt."

"Speaking of manual labor," Deiss says, "the new Fender Stratocaster isn't going to mount itself."

"Fine." Booker gets off the stool and squats out of sight before rising back up to set a laptop on the counter. "Here you go, Fancy Face. Grab a seat."

"She wasn't going to use it here," Deiss says. "She's trying to start her own business."

"Well, she can't take it out of here," Booker says. "I might need it."

Phoebe flicks her eyes toward the ceiling. "You just said you never use it."

"Not using it and not needing it are two different things," Booker says, opening the laptop and turning it toward me enticingly.

"Like you not working and you being fundamentally lazy are two different things?" Phoebe asks.

"Exactly." Booker nods agreeably.

"Liv can take the laptop home," Deiss says, leaning against the wall like he's losing interest in all of us. "Liv, feel free to use it wherever and whenever you'd like."

"You can't just give my laptop away!" Booker looks delighted to have a reason to complain.

"I wouldn't mind working here." I'd love to work here, actually. It would make the loan of the laptop feel less like charity, especially considering how desperately I need said charity. Plus, everyone knows working at home is a recipe for slovenly snacking and procrastination projects. This place has an energy that's preferable to a coffee shop full of caffeine-fueled screenwriters. "And while I'm looking for projects, I could make a real flyer for your next show. It would be a good thing to add to my portfolio. If you give me a dollar for the job, I could even claim the shop as a client."

"What's wrong with my flyer?" Booker asks.

"It's not a flyer," I say. "It's information scribbled on a piece of paper that happens to have been photocopied."

Deiss laughs, and Booker looks at him with a wounded expression that's the definition of overacting.

"I spent hours working on that," he says mournfully.

"If you spent more than two minutes on it," Deiss says, "I'm docking your pay for the difference."

"It took ten seconds," Booker says quickly, turning toward me, "and I look forward to seeing what you can accomplish with more time. Of course, I *will* be charging a dollar for the rental of my laptop, so we'll have to call it even. But it's been a pleasure doing business with you. Welcome to the team!"

"Yes, Liv," Deiss says, "welcome to the team. No need to learn names. Staff changes are imminent if I can't get a hand with the stocking."

"I've got a hand." Booker lifts one eagerly in the air. "Well, look at that, I've got two! And both of them have an affinity for cardboard boxes. Let's put 'em to work, boss."

Deiss lifts an eyebrow and tugs himself off the wall, heading for a door that opens to a set of stairs.

Booker starts after him but turns around, so he's walking backward while facing me. "Password is *Ramones versus Stones.* Capital *R* and *S*, no spaces."

I nod and watch him disappear through the door.

"Yay!" Phoebe gives a little clap of excitement and slaps me on the back like she's mistaken me for a sweaty man covered in football padding. "You got your first client!"

"I guess I did." In spite of myself—and the lack of payment or structure or general explanation of my task—I feel a flare of pride.

CHAPTER 14

I attach Cat Stevens's photo to the email on my phone and hit send. I have to find him. After the terrible meeting I've just had with the bank, the thought of his little face is the only thing keeping me from falling over the edge. It's not like I think he'd provide comfort. Even if he were here, his disdainful gaze would be guaranteed to project nothing but doubt about my abilities. But I need to know he's safe. I've failed to protect myself, but I can't have failed him.

"You're here," Deiss says, coming into the loft and swinging the door shut behind him. I haven't seen him since we walked home from the shop last night and he tilted his chin at me in a silent *good night* before closing his bedroom door behind him.

If it were yesterday or even this morning, I'd probably turn from my spot at the counter and search his voice for any sign of disappointment, wondering if he'd expected me to hide in the spare room or generally stay out of his way. Since it's now, and I'm still reeling from the bank manager's apathy, I nod and finger my bowl of baby carrots absently, my eyes settling blankly on the couch. I've reached out to four shelters, but is that enough? How much ground could a cat cover in a week?

Behind me, I hear Deiss open the fridge. He has it open long enough that its coldness makes its way to the back of my legs, making me feel like my skirt has gotten tucked up inside my panties, leaving my butt exposed. I swat my hand at the flimsy material, making sure I'm covered before nibbling at the carrot. It's dried out, likely because I've opted for the ones discounted due to their sell-by date. My stomach turns, although whether in response to the tiny white cracks in the orange or the general state of my life I couldn't say.

"How did it go at the bank?" he asks over the rustling of whatever it is he's slapped on the counter.

"Fine." I take in the green walls, wishing there really were a burbling brook running through it. I'd like to float away in it. Or elegantly drown myself.

It occurs to me that I can't lie to Deiss. And not just because I'm supposed to have let go of my compulsion to appear perfect. I'm staying in his home. He has the right to know I might become a full-on squatter. Slowly, I turn to find him leaning against the counter, a poorly constructed sandwich in his hand. He meets my eyes and lifts it to his mouth, taking a bite that obliterates an entire quarter of it.

"They think it will be a few weeks before my account is restored." I take a deep breath and train my gaze slightly past his shoulder to the shiny silver of the stove. "*If* I get my money back at all."

"Any clues as to which outcome is more likely?" The minute the words are out of his mouth, he shoves another bite of sandwich in.

As far as reactions go, I find his lacking. In sympathy. In outrage. In shock. I've spent my entire adult life trying to build a nest egg. It would be nice if, for once, Deiss could summon enough energy to acknowledge the drama of the conversation, rather than responding as if we're discussing tomorrow's weather report.

As much as I want to give him a curt *no* and leave him alone to continue testing the capacity of his mouth, I can't ignore the fact that this affects him nearly as much as it does me, even if he hasn't yet realized it. He deserves all the details.

"I got the impression that he was managing my expectations by not guaranteeing I'd get my money back," I say. "But he seemed to indicate he thought I would. Eventually."

Deiss nods. "Good."

I smile tightly. "Sure."

I don't know how I'm supposed to last for what could be weeks or forever. It's one thing to try to live off a credit card and whatever business I can drum up until everything is resolved. It's another to *not know* if it ever will be. How am I supposed to just wake up day after day, pretending that everything is going to work out with no guarantee?

"You should paint it," Deiss says, tilting his chin toward the room I'm staying in.

"What?" I look from him to the room and back again.

"You're stressed about all of this, right?" He makes the claim against my mental state as casually as if he's noting the color of my skirt (which is a lovely shade of lavender that should be making me feel better but is failing miserably).

"It's not my favorite situation I've ever been in," I say dryly.

He shrugs and twists the bread bag back up. "I can't picture you being comfortable in there anyway. You're too . . ." He goes quiet.

"Too what?" I prompt, wanting to know just what it is about

me, exactly, that doesn't fit the color he's chosen for the room he keeps his favorite things in. Am I too uptight? Too musically inadequate?

He tilts his head back and peers at me through lowered lids. "Shiny."

Shiny. I don't know what that means, so it certainly doesn't warrant the flush that starts in my chest and burns up my neck and into my cheeks. I doubt it's the compliment it sounded like. He probably means *overly groomed.* Or *too made-up.*

"Well, thank you for the offer," I say, "but I need to go to your store and get on the laptop. I've got business to drum up, and I certainly don't have money for paint at the moment."

Deiss laughs. "You really think I'd let you pay to paint the walls in my house? If I gave you that kind of ownership, you'd start thinking you had a half stake in the remote or that you could call dibs on the washing machine."

I lift an eyebrow. "Actually, I *am* calling dibs on the washing machine tonight. I had to wash a pair of panties in the sink last night just so I'd have a pair to put on today."

His eyes drop curiously to just below my waist, like he can see through the wispy material to the silky thong beneath. Once again, I feel my cheeks go warm. I wish he'd go back to covering his face with hair, or that I could forget how his lips felt against mine. Despite the fact that my head has always been fully on board with our status as platonic friends, my skin seems to have gotten confused by all the changes.

I clear my throat to break the silence.

"Right," he says, tugging his eyes back up. "And I'm guessing that Booker has activated your pride by declaring the laptop is his, so you're going to insist on using it only at the shop."

My eyes narrow in response. It's not *necessarily* pride that will prevent me from taking their laptop out of the shop. I'd call it *politeness*. They might need it, and I'm too thoughtful to become the reason that need goes unmet.

"Which means," he says, as if my silence is some kind of confirmation, "you won't be working tonight because you'll be doing laundry. So, let's go."

I watch him open the mostly empty fridge and toss the sandwich stuff inside.

"I don't need to repaint the room," I say when he turns back around.

He grabs one of my carrots and pops it in his mouth, causing me to shake my head.

"No," I say sternly, pulling my bowl away from him. "Keep your hands away from my food. We're not animals."

"Speak for yourself." He winks in a way that causes my mouth to twitch with a smile before I can tamp it down.

"And I won't be here long enough to justify repainting the room." I eye him as he grabs his keys off the counter. "So, thank you for the thoughtful offer, but it's unnecessary."

"What color do you think you're going to pick?" He heads toward the door like I haven't even spoken. "Is there a shade of white left, or have you used them all?"

"Oh," I shoot back, following him out, "I think it's too late to try to pull off chic. But if we search the indigo tones, we have a good shot at completing the rainbow."

He crosses his fingers cheekily, and I tug the door shut behind us.

I lie on the wood floor of my temporary bedroom, staring at the new walls. I've gone with a pale blue, the sunny sky to the living room's shaded trees. It's beautiful in a way that my professionally painted walls never managed to be. My back is tight from using the roller brush, and my arms ache. I tilt my head toward Deiss and find him staring past me toward the window. It's open to release the paint fumes, the night stretching blackly beyond it.

I use his distraction to study his profile. He has a smudge of paint on his cheek and flecks of it are mixed into the darkness of his stubble. The effect is strangely appealing. He said he was just going to help me put up tape, but then he started playing records, and the next thing I knew, he had a brush in his hand and was helping me do the trim.

Between the two of us, we got both coats done in a couple of hours. And he was right. Since that call in Africa with the bank, tonight has been the first time I've gone more than a few minutes without my mind being flooded with money worries. Deiss and I didn't even talk much. We just listened to music, the brushstrokes adapting to its rhythm. His gaze turns toward me, and I let my eyes drift, like I haven't been staring at him.

"I need Chinese food," he says, fumbling at his pocket for his phone but giving up before he pulls it out. "Moo goo gai pan and shrimp fried rice."

My stomach growls audibly.

"Does Chinese work for you?" he asks.

I hesitate before nodding. If we split the delivery charge, it shouldn't be too expensive.

He mounts another search and rescue mission for the phone and finds success this time.

"Do you have a go-to order?" he asks. "Or do you want me to pull up the menu?"

"Egg drop soup," I say, averting my eyes. Perfect body aspirations aside, it *is* a Tuesday night and vacation is over. At some point, I have to begin atoning for my sins. Especially now that I've fired my personal trainer. Even my flowy vacation skirts are starting to fit a little too tightly.

To my relief, Deiss says nothing, merely placing the order online. I realize he's likely paid for it with a credit card number saved in his phone, which causes me to panic. I'll have to pay him back with what's left from Mac's hundred-dollar bill. The good news is that I still have most of it. The bad news is that Mac's not likely to get repaid for a while.

I assume Deiss is going to leave the floor once the food is on its way, but instead he stays where he is. He lifts his hand and tucks it beneath his head, exposing a line of taut tanned skin above the waist of his jeans. I only peek at it for long enough to mentally measure the indention of the grooves that point an arrow southward.

"Are you staying in tonight?" I don't plan to ask the question, and I regret it the moment it comes out of my mouth. It probably sounds needy. Or, worse, like I don't want him here. Really, I just want to know if I'll spend the night listening for the sound of his return.

"At least until the food arrives." His head falls toward me, his cheek hovering above the wooden slats of the floor. "Do you have more laundry, or are you going out?"

"I wouldn't even know what to do for entertainment on a Tuesday night," I admit, distracted by the closeness of our positions on the floor. With his full attention on me, it suddenly feels like we're cuddled up together instead of lying three feet apart.

His eyes sharpen with interest at my confession. "What do you normally do?"

"Work. Then gym. By the time I get home, it's usually close

to nine, so I just shower and read in bed for a while until I'm ready to go to sleep." I say it like I'm proud of my discipline, rather than embarrassed by this evidence of the treadmill life he commented on that night in the bar. Still, I brace myself for his judgment, or at least a grin. Deiss probably considers schedules beneath him. He doesn't even seem to eat at normal mealtimes. He just floats through the day, doing whatever he feels like.

"Does your gym have a branch around here?" he asks, surprising me.

"It's not a chain. But it doesn't matter anyway. I've already canceled my membership. I did it the day I went on 'personal leave without pay.'" I smile wryly. "Because I was worried about money. I had no idea then how much more worried I would get."

He grimaces sympathetically, then his brow lifts. "I thought gyms were like a gang. Don't they own you for life?"

The truth in his question makes me laugh. "I've been going there for years, so I aged out of my contract a long time ago. But what I really had on my side was the greater part of a bottle of Baileys, a sugar high, and a drunken coworker cheering me on. I was not someone who was going to take no for an answer."

"Are you ever?" He says it flippantly, but it brings to mind all the noes I've absorbed over the years. *No indulgences*, said the mirror. *No mistakes*, warned the experts. *No, you're* not *enough*, said all the men who made and broke promises to my mom and me.

"I suppose not," I say to the sky blue wall past his cheek.

"And dates?" His lip curls gorgeously when my head jerks back toward him. "I know you go on lots of those. How do they fit into your schedule?"

My eyes narrow as I search him for signs of mockery, but he

gazes back at me with the easy attention of someone merely making conversation. Slowly, I relax, turning onto my side and lifting my hand to my shoulder to prop up my head. "They're for the weekends."

"Never during the week?"

"Weeknight dates mean the man isn't that into you. Unless it's a committed relationship, women should hold out for the primetime nights."

Deiss looks intrigued by the insight. "But what about someone like me, who puts on shows for work on Saturday nights?"

"You're proof of the point," I say confidently. "Notice how you've just managed to ignore the existence of Fridays. You want to pretend that you *can't* ask a woman out on a weekend, but really you don't want to. Because you don't take women seriously. You're never that interested in them."

"I take women seriously." Deiss manages to sound adamant without a hint of defensiveness.

"But you don't want one of them to be your girlfriend." I say this equally adamantly, and he flips over on his side to mirror my position.

"True," he says, shrugging his shoulder.

I knew this. Still, his confirmation settles in my stomach like the dried-out carrots I was choking down earlier. I've always accepted the fact that Deiss doesn't care about much, but I hate the idea that he doesn't care about anything. Except music, of course. Always music. Someone else's emotions poured out in song. Never his—possibly, disappointingly, because he doesn't have any.

"What?" His eyes search my face. "You look . . ."

I lift an eyebrow.

"Like you've tasted something foul," he says.

"Have you ever had a girlfriend?" At my question, I see that same look from yesterday flash across his face. This time, I don't just wonder if it's reluctance. I'm certain of it.

Once again, he answers in spite of it. "When I was younger. She was my neighbor, which was convenient."

"Because you were too young to drive?"

He shakes his head. "I had a '75 Bronco, Brook Blue Poly with a white roof cover. It was the first big thing I ever bought with my *Family Fun* money. I didn't have anywhere to go in it, but that didn't stop me from cruising with the windows down for hours, finding back roads and hitting the gas so hard I'd go up on two wheels when I rounded the curves."

"Sounds perfect," I say. "So, why did you need someone who lived next door?"

"Because there was no one else." His eyes darken, the blue turning from sapphire to midnight. "It had been years since *Family Fun* ended, but I was still nervous to go out in public. If my secret got uncovered, that was it. Maybe it would've been okay if I'd started high school with everyone else, but I hadn't been ready to trade in my freedom for scheduled days. Once I realized there might be benefits to attending—like friends and girls and parties—it was too late. Showing up after everyone had settled into their roles and formed friendships would've brought me too much attention. It would only take one person to spot the Brendan Davis in me."

"That makes sense," I say, being careful to keep my face blank. I know Deiss will retreat at any sign of pity, but I can't help feeling it. I can't imagine what it would be like, hiding away for all that time. Especially as a child, when every day feels like it stretches out for an eternity. "Did she know who you were?"

"No. Catherine knew I couldn't be around other people, but

she thought my family was in the Witness Protection Program." He bites down a smile, and I copy him unthinkingly, nibbling at my own lower lip. "I didn't tell her that, but I might've dropped bread crumbs that led her down that path."

"So, it was a relationship built on honesty." My lip breaks free into a grin. "How could it have gone wrong?"

"Personally, I blame prom."

"You chose a pinned corsage, didn't you?" I say teasingly, shaking my head. "Why do boys never understand that we want the one that goes around our wrists?"

"Robby Stillwell bought the corsage." He bends his knee to distribute the weight of his body against the hard floor. It brushes against mine, making my skin tingle beneath the shorts I've changed into to paint. "He could go to a dance filled with people who grew up watching *Family Fun* without worrying. Just like he could go to football games and parties and everything else a teenage girl wants her boyfriend to be able to do."

"Things you couldn't do," I say softly.

He nods against his arm. "Naturally, she broke up with me."

"For him?"

"I guess. I suppose that sounds better than admitting I couldn't compete with all the other things high school had to offer."

It's a feeling I can relate all too well with. When I was growing up, there was always something better out in the world for the men who came into my life. A better woman. A better daughter. A better home to settle in. It didn't matter how tirelessly my mom and I strived to present ourselves perfectly, we couldn't compete with all the better things the world had to offer.

"And that's it?" I ask the question with a bravado I don't feel. My greatest fear is that it *is* it. That, just like my mother, I'll never have a problem attracting men. But if they stay around long enough, they'll eventually get a peek below the surface, and their disappointment will always send them running away. "It didn't work out, so you've given up on love?"

"I haven't given up on love." For the first time since I met him, he looks genuinely offended. "I love *you*. I love Mac and Phoebe and Simone. I love my parents. I even love Booker, lazy as he is."

I blink in the face of such fervor from him. But that's not what's rendered me speechless. It's the fact that Lucas Deiss has just said he loves me. To my face. And I know it wasn't a romantic declaration, but my stomach feels like someone has strung it up with twinkle lights.

"I wasn't devastated that Catherine broke up with me," he says, seemingly unaware of the way his words have affected me. "It was the fact that I lost her. She was the only friend I had. It never even occurred to me that I was risking that by becoming her boyfriend. I stupidly assumed it would make us closer. But relationships aren't like friendships."

He looks at me for some sign of understanding, but I shake my head. "Are you talking about sex?"

He squints at me. "No, Liv. I'm talking about the fact that friendships aren't declared. They just happen. But a relationship is decided upon. Two people agree that they want each other for a finite period of time. At any point, they're allowed to change their mind." He snaps his fingers, the sound cracking through the room. "No harm, no foul. All memories together are invalidated. They might as well have taken place with a stranger. Doesn't that seem crazy to you? Why would anyone choose to invest their time and emotion into something that tenuous?"

"But friendships can end, too." I don't know why I'm arguing with him. The truth is, what he's saying makes sense. If I could go back to every night I've ever wasted on an ex and spend it with my friends instead, I'd do it in a heartbeat.

"Can they? That's not my experience. It's been twenty years since I worked with the crew of *Family Fun*, but I could call up any one of them and reminisce on the good times we had. If I tried that with Catherine, she'd assume I wanted to rekindle things. Or she'd have a boyfriend or husband who'd take offense."

The doorbell rings, and Deiss sits up straight, shoulders straining against his t-shirt. He uses his hands to push off the floor and heads toward the door.

"I'm right," he says, his voice trailing behind him. "You know I am. You can't go backward once you've seen someone naked."

My mind jerks back to the feel of Deiss's mouth on mine, and I sit up to escape it. It doesn't count, I know it doesn't— that night was so crazy it's easy to believe it was all just a dream—but I can't help wondering what would've happened if Deiss hadn't curtailed the moment with his secret. I clearly wasn't capable of resisting him. What if it had gone further?

It would've ruined everything. But I don't need to worry about that because it *didn't* go further. Deiss didn't let it. He won't ever let it. He doesn't want me like that. The fact might've inspired a twinge of self-consciousness before tonight, but now it fills me with relief.

Lucas Deiss doesn't want me—because he *loves* me. I pull myself up and scurry into the kitchen, letting the words wash over me. All this time, I've worried he'd disappear on me, on *us*, but there's never been any danger of that happening. He loves us. Like I do, he might even need us.

"Couch?" he asks, closing the door and turning around with the bags held out enticingly.

I nod. "Perfect. I'll just grab a water. What are you drinking?"

"A beer would be great, thanks."

I grab the two bottles and join him on the couch, settling into the soft brown leather for the first time since I moved in. It molds like butter against my body, the kind of comfortable that makes you want to catch a cold so you have an excuse to lie on it for days. Deiss unpacks the cartons from the paper bag, spreading them out on the coffee table and waving his hand in invitation as he pops an entire crab rangoon in his mouth and grabs the remote. He flips to what looks to be a reality show about sailing and glances at me with his brow lifted in question. I pull the lid off my soup with a nod, too eager about the bowl's contents to care about anything else.

Deiss swallows with a satisfied groan and reaches for the carton that holds the crab rangoon. "I think I could only eat these for the rest of my life and still die satisfied with the depth of my gustatory experience."

"I can't imagine that someone decided *gustatory* should be the term to describe the act of tasting food. It's got to be the least appetizing word I've ever heard." My mouth waters as I peer in the carton he tilts toward me.

"It could be *pustule* instead," he says, tilting his chin at the offered rangoon. "*Pustuling.*"

I groan and shake my head. "There goes my appetite."

"The rangoon will revive it. Go on. I promise not to say *pustule* again. Or offer the word *smear* as an alternate option for grossness. And I won't even mention *viscous.*"

"Deiss!" I balance the soup in my lap so I can shove his shoulder, and he captures my wrist with strong fingers, guiding it toward the carton. I hesitate over the crispy temptations. I can't reach my hand in there, especially since I chastised him only hours ago about daring to reach into my carrot bowl. "You only have three more."

He scoffs. "You think I'm a rookie? There's another order of them in the bag."

I hold back a grin and pluck one from the carton, taking a dainty bite. It's crispy and salty and creamy and delicious, and a murmur of pleasure escapes me in spite of myself.

"Such an animal." Deiss shakes his head with judgment, his eyes brightening mischievously.

I inhale my surprise, and a part of it goes the wrong way down my throat, making me cough. Deiss reaches for my water bottle, twisting it open and passing it to me with one hand while his other tears open the fried rice. He manages to scoop a heaping pile of it on the chopsticks, getting it all to his mouth without losing a single grain. I lean back, sipping the water and turning toward the TV as I take down the rangoon.

"Have you seen this before?" he asks, nodding at the screen.

I shake my head and spoon some soup into my mouth. It's tasty, but it's no rangoon.

"She's the worst," he says, referring to the blonde in the uniform. "But she's so funny, you can't help liking her. Twenty bucks says she'll pick a fight with someone by the end of the episode."

I look at him in wonderment. "You can't really watch this show."

"Why not?" He holds out his rice and reaches for my soup. Without thinking, I take his carton, allowing the swap. "Granted, I don't make a point of catching every episode. But it makes for great TV. There's beautiful scenery and lots of interesting insights about the boating life."

"That's your excuse?" I lift a skeptical eyebrow. "The educational aspect?"

"Not that I think an appreciation for reality TV warrants an *excuse*, but no. The main draw is the drama. And, of course, it also helps that Jen"—he sloshes my soup toward the blonde on the screen—"has been on every one of the seasons, and her uniform just keeps getting shorter."

I burst out laughing despite myself, distracted by the way his mouth wraps around my spoon. Am I supposed to grab another one from the kitchen? Or does he intend to give that one back to me?

No man I've ever dated has even dared offer me a bite off his fork, much less tried to eat one off mine. It's a level of intimacy for women like Elena, people who are all impulse and no boundaries. Hesitantly—curiously—I reach for the chopsticks Deiss has balanced in his carton of fried rice. With careful precision, I gather a tiny scoop of fried rice and lift it to my lips, wrapping my mouth around the place Deiss's was only moments ago. Unsurprisingly, it's delicious.

"Here it comes," Deiss says, balancing my soup on his knee as his other hand turns up the volume on the remote. On the screen, Jen approaches a deckhand with a scowl on her face. "Someone is about to get eviscerated."

"Do we care why?" I ask, using Deiss's chopsticks to excavate a shrimp out of the rice.

"Nope." He takes another bite of soup and passes it back to me before reaching for the moo goo gai pan.

For the rest of the show, we trade the cartons back and forth between us, keeping up a running commentary on what's happening onscreen. To my delight, when the episode ends, just like magic, another one begins. At some point, I notice that Deiss's thigh is pressed against mine. I study it out of the corner of my eye, noting how natural it looks. It's a perfectly normal amount of closeness for two friends who grew up together.

There's absolutely no reason for it to make my stomach flutter the way it does.

CHAPTER 15

"Five for me," our neighbor Chris calls out a few days later, passing us on the sidewalk as Deiss and I head toward Sounds. We saw him earlier on our run, so he's likely referring to the number of miles he did this morning. "Did I win?"

"Deiss insisted we run six," I say, pretending to complain.

Truthfully, I appreciated the challenge almost as much as I do this casual conversation. Despite all the years I lived in Santa Monica, I never felt like a part of a community. There seemed to be unspoken rules for high-rise living. Neighbors could hold spare keys. They could leave politely worded notes on your door if they disapproved of your noise levels, or even issue complaints through the board. They did not, however, involve themselves in your life.

The casual way I've been folded into the Los Feliz landscape is a marked change. Every morning on my runs with Deiss, someone calls out a greeting or stops us with a cheerful shout. I seem to have been granted genuine neighbor status. And I love it.

"He gets ambitious like that when he feels guilty about his food choices," I add conspiratorially. "I told him spaghetti was too many carbs."

"If anyone should be feeling guilty, it's you," Deiss says, shoving me with his shoulder. "You know that last meatball was mine."

I laugh, despite the fact that I probably *should* feel guilty. I had every intention of cooking for him last night after so many nights in a row of delivery, but then we'd stayed late at Sounds and ended up grabbing takeout on the way home.

"Don't you dare apologize to him, Liv," Chris says, turning to walk backward so he can holler after us. "I haven't seen Deiss run this many days in a row since I moved in. You're like his fitness muse."

I grin at Deiss smugly, but he just shakes his head and squints against the sun like a vampire caught out after dawn. It's a ridiculously beautiful day. Even the birds seem to be celebrating it with their eager chirps. One lands on the sidewalk and waddles for a couple of steps before lifting back into the air. The air sweeps softly against my skin.

"I'm your muse," I say sweetly.

"Because you inspire me to run?" Deiss's mouth twitches with a smile as he pushes open the door to Sounds. "The same could be said about fire."

"Aww, are you trying to tell me you think I'm hot?"

Mia, who usually works the opposite shifts from Booker, groans from behind the counter. "Keep your flirting outside, please. This is a place of business."

I flush, but Deiss just lifts an eyebrow.

"A place of business, you say?" He runs an eye from her inky-black mohawk to the piercing in her lip and down to her

Alien Sex Fiend t-shirt. "Maybe I should consider uniforms then."

She glowers and points a bitten-down fingernail at him. "You wouldn't dare."

"Something pink, maybe," Deiss says, pretending to think it over as he heads into his office. "With bows. And *ruffles.*"

Before Mia can respond, he closes his door. I stifle a laugh and slip behind her. The tips of her mohawk are purple today, and I press as closely as I can to the wall as I pass so she's not tempted to stab me with them. Mia is not the most pleasant person I've ever met, but I choose not to take it personally because she doesn't seem to like anyone. And that includes the customers.

I'd wonder why Deiss keeps her around if I hadn't already realized she's the one who does all the work Booker manages to avoid. She even put up my flyers on her own time, hissing at me like I was trying to steal her job when I offered to do it myself. The only time her territorial shtick seems to abate is after her shift, when Booker is inevitably late, and she allows me to take over the counter to bridge the gap so she can go home. It's a concession she makes begrudgingly rather than gratefully, as if she's the one doing me the favor.

Surprisingly, as fun as it is to work with Booker, I still look forward to Mia's shifts. I get so much more work done when she's aggressively ignoring me than when Booker is blasting music and continuing his unsuccessful quest to convince me to dance with him in front of any customers who happen to be present. Which is why, a couple of hours later, I'm the tiniest bit disappointed to be distracted from my project by the sight of Phoebe strolling through the door

"Hi!" I give a beauty queen smile.

"Are you working on something?" Phoebe directs the question to me but smiles at Mia as she saunters down the aisle between record bins. Naturally, Mia's eyes drop to her shirt, her fingers picking at the hem of her sleeve as if she's found a loose thread that needs urgent addressing. With the sneer on her face accompanying the slight, she might as well stick to one finger and use it to flip Phoebe off.

"A website for a pop-up boutique," I say proudly. It's the third job I've dug up, and by far the most profitable. None of them have paid much, and I've spent as much time searching for clients as I have creating content, but it feels like a start. Not to mention the client list on my website is beginning to look much less sparse.

"Hey, Phoebes." Deiss appears from the back and wanders behind the counter, leaning over my shoulder and peering at the screen. The smell of his cologne hits my nose. There's something dark and smoky about it, like fresh oak barrels swollen with aged bourbon.

"I like the colors," he says, his breath tickling at my ear. I turn to him with a nod, catching the full force of his eyes and mouth up close before he pulls back.

"I think you were right about mixing the light and dark," I say, managing to sound unaffected by his appearance. It means nothing, this appreciation I have for his looks. I also admired Cat Stevens's regality every time I looked at him, but I knew better than to try and pet him. "It needed the more substantial feel to offset the impermanence of the location."

"I want to see," Phoebe says.

I catch Mia eyeing the screen as I flip it around. Unsurprisingly, she says nothing. I should probably be grateful that she's managed to keep her disparagement to herself.

"It looks fantastic!" Phoebe claps her hands together with

delight. "Not that I don't know how great you are, but I'm still always shocked when I see your work. There's something so unique about it."

"Thanks." I think about all the painfully boring things I turned in at Infinity Designs and laugh. "That means more than you know."

Deiss leans against the counter next to me, both elbows resting on it as he lifts his chin at Phoebe. "What are you doing here so early? Do we need to break you out of a bout of writer's block?"

"Actually," Phoebe says, her eyes brightening with excitement, "I came by to tell you that Mac is at lunch with his agent."

Deiss's head tilts. "Right now?"

She grins and nods.

"Let's go," he says, pushing himself off the counter. His hand slips up my arm, cupping the crook and tugging.

I slide off the stool and close my laptop, setting it under the counter with my free arm as I look up at him in question.

"Mac's agent always leaves the tab open," he says, pulling me toward the door. His hand trails down to my wrist before it releases me, and he glances back at Mia. "You've got this?"

"You know it, boss," she says quickly, causing my mouth to fall open in disbelief.

I glance at Phoebe and see the same shock on her face.

"Did she really just call you *boss*?" I ask once the door closes behind us and we're headed toward Phoebe's car.

"Without sarcasm?" Phoebe adds, her voice high with disbelief.

Deiss shrugs.

"I knew she liked you," Phoebe says, "but I didn't know she was actually *nice* to you."

"It's not like she offered to knit me a sweater," Deiss says, opening the door to the front seat and waving me in. "She just said she'd do her job."

"She almost *smiled*," Phoebe says, ducking to climb in behind the wheel.

"That's an exaggeration," Deiss says, closing the door and sliding into the back. "She doesn't even do that when I hand her a paycheck."

I fight the urge to check my makeup in the visor mirror. I did the new, quicker version this morning because of our longer run. I could've stayed behind when Deiss left for work, but it seemed silly not to walk together.

"She smiled at me once," I say.

Phoebe gasps dramatically. "No!"

"Did she really?" Deiss asks.

I nod. "I was coming back from the restroom, and a customer bumped into me and spilled their coffee all over me. It made her smile."

Phoebe snorts. "So, she smiled at your pain."

"You don't know that," I say. "She could've been happy I got burned *or* she could've been happy my favorite pink cotton half-sleeve was ruined."

"Either way," Deiss says, "it was Liv who prompted that joy."

"Exactly." I turn in my seat so I can see him. He's leaning toward us from the hump in the middle, which is funny since he's always been the king of shotgun. "I have brought sunshine and happiness to your employees. You thought you were doing me a favor by letting me use your laptop, but it is I who have turned out to be the true gift."

"'Tis she," Phoebe says grandly.

"You actually look like sunshine today." Deiss's eyes scan

me, taking in my orangey-yellow top, perfectly coordinated with the skirt that doesn't completely cover my thighs while sitting. "But I guess your hair is always kind of sunshiny."

He reaches forward absentmindedly and fingers a lock of it. His touch sends a tingle through my scalp that travels down my neck.

"Ironic, for the Ice Queen." Phoebe flashes me a teasing grin. "Maybe you're melting."

"I'm trapped in vacation clothes." Her words prompt a flush of pleasure that warms my cheeks. It's a strange reaction, seeing as I've never minded the nickname. Have I? *Ice Queen* sounds formidable. Nobody would dare mess with an ice queen. "It's a false illusion that will be rectified once I get my money back."

"I like it," Phoebe says.

To my surprise, I find myself going still, my attention focused on the back seat, even though I don't allow my eyes to follow it. I can't help wondering if Deiss feels the same. He says nothing, though—a lack of response I might feel more acutely if his fingers weren't still in my hair.

If the goal is to pretend we've just happened to discover Mac at lunch with his agent, the effort is a spectacular failure. To be fair, that's more Mac's fault than ours. Actually, it's entirely on him. At the sight of us, he jumps up and waves with both hands, his legs hitting the edge of the table, causing all the glasses and dishes to rattle. Every head in the restaurant swivels toward him, then to us.

This might be fine if it were a fast-casual chain, but it's not.

Bash Crispy is a place to see and be seen, and not one of the three of us has a résumé to justify this kind of attention. You wouldn't know it, though, by the way Phoebe stretches to her full height and leads us through the crowded tables. For all its exclusivity, Bash Crispy is deliberately casual rather than fancy, with bright colors and music loud enough to obscure confidential conversations. In her mismatched layered patterns, exposing just the right amount of smooth, taut skin, Phoebe fits right in.

Beside me, Deiss appears impassive to the scene, like a movie star who's shuttled from one event to the next and has long since resigned himself to inquisitive eyes following him. I breathe deeply, inhaling the scent of freshly baked bread. A handsome man, a few tables over, gives me an appreciative smile, and I flash one back before deliberately breaking eye contact. He looks vaguely familiar, likely an actor of the D-list variety.

Mac grabs Phoebe in a hug that lifts her off the ground and causes the patrons at the next table to flinch as if worried he'll sling her around like a wrecking ball. It's not the most irrational fear. His lunch companion, a thin, overly groomed man with eyebrows so heavily plucked they look like they've been drawn on with a calligraphy pen, rises from his seat.

"You made it," he says, overpronouncing each word.

"He's pretending like he invited you," Mac says, grinning with delight at the revelation, "but he didn't."

"Friends never need an invitation," the man says smoothly before turning toward me. "Although you've been hiding this lovely thing from me. Sebastian Rollbairn, at your service." He proffers a hand.

"Olivia," I say, sliding my hand into his. His skin is soft and a tad slippery, and I'd bet the last seventy-three dollars of Mac's hundred that he sleeps in overnight moisturizing gloves. "It's a pleasure to meet you."

He holds onto my hand for an extra moment while he examines me, likely noticing the fingernails that haven't seen a manicurist in more than two weeks and the absence of cheekbones, which, in the wake of my abandoned diet and personal trainer, even contouring can't resurrect.

"Well, aren't you just perfection personified," he declares at the completion of his assessment.

"She's already represented," Deiss lies smoothly, shifting closer to my side, "and she's deeply committed to her agent." He holds a hand to his mouth as if telling a secret. "Things have gotten *amorous*."

Sebastian's eyes brighten at the gossip. "So, you *are* in the industry. Commercials? A soap?" He waves away the need for me to respond, slipping a card out of his pocket instead. "It doesn't matter. What matters is that sometimes romance and business prove incompatible. If you find yourself in that situation, you call me."

"Of course," I say, serenely. "Mac is always telling us what a dream maker you are."

Sebastian beams. "Speaking of, I've got other clients who need my attention. But you all stay! Have some drinks on me. I only wish I could join you. But there are deals to be done, you know, and money to be made." He winks at Mac as if he's running off specifically to pad Mac's bank account. Then he points a finger at Deiss. "And *you*. I hope you're still considering my offer. I meant it when I said we could find someplace for you in this industry. You've got presence."

Deiss nods and slaps him on the shoulder, making Sebastian's eyes widen in surprise. His hand goes to the spot where

Deiss made contact, and his expression turns pleased, like he's interpreted the sporty display of camaraderie as some kind of acceptance, rather than the blow-off it is.

"*Dream maker?*" Phoebe says the moment Sebastian is out of earshot. Her cackling laugh draws attention from the table next to us.

"You said to flatter him." I grin, grabbing the chair next to the one she's pulling out from the table. Mac slides a marinara-soaked plate on the chair to my right, but Deiss notices it before he sits down and shakes his head.

"Are you twelve?" Demonstrating his own maturity, he places it gently on the table and takes a seat. Then he ruins the effort by flicking a piece of bread crust at Mac's head. It arcs through the air and, by what I assume is at least seventy percent luck, smacks Mac directly between the eyes.

"Children," Phoebe admonishes. But her giggle undercuts the messages.

I'm able to keep a straight face until Mac lets out a high-pitched squeak of incredulity, his hand flying toward the spot of contact as if he's been shot. A snort rips out of me, and he turns my way, cartoon-level betrayal on his face. Rather than dampening my amusement, his expression makes me laugh out loud.

"No drinks for you," he says irrationally.

"What?" I point at Deiss. "He did it."

Mac looks at him. "No drinks for you, either."

"Phoebe laughed first," Deiss says.

Mac looks at her, the reluctance in his expression clear. "Sorry, baby. Fair's fair."

"And I'm sorry, too." Phoebe reaches out and places her hand sympathetically on his. "But you're the one who tried to ruin Deiss's pants with red sauce. That means no drinks for you, either."

Mac's face falls with disappointment, but to his credit, he accepts the ruling with a nod.

"*However,*" Deiss says, leaning back in his chair with his chin tilted up so he can look down on Mac like a benevolent god, "I choose to forgive you. So, you may have free drinks."

Mac perks up and declares his own forgiveness, sanctioning drink distribution for everyone. Within a few minutes, we have an entire page of specialty cocktails in front of us and are trying to narrow it down to the four with the most unusual combination of ingredients. I end up with one that pairs strawberry and peach with basil, while Phoebe's contains elderflower and mint.

"I'm telling you," Deiss says, defending his choice, which involves orange juice and coconut, "it tastes good."

"I'm not saying it doesn't." I squint doubtfully at his glass. "I'm just saying that it reminds me of one of those homemade hangover cures of orange juice and milk designed to make you vomit the previous night's shame."

"That's a lovely image, Liv." Deiss pulls his glass back as if he doesn't want it tainted by my words.

I giggle, already feeling a little drunk after half a glass. It must be the giddiness that comes from free cocktails in the middle of a workday, because everyone seems to feel the same, and none of them are half the lightweight I am. Phoebe keeps eavesdropping on the table behind us and excitedly reciting everything that's been said, despite the fact that each of us has confirmed more than once that it is not, in fact, Margot Robbie she's spying on.

The next couple of rounds are much less strategically ordered. They involve pointing randomly at the menu, then picking our favorite colors when the server arrives with them. I sip at the newly arrived neon-green one and grimace before covertly swapping it out with the untouched one in front of Deiss.

"Where's Simone?" I ask, hoping to distract Deiss from the fact that his cocktail has transformed from a cranberry hue to something that oozes out of sewers in superhero movies. "Did anyone invite her?"

There's a silent pause where I feel, rather than see, the guilt that bounces between them.

"We don't—" Mac says before getting cut off by Deiss.

"We tend to assume the drive is too far for these kinds of impromptu things," Deiss says with a too-casual shrug.

"Plus, it's weird between her and Sebastian now," Phoebe adds quickly. "You know how agents are. He acts like he wants to sign everyone, but of course he just wants everyone to *think* he wants to sign them. But Simone called him daily for months because 'you have to push for what you want.'"

"Phoebe's doing lots of air quotes," Mac says with delight. "That means she feels guilty about something."

Phoebe shoots him a look, but it's unnecessary. I know exactly what she feels guilty about. I wasn't supposed to find out that my adherence to a normal work schedule and the distance of my condo has excluded me from agent-sponsored drink-a-thons—just like I wasn't supposed to discover that Phoebe still sees Deiss and Mac almost daily, while I've been so lonely I sometimes wonder if my voice will dry up entirely from lack of use. It doesn't matter, though, because we're here now. And it feels just like old times. And if I can just stay near them, I'll never have to be lonely again.

"I'm looking at rooms for rent in Silver Lake," I blurt out.

"You are?" Phoebe squeals and clasps her hands together.

"And Los Feliz." I look at Deiss, searching for signs that this is too stalkerish for him, but his eyes drop to his drink.

"Have you found anything?" Phoebe asks.

"I've reached out to a couple of people," I say.

"You have?" Deiss's head jerks up. "When?"

"Whenever I spot a good one. They fill up really quickly, though. I won't be able to pull the trigger on anything until I get my account restored or find a steady repeat client."

I search his face for signs of relief, but it's gone blank. He picks up his drink and side-eyes the one in front of me.

"I'm so excited," Phoebe says, clapping. "I've gotten so used to seeing you every day. I didn't know what I was going to do when you left again."

"So, Deiss is going to have his place to himself again?" Mac asks. "You should let me move in. There's no point in letting an empty room go to waste."

"You have a place to live," Deiss says before lifting his eyebrows at me as if to say, *Look what you've done.*

"But it's always dirty," Mac says.

"Sorry-ola," Deiss says. "Liv is staying."

I look at him in surprise, but he merely smiles smoothly and drags his drink back in front of him. Without breaking eye contact, he pulls the straw out of the sludge-filled glass I've swapped his for and slides it into the lovely red. My eyes narrow.

Sharing is one thing. This reckless color contamination is another. Especially considering Deiss hasn't used a single straw since the rainbow-colored processional of cocktail deliveries began. He's been doing that guy thing where he leaves the straw *in the glass* but pushes it out of the way and drinks around it.

Slowly, with his eyes firmly on me, he bends toward the glass and puts his ridiculously gorgeous mouth on the straw. The liquid inside the glass begins to drop in volume, but he doesn't pull back after a sip. His eyes stay locked on mine as he continues to suck. It's not until his lips curl that I realize he intends to drain it all. With an outraged gasp, I shove his shoulder ineffectually and scoot closer, ducking for the other straw.

My forehead skims against his as a surge of fruity liquor fills my mouth, but I don't pull back. I'm spurred by the way his blue eyes have darkened with intent, the taunting jerk of his Adam's apple as he tries to take more than his share. It's impossible to know if this is just about the beverage I've stolen or if it has more to do with the meatball I snaked off his plate last night. But if it's the latter, it can't go unanswered. My meatball theft was a completely justified response to the coffee he'd robbed me of earlier in the day. Especially given the fact that he complained about the chemical aftertaste of the artificial sweetener after each sip but still managed to come back enough times to drain at least half my cup.

Brain freeze hits as the straw hits dry air with a sputter. I yelp at the same moment Deiss groans, and through the fingers that fly up to press against my forehead, I spot him cupping his own. I don't know if it's the absurdity of our pain, the adrenaline rush from the inhaled cocktail, or just the shot of liquor that's gone to my head, but laughter bubbles out of me, elated and only mildly taunting.

Deiss rolls his eyes, but I spot the smile that tugs at his mouth before he shakes his head at me. "You used to be so classy."

"And you used to have hair." I reach for his chin, sliding the back of my knuckles down the prickly stubble.

He catches my hand as I pull away, tugging it up to rub it over his scalp. "I still have hair."

Just like I imagined, it's softer than it looks, silky even. The feel of it makes my skin go warm as the image of him bent over my body flashes through my mind. Like in some lurid scene out of a dirty film, his mouth explores me, chin scratching at my skin just enough that I can feel every spot he's touched as my hand slips through silk, urging him on. I'm shocked by the thrill the unwanted vision produces, the way the combination of coarse and smooth excites something deep and primal inside of me.

I yank my hand free, flashing a smile to cover my dismay. I've never minded the fact that I'm attracted to Deiss because Lucas Deiss is an empirically attractive person. It wasn't even that disconcerting to discover he could seduce me if he chose to. In my mind, his ability to overcome my senses was more about him than it was about me. *This*, though. Me succumbing to something that can only be defined as lust. Giving in, after all these years, to some silly, throbbing, one-sided crush. It's as ridiculous as it is embarrassing.

And it'd be one hundred percent against the rules.

CHAPTER 16

I blink against the sun as we exit the restaurant. It feels overly bright, as if it's either celebrating our debauchery or chastising us for it. The cheerful breeze that riffles the bottom of my skirt makes it seem like it might be the former, so I smile up at the sky.

"I don't think I've ever been drunk in the middle of a weekday before," I say as our Uber pulls up. Phoebe has gone to Mac's to sober up for the drive home, but we're headed back to Sounds because Deiss doesn't want Mia to get stuck there when Booker inevitably shows up late for his four o'clock shift.

"It's not a weekday," Deiss says after we greet the driver and settle into the back seat of the little green car that smells like fries.

"It's Friday," I say, looking out the window at the colorful signs that line the street and the colorfully dressed people beneath them. With their maps and disposable water bottles, the tourists are easy to spot.

"Friday is part of the weekend. You said so when we were talking about dating."

"No." I roll the window down to feel the wind on my skin. My head is spinning, but in an enjoyable way. "Friday night is part of the weekend. Fri-*day* is part of the workweek, which makes it a weekday."

"But I work on Saturdays," Deiss says, his leg pressing against mine. The heat of it radiates through the thin material of my skirt in an exhilarating way. "Does that make it a weekday?"

"No." I scoot closer toward the door so our legs are no longer touching, but I glance over my shoulder and flash him a grin, my eyes skimming just past his. "That makes you a chump who works on the fun days."

"Nice," he says as I turn back toward the window. "Very supportive."

I laugh, giddy with alcohol and a strange nervousness.

We travel for a few more blocks in silence, and the driver turns on the radio. We've brought a weird energy into his car, with our mindless debate and me so close to the window he probably thinks I'm going to shove my head through it and start barking. My hair flies around my head like a shield of golden whips, which was not intended as a tactic but is a welcome side effect.

"Do you feel sick?" Deiss asks over the tinny pop song that plays through the speakers.

"No." The word twists with defensiveness, and I glance back at him in spite of myself, searching for some explanation for the question.

He meets my eyes, his lighter against the brightness of the sun, glittering like sapphires. My stomach fills with butterflies, fluttering anxiously. I try to turn away, but he places his hand on my arm.

"Hey," he says softly. A strand of hair whips around my

neck, and he reaches up, his fingers sliding across my skin as he pulls it free. "You know I don't really expect you to stay with me forever."

"I know," I mumble, distracted by his hand resting on my shoulder, still holding back my hair.

"It's just that you pretty much stopped looking at me after that conversation." His eyes scan my face like he's searching for answers in the curve of my cheek or the bow of my upper lip.

I force a breezy laugh. "What are you talking about? I've looked at you."

"No, you haven't." His confidence in the assertion is as resolute as it is warranted.

The truth is, I *haven't* looked at him, not since right after that when the bizarre lustiness occurred. I just need a little bit of space to get my head right, to get things back to normal between us. I need him to be the Deiss he was before, enigmatic and distant, not the new, open Deiss.

But that can't be right, is it?

I *like* understanding what makes Deiss so uniquely himself. And I like the closeness between us ever since he picked me up from the airport. I enjoy laughing with him over a bad TV show and drinking coffee with him silently in the morning. He's not the problem. I am.

I've allowed eleven years of friendship to make me stupid. It might sound harsh, but in this situation, harshness is warranted. A smart woman doesn't allow herself to settle into a routine with a man, expecting him to be around night after night.

It's a mistake I haven't made since the tenth grade, when Elliot Davenport's touch and pretty words made my skin tingle with excitement. He pretended not to know me the next day. He didn't even brag about taking my virginity. Clearly, it wasn't valuable enough to be boasted about. But the experience taught me that loss of control leads straight to heartbreak.

Since then, I've only dated men who are attractive in a bland Ken doll way. The kind of men who are likely to reveal a smooth curve of plastic should their pants come off. When I sleep with someone, it's because I've chosen to, not because I couldn't restrain myself. It's after the fifth date, once they've invested an appropriate amount of time and money into me and there's been talk of exclusivity. Sometimes I even enjoy it. But I never, ever lose myself in it.

If I've allowed myself to develop some kind of ill-advised crush on Deiss, I deserve to be defined as stupid. But I don't have to stay that way. I can control this situation.

"Not everyone has to look at you all the time, Deiss." It's a tricky balance, delivering an icy barb while keeping my tone breezy and light.

A flicker of hurt flashes across his face. "I know."

"Do you?" I don't even know what I'm doing. There must be a way to push him away without insulting him, but I don't have time to figure it out. "You did grow up with cameras in your face. Maybe that's why you expect everyone to be obsessed with you."

His eyes narrow, swirling storms of blue that threaten to suck me in. I meet them, keeping mine deliberately blank. A frown tugs at Deiss's mouth.

Then, as quick as the flick of a switch, his brow unfurrows and the storms blink out into two impenetrable seas. An easy smile stretches across his face. "You think so?"

No. I do *not* think so. I know, in fact, that it was a horribly unfair thing to say to him, and he didn't deserve it.

"Maybe." I shrug away my discomfiture. "It makes sense, doesn't it?"

"Perfect sense," he says smoothly.

I blink in the face of his impassivity, feeling like he's just performed a magic trick, transforming from my roommate into the enigma that is Deiss in the blink of an eye. I wish I could hit rewind on this conversation, lob a lighter grenade than the one I'd chosen. Actually, I'd like to rewind the entire last hour. I'd like to go back to somewhere before I started feeling like I've crossed a line.

Back to when he wasn't clearly in the process of easing away from it.

Maybe it's the symmetry of designing a wine label while buzzed, but I'm pretty impressed with the outcome. I've managed to create something eye-catchingly bold that still feels classy, which, in my opinion, is a hard line to balance. I glance up at Deiss for the hundredth time, but once again, he's conveniently busy.

This time, he's talking to an older man in a business suit. The man is probably getting recommendations, looking for something edgy that will make him feel young again. At least Deiss is out of his office now. He spent a full hour in there earlier before he came out and distracted himself organizing the bins. Poor Booker has been desperate for attention, Deiss and I ruining his day by focusing on our work.

At the thought of Booker, I glance over and am surprised to discover him watching me, a knowing smirk on his face. I raise my eyebrows, and Booker wriggles his like a matador wiggling a red cape. He stands up and pulls his stool toward me. It's so close that when he sits back down, his knee presses against mine. He smells faintly of soap and the Skittles he's been savoring one by one for the last hour. Deliberately, he turns away from Deiss so his back is blocking us.

"Did you guys get in a fight at lunch?" he whispers.

"No." I lean around him to make sure Deiss hasn't heard, but he's taken the customer to the front of the store. "Why would you ask that? Does he seem mad?"

Booker laughs. "Deiss? Please. That man never gets mad. He didn't even get mad when I spilled soda on the Ibanez RG5000. And my soda smelled more like Captain Morgan than Dr Pepper, if you know what I mean. You're the one being weird."

My hands go to my face, as if I can pat out the traces of whatever it is he's spotted. "I'm not being weird."

"When Deiss brought us coffees, you practically balanced the cup in your palm to keep his fingers from touching yours."

"You're exaggerating," I say, even though I'm not entirely sure he is.

Booker shakes his head. "I had to double-check his hands to make sure they hadn't sprouted poisonous claws."

"We didn't get into a fight," I say.

"Then what?" He leans forward, searching my face. He's had too much time to think. I should've known I couldn't work silently for hours, leaving him alone with his thoughts, and not have to pay for it later.

"My man-whore of a boss snuck off to the coat check with the waitress, didn't he?" he says confidently. His eyes brighten. "Did you walk in on them and see his hands somewhere disgusting?"

"Booker!" I give an audible gag.

"No," he says, holding up a finger. "You got jealous, didn't you? You realized you love him, and now you can't touch him because you won't be able to ever let go."

I force a laugh, but my stomach churns at how close he's come to the truth. Not about the jealousy or the love or the inability to let go, obviously. But Booker is right that I've been avoiding Deiss's touch since lunch, just like it's still a struggle to make eye contact with him. If a man who accidentally accepted arcade tokens as payment for a record yesterday (Booker believed the customer who claimed they were two-dollar coins) could pick up on that, I have to assume that Deiss has, too.

"I was just drunk," I say firmly. "I always get skittish when I drink too many cocktails. But that's it. Nothing weird happened at lunch, just like there's nothing weird between Deiss and me."

I stand up, determined to prove it. Not just to Booker. Not even to Deiss. To myself. I wasn't supposed to have crazy thoughts about Deiss. It certainly doesn't fit into my perfect version of our friendship.

But it happened.

And I can deal with that. I have quit my job, but managed to accumulate six new clients in my first week of freelancing. I'm all but penniless, but my skin is still tan from a trip to Africa and my belly is full of top-shelf cocktails. I've lost my home for the second time in my life, but I've never felt more happily settled than I have at Deiss's.

If my friendship with him has slipped a little out of my control, I just need to adapt. I'm not going to ruin things by closing myself off. In fact, I'll do the opposite. I'll hang out with him, I'll look him in the eyes, and I'll touch him, casually, because that's what normal friends do. It doesn't matter if I have the tiniest crush on him, because Deiss only thinks of me as a friend. It's why he loves me. It's why we've made the pact.

I cross the store, hovering off to the side until Deiss waves the man in the business suit, who now has a hefty stack of records balanced between his hands, toward the register.

"Hey," I say, closing the distance between us.

Deiss turns and leans back against the bins when he sees me. "Did you get your wine label done?"

I nod. "It was fun. I think it turned out really well."

"Nice." He smiles, teeth flashing white against the dark scruff, and my breath speeds up. He's so complicatingly attractive. "Can I see?"

"Sure." I hold up my hand when he pushes himself up straight. "But first, I wanted to say sorry for what I said in the Uber."

"Not necessary," he says.

"It is, though. I don't even know why I'd say that. I was upset about something else, and I took it out on you." I take a deep breath, feeling like I'm at the end of a diving board. With a sharp exhale, I push myself forward and wrap my arms around him. "Please forget I said anything."

He stiffens beneath my grip, and I freeze, my arms feeling suddenly brittle, like two tree branches I've attempted to embrace him with. But then he relaxes, one arm sliding around my waist and the other wrapping around my back, pulling me into him. His hand palms the back of my neck, sparking unwanted memories of that night in the tent, and I bury my face in his shoulder so he won't see the flush of my cheeks. It feels good, this hug. I can't imagine why it's taken us eleven years to do it.

"Consider it forgotten," he says into my hair.

I nod and pull back, but I forget to let go. His arms stay around me as well, loosening and wandering the length of my back. His body is hard and warm, and when I look up at his face, my eyes get caught on his mouth.

"What were you upset about?" he asks in a low voice, drawing my gaze up.

"Nothing," I say dreamily, distracted by the way his pupils have dilated. It makes them equal parts black and blue, which would translate into a bruise if I tried to re-create it as a design but is unquestionably sexy in person. "I saw someone in the restaurant I didn't want to see."

"Who?" His eyebrows draw together in a very un-Deiss-like way.

I shake my head, not wanting to continue the lie but not knowing how to get away from it. It's not like I can explain that I got freaked out by my attraction to him, especially not while his arms are wrapped around me. It would make my whole apology look like some deviant attempt to cop a feel.

"It doesn't matter," I say, averting my eyes.

"Let's go home," he says, drawing them back. He smiles, but it doesn't match the tension in his face. "We'll grab dinner on the way and find a comedy to watch."

"Okay," I say as the bell above the door dings. Deiss glances up at it, but his arms don't drop from my back.

"You made it back," he says to someone behind me.

"I did," a woman says.

I let go of Deiss, spinning around to find a beautiful woman with dark hair and a familiar face behind me. The sight of her punches me in the chest, making my breath catch in my throat. *Zoe.* Zoe, from St. Lulia. The woman Deiss must have spent his last night of vacation with. My stomach clenches at the way she's smiling at him, so confident and gorgeous. Her legs belong on a runway, which she must know, judging by the four-inch heels she's showcased them in. I feel like I'm back in school in my strappy sandals.

"I remembered the name of this place," Zoe says, "and I thought I'd check it out, see if you were around."

"I'm glad," Deiss says.

I search his face for any sign of what I'm supposed to do, but there's nothing. No excitement to see this woman. No annoyance that she's popped up at his place of business. Deiss has gone blank, his head tilted back lazily, like Zoe is any other customer who's walked through the door today, unexpected but welcome nonetheless.

"Liz, right?" Zoe turns toward me with a wide smile.

"Liv," Deiss corrects her.

Her eyes widen apologetically, and now that we're in better lighting than that at the hotel pool, I can see that they're purple. They must be contacts, but the knowledge doesn't help. Her bronzed skin glows.

"It's good to see you again, Liz," she says brightly, only allowing her gaze to drop for a second to where Deiss's hand is still resting loosely around my waist. "How's the freelancing going?"

"It's good," I say, feeling sick to my stomach. "I was actually just about to get back to it."

"No, you weren't," Deiss says. "We were going to get dinner."

"You should go with Zoe," I say. "She did just get here. Anyway, I should double-check my wine label and get it turned in. If I don't, I'll just spend the rest of the night wondering if they'll like it."

"Let's see it," Deiss says, starting toward the counter.

I allow him to sweep me in front of him, but his hand stays splayed against the small of my back. My skin heats beneath it, either from the feel of his touch or the burning of Zoe's eyes.

"Who's this?" Booker asks as we approach. He scans the length of Zoe appreciatively, slowing as his gaze dips down her tawny legs. "Have we picked up another stray?"

"The name's Zoe," she says, tossing her mane of obsidian hair over a bare shoulder with a smile. "I met Lucas and Liz in St. Lulia."

"Liv," Deiss says, as I slide the laptop across the counter. "Or you can call her Olivia, if Liv is hard to remember."

I bite my lip to stop it from curling up, even though they're both behind me and neither can see my face. Booker is in front of me, and his eyes have widened with interest at the sharpness of Deiss's tone.

"Ugh," Zoe sighs. "I'm terrible. Sorry, Liv. Two weeks of vacation drinking has left my brain totally soggy."

"Well, the rest of you seems to have stayed remarkably firm," Booker says with a wink. "The name's Booker, but you can call me anything you want."

I groan, but Deiss just laughs, reaching around me to flip open the laptop. The label is still up on the screen, and I feel a flush of pride at the sight of it. It looks even better now that I've had a little distance from the process of building and erasing and building again.

"That's amazing." Deiss leans closer, studying the screen like it's an exhibit at a museum rather than a label that's meant to be plastered around a bottle of booze. His hand drapes over my shoulder. "I love how you've managed to make it both whimsical and stately at the same time."

"Thanks," I murmur, pleased at his assessment. A unique spin on a traditional representation is what I kept trying to accomplish at Infinity Designs, but they never wanted anything new or different. Hopefully, this client will. If they don't like it, it will be the first project I've done this week that's been rejected. Everyone else has loved what I've turned in.

"It really is good," Zoe says.

Booker laughs at her higher voice, which betrays her surprise. "You thought it would be bad?"

I turn to Zoe. For the first time since she entered, she looks the slightest bit ruffled.

"No," she says unconvincingly.

Booker laughs again.

"Fine." Zoe shrugs, an apologetic smile stretching across her face. "You hear that someone is going freelance and you can't help assuming they're a novice. You're not, though," she says, turning to me. "You're actually really talented."

"She's been doing this professionally for years," Deiss says. "She's just switching from doing it for a company to doing it for herself."

Zoe's eyes narrow for a split second, and then her smile widens even further.

"That's great, Liv," she says, her hand going to my arm. "There's a ton of work out there to be picked up. In fact, I'm a little overwhelmed myself. I've taken on a new beauty line because the pay was too good to pass up, but I could use a partner on it. We should swap numbers, if you're interested?"

"I'd like that," I say a tad reluctantly.

I know from our chat at the pool that night that it's a great offer. Zoe is well past the period I'm currently in, where you present your services in response to posts from average people offering jobs for set pay. She's worked with big-name companies, many of whom have sought her out, and some of whom she's even had to turn down due to lack of time.

Still, my chest feels tight when I put my number into her phone. It doesn't loosen when Booker and I wave Zoe and Deiss off into the night, where the two of them will eat dinner, and reminisce on their night together in South Africa, and likely opt to relive the experience. I don't know what's wrong with me. I've apologized to Deiss, worked through whatever weirdness was happening in my mind, finished a project, and potentially opened a door to future work. I should be elated.

"That's a fire bunny right there," Booker says, still staring at the door like the ghost of Zoe's ass has lingered in her wake.

I close my eyes and shake my head before giving in to curiosity. "A what?"

"Hot," he says, like he's speaking to child. "Zoe is hot."

"Yeah," I say, abandoning my perfect posture to slump against the counter. "She really is."

"And lucky for you," he says.

"Mmm," I murmur noncommittally.

"I mean, talk about great timing. Deiss happens to hook up with a successful graphic designer right when you're trying to start a new career in that field."

I nod, knowing that Booker has no idea how right he is about the timing. If our friendship, and the pact, and Deiss's general lack of interest in me weren't enough to keep me in line, surely the risk of alienating a potential work partner will be.

"You're right," I sigh. "The timing is perfect."

THEN

Maybe it was foolish, but I'd somehow convinced myself Chad Russel and I were going to get married. Choosing to spend your entire senior year together meant something, didn't it? It was a time of looking forward, planning the rest of your life. We'd spent hours talking about our future careers, what city we wanted to live in. I just assumed we were making decisions. *Together.* Clearly, I'd assumed wrong.

I was upset, not because I truly loved him but because if felt like my fault.

"You don't have time for me," Chad said, standing up from the table where I'd spent a considerable amount of said time waiting for him to show up. His button-up hung stiffly on his lanky frame, like he'd taken the time to iron it to honor the seriousness of his pronouncement. "All you ever want to do is hang out with your friends."

I considered pointing out that, between his studying and his internship at the accounting agency, he was only available on Sundays anyway, but I bit my tongue. I *had* blown him off the last two Sundays, first to cheer on Simone at her powder-puff football game and then to celebrate Mac's birthday. They'd been important events. Much more important than going out to eat so Chad could whine about his internship over an endless basket of bread.

I didn't actually feel hurt until later that afternoon when I spotted him on the Ferris wheel with Lainey Massey, his long-standing "study partner." By the looks of things, they'd transitioned from math to biology a while ago. His hand was up her shirt, and I could see his tongue from the ground. It clearly wasn't a first kiss. He'd been cheating on me, and now he was ready to let everyone see it.

I didn't let myself cry, but I felt my entire body stiffen up, my expression carved entirely of marble. My insides shriveled, and a whooshing sound roared between my ears, drowning out the din of the boardwalk. The late-afternoon sun turned cold, the crashing waves ominous instead of dancing. I'd thought I'd understood how my mom felt, but it was much worse to experience it myself. Chad had seemed to need so little, yet I still hadn't been enough.

It was Phoebe who spotted them first. We were waiting in line for the Ferris wheel, after all. It's not like she could've missed them. She whipped toward me, her eyes wide. I faked a smile.

"Um," Simone said, spotting him next. "Isn't that your boyfriend?"

I couldn't look again. "No. We broke up this afternoon."

Deiss looked at me, but if he was surprised that I hadn't told anyone, he chose to keep his mouth shut. Mac wasn't as discreet.

"Awesome," he said, picking me up and twirling me around. My legs slammed into a stranger unfortunate enough to be passing by. "I hated that guy."

"You did?" I gasped out with the small amount of air his bear hug had left in my lungs.

"We all did," Phoebe said. "He was the human equivalent of a lecture on dust particles."

"*So* boring," Simone agreed.

"Lainey doesn't seem to think so." My words slipped out, pathetic and embarrassing.

"Did he dump you for her?" Mac seemed too shocked.

"Liv dumped *him*," Simone said quickly. "Because he called her mom a bitch."

"Simone!" I shook my head at her. "He did not."

"So, you're mad," Mac said, seeming not to hear me. His eyes lit up.

"I'm not mad," I said.

"She's furious," Simone said.

"She is?" Mac bounced with excitement. "You know what that means. Mad people get to throw stuff."

He grabbed my hand and started to run, dragging me toward the booth with the glass bottles set up in pyramids. Before I could object, Simone had come up behind us and slapped down a hundred-dollar bill.

"Keep 'em coming," she ordered the man behind the counter, gesturing toward the basket of baseballs.

"You can't spend that much on a stupid game," I said, horrified by the wastefulness of it. "It's absurd."

"Please." Simone rolled her eyes. "My parents spent more than that on a bottle of wine at dinner last night. And they didn't even drink half of it."

"My game isn't stupid," the man behind the counter informed me gruffly.

I opened my mouth to apologize, but Phoebe stuffed a wad of bright blue cotton candy in it.

"Throw this," Simone said, folding a ball into my fingers.

I looked for help in Deiss, but he simply lifted his eyebrows.

"I can stand behind you if you want," he said with a smirk. "Show you how it's done."

His flirtation was shocking enough to knock a laugh out of me. To hide my blush, I turned toward the wall at the back of the booth and hurled the ball. To my surprise, it crashed into one of the pyramids, shattering glass and sending it flying. I shrieked with delight, my friends' cheers filling my ears.

"Again," Deiss said, plucking the ball Mac was about to throw from his hand and putting it into mine.

I threw with more confidence this time, laughing when it hit the wall, leaving the bottles intact. Beside me, Mac finally got a ball of his own into the air, and the sound of shattering glass made us scream again. For over an hour, we hurled baseballs, shrieking and laughing until the sun drifted down and our voices grew hoarse.

I didn't think of Chad for hours. And once I did, it was only long enough to admit that he'd been right. I *didn't* have time for him. Not when there was so much more fun to be had with my friends.

CHAPTER 17

*Y*ou look great," Phoebe says, despite the fact that I've shown admirable restraint in not tugging at the leather bustier she's insisted on lending me for tonight's show. I haven't complained about the gray jeans that cling like a second skin, either. There's been no mention from me of the strategic holes in the legs or even the black booties they're tucked into or the eclectic jewelry she's paired with the outfit. In fairness, though, I do like the booties and the jewelry. I wouldn't have picked them for myself, but I definitely would've admired them on Phoebe.

The only giveaway to my trepidation about Phoebe's rock and roll makeover effort is the way my steps have slowed outside Sounds. The storefront windows glow against the darkened night, revealing the crowd within. It's only 9:30. There's still another half hour before the Saturday night concert begins, so I wasn't expecting to see so many people inside. Deiss has always described these shows as gatherings of true music lovers. This, however, looks like a real scene.

"I look like you," I say, giving in and tugging my top up.

The effort proves useless, as the bustier is more like a layer of tar that's been applied to my body than anything that could be categorized as clothing. I don't know what I was thinking when I complained to Phoebe about having to recycle yet another outfit from my suitcase. I knew I couldn't afford to go shopping, just like I knew Phoebe wouldn't pass up an opportunity to play dress-up, especially when it gave her an excuse to get out of helping the guys set up for tonight. Still, a few weeks ago I would've held my ground against the bustier. But if I can quit my job and live out of a bag, I can certainly handle being styled by one of the most fashionable people I've ever met.

"And I always look fantastic," Phoebe says, echoing my thoughts and pulling me toward the door. Her Afro is full and glittering tonight, and she's wearing a jumpsuit that shows off toned arms and plunges in the back. She does, in fact, look fantastic. Unable to argue, I allow myself to be dragged inside.

The room is warm from all the bodies. The mixture of colognes has overridden the shop's usual smell of coffee, dust, and whatever's been ordered for lunch. Some people are hanging out, blocking the aisles as they catch up or flirt, but others are rummaging through the bins for records. Phoebe tugs me to the counter, where there's a line of five people waiting to make purchases. Booker is perched on the stool behind it, ignoring them all while he chats up a girl holding a credit card.

"Deiss wants you downstairs," he says, spotting us.

"Deiss also wants to sell some records," Phoebe says, grabbing the girl's credit card and slapping it on the counter. "So, *sell some.*"

Booker rolls his eyes but picks up the card. "I know you think you work here, but you don't."

"I know you think you don't work here," Phoebe says with a smirk, "but you do."

She leads us to the door downstairs, which has been blocked by a small folding table. Mia is sitting behind it with a lockbox and a scowl. The tips of her hair are green today, and she's finally taken the bandage off her new neck tattoo. It looks like Sanskrit and is still red around the edges.

"Twenty dollars each," she says, giving no indication that she's ever seen us before, much less this morning when I brought her coffee in one of Deiss's travel mugs. I even remembered she likes milk but no sugar.

"I like the tat," Phoebe says. "What does it mean?"

Mia's lips curl at the compliment. "Roughly translated: *Give me twenty dollars.*" She turns toward me, and one pierced eyebrow lifts as she takes in my outfit. "*Each.*"

"I heard Bears in Captivity goes old-school with some power ballads," Phoebe says, referring to tonight's band. She grabs my hand and skirts around Mia's table, giving her a saucy wink as we scurry past. "Don't forget to save me a dance."

"Oh." I breathe the word out as we descend the stairs. "I can't believe you just did that. We're in so much trouble."

"Mac and I come to these shows all the time," Phoebe says, "and we've never paid once."

My eyes widen. "So, just *I'm* in trouble?"

Phoebe glances back at me with an evil grin. "Correct-ola."

I laugh but turn sideways just in case Mia decides to hurl a throwing star at my back. Downstairs, the lights are all on, including the bulbs that line the walls. The band is setting up on the small wooden stage that's raised a few feet off the floor. The back wall is lined with boxes, but the rest of the basement is impressively empty. Someone, likely Deiss, has painted the entire basement a bold fuchsia color. It's an odd choice but surprisingly perfect. It offsets the gray concrete floor well and is toned down by the collection of black-and-white music posters that pepper the wall to the right of the stage. No wonder he's been able to give such helpful advice on my projects. He's got a good eye for design.

The room is mostly empty, but the clicking of our heels causes the few people present to look up. Phoebe waves at the band, but I focus on the group standing in the middle of the room. It's Deiss and Mac, who I expected to see, but Simone's with them, too, standing next to a man I've never met. Notably absent: Zoe.

She texted earlier to set up a time on Monday to meet about the project she's working on, but I haven't seen her since she left with Deiss last night.

I expected to. At least I expected to hear her voice. I sat in my room for hours after I got home, staring at the sky blue walls and missing Cat Stevens, trying to convince myself I wasn't desperate for Deiss to return alone. But when I finally heard the creaking of the front door, I could've wept with relief at the sound of only one set of footsteps.

"This is her. She did it," Mac says, bounding toward me and throwing an arm around my shoulders. He propels me forward, beaming down at me. "These guys like your flyer!"

I smile back at him uncertainly before peeking at Deiss for confirmation, but Deiss's eyes seem to be caught somewhere between my neck and my waist. I inhale sharply. My stomach does an aerial swoop. Even if it is just the novelty of seeing me in Phoebe's clothes, it's intoxicating to discover that Deiss is capable of seeing me as a woman.

"They do?" I ask, still looking at Deiss.

When my words cause him to look up, I smirk knowingly

to distract from the blush I feel blooming on my cheeks. He laughs at my smugness, looking only the slightest bit sheepish at having been caught ogling me.

"Drop the false humility," he says, as if that's the thing that's brought him to laughter. "You know how good it is. Even Mia said so."

"Did she?" I ask, excitement over her approval outweighing my triumph over my temporary release from the friend zone.

"Well," he says, "not *out loud*."

"We love it, though." The stranger takes a step forward, tipping the flat hat on his head like he thinks he's Tommy Shelby. He has two crooked teeth that appear when he smiles. "I'm Max, the band's manager."

"Olivia Bakersfield," I say. "I should've asked before I attached the picture to the band name, but I just wanted to make sure the flyer stood out."

"Clearly, it worked," Deiss says, gesturing above us. "Booker keeps texting to tell me how many people are up there waiting. This is going to be a full house."

"Olivia's right, though," Max says. "It's not best practice to attach an unapproved logo to an established name. But in this case, it's worked out. It's an original, right?"

"It is," I say.

"It is?" He cocks a skeptical eyebrow.

"She just answered you," the drummer says, coming over from the stage. The rest of the group trails after him.

"What made you think to put a hot dog in one of the bears' mouths?" A cute guy with shaggy blond hair and a guitar dangling from his side leans forward with a grin, propping his forearm on Max's shoulder.

I shrug. "It felt right."

His grin widens. "Fair enough. But you have to tell us if the bears are dancing or fighting, because there may or may not be money riding on your answer."

"I wish I could answer that," I say, "but I can't. I tried to make it a little of both, so the viewer would see what they wanted to see."

"Did you hear that, Brad?" He reaches over to shove the drummer. "You've got hidden anger inside you. You should try to see a world that's full of dancing, like me."

"I'll write that down in my goals diary," Brad says wryly before focusing on me. "My anger issues aside, what do you say? Do you want to work with us?"

My pulse quickens as I search his face for signs that he's messing with me.

"Slow down there, Usain Bolt." Max holds up a hand between us, stopping me from answering. "That's not how this works."

"Sure, it is," Brad says. "For once, the whole band likes the same thing. Do you want us arguing over every album cover and piece of merch and all the other stuff that needs to be designed, or do you agree that we should lock down the one person who's brought some harmony to the process?"

Max sighs. "You know you're destroying our bargaining ability, right?"

Brad looks between the two of us impassively.

"I wouldn't have bargained anyway." I manage to get the words out coolly, despite the rapid pounding of my heart. "Talent like mine doesn't come cheap."

"They're going to be big-time," Simone says, leaning against the boxes along the back wall. Next to her, I can feel the offbeat thump of her stiletto against the cardboard. Every-

one has pushed forward to be closer to the band, but it's still thick with people back here. "I mean, just listen to them. They're phenomenal."

"They're good," I agree, sliding my hand in my back pocket to make sure the band manager's card is still there. It's the most precious thing I've ever owned, and I've slid it between my fingers so many times that I'm worried the ink is going to come off.

"And your work is going to be on their album cover." Simone looks at me through heavily lined eyes, only a hint of jealousy piercing her enthusiasm. "They're going to sell t-shirts at their concerts with *your* designs on them."

"Hopefully." I scan the crowd, lit by the bulbs along the walls. Phoebe and Mac are up front dancing, but Deiss is nowhere to be found.

"No, they will. I can't believe you just laid it down like that. *Talent like mine doesn't come cheap.* I've never been so impressed by you."

I laugh at the awe in her voice. "It was false bravado, Simone. I'd already designed the logo for free. I probably would've let them use it anywhere they wanted just for the exposure."

"That just makes it even more badass," she says. "They ate it up, too. What if you end up being the designer for all the bands that pass through here? And then you get so big that other bands start reaching out? You could be a go-to for the whole music industry."

It's a crazy thought, but certainly one I've already had. I don't expect Bears in Captivity to have a massive budget for design, but I know it will be a better haul than what I've been earning piecemeal. More importantly, there's real potential for ongoing work with them. It's a major score for someone so new to the industry. And Simone is right. With this foothold, networking with all the bands that come into Sounds will just get easier and easier.

So many people have showed up that there was actually talk of turning them away, and somehow, my flyer has received credit for the heightened interest. If I can bring more people in week after week, it's good for Deiss, the bands, and my reputation. And it's not just paper advertisements I can offer. Knowing Deiss, I wouldn't be surprised if he does nothing to promote either the store or the shows. He's more the type to rely on word of mouth, preferring the right audience to a large audience.

Maybe it's time for a change, though. For his sake, and for mine.

The music winds down, and the lead singer announces the last song. Beside me, Simone shifts restlessly, causing me to grimace. I know what's coming.

"It's our last chance," she says, confirming my suspicion. "Come on, we still have time to get up there."

It's not the first time she's asked tonight. It's not even the second. She's desperate to get onstage and dance with the band. Apparently, it's trashy if you do it alone but sexy if you do it with a friend. And her Friendsta following adores sexy but has zero tolerance for trashy.

"If you couldn't get me to dance while wearing a Sandy costume at the PKA house, do you really think you're going to get me to rush the stage at my future employers' concert?"

I keep my voice even, but my irritation flares, at her but also at the rest of our friends for leaving us alone. I don't know why Mac and Phoebe always have to run off together like they're still a couple. And Deiss. He's probably tucked back in some corner with a girl far cooler than me. I can't believe I let myself believe he was attracted to me in this faux-rocker costume

Phoebe has dressed me in. Never once in eleven years has he paid me less attention.

"Let's get him up on the stage," Brad, the drummer, says announcer-style into his mic, interrupting the lead singer. For a moment, I think he's backing up Simone and trying to force me up there.

He waves his drumsticks at the crowd, urging on our cheers.

"Deiss, Deiss, Deiss!" he says rhythmically, pulling the audience into his chant.

My eyes widen as the chant builds steam, and I spot Deiss being tugged by Booker from under the stairs to the stage. Even across the dark, crowded room, I can see the way he leans back, as if he's water-skiing, caught in the wake of a speeding boat. He plays it cool, though, once he's on the stage with the light in his face. If I didn't know him so well, I might even think he was amused. Even once it turns into a live commercial, with Mia bringing up the bass guitar and Booker announcing it as a Gibson Thunderbird (color: Tobacco Burst; price: $7500).

Deiss isn't amused, though. He's mad. Madder than I've ever seen him. I can tell by his posture, by the depth of his voice when he begrudgingly agrees to play. I can feel it in the stiffness of his fingers as they move over the strings. The shaggy-haired guitar player pulls Phoebe up to dance, and Deiss doesn't even smile. His face stays blank, betraying nothing, but I know.

And I get it. I get that this attention makes him deeply uncomfortable. But maybe it's more than that. He grew up with cameras pointed at him and people telling him what to do and say. He did what he was told, and his obedience was rewarded with ten years of isolation.

He claims his stint as a child actor wasn't a bad experience, and maybe it wasn't. But what came after couldn't have been good because everything about him is geared toward avoiding the limelight. It's obvious, even in the choice of his instrument. He's not center stage; he's off to the side. He doesn't follow the beat; he sets it. But he's never joined a band because he doesn't want any of this—not the eyes on him or the applause or the expectations.

"I knew I should've stuck with Phoebe," Simone sighs, breaking me out of my Deiss-induced trance. "We'd better go take her picture."

"Who?" I blink with confusion.

"Seriously?" She gestures toward the stage, where the shaggy-haired blond has abandoned his guitar to grind on Phoebe. If they weren't so gorgeous together, it would be obscene. "She's going to want this documented."

"Right." I wrench my phone out of my back pocket and nod at her before plunging into the crowd.

We have to go all the way to the front to get shots that are unobstructed by flying hands or blurred by people bumping into us. Simone videos Phoebe for a moment before spinning her phone around and snapping selfies with the band in the background. During the time it's taken us to get close, the stiffness has seeped from Deiss's body. I can't take my eyes off him. He's lost in the music, his fingers sliding over the strings like they're playing him instead of the other way around. Without thinking, I turn the phone toward him, zooming in on his face.

The blue of his eyes glitter with satisfaction. His teeth tug at his lower lip in concentration. He looks utterly lost in the moment, as if the audience has ceased to exist. And despite the fact that he's ignored me all night, this new form of inaccessibility makes me yearn to run onstage and plead for entry into whatever world it is he's disappeared into.

"I don't know who he is," the girl next to me sighs, "but I know I'm in love with him."

Her phone is also in the air, homed in on Deiss. And it takes everything in me to resist the urge to inform her that I do know who he is. And it's beginning to feel like, as inconvenient as it might be, I know exactly how she feels.

CHAPTER 18

*D*eiss steps off the stage as soon as the song ends, easing through the crowd with the Thunderbird cradled protectively against his chest. I scurry behind him, cringing at the attention he receives on his way out. He shrugs it off, but his back has gone tense again. I can tell by the panic on Mia's and Booker's faces that they've spotted it, too.

He doesn't speak until we all get to the top of the stairs. This floor of the store is empty, which strikes me as a mistake. Surely either Booker or Mia should've stayed up here to make sure nobody walked out with any of the merchandise.

"So, nobody was watching the door?" Deiss snaps, echoing my thoughts.

"I've been up here all night," Mia says. Her usual belligerence has been replaced by an anxiousness that makes her look near tears. If I thought I'd enjoy seeing her taken down a peg, it's now clear I was wrong. "I just came down to bring the Thunderbird."

"If I wanted to play," Deiss says, "I would've brought the Thunderbird down myself."

"Are you mad?" Booker's voice goes high with disbelief.

"Let's see. You just left my store unlocked and unattended, then forced me onstage despite the fact that I've been very clear about my lack of desire to perform. So, yes, Booker." Deiss smiles tightly. "I'm mad."

"But you never get mad," Booker says. "You didn't even get mad when—"

I clear my throat, cutting him off before he can remind Deiss that not only has he ruined an expensive instrument while working, but he was also drunk when it happened. This is not the kind of story anyone should ever remind their boss about, but it's next-level stupid to do it now.

Booker sputters and holds up his hands as if the only way he's capable of shutting up is to physically block his words from exiting.

"When what?" Deiss prompts.

The quiet brightness of the upstairs is eerie after the party-like atmosphere downstairs. The stillness highlights our tension.

"You didn't even get mad," I say quickly, "when that woman tried to bargain over your Sex Pistols album."

Deiss squints at me.

"The nerve of that woman!" Booker grabs onto my effort, stomping his foot dramatically against the floor. "There were only twenty-five thousand copies of that album ever made!"

Deiss's arms cross over his chest.

"We're sorry!" Mia blurts out, her voice quivering. "We thought it would be a good way to advertise the guitar."

"*She* wanted to advertise the guitar," Booker says. "I just wanted an excuse to go onstage."

"So, why didn't you play with the band?" Deiss asks. "Why did you have to volunteer me?"

"All right, here's the deal. *This*," Booker says, sweeping his hand from his hair down across the rest of his body, "is what they call *a look*. It's been carefully cultivated to convey that I work in a music store and—here's the important part—that I work here *because* I am a man who loves music. It's a lot less sad than being an unemployed actor who works behind a counter. But it's just a role I'm playing. Like acting practice, right? I don't know how to play any instruments. I don't even particularly like music. I mean, who listens to it, really? Do they not have a TV? Has their internet been cut off?"

"Stop," I plead, holding up my hands in case it's true and Booker's words only can be contained by physical efforts. It's unnecessary, though, because Deiss surprises us all by letting out a bark of laughter.

"Can your next role be a cleaner?" Deiss asks. "Because I don't want to stick around until the show's over."

"No problem, boss," Mia says quickly, despite the fact that Deiss was clearly speaking to Booker. "We'll take care of this."

"Yes," Booker says, showing the first signs of wisdom he's displayed since we got upstairs. "We're on top of it. You go."

Deiss nods and backs up, his hand reaching for my arm.

"Will you come with me?" His eyes are strangely vulnerable when they meet mine. "Or do you want to catch the end?"

"Of course I'm coming with you," I say without hesitation.

My answer makes him smile, and my heart begins to hammer when he slides his fingers through mine.

"You're going to let her get out of cleaning?" Booker asks.

Deiss's head snaps toward him, but before he can say anything, Mia beats him to it.

"He's told you a hundred times that Olivia doesn't work

here!" Her hands fist at her sides. "She's here because he wants her here, and now they want to leave. So, shut your stupid mouth, get your lazy ass downstairs, and find something to clean!"

Booker tucks tail, fleeing down the stairs.

"I'm really sorry about the ambush," Mia says to Deiss miserably. "I swear to you it'll never happen again."

"It's fine." Deiss steps toward her without letting go of my hand and pulls her into a one-armed hug. "Consider it forgotten."

We leave her looking slightly less despairing, the door dinging cheerfully at our exit. Outside, the wind has kicked up, bringing a chill to the air. The street has that Saturday night energy, peppered with groups and couples talking to each other instead of hiding beneath their headphones. The car lights bounce off the storefront windows.

"Are you all right?" I ask as we start down the sidewalk.

He shrugs. "It's fine."

It's the same thing he's just said to Mia, only this time, I don't believe him.

"It's not fine," I say firmly. "You just had an audience full of camera phones pointed at you, after you spent ten years in hiding to regain your anonymity. At the very least, it's unfortunate."

He looks at me in surprise, but his mouth curls in a way that makes me think I've said the right thing.

"It *is* unfortunate, isn't it?" he says, letting out a wry laugh. "Realistically, I know those videos and pictures will get buried beneath everything else that happened tonight. Very few will make it onto social media, and the only people who will care about those are the posters themselves. But still. It doesn't feel good. If just one wrong person recognizes me, I go from being the guy who owns a record shop to a feature in one of those *Where are they now?* articles."

"Is that really so bad?" I'm not just trying to relieve his anxiety. It's a genuine question. "It's not like you're living in your parents' basement, selling bathtub gin to the neighborhood kids. You own your own successful business."

"Why would I be embarrassed of bathtub gin, Liv?" He fakes a grin, clearly hoping to distract me. "Sure, it doesn't sound like the most sanitary of beverages, but there's something to be said for creating something with your own hands."

"I'm being serious, Deiss."

"I know." He sighs. "But do you really think I'm worried about being perceived as unsuccessful? The problem isn't where I ended up. It's the way people treat you when they've grown up with you onscreen. There's this insatiable curiosity about you, this feeling of ownership. The studio still forwards Brendan Davis's fan mail to me. Obviously, there's less of it these days. But you'd be surprised. Since *Family Fun* became available on streaming, there's a whole new audience of people who want me to say *Funnnn-tastic!* on their voicemail or give them a ride on my private jet."

"You know," I say, feigning coquettishness, "I'm supposed to go back home to Brantley tomorrow for tea with my mother. A private jet would come in handy. It's a *very* long drive."

He rolls his eyes, but his relief at the change in tone is obvious. "No longer than my drive to and from the airport when you crashed our South Africa trip."

"If I wasn't wanted on that trip, there's should've been a lot less guilt thrown my way when I said I couldn't go."

He grins. "We were bluffing."

"Your mistake then."

"You know I don't have a private jet, right?"

I grin back at him. "Why do you think I haven't tried to seduce you?"

"Haven't you?" He leans toward me, blue eyes smoldering. "I thought that was the point of that outfit."

My breath hitches in my throat at his implication. And then it swooshes out as another thought hits me. "Lucas Deiss! Is that why you've been avoiding me all night?"

He drops my hand. "No," he says unconvincingly.

I stop in the middle of the sidewalk, just steps away from the entrance to his building. My hands fly to my hips, even though I really want to use them to cover my face.

"It *is*." If I could melt into a puddle of my own embarrassment, my entire body would be seeping into the cracks in the concrete. How obvious have I been? Could they all see it in my face yesterday at lunch? Is that why he left with Zoe last night?

"I told you to go with Zoe," I remind him, latching onto the one thing I can use in my defense. "I basically sent you off to sleep with someone else. And now you have the nerve to assume I'm trying to seduce you?"

"I didn't mean it like that." Deiss takes a step back, looking toward the door like he's considering making a run for it.

A couple of weeks ago, I would've done the same, taken a cool step back. A woman should never close the distance with a man. It gives him the power. The smarter move is to retreat, triggering the man's biological urge to chase. It's not a couple of weeks ago, though, and I'm done doing what I'm supposed to do.

I move forward, pressing into his personal space.

"You did mean it like that," I say, my embarrassment transforming into something that feels a lot like anger. How dare he act like I have no more pride than to throw myself at a man who doesn't want me? I'm Olivia June Bakersfield. I'm the freaking Ice Queen. "And it *is* why you avoided me all night."

"I was—"

I hold up my hand to stop him, but we're standing so close that it ends up pressing against his chest. "Don't you dare say you were busy."

"I *was* busy." His assertion may be true, but it lacks conviction. He looks down at my hand like he wants to remove it, and I feel another surge of something that could either be embarrassment or anger. The difference between the two has blurred, melted together in the heat they've burned into my skin.

"I'd never try to seduce you," I say sharply. "You're my friend."

"I know." He holds his hands up at his sides as if in surrender, but I spot something in his face, some effort at restraint that makes me suspect he's merely placating me.

"You're not my type," I insist.

"I know."

He's going distant. It's as clear as if I were watching him evaporate into a blur of smoke right in front of me. His eyelids lower the slightest bit, like a curtain sliding closed. The tilt of his chin and the slight curl of his mouth turn him into a mildly amused spectator instead of a participant. The change is infuriating.

"You were holding my hand," I say in an accusatory tone. "The whole way here, you were holding my hand. Why would you do that if you were so concerned I couldn't keep them off of you?"

"You're being ridiculous," he says dispassionately.

"Excuse me?" My fingers curl into his shirt, and I'm not sure if they're forming a fist or attempting to hold onto him so he doesn't disappear entirely. He can't disappear into a puff of smoke before I get the opportunity to eviscerate him. "I'm being *ridiculous*?"

"Yes." Deiss's eyes flash with annoyance, and suddenly he's back, solid and present and leaning toward me with an intensity that throws me completely off balance. "Look at yourself. What are you doing right now?"

My head jerks back like I've been slapped. It feels like I have been.

"Right," I say. "Because how dare I have a genuine response! Silly Liv. Don't I know that I'm supposed to be too cool for that? I'm making everything uncomfortable. What a ridiculous way to behave."

"I wasn't talking about your behavior." He looks so annoyed that I want to stomp on his foot just to give him something real to be annoyed by. "I was talking about the way you've added two and two together and gotten eight. Have a little self-awareness, Olivia. Do you really think I was worried about *you* coming on to *me*? Every man in that place would've set themselves on fire for just five minutes of attention from you."

"They . . ." I trail off as my brain struggles to compute his implication. With a gentle tug, he pulls his shirt free of my grip.

"Every man," I say, my voice coming out embarrassingly breathy, "except you."

His eyes burn into mine, even as he eases back another step.

"I wanted to drag you under the stairs," he says, his tone deceivingly casual, "and peel that leather off you with my teeth."

My pulse speeds up, galloping like a wild horse, as the image explodes in my mind. *His glorious mouth descending on my body. Rough stubble against soft skin. The silky slip of his tongue easing the sting.* I feel every sensation like a tidal wave rolling through my belly.

"Why are you standing out here?" The words come from a distance behind us, jerking me from the fantasy like a splash of cold water. "Are we locked out?"

Deiss's eyes have move past me. With a sharp inhale, I'm able to turn around, feigning the same indifference he's so infuriatingly mastered. Our friends are coming down the sidewalk, Phoebe riding on Mac's back with her arms slung around his neck. Simone is the one who's asked the question, but Mac repeats it like a fact.

"You locked yourselves out?" He laughs, and Phoebe bites his ear. "Dibs on breaking a window!"

"But Liv lives with you now," Simone says. "She's the one who keeps us from doing stupid things like that."

"We aren't locked out," Deiss says easily. "We just didn't go inside yet because we were fighting."

I gasp and widen my eyes, but he shrugs off my reproach.

"What did you do?" Phoebe and Mac ask the question in unison, only her accusation is directed at Deiss, while Mac's clearly speaking to me. Simone, to my shock, has also turned to me in accusation.

My stomach tightens. People always take sides, even when they don't have all the facts. Even when they're supposed to be your friends.

"Liv is pissed at me," Deiss says, "because I didn't give that drummer her number when he asked me for it."

"What is with those guys?" Mac asks before I can properly absorb Deiss's words. His voice cracks with outrage. "That stupid surfer guitarist was all over Phoebe, too."

"But Seth was smart enough to approach me directly," Phoebe says smugly. She turns to me, leaning her cheek against Mac's head. "We're going out next week. Do you want to make it a double date with you and Brad?"

"You're into that drummer?" Simone asks before I've answered Phoebe. "He was gorgeous."

I don't answer her, either. All I can do is stare at Deiss. "He really asked for my number? And you wouldn't give it to him?"

"I believe that's been established." He doesn't bother pretending to be apologetic.

I scowl but am unable to argue without giving us both away. "You had no right to make that decision for me."

"What decision?" Deiss meets my eyes. "You can date whoever you want. I just don't have to facilitate it."

"But the real question is: Why didn't you want to?" Phoebe says.

"Maybe Liv shouldn't be dating someone she's about to work with," Simone says. "I could take her place on a double date with you, Phoebe."

"Guys in bands are the worst," Mac declares emphatically.

"They are not," Phoebe says. "Musicians are sexy."

Mac feigns vomiting, and Deiss uses the distraction to avoid answering for himself. Instead, he pulls out his keys and heads toward the door.

"Have you ever felt a guitar player's fingers?" Mac asks as we follow Deiss inside. "They're eighty percent callus. You make out with that guy, and you're going to go home feeling like you've gotten it on with sandpaper."

"All I know is that Seth earns a living off those fingers," Phoebe says. "He must know how to use them."

"Five minutes of nipple play," Mac says, "and those nubs of

yours will be dust. Nobody will ever be able to tell you're cold again."

"Never refer to my nipples as nubs again," Phoebe says.

"Jujubes?" Mac asks.

Phoebe bites her lip, and I know she's trying not to laugh. I wish I felt the same. I can barely concentrate. My mind is a whirlwind, but my body is hyper-honed in on the straight line of Deiss's back. I can feel him like our skin is touching, as if there were invisible tentacles protruding off him, sparking electricity everywhere they land.

"Nope," Phoebe says once she's gotten control of herself. "New plan: just don't refer to my nipples at all."

"But I love them," Mac says. "They're my fourth favorite part of your body."

Simone groans as Deiss turns on the light and we all head toward the living area. "Please don't list them in order."

"Number one," Mac says, his eyes brightening.

Phoebe clamps a hand over his mouth and promptly shrieks. "He licked me," she says, sliding off his back and falling onto the recliner.

Mac squeezes in with her, then takes the whole thing over, shifting her onto his lap. "Of course I did. If something touches your mouth, you lick it. It's just a basic survival instinct. It's how you figure out if something is poisonous."

Simone side-eyes me as she passes, and I fake a smile, but Deiss's words keep looping through my brain. *I wanted to drag you under the stairs and peel that leather off you with my teeth.* They heat my skin with the friction of their path. Covertly, I watch Deiss saunter into the kitchen. Without making a conscious decision, I follow him.

"You think you find out if something is poisonous by licking it?" Simone asks, settling on the opposite end of the couch from them. "*That's* your survival instinct?"

"Well, I'm not a king," Mac says, as if Simone is the stupid one. "I don't have a cupbearer to do it for me."

Deiss doesn't turn around when I come up behind him. He continues staring into the open liquor cabinet like there's a story written across the labels. I know he's aware of my presence, though. I can see it in the tightening of his back.

"You never answered Phoebe's question." I say the words quietly, even though Simone and Phoebe and Mac are clearly too busy arguing about poison to pay attention to us.

"I didn't," he says without turning around.

"Why didn't you want to give Brad my number?" I ease up to the counter next to him.

He's silent for long enough that I start to think he's not going to answer at all.

"Do you really want to do this?" he says finally. He turns toward me, leaning against the counter so the open cabinet is behind his head. His eyes are hooded when they meet mine. "Let's just hang out with our friends. We'll wake up tomorrow and have coffee and walk to the shop, and everything will stay exactly like it's been."

I nod instinctively, because it's obvious that's what he wants me to do, and because it does sound good. I want everything to stay exactly like it's been, because somehow, despite the fact that everything I've ever worked for has disappeared, these last two weeks have been the happiest of my life.

The problem is those words. *I wanted to drag you under the stairs and peel that leather off you with my teeth.* I can't unhear them, no matter how badly I might want to.

"No," I say firmly. "I want to do this."

He sighs and lifts his hand, rubbing it over his head.

"Deiss," I say sharply. "Why?"

His eyes smolder, and he gives a decisive nod. "Because I didn't want to."

Without taking his eyes off mine, he drops his hand from his head to the expanse of leather beneath my chest. Leaving a trail of fire, it slips down, until it hits the bare skin of my waist just above my pants. I gasp at the feel of his fingertips against my skin, but I stop breathing entirely when he slides two fingers beneath the button of my jeans and curls them toward him, tugging me forward.

He tilts his head down as our bodies meet, his scruffy chin tickling my cheek as he breathes into my ear. His hand slips around to the small of my back, his thumb stroking a trail along the exposed skin. Goose bumps prickle over my body.

"I got jealous," he whispers, "because he's allowed to want you and I'm not."

He moves his hands to either side of my waist, and then, as quickly as he's pulled me in, he shifts me away from him. My legs have gone all wobbly, and I lean against the counter, blinking at him with a combination of wonder and sharp, visceral lust.

"What do you say, guys?" He calls out the words, his eyes still smoldering like he's considering bending me over the counter and having his way with me. "Are we drinking whiskey tonight? Or gin?"

CHAPTER 19

*D*espite pouring a seemingly endless stream of drinks for our friends, Deiss never refills his own. I know because I can't stop watching him. I'm riveted by the way his mouth moves when he talks, captivated by the way it wraps around his glass when he finally takes a sip. If he were a show, I'd be a binge-watcher, memorizing every movement and line.

My obsession is embarrassing, but I can't help myself. It's like a spotlight on him has been turned up, drowning out the rest of the room. Thankfully, I've spent a lifetime putting on a performance of my own. I watch him through my peripheral vision, only allowing myself direct focus when he speaks. If I can't distract myself from him, at least I'm capable of pretending to.

It's our friends that make it possible. We're playing Jenga on the coffee table, Mac and Phoebe sprawled across the floor in front of the TV. Simone sits cross-legged on the couch next to me, serving as a buffer between me and Deiss, who snagged the chair on the other side of her, as far from me as possible. As if a human barrier weren't enough, Deiss has moved from sitting on the chair to leaning against the back of it, adding an extra layer of leather between us.

Two weeks. There's something utterly ridiculous about the fact that I've managed to go ten years without giving into Deiss's magnetism. Now, two weeks into a promise not to touch him, all I can think about is how much I want him. There must be a book for this. *The Practice of Deprogramming Your Desire, or How to Appreciate the Qualities of a Friend without Translating Those into Reasons to Love Him.* As far as titles go, it's a little wordy.

"Not that one," Phoebe says as Mac's finger inches toward a block that is clearly a stabilizer of the tower.

"It has to be this one," Mac says seriously. "I don't choose which pieces to pull out. They choose me."

"You lose every time." Simone shakes her head and slumps back against the couch, her eyes droopy. I've seen her dancing on a table after popping open her second bottle of champagne, but two glasses of whiskey have knocked her out. "If the pieces are guiding you, you should find out why they hate you."

"I don't lose," Mac says. "I always pick the last piece, which means I play the longest of any of you. I'm the last man standing."

I grin, and without thinking, I look to Deiss, expecting him to share my amusement. It's a mistake he's made as well, and for the first time since we were in the kitchen, our eyes meet. I freeze, and his brow furrows. *Look away.* The command pings in my mind, a well-worn principle for maintaining the upper hand. It's a sign of weakness to be the one left staring, but I can't help myself. I'm trapped in the glow of his spotlight.

A clatter startles me out of my haze, and I jerk toward the

rubble of what used to be the Jenga tower. Phoebe and Simone are laughing, and Mac's hand is still midair, a stunned look on his face. I fake a laugh and look back to Deiss, but he's already turned away and is headed toward the kitchen.

"To the last man standing," Phoebe says, tilting her cup toward Mac.

He beams at her as we all give half-hearted cheers.

"I'm going to bed," Deiss calls behind him as he disappears into his room. "Simone, there's a blanket in the closet if you want to stay on the couch."

I tense, trying to keep my face blank.

"You're not going to offer to share your bed?" Simone's words slur together slightly. "It's the gentlemanly thing to do."

"I've never claimed to be a gentleman," he says.

Simone pouts for a second before stretching her long legs out. "I wasn't going to stay anyway. Crashing on sofas is for children."

Relief slips through me like a light breeze, but it dissipates when Deiss comes back out of his room with earbuds dangling from his hand. There's a look on his face that I don't like. A smile that's a little too sweet to be real.

"I assume you have a Disney playlist on your phone?" he asks Simone, squeezing in with her on the couch.

She nods, rightfully looking a little stunned by his thoughtfulness.

Gently, Deiss places the earbuds in her ears, one at a time. "There. Now you can play it as loudly as you want."

My stomach sinks. I know as well as he does that she can't resist such a gesture. She'd sleep on his floor now if he asked her to. Any chance of talking to him tonight has just gone out the window, which I'm certain was the point.

"Liv, can you please get me a pillow and blanket?" Simone says, confirming Deiss's success.

I grab the blanket and a spare pillow off my futon and toss them to her before following Phoebe and Mac to the door, managing not to look at Deiss. I wish I'd never agreed to live here. The problem isn't Deiss. It's too much exposure to him.

Even back in college, I was never with him in such undiluted quantities as I have been over the last two weeks. In my experience, most people begin to grate when you're around them too much. Unfortunately for both of us, that hasn't been the case with Deiss. I was better off not knowing he gets strangely sweet when he's tired or that he tends to look after everyone but in such a subtle way they rarely seem to realize it's happening. Maybe he's right to use Simone as a buffer between us. Maybe I need to build a buffer of my own.

"Text me when you get home safely," I say to Phoebe as Mac drags her out the door. Hopefully, the walk home will sober them up. "And if you talk to Seth, tell him I'm in for a double date with Brad."

"What?" Simone groans from the couch, and I roll my eyes, more to keep them from flicking toward Deiss than in response to Simone. "I wanted to go!"

Phoebe laughs, holding the door open with her foot. "Just last week you were celebrating how many followers you have on Friendsta. Surely some of those fans must be single guys who want to date you."

Simone lifts up, her face appearing over the back of the couch. "Everyone wants to date me. That's not the point."

"What is the point?"

"I want to go on a double date with you and two guys who are members of the same band," Simone says.

"I'll work on Harry Styles and Niall Horan for next month," Phoebe says.

Mac groans, but Simone's eyes widen at the idea.

"Deal," she says with a satisfied smile.

I lie in the dark, silently reminding myself of all the reasons it's a bad idea to attempt to talk to Deiss right now. There are so many, but there's one obvious reason that should make it the easiest: *he doesn't want me to.* I can't push myself on someone else. I can't be so needy.

So there's no explanation for sliding out of bed as quietly as a thief in the night. I sneak on tiptoes past Simone, asleep on the couch. The moonlight shines on her open mouth, glinting off the strand of drool that connects her face to the throw pillow. I shiver, a draft from the open window causing my bare legs to prickle. This is a mistake, but I can't help myself. I try to convince myself I just want to clear things up, but it's not quite believable.

My eyes flicker back to Simone when I knock, and again when Deiss eases his door open, his brow furrowed. I press on the door to open it further and slide inside, but he holds it firm, blocking the gap with his body. I choke at the sight of his bare chest and the two etched lines that arrow into his boxers, then cough awkwardly to cover it.

"I couldn't sleep until I apologized for making things weird. I'm sorry about tonight," I whisper. "Can we just forget it happened?"

His eyes drop to the cleavage popping out beneath my tank top, then dip down past my tiny shorts to my bare legs. Slowly, he drags them back up.

"No problem." He curves a hand around the back of my neck, causing my heart to pound in my chest. Warm fingers tug me forward, and his head dips toward mine, hovering just long enough for me to pray he won't stop. Then his mouth is on mine, shocking me like an electrical current.

I feel his kiss in every part of my body, my skin lights up with it. His scruff scrapes at my chin and his lips burn against mine. He tastes like safaris and concerts and all the things I'm only just discovering are right for me. My arms go around him, nails digging into his bare skin when he deepens the kiss. A moan escapes my throat, and he pulls away, leaving me blinking up at him in dismay.

"We should probably forget that happened, too," he whispers, his hand still in my hair.

My heart falls into the pit of my stomach.

"*Or . . .*" He grins dangerously.

"Or." I exhale the word determinedly. I don't care how bad it might be for our friendship or my heart. It all pales in comparison to the heat of his mouth on mine. "I vote for *or.*"

I barely get through the words before he's lifting me up, wrapping my legs around his waist, and dragging me into his room. Our mouths collide as he pushes the door shut with my back. His hands grip my butt as mine explore the muscles in his back, and he doesn't stop kissing me, not even when he carries me across the room to his bed.

We make out like horny teenagers—stroking and licking and grinding until I'm panting—maybe because this moment has been building since we were. But then his head dips and doesn't come back up. That gorgeous mouth of his keeps traveling downward, tracing a trail of fire the length of my body. The world goes hazy as he slips the straps of my tank top down, nudging it down with his chin as his tongue swirls patterns against my breasts. Scruff scrapes the tender skin, and the silk of a million tiny licks soothes it. I hum my pleasure, feeling like an instrument he's bringing to life.

The sound in my throat gets louder still as his mouth drops lower, skimming my waist, then my thighs, then up again. He breathes heat against the flimsy material that covers me, and I groan with aching desire. My hands go to his head, tugging him forward like they've forgotten a lifetime's training of holding back, and I'm rewarded by his fingers sweeping the layers aside and sliding his tongue in their place. My body disappears, leaving behind a sea of sensations. I am a sky filled with pulsing stars.

I buck beneath the building pressure, whimpering when he pauses long enough to pull my panties and shorts down the length of my legs. He stills at the sound, settling on his knees down by my ankles. I lift my head to look at him but catch sight of myself instead, splayed out ridiculously, my tank top around my waist like a deflated inner tube. My legs are spread apart like I'm awaiting an exam.

Embarrassment hits like a bucket of ice water, dumping over me and extinguishing all of my heat. Never have I so completely lost myself. Years of performing perfunctorily in gorgeous, expensive lingerie, and the one time it really matters, I've shown up like a pig at the county fair. I cringe and tug my knees together.

"Don't," Deiss says in an unrecognizably gruff voice.

I look up apprehensively and discover his eyes scanning the length of me. They're dark beneath his furrowed brow, filled with reverence like he's discovered a priceless piece of art. His fingers run across my leg in featherlight strokes before he lifts it to press a kiss into my ankle. He's shadowed in the weak light that leaks through the window, dark and mysterious and impossibly gorgeous.

"I like you like this," he says, "all wild."

Slowly, he slips my tank top down the length of me, his fingers stroking my hips as they pass and then my thighs. He works his way slowly back up, kissing every inch of me until the world goes hazy again and I'm too filled with pleasure to think of anything but the feel of his mouth against my skin. When his body covers mine completely, he cups his hand beneath my head like I'm something precious.

We kiss slowly this time, not like two people hurrying to make up for the past but two people desperate to hold onto the moment. I press into him, warm and delicious. And when he finally pushes inside me, I feel just as out of control as I did when we started, but in an entirely new way.

"You're amazing," he murmurs into my shoulder after we've collapsed, intertwined and satiated, onto our backs. "I've always been so in awe of you."

"No, you haven't." I don't want his pillow talk. It just reminds me this is normal for him. While I've never experienced anything like what we just did, I have to assume it's always like that for him. After all, he *is* the one who provided the experience.

"I have." He strokes my arm lightly, tracing a line from my wrist to elbow. "I used to study you all the time back in school, trying to figure out how you could be so untouched by it all. Everyone else on campus was copying each other, playing their roles as college kids, but you knew exactly who you wanted to be."

"But I didn't." The confession slips out, even though I'd like nothing more than to let myself believe the pretty picture he's painted. "I only knew who I was *supposed* to be. I was trying to be perfect."

"You think I don't understand that?" He leans over and presses a soft kiss against my shoulder. "I've been watching you for eleven years. But you're missing the point. I was in awe that you tried so hard *for yourself*. You weren't attempting to be perfect so the other girls would be jealous or the boys would want you. You hardly seemed to notice what anyone thought of you at all. It was your own standards that dictated who you wanted to be, and I thought that was inspiring."

"But you told me to get off the treadmill," I argue.

"I suggested it because nobody needs you to be perfect, including you." The corner of his mouth quirks up. "But I certainly didn't tell you to do anything. I'd never dream of telling Olivia Bakersfield how to behave."

I laugh, but my chest swells in a way that's almost painful. This feels like yet another twist I'm unprepared for. First, the closeness. Then, the lust. Now . . . whatever this is. Deiss's appreciation of me? His ability to see me so clearly and translate my flaws into something I can be proud of?

It's overwhelming. Even my mother, the one person who's always known me, chose to pretty me up with makeup so she could view me through a filter. I don't know how to face someone who's managed to see through it all. Even if Deiss does seem to appreciate what he's uncovered.

"I like you." I blurt the words out, flinching as they hit the air. *Never* ever *show your cards first*. "I don't know what any of this means to you, but I do. I like you so much."

"Typical." He shakes his head, a smile stretching across his face.

"*Typical?*" I whisper, my cheeks burning with embarrassment. "I swear on my life, Lucas Deiss, if you're trying to say every woman falls for you the moment you take her to bed, I'm going to push you out the window."

"That sounds fair," he says, still grinning. "But actually, I meant it was typical that you say you *like* me, when just the other day I told you I love you."

His words hit like a bomb. One filled with glitter, stunning me and filling my vision with sparkly flecks. He can't mean it, can he? Not like that. My eyes narrow as I take in his amusement.

"You didn't want me, though," I say. "Not like that."

"I've always wanted you. But it was more important to keep you as a friend. I was scared of losing you."

"And now?"

"I'm still scared," he admits. "Phoebe was right to make the pact, you know. This could ruin everything."

My heart races. "Should we stop?"

"Definitely." Deiss slides me toward him by my waist and captures my mouth with his, kissing me until I'm pressing eagerly into him.

Breathless, I pull back. "Are we going to?"

He slays me with a grin. "Not a chance."

CHAPTER 20

I don't know how we forget that Simone spent the night. Maybe we're distracted by the strangeness of waking up in each other's arms. Or maybe the real distraction is that it feels so right. My pulse quickens as Deiss takes me in, studying me in the watery morning light like he's unsure how I've appeared in his bed. I feel a flair of panic that this is it, that this is where we pretend last night was a drunken mistake. But then he smiles and traces a trail of kisses across my shoulder before pulling me under him.

"I'm not making your coffee," I say firmly, after we've made love and he's trailing me toward the door, his arms wrapped around my waist. "I only make it for you because you always order dinner, but you haven't provided that service in two days."

"Please make me coffee," he murmurs into my ear. "I promise to take you out tonight to make up for the neglect."

A smile stretches across my face, so wide I'm grateful he can't see it. Deiss might not mean it like a date, but I can't help hearing it that way. I can't believe I've slept with someone without having first established a committed relationship. But there's been a lot of stuff over the last couple of weeks that I can't believe I've done, and while I can't exactly claim it's worked out, it *has* been exciting.

"I can't." Somehow, I manage to wipe the disappointment from my words. I do have plans, so I'm not *trying* to play hard to get, but there's no reason to let him know I'd love to fashion myself into a backpack and dangle from his shoulders for the rest of my life. "I'm going home for tea with my mom."

Behind me, he's quiet. I reach for the doorknob.

"Can I come?" He says the words softly, but they still make me freeze. "I'd love to meet her."

My fingers fall from the metal knob and I turn slowly to face him, his grip around my waist keeping him close enough that I have to look up into his face. My bare legs brush against the jeans he's pulled on from the floor. "You want to meet my mom?"

Deiss nods.

"It's a three-hour drive," I say. "Each way."

"We can make small talk," he says with a lazy grin. "We're good at that."

This time, I can't hide my smile.

"Okay," I say, spinning back toward the door before he can be blinded by its full wattage. "We'll go on a road trip."

I swing the door open, and the smile falls from my face. Simone is sitting on the far end of the couch, facing us. Her legs are triangled under her arms like she's trying to ride out an earthquake. Her face is one hundred percent betrayal. It makes my stomach clench, and I pull loose from Deiss's grip, dismayed that we've managed to be so careless. Nervously, I wrap my arms across my chest, wishing I was wearing a baggy t-shirt instead of this skimpy tank top. At least I'm wearing a shirt, though. Deiss's chest is guiltily bare.

"I knew it," Simone says bitterly. "I knew you were sleeping together. You started in St. Lulia, didn't you?"

"Good morning, Simone," Deiss says. "I hope you slept well."

"We all made a pact. Do you remember that?" Simone's scorching eyes follow him as he walks into the kitchen to start the coffee. "You vowed to care more about us and our friendships than your restless dick."

"Okay," I say, cringing. "Let's take this down a notch."

"You know this is going to destroy her, right?" Simone barrels on, ignoring me. All her attention is focused firmly on Deiss. "She's not like us. She doesn't have anyone else. When you drop her, she's going to end up all alone."

Her words cut sharply, making me want to speak up again. But what would I say? We all know she's right. I haven't joined an organized sisterhood or cultivated a following on Friendsta. I haven't bonded with bands or built a home for fellow music lovers. I've kept my world small. Cubicle-sized.

"So, I won't drop her," Deiss says coolly.

"Please." Simone sneers. "Your longest romantic relationship was with a Blow Pop."

"Okay," I say again. "This is not productive. Deiss, can I please get a moment alone with Simone?"

"Yeah." Deiss looks uncertainly between the two of us like he doesn't like the idea of leaving me alone with one of my oldest friends. Finally, he rubs his hand over the back of his head. "I need to go to the shop anyway and make sure they cleaned everything up after the concert. We'll head to Brantley when you're done."

Without waiting for his coffee, he grabs a t-shirt from his room, pulling it over his head as he passes between us. I catch an expression of longing on Simone's face that mirrors my own. The loft goes painfully quiet when the door clicks shut behind him, and I feel a pang of distress at the loss of him and how quickly our romantic morning has deteriorated.

"I'm really sorry," I say, filling the silence. "I'm sorry that we upset you, and that we broke the pact, and I'm especially sorry if you had to hear anything we might've done while we were in his room."

"*We.*" Simone scoffs. "Do you have any idea how stupid you sound right now?"

I flinch at the jab. "I didn't mean—"

"You can't really think you two are some kind of couple," she says, interrupting me. "He's Lucas Deiss. You've witnessed firsthand how many women he's been through. Never once has he referred to one of them as his girlfriend. How delusional are you?"

"Don't talk to me like that." My face is a perfect mask, my eyes dammed against the well of tears that have rushed to the surface. "I know you're annoyed that I broke the pact, but that's no excuse."

"I didn't . . ." Her breathing flares, and she presses the back of her hands to her eyes. Her tone softens. "It's just not fair."

And there it is.

My stomach sinks. I was hoping her pride would keep her from addressing it. After all, it's not like she's been holding out for Lucas Deiss all these years. She even got engaged once, although she dumped the poor sap when her eye was turned by a waiter in Paris. Still, it can't feel good to discover Deiss's interest could be piqued—just by me instead of her.

"You're a beautiful, confident, smart, and funny woman," I say. "Our roles could easily have been reversed."

Her eyes swell before they narrow, turning dark with rage. "Are you seriously giving me some kind of pep talk? Do you think I'm *jealous* of you?"

If words could take physical form, hers would be poisoned steel arrows.

"No," I say quickly. "Of course not."

"I wasn't saying that it wasn't fair that I'm not with a man who has the staying power of a Popsicle in the Sahara. Obviously. I just meant that it's not fair that the rest of us are going to have to pick up the pieces when this thing falls apart. Have you even thought about that, Olivia? Have you considered the rest of us even for a moment?"

I feel a flare of rage of my own. Or maybe it's just panic. "Have *you* considered the fact that it might not fall apart?"

She snickers meanly. "The boy has his charms, but let's face it, Deiss doesn't care about anyone but himself."

"He does," I insist. "He cares about his friends. He loves us."

"If he loved you," she says simply, "he never would've fucked you."

Her words feel like a punch in the chest, but it's the expression on her face that really guts me. It's full of confidence, but also pity. For me and my naivete.

"You're wrong." My words come out weakly.

She shakes her head, so certain it makes me want to cry. "I'm not. And you know it. You're better than this, Liv. Convincing yourself he's someone he's not. That's the kind of stuff other girls do. Desperate, needy girls. Not girls like us."

"I know exactly who Deiss is," I say firmly. But devastation swirls in my belly. Simone has no idea how accurately she's described my mother. "And so do you. If he's so bad, why have you been friends with him for all these years?"

"He isn't bad," Simone says. "He just doesn't care about anything."

I shake my head, unable to argue.

"It's not his fault," Simone says with a sigh. "He can't value anything because he's never had to work for anything."

"And you have?" I exhale the words, shaky and fierce. "Do you have any idea how stupid *you* sound right now? Your idea of a job is drinking champagne while snapping selfies. Deiss had an actual career before he could even walk. I'm pretty sure work isn't a measurement *you* want to use to judge character."

Simone goes still. For a moment, I'm scared my blow has landed too heavy, but there's something about the sharpening of her eyes. She doesn't look hurt. She looks like a snake, sizing up her prey before she strikes.

"A career for babies . . ." Her eyes spark with malevolence.

My stomach clenches at the realization of what I've just done. It could've just been a throwaway comment if Simone didn't know him so well. If only Deiss had offered some lies instead of being so belligerently tight-lipped about his past, maybe Simone wouldn't have leapt at this tiny scrap of detail.

"I didn't mean an actual career," I lie desperately.

"Of course you did." Her eyes are hard. "So, what is it, Liv? What did Deiss do that was so private he could only tell you? It had to have been something where he felt exposed. Something public."

She studies me.

"It was on the trip, right?" She nods at the way my back stiffens. "That's when all the little inside jokes started."

"Please just stop," I plead. "This isn't about Deiss. You're worried about me, remember? How I'm being so desperate and naive and am going to break up the whole group when I get my heart broken?"

"He would've teased you with it." She tilts her head like I haven't spoken. "He likes it when he manages to knock you off balance. So, the question is, what has he said lately that's strange? Something childish."

"Simone," I say, my voice going sharp. "That's enough."

But it's too late. I see the dawn of realization as it lights up her eyes.

"Funnn-tastic," she drawls, clearly pleased with herself.

I open my mouth to lie. But Deiss's face flashes through my mind, his eyes filled with hurt. My stomach turns violently. Spinning on one heel, I reach for the sink, bending over it as I choke. But nothing comes out, even though my entire body is insisting I need to vomit.

Apparently, regret isn't so easy to expel.

I'm in the bathroom, putting on the final touches of my makeup when I hear the door to the loft open and Deiss calls out my name.

"In here," I say. Nervously, I fluff my hair. If my appearance is my armor, I've gone full metal suit. I don't know if I'm hoping my contrived beauty will distract Deiss when I confess how I've betrayed his secret or if I just want him to remember me at my best when he ends whatever this is. I just know that the moment Simone left, I started working on myself with a determination that suggested I could turn myself into an entirely different person if I simply tried hard enough.

Simone said she wouldn't tell. It took a lot of begging, but in the end, she promised she'd keep Deiss's secret for his sake, rather than mine. For one glorious moment, I let myself believe that meant I could keep my mouth shut as well. I know I can't, though. Not if we're about to spend most of the day together. There's omission and then there's lying. The effort required to talk around something so huge for hours can only be categorized as the latter.

"I'll just jump in the shower, and then we can go," he yells.

"I know you didn't get much sleep last night," I call out, smoothing down the lavender skirt he's already seen three times in the last two weeks. I wish I weren't bothered by wearing this again, but I'd feel so much more confident in something new. "You really don't have to come with me if you'd rather take a nap."

I listen for his response, venturing out of the bathroom when none comes. He's leaning against the counter, staring at the couch. His gaze shifts toward me as my heels click against the hardwood floor.

"Simone talked you out of it then," he says with a pained smile. It's such an unnatural expression on him, I want to kiss it away. "I was worried she might."

"Of course she didn't." I stop a few feet away from him, my guilt preventing me from getting too close.

"She tried, though," Deiss says.

"She thinks you'll get tired of me."

"I won't," he says firmly. "It's been eleven years and I haven't yet, have I?"

I smile, and he reaches for me, pulling me into his arms and pressing a kiss against my mouth.

"You look beautiful," he says, releasing me. "Give me five minutes and we'll get on the road."

I nod, staring after him as he disappears into his bedroom. My mother is going to love him. She's going to take one look at him and be utterly charmed. Blue eyes have always been her weakness.

I wish I didn't suspect I'm about to bring another man into her life who won't be coming back.

THEN

The three of us girls were propped up on loungers, the glittering infinity pool stretched out in front of us. Fruity daiquiris that we were finally old enough to order crowded the tiny tables. Mac and Deiss had taken the chairs that bookended us and were tossing a little squeeze ball back and forth over the top of us. Droplets of water flew off of it as it passed, hitting my legs and skidding across the bronzing oil. The coldness of it felt good against my hot skin, but I joined in with the other girls' protests and attempts to slap it out of the air, knowing we were just making the guys want to do it more.

"I'm just saying it's weird," Mac insisted. "If chicken nuggets are just mushed-up chicken parts formed into a nugget, why wouldn't they shape it like a chicken?"

"Because nobody wants to look at a chicken's face while they're eating its corpse," Phoebe said.

"Sure we do," Mac said. "We're savage creatures. Haven't you ever watched a kid eat an animal cookie? They start with the head, every time."

"He has a point," Deiss said, popping the ball up over his head before swinging it back toward Mac.

"Does he, though?" Simone shifted her sunglasses, causing her bikini top to slip a little lower. She'd untied the straps, supposedly to prevent tan lines. As she was reaching down to prevent her breast from fully popping out, her hand froze.

"Crap," she muttered.

"What?" Mac looked around like a dog shaking off a bath.

"Hi, Simone," two girls said in unison, sauntering up in bikinis paired with three-inch wedges.

"Happy birthday," the taller one said in a sickly sweet voice. "It looks like you're having fun."

"Which is so nice," the other one continued, "because everyone at the sorority house was really sad for you that you had to do something with your mother instead of celebrating with us."

"Yeah." If she was ruffled, Simone did a remarkable job of hiding it. "It kind of sucks, but things ended early with my mom because she had to go to the doctor. She's worried one of her breast implants might've slipped. I don't want to be mean, but it looks like the left one got hungry and ate the right one."

I squinted at her because I knew for a fact that Simone's mother had been happily traipsing around Geneva for the last month.

"Really?" The tall one looked delighted by the gossip. "That's awful."

"So gross," the other one said with a gleeful grin.

Deiss chucked the ball over their heads and into the pool, causing Mac to yelp with confusion.

"Beat you to it," Deiss said.

Without hesitation, Mac lunged up and toward the pool.

Deiss did the same, turning at the edge and winking at Simone before cannonballing into the water. A wave exploded over the edge, causing the girls to shriek and scurry out of the line of fire.

"Thanks for the birthday wishes," Simone called after them, before laughing gratefully and blowing a kiss at Deiss for getting rid of them.

I shook my head at Simone's pinkened cheeks. If Deiss didn't stop with his heroics, she was going to start following him around again for sure. He was usually more careful not to lead her on. But only last week he carried her all the way across campus after the Neon Party left her too drunk to walk on her own. She was beginning to gaze at him like her knight in somewhat tarnished armor.

"Your mom is okay, right?" I asked, partly to distract her and partly from concern.

"Oh, yeah," Simone said breezily. "She's never even had her breasts done. I just didn't want them going back and riling the whole house up, telling them I blew them off to hang out with you guys again."

"So, you gave them something better to gossip about?"

Simone tapped her finger to her nose. "Exactly."

"Impressive," Phoebe said. "I think it worked."

"Hopefully," Simone said. "But whatever. I'm not that worried about it. They're sisters."

"Meaning they have to love you?" I asked.

"Meaning they're like family," Simone said. "And you don't choose your family. You only get to choose your friends."

o you think Simone told Phoebe and Mac?" Deiss asks the question as I pull out, almost causing me to panic-crash into the car in front of me.

"What?" I grip the wheel with both hands, too nervous to look at him. Simone must have already texted him, probably addressing him sarcastically as Brendan Davis. I should've known she would. She was still so angry when she left. She tried to hide it, but everything about her was stretched tight, like a rubber band ready to snap.

Maybe this isn't terrible, though. Deiss knows what I've done, but he still chose to come with me. Maybe he understands that I was trying to defend him. Maybe he *wants* to forgive me.

"She swore she wouldn't," I say, stopping the car and turning toward him. "But that doesn't make it okay. I'm so sorry that I betrayed your trust, Deiss."

Deiss chuckles wryly, reaching for a lock of my hair and fingering the end of it. "I'm pretty sure she figured out anything you might've told her the moment she saw you coming out of my bedroom, but I hate that you think I'm trying to keep you a secret, because I'm not. I'll tell everyone myself right now if that's what you want. I just don't want them making us feel guilty."

"Right," I parrot idiotically. My mind races, circling the fact that he doesn't know what I've done before returning gleefully to *us*. Simone laughed at me for using the same term, but it had come so naturally. This isn't something that has happened overnight. Things have been shifting between us for weeks. I've just been too scared to acknowledge it.

"It would just be nice to have one day to enjoy this by ourselves without anyone ruining it, you know?" His hand leaves my hair and trails down my arm, making my skin tingle in its wake.

"I *do* know." Unfortunately, what I know is that *I'm* the one who's at the most danger of ruining it. But Deiss is right. Is it really so much to ask that we get one day to simply enjoy this, without the intrusion of the real world?

"We should turn off our phones," I say impulsively, pushing down my guilt.

"Yeah?"

"Let's leave it all behind for a day," I say. "Just you and me, on the road again."

Like my first day in South Africa, we roll the windows down and wind rushes through the car, making me feel like I'm flying. Unlike that road trip, we never get around to the questions in the small talk game. I've always assumed too much one-on-one time with someone would leave you with no words left to say. But with Deiss, the opposite proves true.

We chat about the shows we've watched and the crazy things Booker and Mia have said. But we also talk about the concert and how many people my flyers brought in. Deiss tells me he regrets serving alcohol to such a large crowd, mainly because there were too many strangers there, but also because he pulled in good revenue without having to resort to it. And I admit that I'm scared to create the flyers for the next band. If they don't draw in as many people, I'll know it wasn't me but the band that brought the crowd.

LA's buildings fall away, replaced by dry, rocky hills and, eventually, the crooked, jutting branches of Joshua trees. The sun burns brighter the farther we travel, and Deiss puts on a pair of sunglasses he finds in the glove compartment. Unsurprisingly, they look unreasonably good on him, and I make the decision to never wear them again. I can't be on the wrong side of a who-wore-it-better contest. It's unacceptable.

"I miss Cat Stevens," I admit after Deiss tells me he used to have a dog. He's been trying to describe his old pet as well as the pictures would if we were allowed to use our phones, and there's something about his attention to detail that's squeezed at my heart. "I know it's silly—he barely tolerated me when he was living rent-free in my home—but I still look for him every time we walk to the shop, like he's out there somewhere, searching for me."

"Maybe we should go check some shelters and see if he's shown up at one of them."

"I've emailed them all his picture," I say, keeping my eyes firmly on the road in case the stinging in them means they're getting red. We've just entered my hometown, which doesn't help with my nostalgia.

"You have?"

I nod. "Surprisingly, not one of them ignored my message.

They were nice enough to respond, but none of them have seen him."

"I'm sorry, Liv."

"It's fine. He's probably happier being on his own."

"Maybe," he says agreeably. "I mean, I'm sure he misses you, but I've heard cats can be . . ."

"What?" I glance over, amused to discover how awkward he suddenly looks. "Skittish? Haughty?"

"Assholes." He lifts his hands unapologetically. "*I* didn't say it."

"You repeated it, though," I say with a laugh. "So, what? You hate cats?"

"I don't hate them," he says. "They just remind me of squirrels."

"And what's your issue with squirrels?"

He grimaces. "They remind me of rats."

"Gross."

"Exactly."

On impulse, I turn toward the animal shelter in town. "I can change your mind."

"About cats? Trust me, you can't," he says confidently. "But if you want to try your powers of persuasion, feel free. If it helps, I can tell you that I'm easily influenced by naked body parts."

"Do you really think I'm going to use my breasts to convince you to like cats?"

"Maybe?" He grins. "I like to imagine breasts could appear at any time. It gets me out the door in the morning."

I roll my eyes, and ten minutes later, we're sitting on a concrete floor, surrounded by cats. The air reeks of litter and pet food, and the meows compete with the barking of dogs from another room. A tiny white kitten is nestled against Deiss's chest, but it's the big ball of fur batting at the hem of my skirt that's making us laugh.

"Have you wronged her in some way we're unaware of?" Deiss asks. "Is that why she's waging war on you?"

"I think your friends were right," I say. "She's just an asshole."

"You love her, though." He pets the kitten, his hand larger than her body, and I can tell by the softness in his eyes that he feels it, too.

"I do." I scoop the feral little cat up and press my cheek into her fur. For a moment, she stills, but then she wriggles around and swipes at my face. "She's perfect."

"I'm naming mine Baby Squirrel," he says, peering down at the tiny purring creature. "What are you naming yours?"

"Fluff Daddy." I put her in my lap, and she tries to bite my finger. "If she were nicer, I'd do as she asked and call her F. Diddy."

"Way to assert your dominance," Deiss says. "It's important to establish yourself as the alpha."

"I think that's dogs." I squint at him. "And if that's what you're trying to do, you'll need to try a lot harder. Baby Squirrel clearly has you wrapped around her little finger."

"I can't help it," he says. "She's so sweet."

I resist the urge to inform him I was just thinking the same thing about him.

Deiss slips his hand around mine as we leave the car for the house I grew up in. It's early afternoon. Clouds have slipped over the sun, turning the day hazy. The lawn is more dirt than grass, and the grass that has survived is brittle and yellowed. The house itself seems smaller than I remember it, likely because I'm viewing it through Deiss's eyes. Before we reach the door, my mom throws it open, cheerleader-clapping with excitement. She looks beautiful, if a little faded. Her makeup has been so well applied, I can't see the lines around her eyes until she's close enough to wrap her arms around me.

She smells like expensive perfume and cheap bleach, a dead giveaway she's deep-cleaned the house in anticipation of my arrival. And I didn't even tell her Deiss was coming. I wonder how she'd feel if she knew I was sleeping on a fold-out couch in his guest room. Hopefully, she'd focus on the fact that I have someone who cares about me enough to take me in rather than fretting over how far off course my life has gone. I'll never know, though, because Deiss has agreed it's my secret to tell. It's not that I think she'd judge me for being robbed. I'm just not ready to discuss it.

"I know you!" My mom lets go of me and hugs Deiss with the same enthusiasm she's just released me from. "You're Liv's friend Lucas. I've seen so many pictures of you!"

"Assembled in her room?" Deiss winks cheekily at me over her shoulder. "Like a shrine?"

"She's talking about magazines," I say. "You know how they'll attach a picture to all those *Watch Out for This Kind of Guy* articles? Your face is usually at the top of them."

"She's teasing, of course," Mom says. "In pictures she texts to show me how much fun she's having in the big city. With you and Phoebe—such great style that one has! And that beautiful boy Mac, and that glamour girl with all the pretty jewelry. So many years, and it's always the same little group."

"We would've made other friends if we could," Deiss says. "But nobody else can tolerate us."

"It's a miracle we found each other," I say with a smirk over Mom's murmured disagreement.

Deiss's eyes soften, and he shifts toward me, his hand pressing into mine for a sweet moment. "That's what I've been trying to tell you."

CHAPTER 22

*O*ver the next few hours, my mom rewrites our history so thoroughly that I find myself wondering if she's gone into a coma without informing me, emerging with someone else's memories. I keep waiting for her to develop an accent. She's charming and bubbly, entertaining Deiss with story after story. Unfortunately, almost every word out of her mouth is a lie.

"I had to get rid of the big house when Liv left," she says as she passes the plate of cookies she's removed from their single-serve wrappers. "It was too empty all on my own. I needed something cozier."

I reach under the table and squeeze her knee, hoping to wake her back to reality. What does she expect Deiss to think when he sees my old bedroom? The stuffed closets and postered walls are dead giveaways that a child grew up there. Is she going to make up a new sibling next? In this alternate reality, did I have a twin who ran away to join the circus?

She squeezes my hand back, like we're doing some weird, under-the-table high five.

I take an unladylike gulp of tea and cough as it goes down wrong.

"Marriage just isn't for me," she says later as she tops Deiss's cup for what must be the fifth time. "I like my freedom too much to settle down. But I'm sure you've seen that same trait in Livvie there. She's had even more proposals than me."

"Is that so?" Deiss leans back in his chair, grinning lazily at me.

"She hasn't told you?" Mom says before I can answer *No, that is certainly* not *so.* "Oh, yes. It's going to take a very special man to lock this one down."

"Like an officer of the law?" I ask. "A psychiatrist? I honestly don't know what we're talking about here."

"Don't be so humble, Liv," Mom says. "Lucas needs to know what a catch you are."

"Yes," Deiss says. "Please tell me where all these men before me went wrong so I can avoid following in their footsteps."

"I wish I could," I mumble, not wanting to embarrass Mom by calling out her fibs, but also unwilling to enhance them.

I expect things to get easier when we settle onto the couch and she drags out the photo albums. Unlike most people, I have no documentation of my awkward phases. My mom has always wanted me to look my best. I can't think of a single photo she's ever taken of me that didn't involve multiple re-shoots and angle changes. Even when I was a baby, she'd smudge a little lipstick on my cheeks to give me a healthy glow.

I reach for the remote and turn on the TV, earning an annoyed look from her. The man in the libido-enhancer commercial doesn't fit the classy scene she's attempting to create. Still, my mom soldiers on, raising her voice over the list of potential side effects. *Rash. Trouble breathing. Blindness.*

She squints as she reads the captions over the photos aloud, unwilling to put on the readers that "make her look old." Deiss plays his part by cooing over my cuteness. But Mom veers wildly off script as she recounts the stories behind the photos.

"This is our old cat, Boots," Mom says, showing Deiss a picture of the cat she discarded in an effort to keep Paul. "We had to give him up when I broke things off with an old boyfriend. Paul was so devastated to lose Liv that it only seemed right to let him take the cat. I thought having a little four-legged friend might keep him going."

I almost snort aloud. Paul had no problem *going*. He practically ran out the door, slamming it shut behind him.

"That was very generous of you," Deiss says. "It must have been difficult to give up your cat."

It was. I feel a flare of anger at what we did to keep that rigid, judgmental man in our lives. Maybe it's my mom's revisionist history that's knocked me out of familiar patterns, because I've never before let myself be angry at the loss of Boots. It's been too easy to focus on pity for my mom, how sad it is that nothing she ever does is enough.

But Boots would've stayed with her. Plus, I loved him. How was it fair to take away something *I* loved in a desperate attempt to hold onto yet another man *she* claimed to love?

I stand up, mumbling something about the bathroom, and slip out of the room. The hallway is dim and dreary. A blown-up photograph of my mother in the tiara she got for winning Miss Brantley smiles at me from behind its frame.

"You should've chosen us over them," I whisper to her younger self.

I don't know if I'm referring to Boots and me or her and me. Either option works. I wish I could say it to her face, but the timing would be cruel. She's so desperate to impress Deiss. And there's nothing she loves more than this part of meeting someone, when she can sparkle brightly enough to distract—when they haven't yet discovered the flaws that lie beneath that perfect facade.

I walk into my bedroom, easing the door closed behind me. The pink duvet has been fluffed, and the dresser gleams from its recent dusting. The pictures tacked on the wall are messy, though, and they're all mine. I smile at the one where my hair is stuck to my head like I've been slimed. Beside me, Phoebe has a trickle of yellow from her hair down to her chin. Next to her, Deiss is holding up one of the eggs we'd meant to unleash on Simone's ex but had ended up hurling at each other instead.

I pull it down, wanting something tangible to replace the ones I lost when my condo got emptied out. My smile falls when I discover the picture beneath it. It's me before prom, wearing the dress Cara Jenkins had lent me. We both knew she'd shoplifted it, even though I pretended to believe her when she said she'd bought it on sale and couldn't return it. I shouldn't have been so surprised when she helped herself to my college money. In the picture, I look beautiful and exuberant, as if I hadn't spent the day terrified that the girls who had been bullying me for years were going to pull some kind of bucket-of-blood *Carrie* prank on me.

"Liv?" Deiss raps lightly on the door.

I open it, and he presses in, moving me backward with his body. A naughty smile plays at his lips, making my stomach swoop. I'm not sure I'll ever get used to Lucas Deiss looking at me like he wants to consume me.

"Is the history lesson over?" I ask, feeling the backs of my legs press against my bed.

"The visual portion of it, at least." He slides his arms around my waist. "I think there are more stories in the tank."

I want to snort at his use of the word *stories*. He has no idea just how fictional the things he's just heard are. His stormy blue eyes dip to my mouth as his hand slips up my back. My stomach lurches again. He's so *much*. So self-assured and dynamic and *real*. He doesn't belong in this house of lies. Neither of us do.

"We should go," I say, nudging him back.

"Yeah?" His arms drop immediately, leaving my back cold.

"It's a long drive," I say.

He nods and turns, heading for the door. Regret surges through me for disappointing him, but he smooths a balm over it when he reaches back for my hand. Our fingers wrap around each other, and I focus on the feeling of connection as I say goodbye to my mom and thank her for the tea.

In the car, I struggle to stay present, but the day has gotten under my skin. The anger about Boots. The lies. The worry that my refusal to tell Deiss that I've given away his secret makes me just like my mom. To compensate for my distraction, I smile and agree with everything he says.

"Yes," I say, my grin widening to something Joker-esque, "she's the best."

"It is," I say, bobbing my head enthusiastically. "The house is always that clean."

We drive for a while, Deiss tapping his thumb against the passenger door to the beat of the radio. It's a pop station, playing songs Mia would never allow in his shop. In front of us, the sun is turning orange, splintering off into pinks as it seeps into the ground.

"Pull over," Deiss says unexpectedly.

Surprised at Deiss's tone, I swerve at the command, coming to a stop on the shoulder of the road without giving any thought to our safety. Loose gravel crunches under my tires.

Before I can ask what's going on, Deiss slides his hand behind my neck, pulling me toward him. He covers my mouth with his, kissing me so soundly that I soon find my fingers in his hair, pulling him even closer. The day disappears, leaving only a quickly fogging windshield and the silk of his tongue tangling with mine. His scruff scrapes my chin in a way that feels deliciously savage. Too soon, he pulls back, leaving me panting as he presses his lips against my forehead.

"I did something wrong today," he murmurs against the skin. "Tell me what it was so that I don't do it again."

I pull back in surprise, the spot where his lips were becoming immediately chilled in their absence. Cars zip past us, sending whooshing sounds through the windows.

"You didn't do anything wrong," I say. "You were great."

His eyes search mine. "But something upset you."

There's something about the way he states it so simply, recognizing the truth without demanding explanation, that makes my heart swell.

"She was lying to you," I blurt out. "All of it was lies."

"Okay," he says.

His pause is an unspoken reassurance that he doesn't need any details I'm not ready to share. It provokes an urge to spill everything. He's entrusted me with his past, despite the fact that he clearly shouldn't have. Can't I do the same?

"I wasn't raised in some charmed mansion where fathers were in abundance," I say, speaking too quickly. "We couldn't get any of them to stick around, and we were so poor we didn't even *have* a home at one point. The kids at school made fun of me for being smelly because we had no place to shower, and it took years of making myself up to perfection to feel confident again. And even as I'm saying this, I want to die because it's so much more information than anyone needs to know, but at least it's real. And I wanted this day to be real, Deiss. I hate that I had the opportunity to share a part of myself with you and instead I let my mom paint over reality until nothing of me was even left."

"You're here now," Deiss says, brushing his thumb over my cheek. "And I see you. I see you more clearly than I ever have. And I've never admired you more."

I feel my face flush, and I avert my gaze. If I were a stronger person, I'd admit that it wasn't just my mom who was concealing the truth. I'd admit what happened this morning with Simone and trust him to keep looking at me the way he is now. But I'm not a stronger person. I'm desperate to keep him for as long as possible.

"Admiration feels like an overreaction," I say, waving it away. I don't pull back, though. I lean closer instead, kissing him lightly. "I didn't mean to make it sound all bad, you know. I mean, the homeless stuff was rough. But my mom and I were in it together. We were partners, as weird as that might sound. It's always been us against the world."

"That's nice," Deiss says. "I've always been close to my parents, too, but they were definitely more parents than friends. Maybe they figured, with all the cast members of *Family Fun*, I had enough adult friends and I'd be better off getting their guidance instead."

"That makes sense." A semi blows by, making the car rattle. I reach for the wheel. "We probably shouldn't keep sitting here."

Deiss nods, and I start down the shoulder, pulling into the road when an opportunity arises.

"I'm sorry about those kids in your school," Deiss says a few minutes later. "That must've made a horrible situation feel even harder."

"It really did."

"Not to compare our situations, because I'm sure yours was infinitely more difficult, but it's interesting that there was a period of time where you didn't have a home and I couldn't leave mine."

I smile at the observation. "Sometimes I think you and I are opposite sides of the same coin."

"I like that," he says. "It means you're stuck with me."

CHAPTER 23

*I*t's strange how odd it feels walking to Studio Sounds the next morning alone, especially considering how *un*-strange waking up in bed next to Deiss felt. Despite how late we got home last night, he insisted we stick to our jogging schedule. And he managed to add a burst of between-the-sheets cardio to our workout session, which is why we ran late enough that he had to head to work while I stayed back to shower and blow-dry my hair.

Truth be told, I can't complain. Even the best yoga class I've ever taken didn't deliver the rush of endorphins today's efforts provided. Nor did it stretch out my thighs quite so thoroughly. I consider stopping for a muffin or something to reward him for a job well done, but I'm not sure what flavor applies to sexual prowess. Banana nut? I cringe at the thought and steer decidedly clear of the coffee shop.

The bell dings over my head as I enter the store, and the customer browsing in the far corner looks up with a grimace. He's communing with the late, great Jim Morrison, and I've had the audacity to interrupt their special moment. I tilt my head apologetically, ignoring Mia's smirk from behind the counter.

"He was waiting by the door when I showed up," she mutters as I slide behind her. "You should've seen the fit he threw when I made him stay out there until we officially opened."

"Maybe he's having a bad day and this is his happy place." I spot Deiss through the windows of his office, but he's on the phone with his back to me.

"He's a loiterer. Apparently, we have two of you now." She gives me a pointed look before returning her attention to the iPad in front of her.

"Wouldn't I qualify more as a squatter?" I ask easily, firing up the laptop. "I do more sitting than loitering."

"As long as you understand that both are equally unwelcome."

"Understood."

Mia jabs aggressively at the screen in front of her as I pull up my portfolio to show Zoe when she arrives. We have a loosely scheduled meeting today to talk about me doing some work with her, and I'm excited but nervous. Today marks one week since I met with the bank. I should be hearing from them soon with either wonderful news or a terrible, life-changing refusal to restore my account. I'm hoping having some more lucrative work lined up with Zoe will take some pressure off the waiting. As it is, I flinch every time my phone buzzes. I'd almost rather know nothing than hear from them. At least then I can maintain hope.

"It's probably an insurance issue," Mia mutters the words. "You being around here all the time like this."

"Because you're tempted to injure me?" I singsong, flying too high from my morning with Deiss to take offense.

A grin tugs at her lips, making me beam, even though I know it's the idea of injuring me that's pleased her. "You're annoying when you're happy," she says.

"Haven't you always found me annoying?"

"This is worse."

"You should see me on sugar," I say. "You'd really hate me then."

"What are you? A toddler?"

I laugh, but she goes back to jabbing at the iPad before I respond. I nod silently and get back to work. A few minutes later, a bag of Skittles flies across the counter and lands on my forearm, causing me to look up in surprise.

"I keep an emergency stash under the counter," Mia says without lifting her eyes from the iPad. "Let's see what you've got."

"Are you looking for an excuse to stab me?"

"Maybe." Her eyes sparkle.

I laugh and open the bag, pouring a few candies into my hand before sliding it toward her. Before she can refuse them, I drop my eyes back to my laptop. It takes a few minutes, but I hear the crinkling of the bag as she picks it up.

Deiss comes out of his office around noon, surprising me by leaning against the counter and kissing me lightly.

"I'm going to order lunch," he says as I sneak a look at Mia. If she's surprised by the romantic shift between us, it doesn't show. Of course, it's possible she's still treading carefully with Deiss after her mistake at the concert. "What are you in the mood for?"

"Luigi's," she says quickly.

"Mmm." Deiss rubs his hands together. "That fried burrata."

"It's the best." Mia fully smiles for the first time since I've known her, and I'm delighted to discover she has teeth that aren't filed into points. They're small and adorably crooked. "I take that back. It's second only to the lasagna fritta."

"Maybe," Deiss says. "I don't know. I think it's too close to call."

"You agreed with me last time," she says, her argument lacking venom.

"Last time," he says, "I was sneaking drinks from Booker's cup."

"Gross." Mia covers her mouth, and I could swear she's hiding another smile. "So was I. No wonder he kept running downstairs to refill it."

"We'll need a sober rematch," Deiss says. "And another opinion in case of a tie. What do you think, Liv? Are you good with ordering Luigi's?"

I nod, struck silent. For years, I nibbled on a nutrition bar at my desk during lunch. I knew my life was lonely, but I'm not sure I ever allowed myself to admit how sad it really was. Sitting here, I want to be involved in these kinds of conversations for as long as possible. I want to continue to create new designs to the tune of good music instead of the incessant ringing of business lines. I want to look up from my laptop and see these colorful walls and bins full of artistic album covers instead of being trapped in a cubicle. And I want to have been included long enough that I can argue over my favorites—with Deiss, but also with Mia or Booker.

And I think I might be able to have it.

Every day, my place here feels more normal. Despite Mia's

constant grumbling about my presence, she's clearly getting used to it. When I'm around, she no longer waits for Deiss to show up to take a bathroom break. Instead, she asks me to watch the store for her. This morning, she didn't even check the register when she came back to make sure I didn't steal anything. Granted, it's entirely possible there's no money in there to take. Still. I felt flattered.

"She'll want the eggplant roll-ups," Mia says.

I scrunch my nose and look to Deiss. "Will I?"

He shrugs. "I haven't had them. You can pull up the menu online if you want, especially if you want your own entrée instead of splitting the other two with us. Mia is an expert orderer, though. If you want to, you can trust her."

"Yeah." Mia smirks, contrary to her words. "Trust me."

"Fine," I say, turning back to Deiss. "Add an order of eggplant roll-ups, please, and we'll all share."

My effort to catch Mia's reaction is thwarted by the ding of a bell. I watch her eyes narrow at whoever has just come through the door. I lean forward to look around Deiss and discover Zoe strolling down the middle aisle like it's a catwalk. She's wearing a skirt that stops so high on her thighs it makes mine look like a family-sized tent. My stomach sinks, even though I know I should be glad she's showed up.

You like her, I remind myself silently. *You liked her when you first met her, and you definitely like her now that she wants to share her business with you.*

It's all true. But what's also true is the fact that *she* likes Deiss. I can see it in the way her eyes light up at the sight of him.

"I made it," Zoe says, throwing up her arms like she's on a game show and we're applauding for her. She drops her arm to slide it through Deiss's and simpers up at him. "Did you miss me?"

Without thinking, I look to Mia. Our eyes meet, matching grimaces tugging at our mouths. Quickly, I grab hold of myself, wiping my expression clean of disdain and turning back to Zoe. Not that it matters. She's one hundred percent focused on Deiss.

"Desperately," he says dryly.

"Don't tease." Her giggle contradicts her words, begging him to give her more. "Can you sneak out of here after I'm done with Liz?"

"It's Liv," I say, wishing it was appropriate to tug her arm free of Deiss's and deposit it firmly back against her side, where it might assist in preventing her skirt from sliding even farther up.

"You're really going to work with someone who can't remember your name?" Mia whispers as I wave at her to shut up. "It's three letters."

"I'm so bad." Zoe laughs and bends over to hug me, which seems more like an excuse to brush against Deiss and show off her cleavage than any real effort to apologize. "I promise, that was the absolute last time."

"I'm going to put in the order," Deiss says, backing up. "Zoe, do you want anything from Luigi's?"

"Aren't you just the sweetest thing." Zoe backs off me like an invisible string is connecting her to Deiss. "I couldn't, though. Gotta shed that vacation weight. You can make it up to me with a drink later, though."

The corner of Deiss's mouth curls with amusement, and I feel the first genuine shot of jealousy rip through me. "I'm supposed to make it up to you that you turned down my offer of food?"

"You offered," she says with a flirtatious cock of an eyebrow, "the wrong thing. I'm giving you the chance to make me a better offer."

He laughs, and a second shot of jealousy roars through me. I'm being ridiculous, though. Lucas Deiss is not my boyfriend. Maybe he really does care about me and has no intention of phasing me out after a couple of weeks like he seems to do with everyone else. That still doesn't change the fact that we've been romantic for less than forty-eight hours. If he knew how protective I was feeling, he'd be horrified. I force my face to go blank.

"As much as I appreciate your generosity," he says, "I'm going to have to pass."

I'm concentrating so hard on keeping my face blank, I don't even allow myself to blink.

"Too many customers?" Zoe makes a show of scanning the mostly empty store.

"I'm seeing someone," Deiss says, glancing at me.

He looks taken aback when he catches sight of my mannequin-esque face, but I'm locked down too tight to allow expression. Do I want him telling my future partner (boss?) that I'm the person he's referring to? Do I want him to see that I'm elated by the implication that I'm the only one he's "seeing"? My mask of indifference feels safest.

"Just one?" Zoe laughs and waves a dismissive hand. She's like a stage performer, all broad gestures and commanding of space. "I figured a guy like you had at least a few of us on the line."

"Just the one," Deiss says. "She's a cat person, though, so it takes up a lot of my time trying to convert her."

"Didn't you also tell me she's way out of your league?" I ask innocently. "I imagine you'll also be expending quite a bit of time on coming up with lavish dates to impress her."

A grin spreads across his face. "I let her paint my bedroom. And I took her for fancy cocktails on Sebastian's tab. What more could a woman want?"

"You made her do manual labor for you and had another man buy her drinks?" I flutter my hand over my heart. "Consider me misinformed. Sounds like you've nailed it."

Deiss's chin tilts up, and his grin widens. "Fine. I'll take her out for a proper date then. Dinner and a show. French food, I suppose, and a film with subtitles. Do you think she'd like that?"

"I think she'd prefer to eat takeout on your couch," I say. "Preferably while watching reality TV."

"She would?" He slides past Zoe and tucks his thumb under my mouth, lifting it so he can kiss me. "That sounds perfect to me. But we'll have time for both."

I nod happily, buzzing too much to consider Zoe's presence. Then I remember, and my eyes slide guiltily toward her. She twirls a lock of hair in a way that looks deliberately nonchalant.

"Oops," she says with a shrug when our eyes meet. "I didn't realize."

"It's new," I say apologetically.

"Clearly," she says. "I asked Deiss about you the other night, but he insisted you were just friends. It's cute that you guys figured it out."

"We're cute," Deiss says with a wink.

"Are you hoping the fried burrata is going to order itself?" Mia asks irritably. "Because it's not."

"Noted." Deiss holds up his phone and pivots on one heel, then strolls toward his office.

I stare after him for a second, wishing I could follow. It seems easier than staying here with Zoe.

"Maybe we should get out of here," I say, turning toward her.

"Your boyfriend is getting you lunch," she says with a saccharine smile.

"He's not . . ." I trail off, not sure how to normalize things. "I'm sorry if that was weird. It's still really new between Deiss and me, so I'm not sure either of us knew how to address it."

"What's weird?" Zoe waves a hand and pulls out her laptop, placing it on the counter next to mine. I offer her my stool, and she takes it with a cool smile. "I'm here to see you. Deiss was just a fun distraction, which I'm sure you can relate to. Why else would you choose to work in this rat hole?"

"Excuse me?" Mia leans toward us, her eyes narrowing.

"No offense," Zoe says, clearly intending to give quite a bit of offense. "All these old records. Some mustiness is only natural."

I sniff furtively as Mia's fingers curl like talons against the wood of the counter. All I smell is the aroma of coffee and a hint of my own perfume.

"So," Zoe turns her attention toward me. "I've seen your wine label and flyer, but what else can you show me? Have you done any work on a beauty brand?"

I show her my portfolio, standing beside her and talking through some of the choices I've made. She nods and murmurs like she's listening, but her gaze keeps drifting toward Deiss's office. I glance at Mia, but she's pretending we're no longer here. Between the two of them, I feel like I've disappeared.

"This one's my favorite," I say, pointing Zoe toward a label I created years ago. I always return to it when I find myself doubting my talent.

Zoe pretends to study it, but her fingers tap restlessly

against the counter, offbeat of the song playing through the speakers. The room seems to grow chilly, despite the fact that Booker hasn't yet arrived to mess with the thermostat.

"I'm sorry," Zoe says finally. "This isn't going to work."

I blink through the hit, staying frozen until I feel able to speak normally. "Are you sure? I really think I have a lot to offer."

"I'm sure you do," she says serenely.

I nod, trying not to ask the question. "Is it because I'm with Deiss?"

She rolls her eyes, but I spot the *yes* in them anyway. It's just the tiniest tic, but it's clear as day. She might as well have said it aloud.

"Don't be ridiculous," she says instead. "Do I look like the kind of girl who gets jealous over a man?"

I shake my head because that's what she wants me to do. "Of course not."

"We just have different ideas," she says, snapping her laptop closed as she slides off the stool.

"Of what?" We haven't even talked strategy. She hasn't given me any of her thoughts on the account she wanted help with, much less asked for mine.

She backs away, looking at me pityingly. "Of what constitutes talent."

Spinning on her heel, she turns, sauntering toward the door. She flicks her hair as the bell dings above her, and then she's gone, leaving me stunned and staring.

"Good riddance," Mia mutters.

"No," I say, "it's really not. I needed her. I needed the work."

"You need work," Mia says, "not *her* work. She's basic, and so were her designs. You'll do better without her."

My eyes widen, and Mia holds out her hand like a five-fingered stop sign.

"I respect your art," she says curtly. "That doesn't mean I like you."

But later, when the food arrives, she passes her precious burrata to me before she's even had any. Deiss's eyebrows shoot up in surprise, and I have to pinch myself to keep from giggling with elation at the gesture.

"You were right about the eggplant roll-ups," I say, exchanging them for the burrata.

"Of course I was," she says, stabbing one of them with her fork.

This time I do laugh out loud, as does Deiss. The store seems to brighten, the music from the speakers swells, and I wonder how I ever could've believed the drive here was too long to be worth making.

I've always been willing to drive hours to get home, and that's exactly what this place has turned out to be.

CHAPTER 24

*T*he rest of the week flies by like some kind of beautiful dream. I spend lots of time working on projects at the shop, one that earns the kind of paycheck that makes me blink in disbelief. Deiss takes me on our first proper date to celebrate. I feel strangely nervous when he knocks on the guest room door to "pick me up," but he looks as unruffled as ever. He also looks like a proper sex panther, as Phoebe would say.

The restaurant on the water where he's made a reservation is perfect. It's not until after dinner that we hit a snag.

The club he takes me to is large, with high ceilings and an upper deck that lines the walls, but it feels small. There are too many people, too much movement. The music is obnoxiously loud, and all I can smell is smoky cologne mingling with sweet perfume. The whole scene is uninhibitedness personified.

"What is this?" I gaze around the pulsing dance floor, feeling sweaty just from the proximity of the writhing bodies.

"Salsa night." Deiss loops an arm around my waist and steers me toward the mass of people.

"I can't dance." I have to lean toward his ear so he can hear me.

"I find it hard to believe there's anything in the world Olivia Bakersfield can't do." Deiss pulls me into his chest, pressing one thigh against mine so his step forward prompts my leg to go backward.

His body moves with mine, smoothly guiding me deeper into the fray. Our eyes lock, and the rest of the room disappears. It's hard to imagine this man has been an enigma to me for so many years. There are so many clues I've missed: The glint in his eyes at his pleasure of our dance. The way his gaze slips down, tracing my neck and the curve of my breasts, following the line of my arm to where my hand folds into his. The curl of his lip at what he sees.

Emboldened by his approval, I squeeze my eyes shut for a moment and relax into his lead, allowing my shoulders to loosen and my hips to sway. The moves aren't difficult to pick up, and I slide into them, feeling the beat pulse its way into my blood. And then Deiss spins me, and I remember what it's like to feel loose and carefree.

Hours later, walking down the sidewalk beneath the glowing streetlights, my body is still buzzing. Music echoes in my head, and I squeeze the beats into Deiss's hand. I want to tell him he's amazing, to thank him for making me feel so alive after so many years of being frozen. Instead, I catch sight of beautiful brunette who passes, and I ask him if he slept with Zoe.

I'm shocked when I hear the words leave my mouth. It's an amateur dating move. Not to mention simple self-preservation suggests a person shouldn't search for answers they don't want to hear. I can't take it back, though. It would involve pretending I don't care, and I'm not sure I'm still the kind of person capable of doing that. Especially not with Deiss.

"I was going to," he says quietly. "I intended to sleep with her in St. Lulia, and I also went out with the intention to hook up the night you moved into the loft."

"And?" I don't know why I want details. Deiss certainly doesn't owe them to me, and my stomach is already queasy at the thought of him on the prowl, all sex panther and irresistible. But I seem to be on a roll.

"And I couldn't do it," he says.

A disbelieving grunt sneaks up from my throat. "You forget that I've met Zoe. I'm fully aware that you *could've*."

"No, Liv." Deiss tugs my hand, pulling me into him, then slides his arms around my waist. He drops his forehead to mine so I can see the sincerity in his expression. "I couldn't. Both times, I knew I was only looking for a distraction from you. And it didn't feel right to use a woman like that."

My heart lurches at his implication, and I thread my fingers behind his neck and tug his mouth toward mine to keep myself from asking more questions. They're unnecessary. I don't need Deiss to explain to me why he didn't act on his attraction. I already understand. Just like me, he learned from his past. We learned that people leave when you let them inside. And he wanted me to stay in his life.

My lips meet his, and I kiss him to say I'm hoping for the exact same thing.

"Well, what do you think?" Phoebe snaps her fingers in front of my face, bringing me back from my endless rationalization over the secrets I'm keeping. She still doesn't know that Deiss and I are together, just like Deiss doesn't know that I've betrayed his confidence to Simone.

I blink at her and feel a pang of guilt. *I'll tell her soon*, I reassure myself for the hundredth time. It makes more sense to wait. The longer Deiss and I date, the more excited Phoebe will be for us, and the less it will appear the two of us are having a fling. And giving Simone time to prove she'll keep Deiss's secret also proves it wasn't so bad that I let it slip in the first place. It's best for everyone if I keep my mouth shut for a little while longer.

Even if this is true, it doesn't justify the fact that I haven't told anyone about the meeting I had on Wednesday with the manager of Bears in Captivity. I'm now officially contracted to do all the graphic work for their band. It's great news, the kind of thing you tell your friends immediately.

It's also the kind of guaranteed income that frees me up to move out of Deiss's loft.

The fact that I haven't informed Deiss of this update to my financial status is unjustifiable. He allowed me to stay with him because I truly needed a place to live. I can't take advantage of his generosity by pretending to be needier than I am. And I certainly can't trick him into making me his live-in girlfriend.

I'm going to tell him. Tonight.

"Liv?" Phoebe frowns. She's dressed me up for tonight's concert at Studio Sounds and is beginning to look frustrated by my lack of response to her efforts.

"This is sexy," I say, forcing myself to focus. Pivoting from side to side, I examine myself in front of Phoebe's full-length mirror. Her room looks like a tornado has blown through, littering its path with thrift store treasures.

"Good sexy or bad sexy?" Phoebe tightens the knot of the

men's Zeppelin t-shirt she's tied to reveal my midriff. She claims its largeness offsets the tininess of the shorts she's had me shimmy into. But her logic doesn't work if we tie the shirt up to be smaller.

"I haven't decided," I say.

"Trick question!" She claps her hands together. "There's no such thing as bad sexy."

She puts on a scarlet slip dress and searches the gold-hooked board of jewelry she's mounted on her wall. With a pleased murmur, she ties a velvet choker with dangling gold in the middle around her neck. She pairs it with simple gold studs in her ears.

"See-ola?" She holds her arms up and spins triumphantly. "I look like I forgot to put on the rest of my clothes, and it's *still* not bad sexy."

I concede to her wisdom and bring up her date with the guitarist again. They went out last night, when I was out with Deiss, and I can't decide if she's being cagey because my excuse for not doubling with the drummer was too vague or because she didn't have a good time.

"He was nice, though, right?" I ask as we walk to the record store. If Seth has done anything to upset her, I can't possibly work with his band. I don't care how great of an opportunity it might be.

"He was wonderful. He's just—" She cuts herself off, pointing at the window display in a boutique across the street. "Check out that dress. Isn't it gorgeous?"

"I guess," I say, squinting at it. The shop is closed and dark. The streetlight barely illuminates it enough to see the outline of the window's contents. "What's going on, Phoebes? Are you not telling me something?"

"What?" She slows, blinking at me with feigned confusion. She's making her innocent face. I've seen her use it hundreds of times, for professors and parents and bosses. She can't possibly believe it would work on me.

I reach for her hand. "You can talk to me, you know. If you want to."

She nods but says nothing, and I feel a pang of hurt, knowing her silence doesn't mean there's nothing to be said. I can't push her, though, not when I'm keeping secrets of my own. Still, it stings. She and I have spent more time together in the last few weeks than we have since college. If she's holding things back from me now, I can only assume she's been doing the same for years and I was simply too out of touch to realize it.

"I just wanted to get back," Phoebe blurts out, her hand tensing in mine. "I was having fun with Seth, but I couldn't stop thinking about getting back."

"Back to what?" I stop and turn toward her, but she tugs me forward, not meeting my eyes.

"Mac," she says, her gaze fixed on the Studio Sounds sign in the distance. A bulb on it is has shorted, and it's begun to flicker erratically. "It always comes back to Mac."

My breath catches at her confession, and my heart floods with conflicting emotions for her. Mac loves her—it's so obvious. But does he love her enough?

"You—"

She cuts me off. "I can't talk about it. If I do, it will be real, and everything will change. Because I can't keep spending all of my time with him if you make me admit that it's preventing me from moving on."

"But what if he—"

She cuts me off again. "He broke up with me once. How could I ever trust he wouldn't do it again?"

"I don't think he'd—"

"Liv." She says my name so plaintively, I break off, despite my determination to finally complete a sentence.

"Seth *did* have a bit of a sheepdog quality," I say, giving in.

"Right?" She exhales a relieved laugh and squeezes my hand. "I kept wanting to chuck a bread roll from the basket, just to see if he'd run and fetch it."

Like last week, Studio Sounds is teeming with bodies. Unlike last week, Deiss is upstairs, mingling with the concertgoers. I spot him the moment I walk in, despite the throng of people between us. He's leaning against a wall, his head tilted back as he listens to someone in the group around him. In a crowd of restless energy, his stillness stands out. Anyone walking in would know immediately this is his store. Or they'd assume he's the guy they came to see onstage. I can't take my eyes off him.

We push our way inside, and Phoebe squeals when Mac appears from nowhere and lifts her off the ground. Deiss looks up, and his smile flashes white against the darkness of his stubble. I grin back, my stomach fluttering.

"Isn't that sweet," Simone says from behind me.

My back tightens, and I turn slowly to face her. It's a bizarre reaction given she's one of my oldest, dearest friends.

"Hi, Simone," I say, attempting to move past it. I can't let this come between us. Even if I have broken the pact, I still believe in the motivation behind it.

"I assume that's still going on then?" She gestures toward Deiss, and I nod. "A whole week. It must be love."

"Practically soul mates." I match her sardonic tone, but my cheeks heat at the sentiment, betraying me.

"Oh, Liv." The anger seeps from her face, and for a moment, she looks like the Simone I've always known. When she speaks again, her voice is pitying. "Please don't do this to yourself."

"I'm not doing anything," I say unconvincingly. "It was a joke."

"You have another week." She doesn't say it meanly. Her hand reaches for my arm consolingly. "Two, tops. You've known him for as long as I have. You must have noticed the pattern."

"My aunt has a shark pattern for cross-stitch." Mac turns around, spinning Phoebe with him. He shuffles closer, pushing Phoebe forward, his arms wrapped around her waist. "She's going to put it on a pillow and give it to me for Christmas."

"Like a throw pillow?" I ask, grateful for the interruption.

"I guess," Mac says. "She just said pillow."

"You know you can't have cross-stitched decor in your apartment, right?" Phoebe twists to look up at him. "Girls are going to assume you live with your grandmother and run for the door."

"Sharks are the best," Mac says, looking flummoxed. "You like them, right? You said you did when we were looking for them in Africa."

Phoebe's eyes soften. "Yeah, they're pretty cool."

"Then who cares if it looks like I live with my grandma," Mac says. "We'll be happy to have it when we're watching TV. You always say my chest is too hard to lie on."

Phoebe grins softly, and I feel the urge to hug Mac. I've

known him for so long that it's easy to pretend he's the same guy I met back in school. He's not, though. He's changing, just like the rest of us. The guy he used to be was reckless and only thought about himself. For all his flaws, those things aren't true anymore. There's nobody Mac thinks about more than Phoebe.

Behind him, Deiss is approaching, flashing enigmatic smiles at the people who try to trap him in conversation.

"Am I missing a group meeting?" he asks, slapping Mac on the back. "You know you're allowed to talk to other people than each other, right?"

"But-ola they-ola won't-ola be-ola able-ola to-ola understand-ola us-ola," Phoebe says.

Deiss shakes his head. "I told Mia not to allow any children in."

"We-ola snuck-ola in-ola the-ola back-ola," I say.

"You, too? I expected better." Deiss tsks, but a grin tugs at his mouth as he moves around them to stand by me. The backs of our hands brush against each other, sending little waves of warmth caressing my skin.

"Good turnout," I say, wishing I could kiss him. I've always considered PDA tacky, but now I can't remember why I ever cared. I like it when I'm working at the counter and he comes over and tilts my chin up to brush his lips against mine. It never feels ostentatious, just sweet.

"You outdid yourself on the flyer," he says. "The band asked about it as soon as they came in. I'm sure they'd love to meet you."

I beam with pride. "Can you introduce me?"

"Whenever you're ready," he says.

"After the show," Phoebe says over Mac, who's high-fiving

me for making the coolest flyer ever, even though I doubt he's seen it, considering he lives in West Hollywood. "You should play hard to get."

"Too late for that," Simone says with an ugly sneer.

I freeze, my hand still in the air, but Deiss doesn't.

He tilts his head toward Simone. "What's that?"

A flush of deep crimson creeps up her neck. "Nothing."

"Are you sure?" Deiss asks calmly. "Because I respect your right to share whatever you feel you need to. Just make sure you're showing that same respect to Liv."

Mac's brow furrows with confusion, and he reaches up and lowers my wrist with his finger.

"Am I missing something?" Phoebe looks back and forth between the three of us.

Deiss and Simone are focused on each other, locked in a silent stare, so I pretend to be distracted by the tweens who have just stumbled through the door in a flurry of giggles. They're a strange sight after Deiss has just mentioned children, and it occurs to me that my advertising might have been too effective. Deiss has always considered his shows to be more of an underground scene for genuine music lovers, and these girls look like they should be at home wearing onesie pajamas and braiding each other's hair.

The awkward moment of silence is interrupted by Booker, who, for once in his life, has managed to appear at exactly the right time.

"Can I just take one bottle of liquor down?" he asks Deiss, ignoring the rest of us. "I heard what you said, but I think you should reconsider. People have come to expect it. It's good for the vibe."

"You mean the tips are good for your wallet," Deiss says, breaking free from his silent showdown with Simone.

"Fine," Booker says. "I need the money. Just let me have this."

"I wish I could," Deiss says. "But we can't do it. We still haven't figured out if the liquor license is going to be worth the investment, and the crowd's gotten too big to control the risk."

"Hi, Booker," Phoebe says, waving a hand in front of his face. "It's me, your friend, Phoebe. You're supposed to greet me when you enter."

Booker steps around her arm without breaking focus on Deiss. "Just one last time. Come on, boss. Don't go all corporate on us. This isn't open mic night at some dumpy coffee joint. It's a freaking rock show."

Deiss looks at me, silently looking for my opinion. As flattered as I am to be included in this decision, I don't know what to tell him. I think he was right to shut it down. But I also know it's not Booker's appeal to his vanity that's making Deiss reconsider. It's the knowledge that Booker needs new headshots, and he was counting on tonight's tips to get them.

"Is this a totally new crowd, or do you know a lot of the people here?" I ask Booker.

He gives me a grateful smile. "Oh, I've seen most of them in here before. We're tight."

"*Tight* sounds like a bit of an oversell," Deiss says dryly.

"What if he kept it covert and stuck to the people he's served before?" I say. "He could stick to the back half of the basement to limit exposure."

"That's stupid," Simone says sharply. "Everyone would catch on anyway."

Deiss and I turn toward her, matching expressions of surprise on our faces. Simone is the last person either of us would expect to be concerned about Deiss's business at this particular moment.

"Don't do it," Simone insists. The intensity of her words doesn't match the casualness of the conversation. "You'll get in trouble."

Deiss's eyes flick toward me again, and I shrug covertly.

"Do you know something?" Deiss asks Simone. But his words are drowned out by the shrieks of four tweens who press into our little circle.

They bounce and squeal, rushing Deiss so that he backs into one of the record bins.

"It's really you!" the tallest girl cries, grabbing his arm. She swings her hair around, grinning triumphantly. "We found Brendan Davis!"

CHAPTER 25

My heart stops. Truly, it quits functioning. There's nothing for one endless second, and then it begins to pound again, thumping so hard the sound of it fills my ears. *I'm the only one he told.* Deiss's secret is out, and I'm the only one he shared it with. It can't be my fault, though. I've only told Simone, and she doesn't know a bunch of young girls. She always says anyone under the age of twenty-one is worthless to her.

They're declaring their love for Deiss as he leans languidly against the record bin. His face is blank, save for a polite smile. If it weren't for the way he keeps reaching up to rub the back of his head, I'd think he's taking this, like everything else I've ever seen him encounter, in stride. The tic gives him away, though. That small show of vulnerability makes me want to forcibly push everyone out the door and deadbolt it behind them.

"What the hell is going on?" Phoebe glares at the girl, who's lifted her phone a foot in front of Deiss's face and begun videoing his discomfort. With a flick of her wrist, Phoebe knocks the phone to the ground without touching the kid.

The girl looks at Phoebe in disbelief.

"Boundaries," Phoebe says. "Learn them."

"Do they think Deiss is famous?" Mac's question is either rhetorical or broadly directed. Without waiting for an answer, he loudly says, "*I'm* the model."

The tall tween scoffs at his claim. "He's Noah Riley."

"First, you said he was Brandon," Mac says, crossing his arms over his chest like he's fully prepared to debate with this child.

"*Bren*-dan." She shakes her head like she's never encountered someone so uneducated as this oversized pretty boy. Behind her, the other two have flanked Deiss and have begun taking selfies. People around us are beginning to stare. "He plays Noah Riley in *Family Fun*, which, by the way, I've seen every episode. *Four times.* I could totally quote most of them by heart. So, I'm, like, his biggest fan."

My mind races as Mac tries to explain to the girl that she's got the wrong guy. Between Lucas and Deiss and aliases and characters, names are flying, but I can't focus on any of them. I need to know that this isn't happening because of me. It has to have been his performance last week at the concert. The video must have gone viral. Somehow, someone recognized him from it.

"That's my picture," Phoebe exclaims, breaking me out of my spiral of panic. She grabs the phone the girl is showing Mac and bends her head over it.

I slip through the growing crowd and peer over her shoulder. My stomach sinks at the sight of the photo she's just enlarged. It's not hers. It's mine. I sent it to her with the shots I took of her dancing on stage. It's one where I zoomed in on Deiss's face.

"What is that?" My voice cracks, and I have to repeat myself to be heard. "What's that picture attached to?"

"A whole article about Deiss." Phoebe clicks off the photo, and I see the words that spell the end of everything. *Brendan Davis*, the headline reads, *Where is he now?*

Together, we read it, my stomach curdling more with every sentence. The author has gone salacious, twisting everything in Deiss's life to appear seedy. They claim he's never had a real relationship, as if he's some kind of sociopath and the eleven years he's spent with the four of us means nothing. According to them, he's a serial bed-hopper who changes identities like other men change their shirts.

They dedicate an entire paragraph to the store. In their version, it's merely a front for his underground raves where he sells drugs and booze to make up for the millions he's lost. The entire article is trash, but there's enough truth in it that they must have had an insider. It's the only way they could know about me, the roommate they claim Deiss has been forced to get to help cover his rent.

"I don't understand," Phoebe says, pulling out her phone and comparing the pictures side by side. "They're identical. Did you post this somewhere?"

"No." I glare at Simone. "A better question is who had access to your texts."

Despite my accusation, I don't fully believe it until I see the flush of guilt on her face. How could I? She's *Simone*.

I was shocked by the way she talked to me the morning she caught me coming out of Deiss's room, but I credited her viciousness to years of unresolved feelings and jealousy. I worried she'd tell Deiss's secret to the others, but it never once occurred to me she'd spread it further. Fights happen, but when it counts, we've always had each other's backs.

Phoebe's eyes flick instinctively toward Mac because who else would have more access to her phone than him? But it's crystal clear he has no idea what's going on.

"Simone?" Phoebe asks. "Is this some kind of prank?"

"I wouldn't make up an entire story about Deiss just to mess with him," Simone says, sidestepping the point. "It's all true. Liv told me. And it looks like I'm not the only person she spilled the secret to."

My mouth falls open in dismay, and I gape at her stupidly, unable to believe she'd do this to me. Then the moment catches up to me, and I jerk toward Deiss. He's looking at me in a way I can't bear, like a puppy that's just been kicked across the room, and the hurt on his face sends tears rushing to my eyes.

"I didn't mean to tell her," I say in a desperate rush. "I was just trying to defend you. She was so mad that morning she caught us coming out of your room together, and she was saying that you couldn't possibly care about me or anything else because you've never had to work for anything. I just wanted her to understand that she was wrong."

Deiss nods slowly, all traces of hurt carefully wiped away. "Got it."

"You do?" I take a step toward him.

"Sure," he says. "It was about you."

My heart speeds up, even though I don't understand. "What?"

"You couldn't let Simone think I wasn't serious about you," he says, "even though I've made it perfectly clear to you that I was."

The back of my neck has grown slick with sweat. His words hold no heat of anger or accusation. In fact, they're said gently, with understanding. But there's something in his eyes, a distance in the way his chin has tilted, and he's begun to speak in past tense.

"I . . ." I trail off, unable to defend myself. Maybe he's right. Maybe, for all the effort I've made, I'm still the same girl, desperate to be seen as perfect.

"Are you guys boning?" Mac bellows the question, an elated grin on his face. If we didn't already have the attention of the entire store, we have it now. He claps delightedly, and I can't determine if he's applauding our relationship or his brilliance in figuring it out. "You're arguing like two people who are totally boning."

The tweens giggle and duck their heads in unison, their fingers flying over the keyboards of their phones.

"Simone thinks so," Deiss says with a placid smile. "That's why she wanted to hurt me. Right, Simone?"

Simone straightens, her mouth twisting. But then her face crumples and her shoulders slump. "I tried to stop you from serving alcohol. Once I read the article, I got worried someone would show up to catch you."

"The article you told them to write?" Once again, Deiss's words are cool with understanding.

Simone shakes her head no, but the guilt in her face is unmistakable. "I was just venting, Deiss. I should've specified that it was off the record. I'm really sorry."

"I'm sorry, too," Deiss says. "I really wanted to believe friendships last forever. It sucks that you had to prove me wrong."

"You don't mean that," I say.

Deiss doesn't bother responding. We all know he's never said anything he didn't mean. It's exactly the reason I shouldn't have blown his secret to convince Simone—and, I might as well face it, *myself*—that he cared about me. I should have trusted him the way he trusted me.

"I should go." Simone eyes Deiss pathetically.

Deiss lifts his chin in response, a silent agreement.

The crowd parts, leaving an open path to the door, where Mia has appeared to hold it open. Her mohawk tips are orangey-red tonight, like glowing embers, and the heat in her eyes as she looks past Simone says she'd gladly use them to set me on fire. Whatever unlikely friendship we might have forged over the last two weeks has disappeared as easily as Simone and Deiss's.

She pushes the door shut behind Simone and turns to face the crowd, her fists pressed against her hips. "The concert starts *now*," she shouts. "If you're not downstairs in two minutes, you're getting kicked out."

The crowd around us surges, hurrying toward the stairs. We've warmed them up with our preshow and now they're hyped and ready for the main act. I've never aspired to entertain the masses, and now I understand why Deiss spent ten years in hiding to escape the spotlight. It's terrible. I feel peeled bare and raw, and I wish I could hide in a tiny ball and forget every second of what's just happened.

Mia follows behind the crowd, ushering them like a rabid sheepdog. When she reaches Deiss, she pauses. "I'll get money from everyone downstairs," she assures him before glowering at the tweens. They're the only ones who have made no effort to follow her directive. "You think your friends will be impressed by a selfie? Wait until they hear you saw Brendan Davis's favorite band play live."

Their eyes widen, and the shrieking begins again as they rush toward the door in a single unit.

"Under-eighteens pay double," Mia hollers after them. She shoots me one last glare before she stalks off to empty everyone's pockets.

My eyes skitter across the room as it empties out, avoiding the people I love most. I can't face any of them. Not Deiss's detached acceptance of the situation and my part in it. Not Phoebe's hurt realization that we've been keeping secrets from her. Not even Mac's inappropriate enthusiasm for our sex life. The temperature of the room drops with the disappearance of so many bodies, and I shiver as I move to reinsert a record someone has left sitting on top of a bin. Through the front windows, the night sky is black.

"So," Phoebe says, her voice abnormally high, "am I to understand that, after all these years, I still don't know your real name?"

Deiss puts a hand on her shoulder, but she shrugs it off. "Of course not, Phoebes. I've never lied to you. Brendan Davis is just a stage name. It's made up, exactly like the character I played. You've always known the real me."

"How can you say that? Apparently, I don't know *anything* about you. You have a whole secret life where you're rich and famous. And sleeping with my best friend." Her voice wavers in question at the end, making me flinch.

Immediately, I understand how bad it is that I haven't told her. It's not the breaking of the pact that will hurt her. It's that she's shared her feelings about Mac with me, while I've chosen to hold mine back from her. I've created an imbalance in our friendship. My silence speaks, and it says I might be the person she tells everything to, but she's not the same for me.

"I wanted to tell you," I say quickly. "I should've. I know

that. It's just so new, and Simone reacted so badly to it. I was scared it would get ruined if we were forced to defend it this early."

"Defend it?" Mac's voice cracks with incredulity. "This is awesome! They broke the pact, Phoebes. It's over. Now we can date."

"Seriously?" She looks at him in disbelief. "All they've done is proven why we needed the pact. Simone has lost her mind and gone Machiavellian on Deiss's life. Who knows if our child superstar is ever going to forgive her for that. And we haven't even gotten to the part where Deiss and the Ice Queen split up. Once that happens, we'll be lucky if any of us ever speak to each other again."

"That's . . ." I start my contradiction without thinking it through. I'd sound idiotic insisting that's not going to happen to us. Especially now, after I failed him so terribly just hours into our relationship.

"I don't care about them," Mac says, filling the silence my nondenial has left behind. "They're stupid."

"Nice." For a moment, Deiss's mouth curls with genuine amusement, making him look like himself again. Just as quickly as it arrived, the smile disappears.

"I mean it." Some internal determination causes Mac to straighten to his full six feet four. His shoulders square, making him larger than life. "I don't care if they break up or if they spend the next ten years holed up in Deiss's bedroom and we never get to see them again. I just want to be with you, babe."

For the second time tonight, my mouth drops open. Phoebe doesn't look nearly as shocked, though, and it occurs to me that she's been keeping secrets of her own. Her feelings aren't one-sided, which strikes me as a pretty big omission.

"This isn't about us," she says. "It's about Liv and Deiss."

I look to Deiss, but he doesn't meet my gaze.

"It's always about everyone else." Mac's eyes sharpen in a way I've never seen. It makes him look like a man instead of a giant boy. "And maybe that was my fault at one point. But that was years ago, Phoebe. It's not where we are anymore. So, you need to figure out if you're down to move forward with me or if this is where we choose to go our separate ways."

As if to illustrate his point, Mac steps around her and walks down the aisle of bins and right out the door. It's almost as shocking as everything he's said; I don't think I've ever seen him go anywhere alone.

"Are you happy now?" Phoebe breaks the stunned silence, hissing the words. Her eyes are glassy with unshed tears. "Everything is ruined."

I feel the accusation like a punch in the gut, because she's not wrong.

For years, I behaved as I was supposed to, and everything was perfectly fine. Now, in merely a few weeks, I've ruined everything. I've lost my home and forced Deiss to share his safe space. I've destroyed my reputation at work and made Mia and Booker uncomfortable by inserting myself into theirs. I've blown up our friend group. I've even lost my chance to collaborate with Zoe, which never would've happened if I hadn't broken the pact like I've broken every other rule.

This plan of mine to live according to my own instincts has been a failure in every possible way. I have to stop. I'm not going to survive it if I don't. None of us will.

"I'm so sorry." I can feel the tears coming, but if I can keep them from breaching the surface, I know I can hide my desolation. "To both of you. I've betrayed your trust, and I don't know how to make up for that. But I can start by moving out of the loft."

Deiss's face tightens. "Liv—"

"I heard from the manager of Bears in Captivity on Wednesday," I say, cutting him off. "They've hired me to do their graphics, and I didn't tell you. I didn't think you'd want me to stay if I had other options. Because we both knew this was never going to last, didn't we?"

I brace myself for one of his cavalier responses, but to my surprise, it doesn't come. Instead, his chin tilts back like he's taken a hit.

"Thank you for everything you've done for me," I say. "It was a fun couple of weeks." For Phoebe's benefit, I add, "I'm sure our time together will only make our friendship stronger."

Using every ounce of willpower I can muster, I stroll out of the shop and into the night.

CHAPTER 26

I spring for a room at an expensive hotel in Santa Monica while I'm looking for a new place to live. It's a ridiculous decision, considering my accounts still haven't been restored and my credit is limited to the one card the bank has issued to me, but it's the kind of place the old Olivia would've been comfortable in, with white walls instead of the smorgasbord of colors that made up Deiss's loft. It has a king-sized bed that I'll sleep in alone.

I avoid the calls from the Bears in Captivity manager and return Marian Hammersmith's call from when I was in St. Lulia. She sounds friendly, despite the fact that it's taken me far too long to respond to her message. Rather than offering lunch again, she suggests I meet her in her office on Friday morning. Nervously, I agree.

When I go to buy new work clothes, I discover I no longer fit into my size. I stare at my body in the dressing room, trying to decide how many meals I'll need to skip to get back into it. A prolonged juice fast will probably do it. But the longer I stand there, the harder it is to imagine a time when I liked my ribs poking through my skin. I look healthier now. My skin is glowing in a way I never was quite able to mimic with makeup. Resolutely, I ask the attendant to bring me the next size up. I leave with several options that will allow me to eat something other than a nutrition bar while wearing them.

I feel so elated on the walk back to the hotel that I change as soon as I get in and head back out for a run. It doesn't feel the same without Deiss, though. I miss the sound of his steps next to me. I miss the way we'd get so wrapped up in a conversation that I'd be shocked when he'd slow in front of his building, thirty minutes gone in the blink of an eye.

Nights are difficult as well. As hard as I try to get my body back on its old schedule, it refuses to adjust. Nine o'clock hits, and it gets fidgety for decadent food and bad TV. My legs slide around the bed as I try to read, like they're so used to tangling with Deiss's that they can't help searching for contact. When I turn out the light, I lie there, blinking in the darkness, unable to sleep.

It's Thursday night that's the worst, though. It's the third Thursday of the month, and for the first time since we graduated seven years ago, my friends and I don't meet up. Or maybe they're out together somewhere, and they've just neglected to invite me. I haven't heard from anyone since the concert Saturday night. Five of the longest days of my life.

I've texted Phoebe, telling her how sorry I am, but she hasn't replied. I've texted Deiss, too—long, rambling messages full of apologies and declarations of love—but I haven't sent them. I'm back on the rules, and they insist if a man wants to hear from you, he'll reach out. And while my reading hasn't unearthed any details on my particular situation, I can only trust that this includes the kind of scenario where you've outed a former child star and unleashed a torrent of amorous tweens on him.

As much as I've convinced myself that I'm back to my old self, Friday morning proves me wrong. I wake up later than planned after tossing and turning and incessantly checking my phone for *We decided to meet up after all! Please come!* texts that never came through. When I attempt to prepare myself for my meeting with Marian Hammersmith, I discover my makeup no longer matches my skin. Weeks of running outdoors has given me a tan.

I cringe at the sight of the contoured cheekbones with the pasty-looking foundation on top of it. I look three-toned, like a little girl who has discovered her mother's makeup and mistakes eyeshadow for blush. It's unfathomable that I haven't realized this before now. Has it really been so long since I made myself up? The last time must have been two weeks ago, when I went to visit my mother with Deiss. It was off then, but manageably so. How is it possible I didn't wear it to the concert last weekend? Washing my face clean, I try again with just mascara and blush, trying to convince myself that the natural look goes better with my grown-out highlights anyway.

Outside, smog has rendered the sky hazy, like the sun has risen but hasn't yet shaken off its slumber. The walk to work takes longer than I remember. There are no greetings from neighbors. The air smells of exhaust and impatience.

Icy air-con hits me as I enter Infinity Designs. "Morning, Sal," I say to the security guard.

"I thought I'd seen the last of you," he says.

"Never," I say. "Someone's got to make cod-liver oil fashionable again."

He laughs and waves me on, but the tiny bit of camaraderie bolsters me. *I belong here*, I remind myself as I wait for the same elevator I've gotten into every morning for the last seven years. *This is where I thrive.*

My conviction falters as the elevator zips upward. It must be because I skip my floor and go straight to Marian Hammersmith's level, which feels a lot like showing up at school and being immediately summoned to see the principal. Her assistant greets me politely, though, and offers me a bottle of water before opening the door. I resist the urge to pat at my skirt.

"Olivia," Marian says, her smile surprisingly warm. She waves me toward the two chairs in front of her desk. "It's lovely to see you again."

"It's lovely to be back." I slide into a seat, crossing my ankles. "I feel like I've been gone forever."

"As do I." She places her hands on the desk and tilts her head calculatingly. "Bob said he felt the need to offer you six weeks of unpaid leave. That is quite . . . unprecedented. Might I inquire as to what precipitated such an offer on his part?"

I have to admire the delicacy with which she's phrased the question. We both know there are several reasons a person might need a block of time like that off—mental or physical health issues, some form of rehabilitation, or a death in the family—and all of them are fully within my right to keep to myself. Still, I don't mind. She's given me the opportunity to defend my actions, and I'm willing to tell her exactly what she wants to hear.

"Of course," I say smoothly. "I've had a bit of personal trouble. My condo got robbed, and the perpetrator managed to get away with everything I own, including my personal laptop. Naturally, that allowed him access to my bank account, which he wiped clean. It's all just been a very long and arduous process which has taken up way more of my time than I cared to give to that criminal. I do hope my time out of the office hasn't thrown any projects off schedule. Mr. Dailey was the one who offered me the opportunity to give the matter my full attention."

"Oh, Olivia." Marian's hand goes to her heart in an elegant display of sympathy. "I had no idea. What a terrible ordeal."

"It's been rough," I admit bravely. "But women like us can't let a little thing like that get us down. And, on the bright side, my account will be restored soon. So, there's shopping to be done. New clothes and furniture and everything, really."

"That explains it then," Marian murmurs, her head tilted.

"My absence?"

"That"—she lifts a finger in the air and drops it to encompass the length of me—"and the rest of it. You don't look quite as . . . *tailored* as you normally do. No offense, of course."

A rush of embarrassment sweeps through me, but I manage to keep my expression neutral. "None taken. Clearly, the lapse is entirely situational."

Our eyes meet, and there's a moment of silence that feels charged with something I don't understand. With a sharp nod, Marian ends it.

"I hope you can get all of your shopping done this weekend. I'd like you back in the office on Monday so we can begin to get things in line." Her gaze intensifies. "I intend to groom you as my replacement."

"You intend . . ." I blink at her, running her words through my head. "You're leaving Infinity Designs?"

"Eventually." Marian leans back in her chair and crosses her legs. "The time has come to shift my focus to other things." With a wry smile, she adds, "In fact, my wife would say that time is well past due."

"You'll be missed," I say honestly.

"As were you," she says. "You do good work, Olivia. But more importantly, you're the kind of woman who understands the value in playing the game. This is a long-term plan, of course. It will probably take a couple of years to position you as the only obvious choice to replace me, but I believe it will be worth the effort. As far as I'm concerned, you're the perfect person to fill my shoes."

"Perfect," I echo stupidly, my eyes dropping to the three-inch heels beneath her desk.

They're a classic black, pointed-toe with a scalloped rim for subtle flair and the red sole to advertise the expense of Louboutin. For lack of a better word, they're absolutely perfect.

And they look terribly, painfully constrictive.

My stomach contracts as I enter the floor where I used to work. I'm not sure I'm ready to see everyone, but my desire to speak to Elena has won out over my skittishness. The office space feels larger than I remembered. It smells of microwave popcorn, an offense that would've irritated me a month ago, although not as badly as Ben's insistence on heating up fish in the shared area. Now, it merely makes me smile. There's something impressively unfettered about the decision to make popcorn at 9:46 in the morning. Is it breakfast? Brunch? It's anyone's guess.

Elena must be lost inside some project on her screen. It's the only explanation for her surprise when I lean over her cubicle wall after greeting several coworkers nearby. At the sight of me, she flinches before quickly covering her nervousness with an enthusiastic greeting. Her reaction makes me feel guilty for not reaching out sooner. It's not like she robbed my condo herself. She was only ever trying to help me out.

"I thought I could convince you to sneak out for a cup of coffee," I say warmly, "but it looks like you're hard at work."

"Looks can be deceiving." She smiles with relief and pops up, sending her chair spinning behind her. "Let's make a break for it. Mr. Dailey's wife has had him on a juice fast all week, and the only time he comes out of his haze of hunger is when he's running for the bathroom. He wouldn't notice if I moved to Toronto, much less disappeared for an hour."

Our footsteps speed up as we head toward the door, as if we really are attempting a prison yard escape. And when the elevator doors close behind us, we erupt into giggles that quickly turn to overlapping apologies. By the time we make it to the street, the sun has battled through the smog and is beaming its approval. What starts as coffee extends into the two of us lying beside my hotel pool in newly purchased bikinis.

Instead of plastic loungers, the hotel has plush cushions on wooden frames. Green plants line the area, and the water in the pool is smooth like glass. A covered area to the left holds a smattering of tables surrounded by flowers, and a group of businessmen have taken them over. They have a small buffet of food lined up against one wall, and they seem to rotate between eating from it and wandering into the pool area to take calls. Other than them, we're the only people here.

"Now I'm really not going to make it back to work," Elena says remorselessly as the cabana boy walks away with our orders for two mojitos and a flatbread to share. "If Mr. Dailey notices I'm missing, I'm going to have to pretend I'm on a juice fast as well. He's spent enough time in the bathroom that he won't have any follow-up questions."

"And I'll be there on Monday to back up your story," I remind her.

She brightens, but as she takes in my expression, her enthusiasm dims. "Are you sure you want to come back?"

"Why wouldn't I?" My eyes skim the length of the pool, deliberately avoiding hers.

"I can't imagine." She leans toward me, smelling of coconut sunscreen. "You've got a real chance at becoming creative director, which is what you've always said you wanted. And who wouldn't? It's more money. More power. And a lot more prestige."

"It's also longer hours, means spending every day alone in an office, and I'll still be looking at an endless supply of food projects."

"I thought you'd be thrilled to get an office," she says, squinting in confusion. "You hate being interrupted while you're working."

My mind flashes to Booker's work avoidance and Mia's sarcastic comments. But especially Deiss. He never failed to encourage me when I was searching through online postings for my next job. As if he had some internal alarm, vigilantly scanning for any doubt that might sneak up on me, he managed to show up with praise every time I began to question my work.

The truth is, between those three people and all the customers that came into Studio Sounds, I was constantly being interrupted. Still, I've never produced more or done better work than I did there. More importantly, I've never enjoyed myself so much.

"I *did* hate it," I say. "But people change."

CHAPTER 27

J 'm not sure the exact moment it hits me that I've made a terrible mistake—possibly because I've known all along. But I realize it when my mojito arrives and it occurs to me that it's full of calories I shouldn't consume if I want to be more *tailored* in order to meet Marian's expectations. And again when I slip the straw in my mouth and drink it anyway.

I realize it when some of the businessmen wander over with a bottle of champagne and begin hitting on us. And again when I pinpoint the safe bet among them but turn down his dinner invitation anyway, despite the fact that Elena has deemed him "surprisingly yummy for a nice guy."

I realize it when Elena goes into detail about the bone broth project she's taken over in my absence.

"I don't think I can go back," I blurt out, interrupting her. "It's a good job. I know it is. And I wish I was like you and had things like the theater to direct my creative energy toward. But I don't. I just have design. And I want to do every kind of project there is to do."

"Okay?" Her face twists with confusion. "So, is this your way of saying you don't want Marian's job?"

"Yes," I say. "But I also don't want a lot of other things. I don't want to be tailored. And I don't want to live alone anymore. And I don't want to play it safe. And I especially don't want to give up on love just because it's messy and I can't predict how it will end up."

"Those all sound like reasonable things," Elena says.

"I don't want to plan for the future anymore when that means giving up living in the now," I add determinedly.

"Still reasonable."

"It's settled then."

Elena laughs. "If you say so."

"Am I missing something?" The sweet pull of my mojito eases my defensiveness. "You don't think I can change?"

"It's pretty obvious you already have," she says, flipping onto her side to face me. "But I don't think you can build a life solely around what you don't want to do. You also have to decide what you *do* want."

"Done." I set my drink on the little square table between us and follow her lead, turning on my side to face her. "I want to use my new ties with Bears in Captivity to connect with other bands. And I want to look for a place in Los Feliz so I can be near my friends again. Because, most importantly, I want to work things out with them. All of them, obviously, but especially Deiss."

"He's the one who brought you home from the airport?" At my nod, Elena licks her lips. "Yeah, I'd want to work things out with him, too. Mainly my thighs."

I hold a hand up before she can elaborate. "You should probably know I'm in love with him."

"You? And the smoldering guy with the sinful mouth?" Her eyes brighten with delight. "But he's not your type at all. You don't go for the bad boys."

"Deiss isn't bad. He's wonderful."

"Tell me how it happened," she orders. "I want every detail from beginning to end."

"We were together for a couple of weeks, but then I ruined everything."

"I'm sure it's not as bad as you think," she says confidently. "We just need to make a plan for you to get him back. Something perfect. Something failproof."

"I'm open to whatever suggestions you might have."

She grins slyly. "First, I'll need details."

My stomach tightens. But if I want to be different, I have to change.

Plus, I do like the sound of a failproof plan.

"Fine." Obediently, I start the story from the very beginning.

"*I need you,*" Phoebe whispers the moment I answer her call.

Elena flashes me an encouraging thumbs-up. We were in the middle of brainstorming plans—most of them too elaborate and outrageous to have any chance of success—when the trill of my phone interrupted us. Obviously, like me, Elena expected to hear something different.

"What?" I wave off Elena's thumbs-up, my stomach tightening like a clamp. "Tell me what to do."

"I'm at the harbor in Marina Del Rey. Please hurry, Liv."

As she gives me the slip number, I jump from the lounger and run toward the server who's given us our drinks, gesturing for the check. My heart races at the muted tone of her voice. Phoebe, who is always so much larger than life. It's terrifying to hear her sound so small.

"Are you okay?" I squeeze my eyes shut as I wait for her answer, but I don't get the reassurance I'm so desperate for.

"Just hurry," she repeats before the phone goes dead.

"Charge everything to room 214," I tell the server. "Do you need me to sign something?"

He shakes his head like he's scared to answer wrong.

"Thank you," I say, turning to run back to my chair.

It's unnecessary, though, because Elena is already running toward me with all of our belongings wadded into her arms.

"What's happening?" Her sunglasses have slid down her nose and are perched precariously on the tip.

"I have to go to the harbor." I reach to pull my purse from her arm, but she takes a step back, holding it away from me.

"Something's wrong with Phoebe," I say desperately.

Rather than respond, Elena begins to run. I follow after her.

"You can't come," I call behind her. "It might be dangerous."

She doesn't acknowledge me. There's a taxi outside the hotel, and she manages to whip the back door open despite the mess of stuff in her arms. Sliding inside, she barks "Marina Del Rey harbor" at the driver. It's a miracle that I make it inside the car before he hits the gas.

"What's happening?" she asks as the driver lurches into traffic, cementing her inclusion in whatever this is.

"I don't know." Sunscreen stings my eyes, and my heart pounds in my chest. What *is* happening? "I'm worried, though. Phoebe wouldn't ask for help unless it was bad."

I think of the time we hiked to the Hollywood sign and she refused to let Mac carry her the rest of the way down after she got knocked off the path by an unleashed dog. We didn't realize she'd fractured her ankle until the next day.

"We're lucky we were so close," Elena says. "We'll be there in ten minutes. Whatever it is, it's going to be fine."

I try to smile at her, but my face feels frozen. If anything happens to Phoebe, I'll never forgive myself. I lean forward in my seat for the rest of the ride, like my body is a rudder guiding the car. Miraculously, traffic is not terrible.

"You should stay here," I tell Elena when the driver drops us off in the parking lot. Before the words are out, I begin to run, calling the rest out over my shoulder. "I don't know what we're walking into."

Once again, Elena ignores me, following close on my heels. The orange and pinks of the slowly setting sun bounce off the gleaming white boats, making them look like they're in danger of catching fire. My sandals slap against the dock as I run faster.

"Phoebe!" I shout her name as I draw near to the number she gave me, panting with relief that the slip is still occupied.

"Liv?" She appears at the edge of an upper deck, smiling down at me. With a champagne glass in her hand and a white dress that flutters in the wind, she looks like the kind of woman who'd own this two-story yacht, not be held hostage on it. "You made it! Come on up."

Relief crashes over me, making my knees go weak, but I manage to scramble on board. Elena comes with me, our arms brushing against each other, sticky with sweat and sunscreen. Despite my lingering panic, I find myself pausing for a moment to take in the covered sitting area with its navy-blue cushioned bench seating and adorable wooden table.

"If this is some kind of prison," Elena says, echoing my thoughts, "your friend could do worse."

"Shh." I put a finger to my lips. "She might be pretending to be okay because someone is watching her."

Elena's eyes widen, at the same moment I notice the slight movement beneath me. With the smoothness of butter, the vessel eases forward, slipping away from the dock and into the deep, vast ocean. A flare of panic shoots through me.

We're trapped.

CHAPTER 28

Stealthily, Elena and I make our way to the upper deck. To my shock, Phoebe isn't climbing the rail, preparing to leap overboard. Instead, she's leaning against the console, chatting with a man behind the captain's wheel. Rather than having a rope tied around her ankles like I imagined she might, she has a white flower pinned in her hair.

"Stop the boat!" I demand, using my most imposing voice.

"It's okay." Phoebe laughs and holds out her champagne, as if I might like to toast to our kidnapping instead of stop it. "I'm sorry if I freaked you out. I just wanted to get you here quickly."

"You . . ." I trail off, unable to comprehend the idea that I've been so terrified for nothing. "I . . ."

"Are you mad?" Phoebe looks ruffled for the briefest moment but quickly shakes it off. "Well, you can't be. Because it's my day. I'm the bride."

I gape at her, and she lifts her other hand so they're both in the air.

"We're getting married!" She beams.

"You're . . ." I trail off again. It's possible my brain has not made it to sea with us and is sunbathing somewhere back on dry land. Uncomprehendingly, I look back and forth between her and the broad-shouldered man glancing back over his shoulder with a rakish smile. "Do you even *know* this guy?"

There's nothing discernibly wrong with him. He's nice to look at, and he does seem capable of handling a boat, which I imagine is a nice quality to have in a husband. But I've never met him before. More importantly, he's not Mac.

"Connor Collins," he says. "Pleasure to make your acquaintance."

"Are you holding this woman against her will, Connor Collins?" Elena asks.

"I'm not," he says, as if this is an entirely normal question.

His confirmation doesn't bring the relief it should. Phoebe can't marry this man, even if it *is* entirely of her own volition. Maybe there was a time when I could've focused on the implied wealth of boat ownership and been impressed that this man was willing to legally tie his life to Phoebe's. But now I know how it feels to wake up in the arms of someone you truly adore. I've been lucky enough to experience being in love with your best friend, even if I wasn't quite lucky enough to hold onto it.

"Please don't do this," I blurt, clasping my hands together. "It's too fast. Marriage is too big to be decided on flippantly. It lasts forever."

"But don't you see?" Phoebe says, despite the fact that I clearly don't. "That's exactly the point. We've found a loophole. The pact was created because of potential breakups. But Mac and I aren't just getting back together. We're committing the rest of our lives to each other."

"You and Mac?" Relief soars through me, and my head tilts back, filling my vision with the colorful sky. "You're getting married to *Mac*."

"In front of this stranger, apparently," Phoebe says. When I lower my chin, I discover her studying Elena curiously, like an alien life form or a particularly vibrant butterfly. "Why have you brought someone I've never met to my wedding?"

"Did I not indicate that on my RSVP?" I ask dryly. There's no point reminding her that a whispered "I need you" doesn't traditionally translate into a wedding announcement. "I could've sworn I ticked the plus-one box."

"Your date is down there," Phoebe says, motioning toward the front of the boat. "Work it out, and quickly. My maid of honor can't be fighting with the best man."

I freeze for a moment. In all the plans Elena and I devised this afternoon, not one of them involved seeing Deiss for the first time since everything fell apart while wearing a loose-fitting sundress over a bikini, my skin oily with sunscreen and pink with the early stages of a burn. Tentatively, I step toward the rail. My stomach gives an enthusiastic leap at the sight of his short dark hair. Naturally, he's leaned back against one seat, his legs kicked up to rest on another.

"He's with Simone," I say, turning back around.

"I'll take care of that." Elena grabs my hand, leading me firmly forward.

"I like her," Phoebe says to me before redirecting her attention to Elena. "You're now an usher."

"I won't let you down," Elena says with a salute before dragging me downstairs.

The boat is picking up speed, and the wind whips my hair around my shoulders as we move out onto the bow. Deiss looks up, his eyes bluer than the darkening water behind him. He meets my gaze and holds it, showing no surprise at my sudden appearance.

Simone, on the other hand, leaps to her feet. "Hey," she says nervously before rushing forward and wrapping her arms around me. "I'm so sorry, Liv. For everything."

"I know," I say into her shoulder. And I do. One bad week could never make me forget eleven good years. "We'll get past this."

"I didn't set out to do it," she says, pulling back and looking at me plaintively. "I know that doesn't make it better, because I *am* the reason Deiss's past got exposed. But I was just upset, and I vented about it to a friend who just happens to be a journalist, and it turned out her job meant more to her than our friendship."

For a moment, I'm tempted to scoff. It's rich, the clear disappointment she has at a friend's betrayal when she was so eager to let me take the fall for her own. I don't, though. She was right when she said that we choose our friends. For better or for worse, I've chosen her.

"You must be Simone," Elena says. "I'm the usher, and I'm going to need you to come with me."

"Where are we going?" she asks, her eyes widening as Elena tugs her toward the back of the boat.

"To see if this boat has a plank." Elena flashes an ominous smile at her.

I laugh, but it's ninety percent fueled by nerves at finding myself alone with Deiss. Unlike me, he doesn't seem to be the slightest bit affected by our sudden proximity. His gaze is clear and steady as it meets mine. Rather than calming my nerves, this only makes me more flustered.

"I had a plan," I say inanely, swaying in front of him.

"A plan to what?"

"To make things better." I offer a hopeful smile that he doesn't return. "To get you to give me another chance."

"What was it?" His voice betrays nothing.

"We thought of a couple, actually." I begin to pace in front of him, taking three short steps to one side of the boat before crossing to the other. My hair whips against my face. The sunset is getting sharper now. Instead of making the entire sky glow, the oranges and reds are getting more concentrated, separating themselves into individual strips. "But I'm leaning toward the one where I convince a bunch of journalists that someone else is Brendan Davis. I haven't figured out who yet. Maybe some guy who's already dead? And the goal would be to flood the internet with that, so it would drown out the reports about you."

"Sounds ambitious," he says dryly.

"I think it could work, though." My voice flares frantically. "If I just try hard enough. I could make up fake Twitter accounts and try to spread it there. And put up a billboard. Maybe I could even get a real newspaper to pick it up."

He rises to his feet as I pass, smooth as a panther, and catches me around the waist with one arm, stopping me in my tracks before I realize what's happening. "I just wanted a call," he says quietly, his gorgeous mouth suddenly inches from mine.

I blink at him, too mesmerized by his closeness to be able to formulate a response.

"Do you know how many people have come into Sounds this week looking for Brendan Davis?" he asks.

I shake my head, not wanting to know.

"Too many," he says simply. "Way too many to undo it. It's

out now, and that's fine. It has to be. What's not fine is that you left."

"I wish I hadn't." The honesty of my words sends tears rushing to my eyes, and for once, I'm unsuccessful at holding them in. They burn as they push their way out, the feel of them shocking against my cheeks.

"You said we weren't meant to last," he reminds me.

I nod miserably.

"But we could," he says, surprising me with his insistence.

"We could." I mean to agree with him, but my words come out too high, like I'm asking a question.

"We could," he repeats firmly, sweeping a warm thumb across my cheek to wipe my tears away. "I love you, Liv. I've loved you for a third of my life, and I'll continue to love you for the rest of it. And I can do that as a friend if that's what you need. But if you want more, you have to know that I'm not going anywhere."

My heart rate picks up speed with every word he says, and by the end it's racing. Strangely, my euphoria doesn't stop the tears. It seems to fuel them. Not in my wildest dreams have I imagined Lucas Deiss promising to love me for the rest of his life.

"I want more," I blurt stupidly as a rogue tear makes it all the way down to my neck.

Deiss laughs and covers my mouth with his, kissing me in a way that makes my knees weak.

"Sorry to interrupt," says an unwelcome voice I recognize as Mac's. "But this thing is trying to kill me."

Deiss's arm tightens around my waist before he reluctantly pulls back. "We're having a moment here."

"It's *my* wedding day," Mac says, holding his arms out in front of him as a wriggling ball of fur claws at his hands. He looks casually gorgeous in his khakis and white linen button-up, except for the red marks that line his left arm. "And now I'm going to be all scratched up in the photos."

"Sorry," Deiss says. "She was at Sounds with me when you called and told me you were in trouble. Maybe if you'd just been a normal person and said you wanted to meet up, I would've realized I had time to drop her at home."

"Is that . . ." I squint at the proffered kitten before pulling loose from Deiss to grab her. "Fluff Daddy!"

I cradle her to my chest, and miraculously, she calms, staring up at me as if she remembers me. "How did you get her?" I ask, staring back at her in disbelief.

"I took a little drive down to Brantley," Deiss says, sliding his hand down her side and eliciting a rumbling purr before she swipes at him. "I thought we could raise her together. If you want to move back in, that is. If not, I'm willing to cede custody to you."

"But I don't understand," I say, despite the fact that everything in me is warning me not to ask questions and simply say, *Yes! Yes, please! I'd love to move back in with you and this perfect, gleefully violent creature!* "I walked away. Why would you drive all that way just to get a cat for me?"

"Because I knew you missed Cat Stevens," Deiss says. "And whether we ended up together or not, I thought Fluff Daddy would make you happy."

"I love you." I breathe the words, feeling as if they're coming somewhere from deep inside my soul.

"Then you're going to love me even more when I tell you I've found Cat Stevens."

I gasp, my heart squeezing. "You did?"

"Well, not exactly *me*," he admits. "But it turns out there are upsides to having an army of self-proclaimed fans who won't leave you alone. Those tweens are *savvy* online. It only took them four days to hunt him down. Apparently, a couple came home and discovered he'd gotten in the cat door while they were out of town. They turned him into a shelter on Wednesday."

I close my eyes, not wanting more tears to spill over. "And he's okay?"

"They said he tilts his nose up at everyone and turns his back when the other cats attempt to engage him."

I choke out a laugh. "Then he's okay."

"Perfect-ola," Mac says before Deiss can respond. He lets out a piercing whistle, waving Phoebe down when she peers over the edge of the top deck. "You guys are good. And everyone's good with Simone. Now, Phoebe will let me marry her."

"Does that mean that Phoebe is good with me?" I ask hopefully. "Because she hasn't returned any of my calls all week."

Mac scoffs. "That wasn't because she was mad. We were just on our honeymoon. Everyone knows you don't take calls on your honeymoon."

"You took your honeymoon *before* the wedding?" I ask.

Mac shrugs, his attention fully on the stairs where Phoebe is descending. "Why not?"

Watching his eyes light up at the sight of her, I don't even consider arguing. What would I even say? Love rarely follows the rules.

The wedding lasts for two and a half songs, played on Deiss's phone, which he holds in the air. It's just long enough for Mac and Phoebe's vows, the former of which gets a little ramble-y when Mac decides to list the things he loves about her. The sunset is in its final, most magnificent blaze as Connor declares them man and wife, and Elena yells at us to squeeze together while they're still kissing, capturing the dying day before the bright colors burn out.

Deiss winces as Phoebe demands he play "I Will Always Love You" but acquiesces, reaching for my hand as she and Mac begin to dance. He pulls me to him, scooping the sleeping cat from my arms and passing him to Connor, who is too unaware to be properly afraid. Then he dips me, tugging me into his chest as I come back up, and together we sway to the movement of the waves.

"I'd like to move back in with you," I whisper in his ear as the song swells. "If you don't think it would be moving too quickly."

He grins lazily, his hand drifting down my back. "It's been eleven years in the making, Liv. We need to make up for lost time."

And for a moment, I allow myself to picture it: a future with Lucas Deiss.

I can see it so clearly. Our walls changing colors over the years. Coffee in the mornings. Me, building my graphic design business from the counter in his shop. Him, teaching guitar to our child in the back. Our feral little cat, terrorizing everyone. And Cat Stevens, peering at us from under the bed, his eyes sharp with disdain.

It's breathtakingly perfect.

But then I look around at the little lighted bow, glowing brightly in the middle of a deep dark ocean. Phoebe is shrieking with laughter as Mac spins her around, the white flower in her hair catching in the wind and disappearing from view.

Simone is forcing Elena to be in one of her selfies. Stars twinkle up in the distance, like the sky has strung party lights just for us. And I realize there's no point in looking toward the future.

The present will do just fine.

Acknowledgments

Isaac Waldon, you will always be first on my list of people to thank. You probably assume that's because you talk me through every single plot point and make me laugh when I'm otherwise tempted to hurl my laptop across the patio. You'd be wrong. I will always thank you first because you're the voice in my head telling me I can do anything that I put my mind to. You're my strength and my joy and my heart. You are my everything.

(But also, if I do anything wrong, remember that you just agreed that you're the voice in my head.)

Thank you to Claire Friedman for being the best agent I could ever ask for. I thought you'd sell my books. I never imagined that you'd also be such a big part in making them. I'm so grateful to have you as a partner. (Seriously, though. My book is super pretty, right? SAY IT.)

Thank you to my editor, Kate Dresser, for all of your brilliant suggestions and guidance. This book is every bit as much yours as it is mine. From our very first conversation, I knew I was lucky to work with you. Naturally, I was right.

Thank you to the amazing team at Putnam. You're all rock stars, and I'm so grateful that you took a chance on me. Thank you so much for not blocking my email address when I used it in excess.

I wrote this book during the pandemic, so my world felt a lot smaller than normal. I could've disappeared inside the writing cave and forgotten that the Earth was still turning outside. These are the people who didn't allow me to:

Thank you to Autumn, Christina, David, Bill, Little Isaac, Davey, and Riley for being the greatest pod ever. Family Day was the bright spot of every week. I loved it almost as much as I love Trash TV Night. DC wouldn't be home without all of you.

Thank you to Tina, Amanda, and Keri for being my besties. I love that we could be separated for an entire year but still talk as much as ever. It's basically scientific proof that nothing will ever be able to keep us apart.

Thank you to Jamie and Dana for expanding our numbers. I feel like Kai might become the voice of reason when Isaac and Jamie are determined to injure themselves.

Thank you to Jennifer, Rhonda, and Charity for being the ultimate crew. You were always there to remind me to celebrate *The Layover* when I was too caught up in this book to remember to stay present. I'm so grateful the Scheduling Gods brought us together.

Thank you to Jane, Bob, Staci, and Missi for being the best parents and sisters a girl could ask for. I love you!

Thank you to the sqaf-ers for proving it's actually possible to make new friends during a pandemic. Your kindness and enthusiasm and support has been such an unexpected source of delight. Now, I'm just waiting on Cindy to sum this whole thing up in the most irreverent manner possible.

When I wrote my acknowledgments for *The Layover*, I wasn't thinking about all the people who would read it. I didn't know how much your messages would mean or how a good review would make my day. This time, I do. Thank you so much for picking this book up! Every person who reads this makes it more possible for me to continue publishing books. Thank you for being a part of this journey and helping to make that dream come true.

Discussion Questions

1. *From the Jump* introduces us to a group of close friends who met in college and moved through adulthood together. Discuss the dynamics of the group and who you resonated most with.

2. The novel's heroine, Liv, is desperate to break free from the self-imposed constraints of her life. What does she no longer find gratifying? What urges her to finally say "no"? How does she change after that point?

3. How does Deiss and Liv's relationship progress throughout the story? How does the trip to South Africa change it? What are the moments where you picked up on their chemistry the most?

4. *From the Jump* is a friends-to-lovers romance. What is your favorite romantic trope? Enemies to lovers? Second chance romance? Or something else? Discuss how Waldon utilizes the friends-to-lovers arc to build tension.

5. After Liv quits her job and joins her friends on vacation, the novel includes immersive and vivid details about South Africa. If you could hop on a plane to any country, where would you go?

6. Discuss the pact that Liv makes on the trip. What does she hope it will accomplish and what actually happens?

7. Discuss how Deiss's childhood years end up impacting his life as an adult. How does the truth behind his identity bring him and Liv together?

8. Why does Liv ultimately end up letting herself fall for Deiss? Why are they a good match for each other?

9. Besides the romance, *From the Jump* also explores the importance of friendship and honesty. Despite their mistakes, how does the group end up coming together?

10. What were your thoughts on the ending? What do you think is in store for Liv, Deiss, and the rest of the group?

About the Author

Lacie Waldon is a writer with her head in the clouds—literally. A flight attendant based in Washington, DC, Waldon spends her days writing from the jump seat and searching the world for new stories. She is also the author of *The Layover*.

Visit Lacie Waldon Online

laciewaldon.com
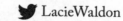 LacieWaldon
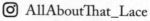 AllAboutThat_Lace